D1032519

THE *Lady* AND THE
LIONHEART

Center Point
Large Print

Books by Joanne Bischof:

Sons of Blackbird Mountain
This Quiet Sky
To Get to You
The Swelling Sea (Message in a
  Bottle Collection)

The Cadence of Grace Series:
Be Still My Soul
Though My Heart is Torn
My Hope is Found

THE *Lady* AND THE LIONHEART

JOANNE BISCHOF

CENTER POINT LARGE PRINT
THORNDIKE, MAINE

The text of this Large Print edition is unabridged.
In other aspects, this book may vary
from the original edition.
Printed in the United States of America
on permanent paper.
Set in 16-point Times New Roman type.

ISBN: 978-1-68324-784-5

Library of Congress Cataloging-in-Publication Data

Names: Bischof, Joanne, author.
Title: The lady and the lionheart / Joanne Bischof.
Description: Center Point Large Print edition. | Thorndike, Maine :
  Center Point Large Print, 2018.
Identifiers: LCCN 2018005442 | ISBN 9781683247845
  (hardcover : alk. paper)
Subjects: LCSH: Large type books.
Classification: LCC PS3602.I75 L33 2018 | DDC 813/.6—dc23
LC record available at https://lccn.loc.gov/2018005442

To Amanda, for everything

THE *Lady* AND THE
LIONHEART

Permanent may be the scars that we bear,
but there is a love that makes all things new.

ONE

Roanoke, Virginia
Spring, 1890

With the hiss of smoothing irons and the starchy scent of soap trailing her, Ella toted a bundle of hospital linens up the steps. Snowy evening light whispered cool and gray through the stairwell window of the converted townhouse, and after an afternoon spent below ground, even the sight of fog and gentle flakes bolstered her spirit. Something so simple, but these days—years, really—she was thankful for *anything*. The wind curled the snow in swirls down the street and she halted at a flash of color drifting along with it. A string of pennants. Wet with the weather, the vibrant strand of cheery flags tumbled along the snow. Ella stepped closer to the window, but they vanished from sight.

Even so, she smiled.

"Excuse me, little miss *scullery maid*."

At the sound of Clara's voice, Ella slid out of the way as best she could. "Room to pass?"

Clara's eyes were on her as she inched by. "Barely. And I've been waiting for those sheets all day." Hair a few shades darker than Ella's pale yellow, Clara slid a nursing cap into place as if back from a break. With a dismissive click of her tongue, the nurse pushed past, nearly making Ella drop her heavy bundle. Steadying both patience and feet, Ella lifted her eyes. One more flight to go. And she wasn't a maid. She was a nurse.

Well . . . almost.

Upon applying at Dr. Penske's private practice, the physician had wasted no time pulling it out of Ella that she'd had little schooling. While she *had* attended several years at the one-room schoolhouse where she was raised, she'd left altogether before completing her exams and instead had gone on to teach herself the art of nursing at home as best she could, even adding medical journals to the standard studies.

Of which he was not impressed.

Yet he'd given her a position under the strict understanding that she would be in the scullery—tidying jars and linens, boiling water, or running errands. Certainly not assisting patients. Though now and again, necessity allowed her to step in and help where needed. Proper education or not.

School. Oh, the very word she loathed. Just one of the failures that haunted her.

But there had been no time to finish school. Not when she was barely fifteen, knelt in her bed, giving birth to a stranger's child. Eight months of fear and worry and then hours of suffering, only to crawl away from it all with empty arms and a cracked heart. Society's righteous murmurs of how she was better off—*God be thanked.*

Yet her son's death felt a wretched distance from the mercy they claimed it to be.

Hot chills covered her skin as she fought the memories of those dark, friendless days. She toted the clean laundry upwards, and when she neared the top hallway, the sound of violent footsteps had her turning. A tree of a man nearly crashed into her. Every stormy, trench-coated pound of him.

A yelp lodged in her throat, then Ella swung to a halt at the sight of a baby in his arms. Sheer surprise had her dropping the bound linens, and he gripped the handrail, steadying himself.

His wild brown hair stood on end as if tugged by a thousand worries. "I need a doctor," he panted, using a ledge to climb around her mess with a balance that defied logic—and when he silently landed much too close on the other side, decorum. Her senses were struck with the scent of coal smoke and . . .

Caramel?

Ella made to step back, but there was nowhere to go. It mattered not when she looked once again to who he held. Bundled in a snow-dusted blanket, the baby glistened with sweat and perhaps tears. She reached for the babe, but he tightened his grip.

"A doctor!" Pale green eyes glittered fiercely.

Stunned to silence, Ella had to work to find her voice. "Uh . . . follow me."

She shoved the linens aside then hurried up the last few stairs, him beside her. A few more steps and she pushed past the door that led them into the children's ward.

"In here," she called over her shoulder, then searched for the doctor. "Dr. Penske. I've a baby here who seems to be running a fever."

Turning from the boy he was tending, Dr. Penske glanced from the man's patched coat to the unlaced boots which thundered to a halt beside Ella's. The stranger's chest heaved as he swallowed a breath.

"Seems to be?" Dr. Penske's tone was as dismissive as his gaze.

"I—I haven't examined the child," she said.

The doctor glanced around the children's ward where two other nurses bustled with tasks. Using the back of his hand, he swiped a lock of hair from his forehead. "Well, why don't you get to it?"

Me? She was only given the most mundane tasks from emptying chamber pots to changing linens. Hopefully the stranger didn't sense that. "Please lay her here." Ella moved to an open crib bed and lowered one side down. "I'll check her temperature."

The man eyed her warily but did as she asked. Ella's fingers were suddenly unsteady as she

14

adjusted the pillow beneath the tiny, blonde head. She'd never been assigned a patient before. Not once on her own. But she'd read the nursing encyclopedia forward and back and watched the nurses day in and day out. Besides, she was the oldest of five brothers and sisters. Ella forced herself to remain calm. When it came to fevers, she knew what to do.

A check of the girl's pulse said it was just over one hundred and twenty beats per minute.

Ella unbundled her down to a wrinkled dress and sweater, then cast the blanket to the foot of the bed. "The child's name?"

After lowering the other side of the crib, the man knelt there. "Holland."

Flicking a glance to his face showed that he was serious. Ella pressed the back of her hand to the babe's round cheek. She nabbed a thermometer and loosened her clothing enough to ease the glass tip under the girl's arm. "How old is she?"

"Seven months."

"How long has she had a fever?"

"A few days. But it's gotten worse today."

The mercury rose. "It's a good thing you brought her in." Ella waited another minute, freed the thermometer, and at the numbers, blew out a controlled breath. A very good thing. "Has she been seizing at all?" Ella tugged off the baby's leather booties.

"No."

"You're certain?"

"I would know." Irritation edged his voice.

Ella held up a hand to pacify him. "The doctor'll be with her shortly. Please have a seat."

She motioned toward the chair beside the bed and he pulled it forward, sitting as near to the girl as he could.

"Has she been taking fluids?" Ella asked. "Any food?"

"Not much food. A little water." Looking lost, he glanced around the room, then back to the child. "We've had a hard time getting her to drink. She's so sleepy." The man leaned forward and touched the baby's tiny fingers with a hand that looked like it could heft her in one scoop. "Hey." He smoothed those pale blonde curls. "Wake up, baby girl."

"She's lethargic," Ella said in response to the girl's unmoving lashes. "I'll mix her up a tea and see if we can't get a little fluid into her."

Excusing herself, Ella hurried away. In the scullery, she filled a dish with warm water and added licorice root, then a hearty pinch of sugar.

"Is he *human?*"

Ella needn't look up to know the whispered question was from her friend, Abigail. "What are you talking about?"

"Look at that face." Abigail wagged her eyebrows then faked a shudder, which was voided by her mischievous smile. "Seems rather intense

16

to be the doting father. How can someone so handsome be *so* broody?"

"He's just a little odd. I think." Ella tugged on the strap of her apron, straightening the clinic-issued uniform. A reach for rags almost knocked over a basket of bandages in her haste.

"He's a bit more than that, wouldn't you say? Which has me wondering . . ."

"Don't you have something to be doing?" Ella rummaged for a glass dropper, and finding one, prepared a tray.

"There are plenty of odd folk about with the circus in town. They came in on the front end of the storm and I hear they've been stranded with the weather." Abigail's eyes lit with her discovery. "I bet that's where he comes from."

"The circus?" Ella thought of the colorful pennants that had tumbled along with the wind.

"Don't you read the newspaper? And that bizarre sound this morning—apparently those were elephants."

Ella had to resist peeking out of the scullery as she caught Abigail's final whisper that it was too bad the man hadn't bumped into *her*.

"He didn't bump into me," Ella muttered as Abigail bustled out and Dr. Penske poked his head in.

"I just looked at the child. What was her temperature?" He polished his spectacles on the hem of his coat.

17

"One hundred and two point eight."

He eyed the tea she was straining. "Good. Administer fluids, keep her uncovered, cool compresses. I'll be by again shortly. Keep a close watch on her."

"Yes, sir." A little thrill coursing through her at such a task, Ella carried the tray back to the bedside.

The man in the chair watched the baby so intensely that Ella's feet slowed. Dark circles rimmed his eyes. She'd seen many a worried parent before, but everything about him was amplified. He pulled at his hair just as his fierce gaze slid to Ella. Unsettled, she set the rattling tray down. The man straightened, but his watchful study of her didn't waver.

The circus . . .

Her fingers started on the buttons of the baby's sweater. Now was probably *not* the time to mention that she wasn't officially a nurse. Perhaps she'd just keep it to herself entirely. The man rubbed at the side of his lightly bristled jaw. Glancing at him, Ella had to work very hard to pretend she didn't know what Abigail's swooning had been about. Olive skin set off pale green eyes that were still watching her so closely, she almost popped the final button of the little yellow sweater clean off.

Though she wasn't sure she'd ever seen one, the word *Gypsy* flitted to mind.

She lifted a damp rag and pressed it to the baby's cheek.

Brow furrowed, the man leaned forward and rested his forearms on his thighs, hands clasped. Though they fluttered, the baby's lashes didn't open.

Ella smoothed a damp tendril of the girl's hair. "Holland," she said softly, taken aback by the sound of such a name, surprisingly befitting this tiny sprite with her blonde curls and rosebud lips. Such a wee thing. And in the care of this man . . .

"She is yours?"

The man nodded as Ella slipped the sweater off.

"Do I need to pay something?" He reached into his pocket.

"Not now. We can worry about that later."

"Are you sure?"

"Positive." She gave him what she hoped was a reassuring smile, and settling on the bed, lifted the baby onto her lap. Holland was limp, just as she feared. "Hello, little one," Ella whispered. The girl's plump, tiny form declared just how young she was. Her dress was a series of colorful patches, stockings frayed in the knees. Paired with the pointed knit cap Ella had set aside, she looked every bit a Gypsy as her father. Ella filled the dropper with fluid and coaxed it past the baby's sleeping mouth. Giving the tip a squeeze, a few drops slipped out and Holland's mouth worked.

"Very good, sweet one." She felt the man's gaze boring a hole into her.

Ella caught a faint dribble with a rag, then settled the baby back in the crook of her arm. Another attempt proved successful, and soon the dropper was empty.

She looked at the man. "We'll give her an ounce of fluid every fifteen minutes for now. I can try some ice chips as well. I'll go prepare some."

He nodded.

Worried over the way the baby winced at the movement, Ella nestled her onto the bed and raised the side up again. She swiped the girl's brow, then handed the rag to the man and motioned for him to do as she had done. But, oh—she was supposed to note all patients in the nursing log. Dr. Penske ran a tight ship at his practice.

"Just a moment, I'll be right back." Ella dashed away for the thick book and returned just as quick. Pencil poised, she spoke as authoritatively as she could. "Your surname? Holland's?"

He hesitated for the briefest of moments. "Lionheart."

Ella tipped her head slightly and knew a lift of her eyebrows betrayed her.

He arced a hand toward the ledger. "Just *write it down*."

She nearly apologized as she scribbled it and was mildly afraid to ask. "Your name, sir?"

"Charlie. And the same—Lionheart."

Before jotting that down, she flicked him a glance. "Charlie. As in Charles?"

"No, as in Richard. Like the king."

She smiled despite herself.

"My parents had a sense of humor." His eyebrows dipped sharply. "Just . . ." He scribbled through the air with an invisible pencil.

She finished her notations and slid the book aside. Seeing that Holland was still flushed, Ella made quick work of the patched dress, stripping her down to a pinned diaper. Picking up the baby, Ella held the child to her chest and felt her steamy back. "Oh, my sweet one."

She bounced softly, hoping the cool air on the baby's skin might help. Ella tried to ignore what the girl's shape—the gentle weight of her—did to her heart. Charlie Lionheart watched, expression vulnerable. Strikingly so.

He bore the same thick lashes as the baby, and though his coloring was darker, their profiles showed a remarkable resemblance, the parentage clear. With the settled silence, he tugged a slip of black silk from around his neck. He crammed the scarf in his pocket, flashing dark, fingerless gloves.

"You are a performer?" Ella asked hoping to set him at ease as she rocked Holland.

"I'm sorry?" He ran a broad hand down the side of his face that had been in want of a razor for several days.

"The circus. You are a circus . . . person?"

His hand stilled.

Oh dear, that was the wrong thing to say.

Clearly not about to answer that, he reached into his pocket. "Is this . . ." He pulled out a handful of coins. "Is this going to be enough?" The uncertainty in his eyes could have answered his own question.

It took Ella but a moment to tally the small sum. She breathed in slowly through her nose. "Yes." But it felt like a lie.

He must have sensed it. "For how long?"

"One night." Barely. Ella smoothed a palm down the side of Holland's hot cheek. How she wished that wasn't the case, but Dr. Penske had strict policies when it came to this hospital that catered to Roanoke's upper crust. They were, after all, in the doctor's home, and a philanthropist he was not. Surely this stranger would have had no idea of that when he spotted the three-story establishment from the street. While Dr. Penske occasionally allowed payment installments, if this man was traveling, she didn't know how gracious the doctor would be.

Charlie blinked quickly. "All right. Um . . . is that enough time for her to get well?"

Ella tried to guard her reaction but knew it

showed when he quick-glanced around the room. "Is there something I can do?" He looked back at her. "This is all I have."

"Everything?" It was barely enough to buy a hot meal.

"Do you *want* the clothes on my back?"

"No."

Holland whimpered against her shoulder and Ella rocked gently.

"Mr. Lionheart—"

"Charlie."

"Charlie, sir . . . let's just focus on tonight and Holland. She may be greatly improved in the morning. We'll keep a close eye on her and give her the best attention we can. If she needs more care, we'll cross that bridge when we come to it." Ella held his gaze, praying the doctor wouldn't make a liar of her. "We won't let anything happen to Holland on account of money."

His expression seemed to soften on the way she called his little one by name. Finally, he nodded. She sensed a shift in the air between them as he looked at her almost trustingly.

"Thank you," he said.

"You're welcome. Should . . . is there some way you can get word to the child's mother?"

"Her mother."

"Your wife?"

He peered down at the mattress then smeared fingertips over his forehead without looking up.

"I've never had a wife." His tone was a drip of hot wax—sealing the conversation to a close.

Abigail rushed by, asking Ella to help her find the tincture of camphor in the scullery, ripping Ella's thoughts from what the man had just alluded to and onto duties that needed to be done. It pained her to set the baby down, but she settled Holland onto the small mattress. Then she remembered the ice. "I'll be by in a few minutes." She tidied the tray so the cool rags were in his reach.

Nodding gently, Charlie thanked her.

When Ella stepped away, he leaned forward and kissed Holland on the forehead. Tucking the dropper into the scullery sink, Ella peered back over when she heard him whispering soft words to the baby—almost lyrical. He wasn't singing, not exactly, but she realized it was some kind of hymn. One she felt she knew. His large hand smoothed back the infant's blonde curls again, arm cradling her as if the simple touch might hold at bay all that could step in and separate them.

His aching tangible, Ella had to pull her gaze away, remembering her own kind of fear afresh and how it mattered not that she'd clung to hope. She had still found herself kneeling—nothing to her fingertips but cool earth and cold stone as she pressed flowers to a grave so small, it might have been missed. Her grief so deep, she'd given no thought to those who called her a harlot. They didn't care to find out that she'd been in the wrong place at the wrong time. That you don't have to sell your soul for it to be stolen regardless.

Peering once more over her shoulder, Ella watched as Charlie stood to adjust Holland's pillow before sitting on the edge of his chair again.

Perhaps this was a bad idea. Perhaps the scullery was the best place for Ella after all. It was safe there. Her heart didn't beat back to life surrounded by bowls, bottles, and scrub brushes.

Feeling every ache over a little girl named Holland . . . and a little boy whose mother couldn't bring herself to name, Ella stepped away.

Two

Charlie leaned back in his chair, which sent his coat slipping from the top rail. He picked it up and crammed his gloves and scarf back in the pocket. Remembering Holland's tiny stuffed tiger in the other, he slipped the animal out and into the crook of her plump arm. The tiger was small and the velvet threadbare, but rarely was it not in her grasp as she crawled around their tent or flapped it up and down on his mattress in the wagon. Those blue eyes of hers bright with mischief.

His throat went tight.

It killed him to sit here and do nothing, but he held on to what had been prescribed—fluids, cool compresses, and medicines they hadn't access to apart from here. As the hours passed and with that woman's help, Holland's temperature had lowered. Even as he thought it, Charlie lifted the damp rag again and gently swiped it down the side of her neck, her bare chest.

"Hey," he whispered, shifting forward to rest his forearms on the bed. "You need to get better. Because I need you. And Regina needs you. And everyone else does, too, all right?"

Holland breathed slowly, sleepily. Her chest lifted and lowered, and resting his chin on his folded arms, Charlie watched her small ribs rise and fall. Her hand lay fisted and he traced his finger along it, his thumb almost as thick as her wrist.

Rock of Ages . . . cleft for me.

The hymn kept circling his mind—over and over and over as it always did when he didn't know what to do, when the air closed in on him.

Let me hide myself in thee.

He stared at her pale skin, remembering how easily those tiny, round fingers could tug at his hair, his top hat, anything he had worth catching. Imagined her belly laugh and the way he could coax it out of her with a few animated kisses to her neck, her cheeks . . . those pudgy feet. Charlie smiled at the thought and lifted Holland's limp fingers to his mouth to press his lips there.

"How is she doing?"

At the voice, he looked up into the blue eyes of the nurse who'd been coming and going. The young woman placed used rags into a bucket. What was her name again? She filled the dropper and repeated the task of getting Holland to take some. When the baby struggled, the nurse mentioned fetching more ice chips.

Holland's blue knit hat in his hands, he folded it. Unfolded it.

How many times he didn't know.

The nurse worked quietly another minute. "Her temperature is down again. It often does that

come morning. It will give her a little reprieve."
She checked Holland more closely, looking into
her mouth and feeling around her throat. "I fear
this may not be a common cold. I'll have to do
some reading today."

"What about the doctor?"

The one who had barely spent two minutes with
Holland.

Charlie didn't like the way the nurse's
gaze moved to the man with the rolled-back
shirtsleeves across the ward. Nor the distrust
that lived in her expression. Unsettled, Charlie
glanced from the doctor, then back to the nurse.
"I forgot to ask your name."

She tipped her head down—flashing a crown
of golden braids coiled around her head. "Ella.
A very plain and boring Ella." She gave him a
little smile. "My parents forgot their sense of
humor."

He searched her face and saw that she was
teasing. One more person poking fun at his name.
Sarcasm crept up his throat. "You're quite funny,
do you know that?"

She rolled her eyes, and he would have
regretted his condescension if she hadn't
deserved it. And here he had been liking her. A
glance out the window showed it was still foggy
with a lightly falling snow. One more day the
carnival couldn't open. "Does it always snow in
Roanoke this time of year?" He said it absently,

28

not thinking to make conversation anymore with *plain and boring* Ella.

She answered anyway. "Not that I can ever recall. It's quite late. Just when I thought spring was here . . ."

So had the circus. They'd all thought they'd just be passing through—three days to perform—then move on as usual. Instead, they were trapped in this town. He looked at Holland on the bed and knew it was for the best that he had the day free.

Gaze to the nurse, he watched her, too closely, he realized, when she blushed. "What time is it?" he blurted awkwardly.

Which didn't seem to jar her one bit as she looked to the far wall.

Maybe he could still like her.

"Almost five in the morning."

"How long do you stay here?" he asked.

"I'll be leaving in an hour and another nurse will care for Holland. She's very good at what she does and very kind."

"Thank you." But he didn't want this lady to go. Despite the fact that she was mildly annoying, she was doing a good job with Holland.

Just then, the doctor strode over, ebony hair askew in a wake of clear frustration. He grumbled something about missing linens, and Ella's cheeks tinted as she admitted to having left them in the hall. The doctor escorted her to a nearby cupboard where a lengthy lecture on cleanliness and promptness followed. Though Charlie tried not to listen, he overheard the man saying he would need to dock her pay.

Charlie straightened and glanced over.

Ella apologized and then left for several minutes, perhaps to the laundry. Upon returning, she went back to her work of quietly tidying Holland's bedside table. Charlie rubbed the side of his head. Maybe he should tell the doctor that it was his fault she'd set that bundle aside. But he had a hunch it would only get her in more trouble.

The pale shadows under her eyes reminded him that she hadn't slept, which meant he hadn't either. Or eaten. Good grief, he was still wearing half his costume from yesterday's snowed out parade. The waistcoat now hung open and he'd pulled off his gloves, but it was unseemly for him to be in public without them. He thought about putting the gloves back on, but exhaustion kept him still.

Since they'd landed in town, he'd left Holland only to work, and even then, he'd been back to his tent as quick as possible. Except as he'd tugged off his coat yesterday, he'd knelt beside Holland's box bed and knew she wasn't getting better . . . she was getting worse.

Charlie rubbed his fingers and thumb over his forehead at the headache forming. Since she was asleep, he should close his eyes. Even for just a few minutes.

"What does that mean?" the nurse asked softly.

"The writing."

He looked up at her. "Huh?"

"On your hand."

He turned his wrist to see which one she was referring to. "Um . . . *Carpe Diem*." He rubbed his head again, then dropped his arm. A question in her eyes, he added, "It means 'seize the day.' "

"Oh." Her voice was small. She eyed the side of his hand again. "Is it a . . ."

He narrowed his gaze, waiting. She bit her lip timidly.

"A tattoo," he finished for her.

She looked back to the fine, black script. "Was that painful?"

He gave it a quick glance. "Not *this* one." When her eyes widened, he knew that was a dumb thing to say. "Does that offend you?"

She pursed her lips, face a blank slate. "Why did you do it?"

"So I wouldn't forget."

Her brows lifted. "Will it never come off?"

Words eluding him, he shook his head, soaking in the sight of her face. The unspoken thoughts that traced her brow. He didn't mean to shock her but was somehow doing it anyway. He rarely spoke to *rubes*—townies. At least not away from the lot. Not candidly. Something about it

31

fascinated him. Especially since she didn't know who—and what—she was talking to.

If so, she'd blanch a lot more than she had over his hand.

"Did the doctor happen to see it?" she asked gently.

"I don't know. Why? Is he gonna think I'm a criminal?"

Her mouth pressed slim and she looked toward the dark-haired man. Answer enough when she blinked quickly as if shaking off some silent worry. She placed an empty bowl on the tray along with a cup. "I'll be along to check on Holland before I go. Would you like some water? Or something to eat? You must be hungry."

"No, thank you. I'm fine." He didn't want to trouble her.

The nurse—Ella—moved to walk away, but stilled at the foot of the bed. He looked at her and the shift in his neck made his head throb worse.

"Seize the day," she said. "It's a pleasant thought."

Despite himself, he smiled a little. "Yeah, I suppose it could be something worse."

Her own smile reached her eyes, and a few minutes later, she brought him a cup of water and a piece of bread anyway.

Coat pulled tight against the cold, Ella shivered. *May flowers, indeed.* She ducked chin to collar and crossed the muddy intersection of Campbell and Second, nearly missing the cream and black poster hanging on the fence in front of Rorer Hall. She stepped closer and touched the paper where an inky drawing of a trapeze artist swung above the bold, etched font of *The Most Spectacular Show.* Her finger slid down to a silhouette of three lions. A clown on a unicycle. *One dime to enter,* it said. *Three days only.* The dates were crossed out and adjusted for later on in the week, and she smiled softly, realizing that meant more rest for Holland.

Ella hurried the last block home to her apartment building, feet complaining at the next three flights that led to her door where she slid the key in the lock. She pushed into the small space that was one part parlor and one part kitchen. Nestled off to the side was the bedroom she shared with her roommate Margaret, who often worked opposite shifts. Settling down on the faded sofa, Ella unlaced damp boots and slid them closer to the warmth of the Quaker stove.

With a cup of tea beckoning, she added a scoop of coal to the stove. While the kettle steamed, she washed both face and hands. Pulling a few pins released her rounded braid and Ella tossed it over her shoulder. She blew at wisps of pale yellow hair as she crossed the small room. After hanging up her apron, her fingers slid down the square bodice and she thought of the little girl she'd held there for much of the night. Holland's labored breathing. Whimpers whenever Ella moved her too much. Which made her wonder . . .

Ella snatched the nursing encyclopedia off the bookshelf, fixed a cup of tea, and after changing into a nightgown, crawled into bed and pulled the wool blanket snug. A sip of hot brew, and she nestled in deeper.

She flipped through the book, reading first on adenoids. No. That wasn't it. She shuffled to the index and hunted for pneumonia. *Page 564.* Ella turned there and read, *"A common disease in childhood."* She read on. *"The cough is usually persistent and troublesome."* Holland didn't have a cough. Ella finished the page, then sipped her tea. "Hmm . . ." An idea sparking, she searched for Rheumatic fever, finding the section.

"Rheumatic fever—an acute infectious disease. Inflammation of the joints resulting in pain."

Ella twisted her mouth to the side.

"The predisposing causes are tonsillitis, exposure to cold and damp, and lack of proper nourishment." She thought of Charlie and his mere coins. The storm that had blown in so unexpected. Holland's threadbare dress. Ella's heart tightened as she read on. *"The patient's temperature varies from 102 to 104 with marked remissions."*

Starting back at the beginning, Ella read of the

fever once more, noting the baby's symptoms, and the events of the past twelve hours fell into place. She took care to study the advised treatment, glad she'd done what she could, though a few new remedies came to mind for tomorrow.

"The patient should never be allowed to exert himself in the least, for anything that will give the heart extra work is to be avoided."

Ella would take care to keep Holland as comfortable as possible. She'd also look closely for a developing rash.

Settling lower, she took one last sip of tea. Her gaze flashed over the rim of the cup and she remembered the dark look Dr. Penske had given Holland's father. The way he'd avoided him.

"I don't know, why? Is he gonna think I'm a criminal?" Charlie had asked.

She thought back to earlier in the winter when a sailor had come in, an imprint of an anchor on his shoulder. The doctor had treated the man poorly indeed. Told the staff of a study he'd read declaring that such markings were an easy way to identify felons since they were most often obtained in jail. He'd cautioned the nurses to take care with such unsavory characters.

Ella thought back to Charlie and the black script that went from his wrist to the base of his sturdy thumb. She thought on the gentle protectiveness he had for his little girl and tried to make sense of it all. Then she glanced at the clock, and seeing she was but a quick sleep away from the start of her next shift, she rose, crammed the curtains closed against the light, and slipped back into bed.

THREE

The five blocks from Ella's apartment to Dr. Penske's hospital felt long indeed on this cold afternoon as she walked toward the converted townhome with its white sash windows and wrought iron flower boxes. While only a few flakes of snow fell today, heavy fog made it hard to see up the road. The scent of soot hung in the air as a distant train whistle blew, and on the nearest corner, a man with a political badge pinned to his coat was rallying a crowd. Ella ducked her head and hurried across the street.

In hand she carried her wooden box of herbs and medicines, and if Dr. Penske granted permission, several to use for Holland. Though the hospital surely stocked everything she had in her small latched case, Ella hoped the offering might ease some of the fees between Charlie and the doctor.

She spotted Clara standing on the top step of the sprawling porch, adjusting her little white nursing cap. "Everything all right?" Ella asked as she stepped onto the sidewalk.

"I'm watching for the ambulance. I thought I heard it coming."

Ella listened for the wagon but only heard a ruckus from somewhere upstairs. "What's going on?"

Voices rose one over the other from the third floor windows.

Clara threw her a glare. "I'm sorry that his little girl has a cold. But it doesn't mean he has to shout."

"Who?"

"That man!"

"Which man? What's happened?" Ella moved to the bottom step, already afraid of the answer.

"The one with the baby. He's up there terrorizing the place because they're sending her home."

"Home?"

"Her temperature went down."

"It's meant to fluctuate." Ella hurried up the front stairs.

"She's fine," Clara called after her.

Ella ran into the foyer, then started on the carpeted flights that led to the top floor. Her pulse raced in her ears as she rounded the corner of the children's ward only to see the room in a tizzy. From the far corner, she could hear Charlie shouting. And Holland wailing. A sound so choked, so terrified, that Ella could scarcely breathe.

"It goes down sometimes and then it comes right back up!" Charlie said. "Her fever did it the day before. And the day before that. Which is why I brought her here."

"What's going on?" Ella asked a nurse who hefted a spindled chair down the aisle way.

"Some rough men came in early this morning, got treated for blistered hands, then split before they could be billed. Took whiskey from one of the cabinets. Doctor's furious. Is certain they were with the circus, so he asked the man with the baby to pay up front and he can't."

Mouth gaping, Ella picked her way to where Dr. Penske stood toe to toe with Charlie. Holland was pressed to Charlie's chest, her wails scratchy, his dark trench brushing his boots.

"I didn't even know those men! If you just give me a few minutes, I can get money wired through the bank. I have an account in New York and one in New Orleans."

"Oh, I'm *sure* you do." A lock of Dr. Penske's hair fell limp across his brow. "Get out of my hospital."

"You can't do this!" Charlie shouted.

"Oh, yes, I can!" the doctor yelled back.

With a growl, Charlie stomped to the bed, grabbed Holland's things from the bedside table, then barreled down the aisle. He seemed to notice Ella for the first time, and in passing, the rage in his eyes shifted to brokenness. Holland, curled up against his chest, tugged at her ear as if it hurt, her cries all that lingered as he disappeared around the bend.

Ella rushed up to Dr. Penske. "Has her fever broken?"

He pulled off his spectacles and used the edge of his coat to wipe the eyepieces. "She'll be just fine. I gave her father instructions—no different than what's been done for the girl here. There's little to do for a simple fever. A bit of time and comfort is all that she needs. Trust me." The side of his mouth quirked up. "We're doing him a favor by sending them on home."

"But she may have Rheumatic fever!"

"Are you a physician now?"

"She had the makings of it last night. Aches. And her throat. All the signs—"

"Did you read about that in one of your books?" he snapped.

"Did you check her this afternoon?"

"She's fine. We need these beds for patients who have dire injuries and can actually pay for their care." His glare followed Charlie's path, voice low. "The last thing we need here is some gutter-rat illness. The pair of them can go back to whatever hole they crawled out of."

Jaw open, Ella backed away. Heart pounding. His gaze flicked to the box she held then back up. Dr. Penske eyed her sharply and she took another step and then another.

"What are you doing?" he asked.

Truly, she didn't know.

"Walk out that door, young lady, and you will no longer have a position here."

Her chest heaved as she stared at the man. She'd worked hard for this position. A job many wanted, and she'd managed to get on staff.

But all she could think of were Holland's cries. The possibility of Rheumatic fever and the damage it would do to her heart if left untreated. Ella took another step back.

"I mean it, Miss Beckley."

She nodded slowly. Glanced around the ward at the small faces—thinking of one. No . . . two.

Holland. And the tiny boy she hadn't had the power to save. But this time . . .

The decision snapped into place and Ella hurried out, fearing Holland was long gone.

Down the stairs and into the fog, she glanced up the street, having no idea where the two had headed. She closed her eyes, trying to recall what the poster had said of the circus' location. Just past Campbell. Three blocks from her apartment. She dashed down the street, scurrying around a coal and coke wagon, then over a puddle and up on the other sidewalk. Holding her skirts, she rushed over the slushy walks. Brick buildings loomed all around, and even among the chilly shadows, her skin warmed from running.

She turned the corner and hurried across a quiet, snow-dusted road, then spotted a man in the distance. As tall and wide of shoulder as she remembered Charlie. Ella called his name.

He glanced back without slowing—flashing the profile she now knew.

Reaching him, Ella was breathless as she peered up into grief-stricken eyes. He held his coat tight around the shivering baby. Ella hadn't realized they'd stopped in front of one of the grocers until a woman bustled out and nearly dropped her bundles. It was the same blushing fumble that had plagued several of Dr. Penske's nurses the last two days. But Charlie didn't seem to notice the woman's awed stare as he peered down at Ella.

"What are you doing here?" His brow knotted.

"I want to help you."

His forehead pinched tighter.

She looked at the seven-month-old whose tiny face peeked out from the folds of his collar, eyes closed—asleep. Tears had dried to her cheeks.

"I think I know what might help her." Ella motioned for him to walk on.

He did, peering sideways at her. "You want to help her?" His gaze fell to the box of medicines she held.

"I'll need to come with you."

"Now?" he said it with uncertainty. As though she didn't mean it.

She hesitated. "I have some time today."

Swallowing, he looked the way they had come,

then where he was headed. As if she'd just asked him to break the law, he gripped the back of his neck. Squeezed his eyes closed. Indecision hung heavy until he peered down at her again. "Okay." Such a simple word and then he quickened his pace, glancing back just briefly.

The fog rolled cold over her as they hurried along. The blocks passed in a blur. Oft-walked streets now obscuring in mind. All she could see was the determined shape of Charlie's shoulders as he towered ahead, dark coat nearly dusting the street beside his thunderous boots. He spoke to no one and no one spoke to him.

A chill settled around her, and then Ella spotted a trio of massive flags whipping in the wind. Blurred by the thick fog, more like ghosts of flags. Charlie walked toward them and Ella almost tripped over her feet at the sudden burst of a voice.

"Ey! Charlie, love. Where've you been all my life?"

Ella's head shot up. Charlie passed through what had to be the circus entrance as it was flanked by two booths, one inhabited by that strange female voice.

"Practicing my card game," Charlie said distractedly as he opened a low gate.

"Aw, you still sore about that?"

It was then that Ella spotted a large woman who nearly filled the entire booth. She had a cigarette held by her ear, hair pulled back in a wild bun. Fiery rouge on her cheeks. Above loomed a banner that read *Graven Brothers Circus*.

"Not so fast, missy. Who do you think you is?" The woman held a wooden baton out and Ella slammed to a halt, staring at a forearm as pale and thick as a mound of dough.

Charlie halted. "She's with me, Lorelai."

"None of that nonsense, now. I'll have no strange women about. Not on me grounds."

"Lorelai, she's a *nurse*. She's come for Holland."

"She bett'a be." The woman's face softened when it shifted to Charlie. Her baton lowered. "Aw, but me Charlie-boy's a good lad. Give us a kiss, love, and I didn't see nothin'."

Charlie kissed a painted cheek in passing. "You're too good to me." He held the gate open for Ella who swallowed the pulsing that had shot into her throat.

"Give 'olland me love," the woman said. Then she eyed Ella sharply.

Charlie walked backwards and the woman blew a kiss toward the baby who had stirred awake. He spun back down the path, his pace resuming its force. Ella skittered over the thin traces of muddy snow to catch up just as a pair of men hanging a sign threw a wave to him. Her town— her world—but a memory now.

"Are we opening tomorrow?" Charlie called.

"Yep!" one of the men bellowed before

glancing toward the giant, striped tent in the distance. "Not likely for a blowdown now!"

Charlie nodded at that even as he steered around a painted cart. A bit too quick and Ella nearly crashed into it, her nose inches from a peeling painting of two frowning clowns. She bit back a yelp and hurried to keep up.

Strange voices greeted Charlie all around. One man hollered out a "G'day, Preach!" while a gentleman pushing a wheelbarrow full of straw asked after "wee Holland."

A few moments later, Charlie stopped in front of a Gypsy wagon with a green, rounded top. A woman was there—light brown skin stunningly beautiful, long black hair draped with a colorful silk scarf. Ella stayed clear of the sign advertising palm readings for five cents while he swapped a coin in exchange for a jar of milk. The woman pocketed his money with a wink, said something in a language Ella didn't understand, then strode up the steps of her wagon and disappeared behind a beaded curtain.

A goat bleated a farewell as Charlie continued on.

"You know a lot of people here," Ella said, hoping it might calm her nerves and just to make sure he knew she was still following him. Or maybe he'd forgotten.

He spoke without slowing. "Is there a reason I shouldn't?"

A hunched man with a monkey on his shoulder crossed in front of their path. Charlie slowed, but suddenly focused on a nearby worker leading a brown bear on a leash. Ella didn't notice Charlie had halted until she'd crashed into him. He looked back, expression unreadable.

"Um . . . sorry." Ella swallowed hard and fought the urge to rub her nose.

Charlie went to take a step then lifted his arm and looked at his sleeve. Ella realized she was clutching onto it for dear life.

She quickly let go.

"Are you all right?"

"Oh, yes," she squeaked eying the beast of a bear. This was perfectly normal. Just your everyday kind of outing.

He rolled his eyes and started on faster than the beating of Ella's heart as she rushed to keep up, cold to the bone and utterly alone except for this man who she didn't know. The wisdom of this choice was starting to feel very thin.

"Mr. Lionheart . . . Charlie . . . I . . ."

He cast a look over his shoulder as they crossed over a small decorative bridge. Her face must have been flooded with angst because he stopped.

"Is something wrong?" he asked, glancing around. Spotting a crowd of laborers, he turned his back to them, ducking his face closer to Ella as if to keep their presence here as subtle as possible.

"I just . . . where are we going?"

"Home—to lay Holland down. Which is this way. I need to get her inside." His nerves were showing. "And quite frankly, *you* as well."

"Me?" Did he sense that she wanted to turn around and flee? Go home and shake the mud of this place off her shoes? A part of her did. But then she glimpsed the tiny face peeking out of Charlie's coat. His arms wrapping the tiny form as best he could. Ella looked into little blue eyes brimming with tears.

Tipped her chin up. "Never mind."

"Home's just over there." He pointed to one of the plain, canvas tents in the foggy distance.

"That's where you live?" she breathed, not meaning to say that aloud.

He spared a curious glance. They walked on a few paces, her heading into a tent with a man whose conduct she didn't know. What if it were just the two of them in there?

"You don't live . . . alone . . . do you?" Her voice was high.

He didn't seem to hear her as he halted in front of a wagon that held wedges of wood. Charlie bartered with the wagon owner for a few pieces, promising to return within the hour to fetch them. Then he motioned for Ella to walk on.

Her question still unanswered, Ella tried a different approach, desperate for some kind of insight into his character. "Where do you leave Holland? When you're working."

"Do you think I leave her alone?"

"Of—of course not."

Charlie glanced back at the wood, then to Ella. "She stays with a woman who lives with me. Her name is Regina."

Nearly tripping, Ella envisioned the Gypsy lass who had this man. But before another moment passed, she was hit by the shock of what he had just alluded to.

Her gaze flew to him as he wove around the nearest tent. How much was different for this bohemian people and their moral compass? When she didn't respond, his green eyes flashed back to her. Lingering.

"Regina," he said, clearly seeing that he was going to have to elaborate. "She's a costume mistress. I share my tent with her, my wagon. I take care of her. And in exchange, she tends to Holland as though she were her own."

"Are you saying that this woman living with you is not even the child's mother?"

The side of his mouth lifted. "No." He looked amused. "She's not the child's mother."

Ella wet her lips. He hesitated a moment as if trying to read her expression. His own was horridly unguilty.

He pulled a hand forward through his cropped tangle of hair. "Does this bother you?"

"I . . ." She gulped, unwilling to acknowledge what it did to her. The cold wash of memories that spread within as she stood before a man who clearly had no regard for women. So stiff, lifeless words slipped out instead. "It's certainly frowned upon."

He stopped in front of a tent. The opening was tied closed and he worked on the first loop. "You don't say?" He loosened another.

She ignored his sarcasm.

"People can frown all they want then." His voice fell to a whisper as he freed the third. "It's not their life. Besides, Regina . . . she means a lot to us. To me."

"All right."

"I need her." He straightened. "And Holland adores her. They're good together. Do people care about that?"

"I . . . don't . . . know."

"Then *don't* bring them into it." He yanked back the flap and motioned Ella in.

"After you." Her sharp tone matched his.

He slammed his eyes closed a moment. "Look. I'm sorry to be so short, but I could get in trouble for this. Do you understand?"

"Because of me?"

He nodded, and by the look he flashed, it was more than a little trouble. "It's against the rules."

"You have rules?"

"*Every time* I say something you ask me another

question." He quickly glanced around. "Can we just get inside? Please. I'll tell you whatever you want, inside."

His gaze raked her and she wondered how she—five foot five in a gray nurse's dress with puffy sleeves and sweating palms—could possibly hold a threat to him.

Ella clutched her box close and followed him in.

Surrounded by nothing but white canvas, dim light seeped through, making the makeshift room bright.

He gestured toward a stout woman standing at a tiny black stove. "Ella. Meet Regina. Regina, this is Ella, a nurse from town."

The heavy-set woman looked over her shoulder and smiled, revealing a gap between her teeth. Her dark hair was threaded deeply with silver and pulled back into a rope of a braid. Standing on a crate to better reach the stove, she couldn't have been but three feet tall. A few seconds passed and she arched a thick eyebrow. "Were you expecting Sleeping Beauty, *cara*?"

The question hung in the air for a moment. Then two.

Ella felt Charlie behind her, so close with his mouth lowered to her ear that she nearly jumped. "That means don't stare," he whispered loudly.

FOUR

Gulping, Ella glanced around the square tent that was surprisingly roomy and warm. Only three walls were of canvas. The fourth was made up by the open side of a painted green wagon. She'd seen a picture of a circus wagon before in a story book, but it paled in comparison with what she'd seen today. Particularly this one, near and solid, with its ornate trimmings, guttered rooftop, and gold-painted wheels. The tent butted up against it, strapped snug where canvas met wood so that not even a breeze snuck in.

Regina ambled over and gently took the jar of milk.

"It's nice to meet you," Ella said softly.

The woman returned the sentiment, but concern showed in the way she pressed a stubby hand against her brown cheek. Her dark eyes tilted in Charlie's direction as he stepped toward a small wooden bed. He lowered the baby onto a fringed blanket where just below an ornate rug covered most of the grass. The woman's gaze returned to Ella.

Ella knelt there at Holland's side as Charlie slipped off the baby's hat.

He looked at her and Ella braced for whatever

51

comment was to come, but he simply said, "Thank you."

Drawing a breath, she held his gaze the moment he allowed. She searched her mind for where to begin. "Do you have any oil? And hot water to make her tea? Also, a little pot, please."

He stepped away and returned with a glass bottle and a copper pot. "Like this?"

Regina hefted a kettle onto the small potbelly stove.

With a snap, Ella opened up her wooden case. She freed a tiny glass jar of dried eucalyptus and mixed a hearty spoonful into the oil. At her bidding, Charlie set the pot on the stove. Ella asked him to fill another with water and add a teaspoon from the same jar she'd used. Next Ella carefully stripped the baby of her dress. Though the oil would take time to properly stew, she dabbed some and with the warm herby oil to her fingertips, made slow circles on Holland's chest. She named a few other things that would be needed.

Charlie moved away and pulled apart two small curtains that hung from the broad side of the wagon. Several crates formed makeshift steps into what looked like an oversized, raised bed. Pillows and blankets were scattered everywhere. He rummaged, and as he did, Ella glimpsed a crate of folded clothes, a hanging top hat and a pair of high-polished boots. After taking up a pencil and leather-bound notebook, Charlie scribbled a fast note then tore out the sheet of paper. Climbing down, he must have caught her study of his private space because he pulled the curtains together to block it all from view.

He gave the note to Regina. "Give this to Mr. Graven. He'll cover everything you need and he can take it out of this week's payment."

Nodding, Regina accepted it, but she glanced to Ella. "She cannot be here. You know that."

Holland pulled at her little ear and Ella stopped circling to feel under the baby's jaw for swollen lymph nodes. The girl peered up and Ella smiled gently.

Regina spoke softly. "If Madame Broussard finds out—"

"Then she *won't*." Charlie ran a hand over the back of his neck. "And it's just for a short while." He was quiet a few moments, and when he spoke again, his voice was as soft as ever. "I don't know what else to do."

Reaching up, Regina squeezed his arm in a motherly way.

Awash with how little she understood about this man—these people—Ella looked away. But Charlie moved back to the bed and knelt beside her. Though his stature was as broad and looming as ever, there was a gentleness in the way he took off Holland's booties, then her stockings. He set both aside. "What else do we do for her?"

Ella drew in a slow breath and hoped with every ounce of her being that she had the right answer to that.

If word got out that he brought a young woman here, he was going to have a lot more on his trail than a disgruntled doctor. Charlie tried not to think about that as Ella pulled off her coat and set it aside.

"We need cider vinegar. Do you have any?" she asked. "Also licorice drops which we can break up into tiny pieces."

He looked over at Regina who reached for her shawl.

"I will find some. Anything else?" Regina asked.

Ella requested items that included molasses, brandy, and more rags for compresses. Regina set about dampening a rag and handed it to Ella.

"How will we get her to take these things?" Charlie asked when Regina was gone.

"I'm not sure yet." Ella dug through her case of medicines, eyeing several bottles. She set two on the edge of the bed. "We might have to tuck them into something she *will* take. Which is why the molasses is handy. Also applesauce." She nodded toward the bottle of herbs that had already been sprinkled into the pots. "The steaming eucalyptus should provide some relief for her. The other herbs should all help with her throat, which I fear has an infection. That's what's causing the fever. Treating the fever alone at this point won't do much good. Though we do need to keep it as low as we can." She felt Holland's diaper and began to loosen the pins.

"I'll do that." Charlie pulled a basket close. He worked quietly, taking care with the pins so as not to poke the baby, then set the damp diaper aside. He'd wash it with the rest of the diapers tomorrow. He realized the nurse was staring at him.

She pressed the back of a hand to Holland's cheek. "You are good with her."

"Well, that's a relief because I'm all she has." He regretted his sarcasm when Ella looked up with sad eyes.

She adjusted the compress from Holland's forehead to her chest. "The baby's mother . . . she is gone?"

Charlie moved the diaper to the laundry pile.

He didn't tell rubes about his private life. Not ever. Why was this woman so danged curious? But an answer paled in comparison to what he owed her, so he found the words coming out. "Holland's mother died when the baby was five weeks old."

"I'm sorry."

"It happens." Not wanting to talk about that, he moved to the stove and checked the kettle. But grief needled into his chest anyway. He picked up an empty tin cup from beside the baby's bed, then plopped it in the washtub, thoughts suddenly as scattered as his messes. Whatever Ella had made him add to the water was filling the room with a tangy, rich scent. It tingled in his chest with every breath he took, so cooling that he was thankful Holland was breathing this air. "I appreciate you coming here. Helping. Thank you."

Ella gave him a muted smile.

"When do you need to be back to the hospital?"

She folded the damp cloth and ran it down the baby's arm. The words came out slowly. "I don't need to go back today."

"I'll pay you for your time."

"I don't want you to pay me."

"I'd like to all the same." He rubbed knuckles to jaw. "I'll get paid soon. If you can just help her, I'll give you that and anything else I have."

Her blue eyes seemed sad.

"What can I do?" he asked.

"Honestly? Just sit a moment. There's not much to do until I can make those tinctures and teas. For the time being, she seems comfortable."

With them alone, he pulled a crate to the tent flap and sat, giving her space, setting himself where he could be seen by anyone who might pass by. The sky was growing lighter.

"I take it you don't have work to do today, either?" she asked.

"Until the circus opens, not publicly."

56

She tucked her bottom lip between her teeth and looked about to ask what the public kind might be. He was glad when she didn't. No sense overwhelming her completely. Charlie looked around, feeling strange to be alone with a woman who wasn't Regina. He clasped his hands, and not wanting the nurse to be uncomfortable, kept his gaze on Holland. She seemed to be sleeping well.

He cleared his throat. "I've never brought a townsperson here before," he confessed. Not to the circus and certainly not to his tent. "I'm sorry that I've been rude to you. I just don't know what to do or say because this is new to me. I don't talk with people like you very often."

"People like me?"

He felt a small grin betray him. "A rube."

"Rube?"

"People who pay. To watch us."

"Oh."

"So if I was . . . gruff, I'm sorry. I'm just not good at this. That's not meant to be an excuse. I want to apologize for not being more polite." This was coming out all wrong. "I'll do better. At least, I'll try."

She smiled as if that was the strangest apology she'd ever received. "Thank you. I'm glad to be able to help."

He dipped his head in a nod.

Ella set the rag aside and brushed a curl away

from Holland's forehead. Charlie noted the nurse's hair was the same pale color. She looked over at him, eyes kind. "How did you come to live here with Regina?"

Charlie drew in a slow breath. Early evening air wafted cold through the slit in the tent. He tugged the canvas somewhat closed. "She's been a friend of my family's for a long time. Her husband died some years ago, and when it was just me and Holland, she moved in with us to help."

"That's so kind."

"That's Regina. You won't find a better soul. Her contract states that she's my costume mistress, but you could say she's my godmother."

At that Ella beamed as though Regina were her godmother too. It was such a sweet expression, he wished it lasted longer. But she turned back to the baby as she spoke. "Just keep administering fluids as often as she'll take them. Try and keep her comfortable. And still. The best thing is sleep. The steam will be beneficial so keep water boiling all night long."

Seeing Regina through the slit, Charlie rose and opened the flap.

The stout woman held a filled basket. "I found most everything and Angelina offered to go to the confectioners for the licorice drops. She'll bring them along when she gets back." Regina gave Charlie an envelope. "And Mr. Graven advanced half your pay."

Charlie blew out a breath of relief, peeked inside the envelope, and thumbed through the money. He slid out a bill to give to Ella but she shook her head so Charlie folded it up and slipped it in her medic case.

She pulled it back out and wedged it beneath a pair of books on a crate.

Charlie rolled his eyes and she smiled. That wasn't the end of that game.

Ella spent the next few minutes going over all that Regina had scrounged up. The pair of them chatted easily as Ella prepared what must have been a tincture and gave Regina suggestions for the evening. "When she wakes, give her some of the tea in the blue jar, then mix up some of the chamomile after that."

"This one?" Regina pulled a narrow, cloth bag from the basket.

"That's the one. The first will battle the infection and this will help her stay restful. She's going to be sleepy but whenever she's awake, offer her bits of licorice drops. Just smash them up nice and small." Ella glanced over at Charlie and hesitated a few moments before saying, "I should be going now. I can come back tomorrow and see how she's doing." She took up her coat. "Perhaps you don't have any ice."

He shook his head.

"I'll bring some. Should I . . . should I go out the way we came in?"

"It'd be better for me to walk you," he said. "Tomorrow I'll meet you at the entrance. What time?"

She slid back into her coat. "How about nine o'clock?"

He nodded at that.

Though sunset was but an hour away, the sky was brighter when they stepped outside. The clouds parting. "It looks like there will be finer weather for you tomorrow," she said.

He tilted his head toward the faint warmth. They walked side by side and he made it a point not to rush her as quickly this time. There were plenty of circus folk milling about on the eight-acre lot, busy with all that needed to be done and dried out by tomorrow. Colorful valentines— which rubes called posters—were being nailed around, advertising everything from the main matinee to dozens of sideshows.

Knowing the consequence for being spotted with an outsider, *especially* a young woman, Charlie thought about stepping away from Ella some, but he didn't want to be rude, so he just crammed his hands in his pockets and focused on not letting his shoulder bump into hers.

"I'm sorry that I accused you of . . . well, of . . ." Her voice was unsteady as he led them around the back of the Big Top where they were less likely to be seen.

He smiled over at her, which was probably the

wrong thing to do since that accusation had been his overindulgence in women. Living with a lover out of wedlock—or whatever she'd assumed he was up to.

"Despite what you may think, I *was* taught morality." Hand pressed to his heart, he moved to her other side. "I also try not to break the law."

She pursed her lips.

"Especially in the state of Virginia," he quipped, pretty sure that's where they were. His determination aside, there was a fine for what she'd accused him of.

Her eyes flashed with regret, and then she looked like she was about to apologize. Or faint. He smiled as they rounded the striped tent. Here he'd thought making friends with rubes would be hard.

Look how well he was doing.

The ring of a hammer sounded nearby. Ella peered that way. Whether to cool the blush in her cheeks or to sightsee, he didn't know.

A moment later, he watched that round mouth of hers drop when they passed the elephants being led back to the menagerie tent. He looked at the six-ton animals, straining to see them as she might. Tried to imagine that their busy trunks and floppy ears were something out of the ordinary. Trying and failing, he simply walked Ella to the entrance and saw her through.

He bid her farewell and watched her cross

the street. On the opposite corner, she gave him a small wave and a promise to be back at nine tomorrow. If his father were standing beside him, he would warn Charlie to not get attached. Charlie pressed on the knuckles of one hand, then the other, and tried to drive that warning to heart as he walked away.

FIVE

"Ella Beckley! I can't believe you did that!"

"I know," Ella groaned and lowered her face onto her folded arms.

Seated at the breakfast table across from her roommate, Margaret, she knew a lecture was coming and deservedly so.

"All the other nurses were in a tizzy. You just walked out on Dr. Penske!"

"I know. I know!" She straightened. "I don't know what to do now. Thank you for bringing my things home."

"He practically *shoved* it all into my arms." Margaret smirked then leaned forward. "Rumor has it that you walked out because of a patient. Was it Mr. Circus?" Her brows bobbed. "I heard the ruckus *he* made."

Ella winced under her friend's scrutiny.

"It *was* him!"

She nodded.

"Ella! What happened?"

She relayed the story, finishing with the part about Charlie and Holland and the carnival grounds yesterday. Margaret shook her head, mouth ajar.

"I can't believe it," the brunette whispered.

"It's very true."

"And you're going back today?"

Ella nodded. "To check on her and to bring ice."

"How exciting!" Margaret's eyes went wide.

Exciting? "Margaret, I don't know what I'm going to do. I quit my job." Ella reached out and touched her friend's arm. "I promise I won't skimp on this month's rent. You can count on me." She just wasn't sure how. Ella thought of the money Charlie had offered her but she was going to have to think about that.

Margaret squeezed her hand. "Don't worry. We'll think of something."

Even as she tallied what was in her small savings, Ella took another sip of coffee. She lifted her eyes to the clock then slammed the cup down. "Oh, I've got to go!"

"Why the rush?"

"I promised to meet him at nine and I'm going to be late." Ella grabbed a shawl and the box of herbs and medicines, then darted down the steps to the street below, resenting all three floors as she thundered back up into the apartment for the ice she'd forgotten. From the icebox, she tugged a small chunk, wrapped it in a strip of cheesecloth, and darted to the sidewalk.

A moment's glance in each direction and she crossed the street. It was three blocks to the circus and Ella nearly ran each step. The sidewalks were all but empty, some businesses even closed. In the distance, a throng of townsfolk was gathering for opening day—people braving the mud for a day at the circus.

It took several minutes to find Charlie among the crowd and Ella knew she was late when she spotted him leaning against one of the brightly-painted booths, arms folded over his chest. He seemed to study something in the far distance, the morning light warm on his brown hair. He wore a white shirt that was untucked and wrinkled, suspenders abandoned about his hips. Then he glanced over at Ella and straightened.

"You're late, *plain and boring* Ella."

"I'm sorry."

His mouth quirked and she could see that he was teasing. "This way." He tipped his head toward the entrance they'd used the day before. He swerved around the thick lines—a few complaints rising from the press of people waiting to purchase a day's admittance at the ticket wagon.

"Oh, keep your shirts on," he muttered under his breath. With a hand pressed to the top board of a low barricade, he hopped over and turned, hands at her waist. To lift her over as well?

She stepped back.

As if regretting his actions, he took the ice and pocketed it, then hefted up her box. He held her arm as she climbed the boards that made up the gate. She landed with an "oof" on the other side and he flicked one of the entrance workers a coin.

Charlie started on and Ella fell in step beside him. Everything was different than the day before. With the sun piercing through clouds, the giant lot was no longer a frosty land of shadows, and although a fresh sprinkling of rain had washed away the thin snow, turning the ground to mud, hordes of people milled about. Two workers shoveled sawdust onto the main walkways and a man on stilts lumbered over the heads of a huddle of giggling children. The air held the earthy smells of distant rain, wet straw, and manure. From somewhere in the distance, exotic birds called to one another.

"I'm sorry to be in such a hurry," Charlie said. "But I have to be to the Big Top soon. My act doesn't start until one, but I need to sort some things out with my boys."

"How is Holland doing?"

"She seems good," he sighed in relief. "A little better."

"That's wonderful to hear." Ella smiled up at him and shouldn't have, for he gripped her elbow and swerved her around a man juggling wooden balls.

He let go as they walked on.

"What do you do here?" she asked to cover up her embarrassment.

Hands in his pockets, he tipped up his freshly-shaved jaw. "I'll give you two guesses."

She eyed him from head to toe, not daring to confess all the ideas she'd drummed up last night. She went with the wildest. "Sword . . . swallower."

At that he laughed. "No, or I'd have been to see you much sooner. One more guess. And I'll give you a hint since you're clearly very bad at this." The amusement in his expression warmed her more than the parting of the clouds.

She looked at him, then around, then back. Felt her brows pinch. The smile lines around his eyes deepening, he thumbed over his shoulder to where a poster hung from the partition. She moved closer to see that it depicted him in a top hat that was pulled low, expression intense, lions flanking him. Ella's eyes shot wide as she read, "Ferocious lions under the Big Top. Live and untamed." She looked at him. "You work with lions?"

He nodded.

"Is that safe?"

He tipped his head to the side, sunlight shining on his olive skin. "Would I be standing here talking to you if it wasn't?" He motioned for them to walk on.

Fair. The tents that billowed in the breeze were growing plainer. Ornate wagons looking more like homes than showcases with their glass windows, little curtains, and even a few potted plants. Which meant his own tent and wagon weren't too far off. Ella was eager to hurry to Holland, but her feet slowed. "They're not . . . nearby, are they? The lions?" Surely he wouldn't keep them close to the baby.

He chuckled and touched her lower back to have her walk on. "They stay near the Big Top."

"And you just came from there?"

He nodded, touch falling away. "I spend my mornings working with them but wasn't there yesterday—which isn't ideal. They have a nasty habit of misbehaving when they get jealous." He winked.

She was mildly tempted to ask what a misbehaving lion entailed.

At his tent, Regina stood just outside, bartering with a man for coal. She paused and spoke to Charlie. "She's just woken. And our lovely Angelina brought by a jar of honey for Axel."

Saying she was a dear, Charlie pulled back the tent flap for Ella who ducked in. Light played through the canvas walls, the space as homey as she remembered. Then she froze.

There, lying on the bed with the stuffed tiger nestled against her, was Holland. She stared up at the canvas ceiling as air lifted it up and down—like grass on an open plain. Ella moved beside the baby and knelt on the rug. Holland peered over at her.

"Hello, sweet one." Ella pulled a locket timepiece from her medicine case, then slid her thumb into place to take the baby's pulse.

"She didn't sleep well last night, but is doing better this morning," Charlie said.

Checking the timepiece confirmed that Holland's pulse was lower today—one hundred and twelve beats per minute. Much better than it had been. Ella kissed her forehead. The baby blinked from her to Charlie with vibrant eyes. Her little mouth worked as she sucked what must have been a chip of licorice drop.

Sliding on the locket, Ella motioned to the melting ice. "Will you smash that up?"

Charlie moved to the shelf beside the stove and began banging about, returning a minute later with a dish of powdered ice.

"Perfect." Before Ella could ask for a spoon, he brought one.

"She still won't eat much." Charlie knelt.

Ella touched Holland's forehead then gently lifted the baby to sit against her. "The fever is still there." She held the spoon to the baby's lips and Holland hesitated then suckled a taste of the ice.

Charlie watched. "But she drank some."

"That's a good sign."

He used his finger to tap off a list. "I did the tea . . . the tincture . . . and the oil rub." His eyebrows scrunched. "And something else that I can't remember."

Ella smiled and with the air still fragrant with the scent of eucalyptus, she had a hunch what that was. Then she noted the shadows under his eyes. "Did *you* sleep?"

"Like a king." But by the way he rose, she sensed he was evading her question. He set about tidying up the small space.

"You're making yourself late, Charlie," Regina said.

Ella held the spoon and Holland nibbled more of the powdery ice. Charlie's shirt was still untucked and wrinkled, and for the first time she noticed that the hem was spliced in several spots.

"Was that from a lion?"

Charlie peered down at the frayed edges, having to shove the front of his hair back as he did. "Oh. Yeah. Han and Kristov like to bring their claws out when we wrestle. But Axel has better manners." As if that were the most normal thing to say, he walked up the crates and ducking, stepped into the wagon where he closed the curtains. "Did you see the new bills they hung around?" he called through.

"Yes," Regina said. "They're excellent. You look very fierce."

Then his voice through the curtain, "I smiled, but no one ever draws me that way."

Regina winked over at Ella.

"Have you seen the tin of greasepaint?" he asked.

"It's here on the shelf."

His muffled voice, "And here I was hoping it got lost."

Regina whispered to Ella, "He doesn't like it." The small woman stirred her pot and Ella nodded like she understood what they were talking about.

When Holland had chewed and swallowed another taste of ice, Ella filled the tiny spoon again. Charlie called out for his shirt and Regina ambled over to where it sat folded on a chair. She slipped it to him through the curtain, taking the other in exchange. Ella kept her eyes away from the slim part and tried not to notice the way he was thunking about. Regina set the tattered shirt on top of a sewing box that had several others waiting to be mended. Then she ducked behind a small, folding partition that must have hidden her bed from view because she stepped back around with a folded blanket.

By the time Ella coaxed a smile from Holland, the curtain opened and Charlie climbed out. Dressed in black pants and tall, polished boots, he seemed more commanding than ever. He'd carefully tucked a crisp white shirt beneath an embroidered waistcoat and from a peg on the wall pulled down a green velvet jacket that was so dark it was almost black. Cropped in the front and longer in back, he slid it over his sturdy shoulders. Ella could only stare as he knotted a black cravat around his neck, tucking it with hurried hands beneath his vest. He finished by casually touching the top button at his collar, then the cuff links on each sleeve.

She must have stared overlong because he stopped his tugging and straightening and smiled at her. She slammed her mouth closed.

Chuckling, he turned to a mirror on the wall, leaned toward it, and dampened his hair from the washstand. Next he opened a tin of pomade and ran some through. Ella smoothed her hand over Holland's fingers and watched as Regina brought Charlie a comb. He slicked his hair back, parting it to the side, combing it until it was perfectly smooth.

His gaze found hers in the mirror.

And drat, she was still staring. Ella set the empty cup of ice aside and Holland played with the spoon, twisting it and turning it in pudgy hands. She dropped it to pull at her ear and Ella handed it back. Using a small rag, Ella dabbed gently at the baby's runny nose. The moisture there, combined with the lack of a rash, both blessed indication that this was likely tonsillitis that hadn't bloomed into its more fatal cousin, Rheumatic fever.

Charlie moved another tin down from a shelf and pulled out a few things.

"The white—do the white," Regina said.

"I don't want to." He rubbed at his smooth jaw.

"It's opening day, they'll expect it."

"I don't have time."

"Sit down. I'll do it." When Charlie grinned, Regina smiled over at Ella. "Do you see how I spoil him?"

Ella peered down to see that Holland was blinking asleep. Despite herself, she pressed a kiss to the baby's forehead once more. Charlie watched the exchange with a curious expression. Then something Regina said snapped him back to attention. He tugged a crate over to where the woman was waiting with the tin.

He sat, closed his eyes, and bent his head back. Regina smeared powder over his face until it was white, then took a black pencil from the box. With expert movements, she drew the shape of a masquerade mask, then around his eyes angled, cat-like openings. She shaded the mask in with gentle strokes from a jar of black coloring until it was as solid as midnight. The effect was both peculiar and intriguing.

"Do you do this every time you perform?" Ella asked.

Charlie squinted over at her, his expression slightly guarded as if he knew how uncommon this was. "Yes, but thankfully Regina is very good at what she does."

The small woman told him to hold still. "He only says that so he doesn't have to do it." A few more strokes of her pencil, then Regina leaned back and studied the masquerade effect. "Now

73

you're really going to be late." She wiped her stout hands on a rag.

Charlie moved about before returning to the center of the tent with a brass-topped cane and a pair of white gloves. "My hat?"

Regina pointed to his wagon bed and Charlie fetched a black top hat, wearing it for several seconds before he swapped it for another.

"See you this afternoon," Regina said.

Charlie bid her farewell, then set the new hat on his head, tilting it down and a hint to the side, shading his brow. He gave Ella a mischievous smile, his face just as handsome with the paint as without.

"Goodbye, Miss Holland." He tipped his hat toward the baby, strode to the tent opening, then glanced back, his green eyes somehow more vivid now. "Thank you, Ella. If you're here when I'm done, I'll walk you out." He smiled, then was gone.

Ella hadn't realized her mouth was ajar until Regina strode back to her pot saying, "If the wind changes, your face will stay that way."

Swiveling toward the woman, Ella knew she needed to speak the question that lay waiting to be acknowledged, and even now she was sure to sound like a ridiculous schoolgirl. "How long . . . how long are you here? In Roanoke?"

"We perform for three days. By tomorrow, we'll have two left. Then it's farther north."

Holland's soft breathing filled the silence.

Ella peered down at the baby, then to the slit in the tent where Charlie had vanished. "And then you're all gone. Just like that."

Regina gave Ella a sad smile, as if understanding. "Just like that, *mia cara*." She said it gently, then pressed a small, soft hand to Ella's cheek. "It is like the wind, you will find. He is here one moment, then gone the next. No trace of anything, just memory." She pulled away, and started back to her stove.

Ella feared what may have shown in her face, and when Regina spoke again, knew it had been enough. "If I could have a pearl for every broken heart that trailed that man . . ." Regina's whispered voice fell to silence, but Ella had a hunch she'd be a wealthy woman.

Six

With his sights set on the back yard of the lot, Charlie strode through the crowd. Rubes always stared when he was dressed up. Especially after all of those people had been in the matinee. Because conversation always turned personal, he'd learned to keep moving, but he did wave to a pair of boys who stood gaping as if they had a million burning questions. Their hope visibly fell when he strode by.

Conscience kicking in, Charlie slowed then circled back a few steps. They bolted up to him.

"Do you feed the lions zebra?" the oldest of the pair asked.

"Only when we run out of little boys."

They grinned and their mother smirked.

Charlie tipped his hat to her then took a knee as her sons pelted him with more curiosities.

"Where do they sleep at night?"

"Do they purr?"

"Are their manes pokey?"

No space to get a word in edgewise, Charlie simply tousled the youngest lad's hair when the boy asked, "How do you tame a lion?"

Charlie peered into the two freckled faces and saw eyes—souls—that would one day be men's.

Men with children and wives entrusted to their care. "You really want to know how to tame a lion?"

They nodded quickly. He waved them closer, and a small, brave hand grazed the gold braiding on the side of his sleeve. Charlie smiled, then spoke soft and low, the answer for their ears alone.

They stepped back but a moment later, expressions awed. Surprised.

"Truly?" the oldest asked.

Charlie made a show of crossing his heart. "You remember that." He rose, nodded toward their mother and the crowd that had gathered, then bid the lads goodbye before starting back on his way.

The show had gone well, and as much as he'd wanted to hurry home today, he didn't want to abandon his post at the lions' feeding. His cats were fed twice a week, about twenty pounds of meat apiece, and Charlie made it a habit—just as his father before him—to oversee the process. Some trainers believed that a fat lion was docile, more easily pacified, while other circuses fed their big cats less than desirable fare to cut costs. Disagreeing heartily on both accounts, Charlie liked seeing his lions happy and healthy, and overseeing the quality of their meals was crucial to that.

But it had also delayed him longer than he'd

accounted for when he'd promised to walk Ella home.

Back in his tent, he was met with nothing other than a note. Charlie hung up his coat and hat. He yanked off the waistcoat and tossed it on his bed, followed by the cravat. Smearing a dab of oil over his face freed the greasepaint then he scrubbed his skin clean with a rag at the washstand. Aiming to get a sandwich, he walked out, the note from Ella folded in hand.

Charlie fetched his dinner and ate it in the shade of the cookhouse tent while workers and performers filed in and out. After polishing off a glass of lemonade, he headed for the crowded midway. A pair of Romani men walked by juggling colored pins, and beyond that a cluster of people *aaah'd* as three clowns spun plates on striped sticks. Charlie strolled along, not needing to watch to know how the act would end. He'd seen it more times than he could count.

Seated on a stool in the middle of the midway, a man played a bright red calliope—his fingers tapping out a cheery riverboat tune through the golden pipes of the steam piano. A monkey at his feet held out a hat, accepting tips.

The crowd was beyond thick and two ladies waiting in line for a palm reading studied Charlie openly as he inched by them. Their gowns were fashionable, lace collars high to their chins, dainty hats bedecked with feathers. The scent of perfume hung thick around them. They put a bit of sugar into their smiles and he gave a cordial one back, but what he *wanted* was to find Ella.

And then he spotted her. Standing in the sunlight beside the Big Top, looking at a cage with brightly colored birds. She bounced gently, Holland bound snug in the sling.

Charlie broke through the crowd and walked up behind her. "You shouldn't be out here," he said softly.

Ella turned and searched his face. "I'm sorry. Regina was heading to the market and Holland was fussy, so I thought if I walked her, she'd settle easier. She ate all the crushed ice and seemed to want more. I wish I'd brought more. I thought some sunlight and fresh air might distract her." She touched the soft fabric of the sling that was usually draped across his own chest. "Regina helped me tie it. Holland fell right to sleep."

Charlie peered down. Holland's round cheek was pressed against the front of Ella's dress, her tiny lips parted, and she lay so still, he doubted a hundred cymbals would wake her now. "You have a way with her," he said, meaning it and trying to set Ella at ease as he touched her elbow and gently turned them away from the cage. "I need to get you back inside, though."

"I'm sorry."

"Please don't be." He winced, already regretting his next words. "Do you remember when I told you it was against the rules for you to be here . . . with me?"

She nodded soberly.

"I meant that. If it was just you out it would be fine. But with Holland, too many people around could recognize her and . . ." he hated to say this, "trace you back to me."

She appeared uneasy as he led her on. "What does that mean?" she whispered.

"It just means that . . ." He ran a hand through his hair as he walked them forward. "It means that I'm not supposed to have any kind of company. Not with townies. Even standing out here talking to you is—"

"Even though I'm just a nurse?" She peered up so kindly that the line between *Ella* and *Ella the nurse* felt very blurred.

And now that he was being honest with himself, it had blurred sooner than this moment.

But he formed the words anyway, knowing they were safer. "Even if you're just the nurse. And a nosy one at that." He smirked and walked backwards, still watching her. Then he slowed. "I can take Holland now."

Her hand slid over Holland's head in that way it seemed to always do. A circling over her curls as though Holland were too good to be true. Eyes downcast, Ella went to loosen the knot of the sling when Charlie stepped closer.

In a motion that appeared to surprise her, he

slid his fingers along the edge of her shawl that had slipped down her arm. He pulled the shawl over her shoulders, her front, covering Holland. A veil over the sight of the baby in her arms that made him a little less uneasy.

Without speaking, Ella looked up at him.

"Was that wrong to do?" He hadn't meant to be unseemly. But he could see that might have been. He tried to think of something to say and probably chose wrong with, "I'll walk over here and you walk over there. We'll head to the entrance separately today."

She stilled. "I've left my box in your tent."

He looked around a moment, saw the sun low in the sky. "I have another show I need to get ready for soon. Is it okay to leave it and you can get it tomorrow? Or I can bring it to you."

"Are you sure I should come back tomorrow?"

Had he offended her? He feared he may have. "Only if you're free. Either way, I *will* pay you for your time and the ice."

She shook her head again at that. "No payment, but I am free."

He tried to think of how to respond to that, but then someone was calling out to him.

"Well, if it isn'a Bonnie Prince Charlie."

He looked over to see Ruth giving him one of her smiles.

"Have'na seen ye all week," she said.

"Ruth." He gave a cordial nod to the other two

aerialists beside her. Dressed in little ruffled bloomers and corsets, their faces painted like dolls, they had a swarm of murmuring onlookers around them who were no doubt awed by their coverings of thin tights from toe to hip. A fact he knew Ruth enjoyed.

The young Scotswoman put her hands on her hips as he passed by, the latter of which she gave her signature swivel. "When are you going to come and see me?"

"When are you gonna come and see *me?*" He walked backwards, thinking to find Ella.

The feathers on Ruth's lace garter fluttered. "Ye ken I haven'a the time for that nonsense."

"And that, my dear," he halted and pressed a hand to his heart, "is why we part ways."

She feigned the same pout she'd used since they were kids.

He turned away for Ella.

"A fair bit of work you did in the show today," Ruth blurted.

"And you too," he said, looking back only a moment. "All of you . . . nice . . . twirling." He scanned the crowd for Ella.

She'd moved to the other side of the path. That's right. He'd told her to. He braved another glance across the midway and even from here could see that Ella's cheeks were flushed.

Which had him looking back at the aerialists to try and see them the way Ella did. Lace, tights, and revealing corsets that when compared to the way city women dressed was quite insufficient. Scandalously so. He pulled his gaze back to Ella. And now her cheeks were redder.

When they neared the exit and the congestion was that of only townsfolk—strangers—he moved back to her side. She was quiet as they followed the path that drained onto the city street. Horses and wagons rambled by and children wove between them, clutching school books. Suddenly lost, Charlie looked around. But Ella was storming onward. He jogged after her. Not only had he promised to walk her home, but she had to give Holland back.

He slowed when he reached her and shoved his hands in his pockets. This was probably a good time for small talk so he thought of what that entailed. Maybe the weather? He looked up at the sky to try and form some kind of normal, everyday, non-carny conversation.

"What was her name? Holland's mother?" Ella asked softly.

Or . . . they could talk about that.

"Um." He blinked, trying to get his bearings. He never spoke of his private life, but was getting so used to this woman's questions, that something had him blurting it out. "Her name was Jessamine, but I never really called her that." Just thinking of her sunny smile made his heart ache afresh.

He followed Ella around the corner and she stayed quiet for half a block.

"What are you thinking?" he asked.

"I'm just wondering . . . why all those women . . ." She studied him closely, as if she could make out his character right there on the corner of whatever street it was they were standing on. "Did they know her? They don't seem very . . . um . . . *patient.*"

"What are you talking about?"

"Holland's mother. I'm sorry to bring up such a difficult subject, but I'm trying to figure you out, Charlie Lionheart."

"Figure what out?"

"Well." She shook her head, seeming to hunt for the words. "Do you regret having not . . . legalized matters?"

He blinked down at the ground. Legalized matters? Was she talking about Holland? How did she know about that? He could see that the words pained Ella. But something else was moving through his mind and he tried to piece together her words.

Tried and failed. *"What?"* The word clipped off his tongue in utter confusion.

"I'm sorry. It's not my business. I'm just . . . just confused." Ella pursed her lips and he folded his arms, waiting. "Well, I confess," she began again, "I wasn't sure what to make of this all. You and Holland's mother. You and these other women."

"I rarely even speak to those ladies."

"You weren't acting that way. With all that talk of *'when are you going to come and visit me?'*" She waved a hand back the way they'd come.

Her accusation crawled hot fingers up his skin. "What? Are you my mother now? I was talking about church, Ella."

"Church?" Those brows might as well have been pinned to the sky, they spent so much time there. "That didn't sound like church talk to me."

Charlie blew out a slow breath then leveled her with a gaze. He was going to regret this because it wasn't true. "Well, I don't really care what you think."

"She deserves more respect. From those women." Ella looked disgusted with him. "And from you. She was a real person."

"Who?"

"Holland's mother!" The words slammed off her lips, eyes snapping.

He looked at the sidewalk, then at the baby, and then at Ella. He squinted. "I don't understand." He took a step closer, but she moved back, and for a second he thought she was going to slap him. Confounded woman, what was wrong with her? Then her implication hit him—slammed into his chest, shoving the words out. "Ella! Jessamine was my *sister*. Holland's *not* my daughter."

Ella's eyes went wide.

"She's my niece. Did you think I was her father?"

"You said Holland was yours."

"She is mine—*now*." For he was the only person Holland had. And he'd given everything he had to get her back. God help him, he was trying to make that count for something.

"Ohhh . . ." It came out an airy groan and Ella felt around with her hands as if to find a seat to collapse on.

"Had you thought . . . ?" He shook his head, at a loss for how to phrase it delicately. Why did she keep assuming that he bedded every woman who breathed? "You're upset with me."

She shook her head. Nodded. Shook her head again.

A smile formed without his permission.

"That was a dirty trick to play," she said.

It vanished just as quick. "I didn't trick you." He searched her face. He'd been more open with her than he'd ever been with a stranger in his life. "Ella, please know that. I didn't think you'd jumped to that conclusion."

She made a little sound in her throat.

"I can see now that it was an easy mistake for you to make."

And then there was that sound again. Except this time she was glaring at him.

"Blast it, Ella! I really don't know what to do with you. You're so . . . difficult!"

"I'm difficult? You could have just *told* me she was your sister's from the start."

"Well, I don't like to explain my life to people." Two men in bowler hats eyed them in passing, so Charlie lowered his voice. "But you ask too many questions and you're always reacting to all the answers and this is why I don't do this." With a hand, he motioned between them. He never should have let an outsider into his life. His home. He should have let her tend to Holland that day, then politely had her go back the way she came. He hadn't expected *this*. This thing he had no name for. But it was inching inside him every second he was with her now.

His eyes traced her blonde braid that was wound loose and nearly free, barely restrained with a ribbon. And now he was saying words that he felt he would regret. "When I'm around you I feel like I'm doing something wrong." Wetting his lips, he braved more. "It's not that way with other people I know. Look at Ruth. I've known her since she was three. And it's always been exactly like what you saw. Well, not *exactly*."

Ella's eyes narrowed. So much for his shot at humor.

"We've never seen eye to eye, Ruth and I. But she doesn't get upset and shout at me. She just walks away." And she'd be recovered the next time he saw her. Ruth was easy to figure out.

Ella pursed her lips. Then her chin trembled.

Oh no.

Charlie closed his eyes. He held his breath a moment, then released it, opening his eyes again only to see her lift Holland from the sling. Something lived in her face. So deep and pained that he feared there had been a lot more to what she'd been trying to say. He thought about remedying that, asking what it was that had her so troubled—

"You know what to do. For Holland." Ella's chin trembled again. She hesitated, then her fingers softly dented Holland's pudgy form as she held her out. A grip that made her seem like she could hold on forever.

He nodded absently and took the baby who was squirming awake.

"If something should change, this is where you can find me." Ella glanced up to the center windows on the third floor. "But I think a few more days of the treatments and she'll be right back to her old self." Her voice cracked. "Goodbye, Charlie." She pulled away, looked at him from beneath wet lashes, and then hurried up the steps to her apartment building.

It hurt when he knocked his forehead against the tall frame of the wagon, but Charlie did it twice for good measure. He felt Regina watching him from where she rocked in her pint-sized chair.

"Something has gone wrong," she said.

He banged his head one more time then shot her a glance.

"The nurse," she said. "Ella?"

He nodded.

"Perhaps this is for the best."

It was. So why did he want to walk back and tell Ella he was sorry? Sorry for not being more careful with her. For telling her she was odd, and at least twice he'd called her boring. Worse than that, he'd snapped at her. Made her cry. Said he didn't care what she thought.

No wonder he'd never had any friends outside of show business.

Don't try and make friends with rubes. There is no point.

His parents had told him that over and over growing up, and he'd watched from beneath the midway booths as the townie children ran through the circus—having the time of their lives. Charlie had known better than to try to so much as talk to them. He'd never see them again.

No wonder he'd messed everything up. He had no idea what he was doing with Ella. Had to remind himself that he would never see her again, too. Charlie ran fingertips over his forehead as Regina slid the lid off the tin of greasepaint. That was his cue. He pressed his eyes closed, took a breath, then opened them.

Charlie looked to Holland sleeping in her bed, a damp rag on her forehead.

He could do this.

Pulling a crate in front of Regina's chair, he sat and she lowered the tin to her lap. Leaning his head back, Charlie closed his eyes . . .

And let Regina paint away the last shred of peace he had.

He inhaled slowly. And then out. Having to remind himself that this wasn't who he was. It was simply a show. One more, of a different kind. No lions. Just him. He felt the cool brush of Regina's fingers around his eyes where she was blackening the skin. The haunted look she created so well. Just as was required of him in the contract.

The paper that bore his signature. That he would give his body. His life. For Holland's.

It was worth it. His chest heaved. It was worth it.

"Charlie," Regina whispered.

Eyes still closed, he cleared his throat.

"Breathe, my boy."

When she paused and pulled her hands away, he nodded fiercely.

"You won't have to do this much longer." Her voice rasped out a cry of hope. "The debt is nearly paid. You're *almost* finished."

He nodded again, mouth dry. Just one year. Holland's first year. As was his promise.

But his pulse was racing. It was always hardest on opening night. A new crowd. New faces. Jeers from people who had never seen him. The sting, the pain of it always drove deeper this night. A piece of him dying—the piece of him that always dreamt that with each new city came the chance for a new beginning. But each time, at the hands of Regina and her skill with a brush . . . and all that he'd given to Madame Broussard . . . a fresh start was lost to him.

Those very people he wanted to be normal around were about to pay good money to gawk at him in her show.

He was glad Ella was safe outside his world tonight.

"Rock of Ages," Regina said softly, "cleft for me."

And he realized his breath was racing. Charlie tried to slow it. Searched his heart for the hymn. All that he clung to daily and during these dark nights, the only thing that kept him from losing his mind.

"Let me hide myself in thee," Regina sang softly for his benefit.

The next words moved through his mind and he exhaled. Regina finished darkening his eyes. There would be no looking in the mirror tonight. It was a face he hated seeing.

When she pressed the lid back on the tin, he stood. "All done?"

"You will draw a good crowd." She meant it in compliment; it felt anything but.

He nodded, trying to rally his strength, his heart. So tiny, almost lost in his shadow, Regina squeezed his hand. When she pulled away, Charlie tugged at his sleeve cuff where *Carpe Diem* faded into other dark markings. "I don't think I can—"

"Holland's stirring." Regina's voice hinted caution. The only answer he would get; they both knew he had no choice.

"Please get her." He didn't want Holland to see him like this.

Regina rose and the baby's cries quieted. Charlie moved to the slit in the tent that led into the black night. As if knowing he was leaving, Holland started to fuss. His face still turned away, he reached for the black cloak that hung from the nearest tent pole.

Her whimpers turned into a wail as he draped the cloak over his shoulders and pulled up the hood to shade his face from view. Through the slit of the tent, distant torch lights flickered. Beckoned. Reminded him that by their light, he would fall to his knees as nothing but a showpiece.

Holland's raspy cries made his heart feel like it would snap. His arms burned to hold her. To bring her close. To pretend like all of this was a bad dream. But that was *why* he was doing this.

So he could hold her close. So that this despair wouldn't be her future.

Though he knew . . .

Her reality would have been much different. *Much worse.*

Which was all the prompt he needed to square his shoulders and tip up his head. If he simply walked into the dark and gave the crowd the thrill it hungered for . . . he could return to Holland, pick her up, and know that she was safe. For that reason alone, he stepped out into the night. And for that reason alone, he would do it again tomorrow.

SEVEN

Morning light spilled through the window as Ella sat at the table, arms resting astride the newspaper she was poring over. It had rained through the night, but now a clear day bloomed through departing clouds.

Margaret stood beside her, fussing over the contents of a box of lace and bows. Ella scanned the typeset advertisements, hoping to spot an open position. Maybe a nursemaid or a laundress. She'd happily waitress as well since she could do most any domestic work and her savings would be gone after this month's rent was paid . . . and Charlie was *not* Holland's father.

Or so had gone her focus all morning.

When she peered down on the sidewalk where he had stood the evening before, her emotions were more tangled than the handful of ribbons Margaret was attempting to unravel.

Margaret bustled back into the bedroom and returned ribbonless. "What's the point of having time off only to spend it cooped up in this apartment?"

Ella looked at her friend.

"I was thinking of going to the circus. Why don't you come with me?" Margaret adjusted a ruffle on her flounce skirt then poured a cup of coffee. "This will be here later."

Ella sighed. "I'd go with you, but I really need to find work."

Margaret conceded the truth with a nod. "I know. But . . ." She gave a pleading look. "Come along with me. Please. The banners say they close after tomorrow, and this is my only day off. I hear it's quite spectacular. They have different shows . . . oh, the animals!" Margaret lifted a scone from the plate in the middle of the table, broke it, then popped a small bit in her mouth. "I've a hankering to see an elephant. And," she made a show of fanning herself, "some of the dashing gents I keep hearing about."

Ella smiled sadly. She *really* didn't want to go. For reasons she couldn't explain. But there was a reason that would make sense and was unfortunately very true. "I need to save every cent I have." Meager as that was. "For this month's rent."

"I'll get you in. I'll pay your way."

Ella let out a little laugh.

"What's so funny?"

"Nothing." But oh, the irony. And then she was struck with the way Charlie had helped her over the wooden barrier. Her hand in his. How she hadn't let herself think much of it then, but now, after their argument and all that had passed, she

95

studied her fingertips, trying to draw his touch to memory.

"Hello in there . . ." Margaret pretended to knock on Ella's head. "Where did you go?"

Ella blinked quickly. "Sorry. Have a good time. Tell me all about it."

Margaret sighed. "All right then. Off I go to the circus . . . all on my lonesome."

A bittersweet smile surfaced—as did the temptation to wander down there with Margaret, see the sights and have some popcorn and lemonade, all for the chance to lay eyes on the lion tamer one last time. Even if only from afar.

Just sitting here she could nearly imagine Charlie in the center ring with his commanding presence and ferocious companions. So dashing with his slicked, dark hair, pristine gloves, and painted face. Vibrant eyes concealing a most mysterious reality. Did his audience know who he was? How he cared for a child who wasn't even his own? An orphaned baby who held his heart?

Swallowing a twinge in her throat, Ella tried to raise a smile for her friend's sake.

Easier would be to add the pearl she owed to Regina's necklace.

Bidding farewell, Margaret headed downstairs and Ella tore out the page of advertisements, three of which she'd circled—a need for a seamstress on Fifth, a laundress in a wealthy home, and a nanny for a trio of boys.

Regret would be her only companion if she remained indoors, so downstairs she went, coat in hand. Her mother had taught her and her sisters to be handy with a needle, but the seamstress position would be a rather far walk every day. Perhaps a little too far, but certainly worth a try. The laundress position in the wealthy home was only a few blocks away, and the nanny advertisement stemmed from one of the finer homes on the edge of town. This address she committed to heart as she tried to rally courage.

Outside, the morning beamed down with a cheery sun and Ella started westward. A clear, quiet day blew her the few blocks there, and when she knocked on the door of the fine townhome, she was greeted by a male servant, then ushered into a den. A tall, slender man conducted the interview, and from his introduction, Ella learned right away that he was the boys' father. Triplets. She'd never met triplets before, and the longer the father posed questions, his eyes on her with a brash smile, the more uncomfortable she felt.

Worse was when he asked her how someone so young and pretty could be out of work. He winked and she conjured up a reason why she wouldn't be able to fill the position.

Her skin still crawled with the memory of him even when she left in the direction of the next post. At the home seeking a laundress, she knocked and was greeted by a maid.

Ella held out the advertisement. "I'm here to see about—"

"Our apologies, but the position has been filled."

"Filled?"

The maid tipped a nod, then asked if there was anything else Ella needed.

"No, thank you." Back on the sidewalk, Ella sat a moment in the speckled shadows of a leafless maple and studied the final job position— seamstress. She really didn't want to walk two miles to work every day, but options were sparse.

The sun was high overhead when she arrived at a narrow brick building, and after meeting the family, Ella learned that while the job paid only fifteen cents a day for long hours, it included room and board. She followed the mistress of the house to a closet where the woman pulled out a dozen stylish gowns that the last seamstress had fashioned. Ella gulped and confessed she was best with mending and buttons. The homeowner politely showed her out.

Ella walked to her apartment with sore feet, the flame of hope fizzled. Perhaps the next paper would have the right position.

Back home, she set about cleaning to keep busy. With a beautiful spring day out, she carried bedding up to the roof to air. She checked her pots of herbs in the corner of the small greenhouse that the landlord let her use. The parsley was bright and green and she fingered ripening strawberries, then plucked a few sprigs of chives and carried them back down to her apartment.

Margaret came home not long after, cheeks glowing as she shared about all the sights she'd seen. The girl exuded delight over the matinee. She described the tent, the cheer of the audience, and the magnificent performances from aerialists and animals alike. "And when I was looking for the privy, I saw something you wouldn't believe! There were some wagons stuck in the mud— those fancy circus ones, you know." She waggled her hand. "A bunch of workers were trying to get one of them loose. And guess what?" Her brown eyes were wide, sparkling.

So much so that Ella smiled. *"What?"* she asked theatrically.

"There was *an elephant* pushing the whole operation. You should have seen it. It was such a sight! They couldn't get the wagon out, though, not even with all the horses at the hitch. Snapped the wagon right off the axle and they had to yell to the poor elephant to stop shoving the front into the mud."

Ella nodded gravely, remembering how Charlie had mentioned them being stranded. He wasn't kidding.

"And oh the men. Ever so many of them!" Margaret tugged off lace gloves. "But I only managed to catch the eye of a country bumpkin. Too backwoods for me. He and his friends didn't have a proper hat among them, and one of the young ladies in tow couldn't even tie up her stockings right. You'd think she'd know better—" Margret's hands froze. "I'm so sorry, I shouldn't have said that."

Ella shook her head—not offended in the slightest. She had no shame of being raised far from city life or having a family who was as poor as those people surely were. She'd once had loose stockings as well.

When Margaret draped the gloves over a chair, Ella spoke. "Did you see any lions?"

Margaret's eyebrows danced. "I saw Mr. Circus, if that's what you mean. And later, he was there with that wagon. Shoveling mud with the others before it snapped. I hardly recognized him without all that stuff on his face and the fancy getup. He looked just like one of the workers."

A pang struck her heart, and afraid to hear more, Ella quickly offered to fix supper.

"You're a doll." Margaret tugged off her button-up shoes. "I'll do the dishes."

Ella made a simple meal of toasted bread, slices of cheese from the icebox, and used the last of the honey to whip up honey butter. Margaret asked about her job search and Ella shared about it as they ate. Short story as it was. When Margaret set about tidying up the kitchen, Ella said good night and turned in early.

Her feet ached, and truth be told . . . her heart did too.

Curling up under her blankets, she felt sleep taking her. It seemed only a few hours later when a strange sound awoke her to the dark. The streets below silent. Everything quiet if not for the thunking in the hallway. Footsteps. Then a knock on their door.

Ella sat up. Heart pounding, she listened as the knock came again. She slipped from the covers and looked over at Margaret who was asleep in the other narrow bed. At the third knock, Ella crossed the bedroom floor and peeked into the main room toward the door that blocked her from whoever it was that was there. Quite certain she didn't want to answer it, she considered waking Margaret for help.

But then the knocking turned to a pounding and someone was calling her name.

She knew that voice.

"Ella. It's Charlie," he called through the slab, and Ella heard a baby's fussing. "Are you home? I have Holland here. She's—"

Ella was at the door, twisting the lock. A yank on the handle and suddenly Charlie was peering down, Holland in his arms.

"Come in." She held the door open and his trench coat brushed over the threshold.

Gripping the paw of a stuffed tiger, the baby whimpered, cheeks stained with tears.

"She won't eat or drink and she won't sleep," Charlie panted.

"Have you tried ice?" Ella asked as he set a limp canvas sack by the door.

"I don't have ice."

Of course. That's why he was here. Ella hurried to the icebox, lifted the brass handle, and tugged the small frozen block from the wooden chest. She dropped it on the table and shuffled through a crock of knives for a mallet and a butter knife. Once a piece was chipped off, she used the mallet to tap it into powdery chunks. Charlie moved to her side as she filled a spoon.

Ella pressed her shoulder to his and lifted the spoon to the baby's mouth. "Here, my little love," she whispered. "Try this." Ella slipped some between Holland's bright lips and the girl suckled the frosty bits. "That's a good girl." A few icy specks hit the collar of Holland's nightgown and Ella brushed them away.

Holland swallowed, winced, and began to cry again. Ella checked that the bedroom door was closed and filled the spoon again. She repeated the motion several times until the baby's cries quieted, the cold ice no doubt comforting her throat and bringing much-needed fluids. Holland pressed a tear-stained cheek to Charlie's chest and rubbed her face against his shirt.

Ella smoothed a hand down the baby's back. "She may sleep now."

"I'll just hold her."

"You should sit down."

He looked tired. Ella moved a crumpled blanket from the sofa, but Charlie was already sinking to the floor in front of the piece of furniture.

The bedroom door opened and Margaret peeked out. A glance to Charlie and Margaret's eyes couldn't have gone any wider.

"It's all right," Ella said. "He's a . . . friend . . . of mine." She offered his name and hoped Margaret wouldn't let on that they'd already spoken of him.

"What is he doing here?" Margaret whispered.

Charlie glanced to Ella. Kneeling beside him, she waved her roommate over. "His little girl is still sick."

Margaret vanished, then returned with a robe on. Looking warily at Charlie, she slid in beside Ella and knelt. Then a touch to Holland's forehead. "Oh, she's feverish."

"She's been fighting an infection." Ella rattled off the list of things they'd been doing from the warm teas to the herbal tinctures.

Charlie looked from her, then to Margaret, then back to Ella where his gaze lingered.

"I just gave her some ice chips. Do you have any other ideas?" Ella asked Margaret.

"No. But I know these things take time. Days, really. Is she getting better or worse?"

Ella peered over to Charlie.

"I thought she was getting better," he said. "But she hasn't eaten all day and I can barely get her to drink. She's taken some of the tincture but nothing else. I haven't been able to get her to go to sleep yet tonight, and I think she's hungry. I didn't know what else to do so I came here." His lashes lifted and lowered as he studied Ella's face.

Her voice felt weak. "That's normal, wouldn't you say, Margaret? To not take much food?"

Margaret nodded. "Even with only a little food, as long as she's taking some fluids, she should fare just fine. The infection in her throat is making it painful to swallow, but once that passes, it'll be easier and easier for her." She mostly spoke to Ella, but upon finishing peered briefly at Charlie. Margaret was as outgoing as they came and her uncertainty only amplified the untoward nature of all of this. A man in their apartment.

Ella sifted through her own mind and heart searching for a trace of fear but found none. She peeked over at Charlie, unsure of how to make sense of what she *did* find.

"What do I do? For tonight?" he asked. "Just do what I can to keep her comfortable?"

"Have you been trying to get her to sleep all this time?" Ella glanced at the clock to see that it was quarter to three. Nearly morning.

"Trying, yes." He lifted his hand from Holland's head to swipe it down his face. "She was like this last night, too."

Ella watched him. "Charlie?"

He looked at her, his once-brilliant eyes almost unfocused.

"Have you slept?"

He didn't answer.

"Charlie, please be honest with me. Have you slept at all?"

Slowly, he shook his head.

"And you worked last night and you have to work today, don't you?"

He nodded.

Fearing the sofa was unsafe for the baby, Ella hurried into the bedroom, stripped the coverings off her bed, and made Holland a plump nest beside Charlie. She motioned for him to lay the sleeping girl down, then told Margaret to please not stay up on account of them. Knowing her friend had a morning shift, Ella was happy when she heard Margaret crawl back into bed.

"What time do you need to be to work today?" Ella asked, carefully covering the baby.

Charlie cleared his throat. "I need to be to the lions by eight. Seven would be better."

"And have you eaten?"

At his silence, she fought the urge to click her tongue at him. "Holland's asleep now. Let her rest for a bit. You can lay down right here beside her and close your eyes while I fix something to eat. You can rest, then eat, and be home in plenty of time."

He looked to her face where his gaze roved freely. With strands of hair spilling out of her braid, she shoved them back. She spoke his name softly, but he just stared at her. So long that her heart began to hurt for she remembered the words she ached to say.

Moving closer, Ella knelt beside him. "Charlie." She touched his sleeve, just brushing the fabric before pulling away.

His gaze followed the movement then up to her face.

"I'm so sorry," she said. "Will you please forgive me? For yesterday?"

He blinked several times.

"I treated you unfairly and was unkind. I'm so very sorry."

He simply stared at her and she wished she could know what he was thinking. But surely he was just exhausted.

She swallowed hard. "Will you please rest and let me make you something to eat?"

Finally, he lowered his head and ran a hand through his tousled hair. Was that a nod?

"That would be fine," he said, his voice husky. His eyes found hers. "Thank you."

Ella rose, and after adding more coal to the dying fire, moved to the cupboard. What could she make quickly? She found a jar of corn, a box of meal, and with eggs in the icebox, set about whipping up a batch of corn cakes.

Remembering the block of ice, she put the melting mess away. Ella poked about in the icebox and grabbed the chives along with a slice of ham that Margaret—bless her—had gotten at the market. Ella vowed to pay her friend back as she cut off a piece and added tiny dices to the batter. She would need to buy another block of ice as well. Deciding to shove thoughts of her tiny savings aside, she set a cast iron skillet to heat, added butter, and poured out three small cakes. Leaving them to brown and bubble, she moved around the sofa to where Charlie and Holland were.

She was about to call out to him and was glad she hadn't because there he was, lying on the floor, his head on the mound of blankets, an arm draped over Holland. And they were both asleep. Her heart stirring in a way she'd never felt before, Ella moved closer, plucked the blanket off the sofa, and lightly draped it over both father and child.

Not father, she reminded herself. But looking at the way he held her . . . the way he seemed to give everything he had for her, she couldn't think of him as anything but. She eased the blanket over his shoulder.

"Good night, Charlie," she whispered.

Smelling the corncakes, Ella moved back to the stove and flipped them, relieved that they would be just as tasty cold. At least he would have breakfast. And then maybe she could show him that she'd meant what she'd said. Lord willing, ease the ache in his eyes—the one she'd put there.

EIGHT

"Ella," a man's voice said softly.

She stirred, the light on her face so bright.

"Ella."

It was Charlie speaking. Remembering everything from a few hours before, Ella blinked into the yellow haze of morning and sat up.

He was crouched in front of her. "Do you always sleep in front of the door?"

She pulled her legs deeper under her nightgown, stunned at having fallen asleep so quickly. With a stranger in the apartment, no less. "No." Sitting up, everything hurt. "I just didn't want you to leave without something to eat." She'd sat down there and hadn't meant to drift off. She couldn't even remember how it had happened.

"Holding me hostage?" He took a bite of the corncake that was already in hand. "Over breakfast?" He smiled.

She felt utterly awkward in a nightgown and robe in broad daylight. With him fully dressed, including coat and boots, no less. "I see I didn't need to worry." When she went to stand, he helped her. The sensation of his gentle grip lingered even after he let go. "How is Holland?"

"Still asleep."

"How long have you been awake?"

"A while."

"And you just left me there sleeping in front of the door?"

His eyebrows clamped together. "Should I have carried you to your bed?"

"No!" She almost yelped it and felt her cheeks heat. "I meant—you could have woken me."

"But you seemed so peaceful." His expression was still curious.

Never mind. She was not going to get far with this. "I should go get dressed. It will just take a few minutes. Will you still be here?"

"I can be."

Did that sound forward? As though wanting him to stay. She brushed around him, trying to ignore the way he watched. But she glanced over her shoulder before disappearing into the bedroom and nearly smacked into the doorjamb.

Great, and now he was chuckling.

Ella closed the door and dressed quickly, careful not to disturb Margaret who was a slow riser. Ella combed her hair and plaited it with hurried fingers. With a whisper of thanks over the water in the pitcher, she rinsed her face and mouth. She scrubbed her cheeks with a towel, plucked a sweater off the back of the door, and slid it over her yellow seersucker dress. Pausing at the mirror gave a moment to check her reflection. Haunted, lonely eyes looked back. "He's leaving tomorrow," Ella said softly. *"Tomorrow."* She pushed a stray lock of hair into her braid. "You need to make amends with that."

Steeling her emotions—her heart—she stepped out and skirted the sofa to peek on Holland.

Charlie crouched in front of the stove and put a scoop of coal in.

Had he lit the fire for them? He must have. Margaret hadn't woken yet, and even if she had, Ella doubted her roommate would have braved coming out with a dozing lion tamer on the floor.

"Thank you," Ella said when he closed the square iron door.

"Thank *you*." He dipped his head. "For break-fast . . . and the nap." He smiled again, then rubbed idly at his wrist. It was nice, his smile. "And thank you for helping us last night. I didn't know what to do." He rubbed gently at his other wrist. "Are you all right?"

Swallowing hard, Ella moved back to the mound of blankets where the baby slumbered with her pudgy cheek squished against a damask pillow. Settling down beside the dear, Ella felt Holland's skin, relieved at how cool it was. "I think some sleep was just what she needed," Ella said. "And now she might even eat. I can make something softer if she won't take a corn cake."

He was watching Ella warily—as if sensing the battle inside her. "We should be going. Can I take it with me?"

She slid her mouth to the side as a plan

unfolded. A way to help him and Holland, one last time. "What about this. I can feed her some breakfast, maybe even give her a bath. I could bring her along to you shortly. If you'd let me."

"Don't you have to work today?"

She was about to shake her head, but it was time to give a better answer. "No." Rising slowly, she brushed at her hands. "I don't work there anymore."

His eyes searched her face. Would the reasons show?

"It's not because . . ." He looked to be trying to piece it together. "You followed me," he whispered. "Did they fire you over that?"

She nearly nodded.

"Ella."

"I think I might have quit." Perhaps it was a little bit of both.

"Over Holland." It wasn't a question.

She gave him a soft, "Yes."

"Ella." The way he breathed her name again made her suddenly feel like everything was going to be all right. Like someone was on her side. Someone strong and capable and caring. But the feeling vanished as soon as it formed. She barely knew him. And he was leaving soon. *Very* soon. Ella looked up into his face, skimming her gaze across his smooth forehead to his lightly bristled jaw, letting her attention rest for the briefest of moments on his mouth before turning all focus to the eyes that watched her with a tender openness. What was Charlie Lionheart to her?

What could she possibly be to him?

Remembering her offer, she put on what was hopefully a convincing smile. "Trust me. I'll get Holland all settled and fed and then bring her along. It would be a joy." Perhaps humor would be the best approach. "I don't have anything else to do today and she'd save me from hours of boredom."

"Is that so?" A small smile.

Ella nodded.

He looked down at the baby who was still sound asleep and for the first time in days looked peaceful. "I suppose . . ." He eyed Ella again as if to make sure she wasn't about to sprout horns. "There's no harm in letting her sleep. As long as you don't mind bringing her along."

"It would be my pleasure."

He studied her a moment longer, and she realized that his scrutiny was of a different kind. One that had her feeling very much a woman and him a man. Then their heads turned in unison at the sound of shuffling on the other side of the bedroom door. The shuffling stopped, Margaret perhaps listening just on the other side.

"I should probably go so your roommate can come out now. I think she's feeling held hostage." He moved his face so near to Ella's ear that a little shiver slid down her neck. "I do think she's scared of me."

Ella peered up into his face as it slowly moved away. In a quick glance, she took in his striking form from the black coat that brushed the ground wherever he walked to his tall boots with the clattering buckles that served who-knew-what purpose.

"You are rather intimidating," she said half in honesty and half in jest.

He smiled and looked once more at Holland before moving toward the door. "Oh." One hand slipped into a pocket and he pulled out a dime.

She sensed it was the only one he had from the soft sound of his pocket.

"So you can get in." He gave it to her. "And Ella," he formed a fist with one hand, smoothing a broad thumb back and forth over his fingers, "I do forgive you . . . and I hope you'll forgive me."

Suddenly her throat was tight. She drudged up a nod then a smile. "Thank you, Charlie."

His Adam's apple dipped and he looked around the apartment. "There's something else I need to tell you. We . . . we would be leaving tomorrow. Today would be our last performances. But we've got a situation with some wagons. On top of that, the roads to Charlottesville are still muddy. So much so that the roustabouts who went ahead could barely get through. The caravan won't make it."

Ella drew in a breath. Held it.

"They've come back, and after last night's rain, it's been decided that we're going to have to wait for it to dry out more."

What was he saying?

In the distance, a cannon boomed, followed by the distant roar of cheers.

Charlie grinned. "We'll be here for a few more days. I hope you Roanokeians don't mind. We promise to put on a good show." His eyes searched hers so deeply, she had to remind herself to exhale. "You're stuck with us for a little while longer."

Her chest filled. A few days. So small a thing. But for some reason, those words pooled within her as warmth and hope—and she dared to ignore what dimness loomed beyond. Did her expression hold the same wonder as his own? All she could do was smile. It seemed all right, for he was doing the same.

NINE

While Holland slept, Ella tiptoed around the apartment, cleaning up her cooking mess and answering Margaret's countless questions . . .

How long has Charlie been with the circus? *I don't know.*

Why is his last name Lionheart? *I've wondered that myself.*

Why is the baby named after a country? *I'm quite certain it's not a country.*

Don't you find him a little frightening? *Maybe at first. But . . . no.*

And why that was, she was still trying to understand.

There was a large part of her that knew she should be afraid of men, but to her bewilderment, she wasn't. At least not with all of them as a whole. She was merely fearful of those who claimed to be spiritual, as she knew what evils could lurk beneath the surface. Much better for a man to be upfront about who he was. Not hide in the shadow of some hogwash about grace and mercy.

Ella gripped the bowl she was washing and forced rising memories away. A slow inhale burned until she released it.

Margaret hurried about, getting ready for her

shift. At a knock on the door, Ella met and paid the milkman and bade farewell to Margaret who slipped out with a wave. At the stove, Ella slid a small pot into place, added a splash of the milk, a dash of sugar, then left it to warm.

Thankful that Charlie had had the presence of mind last night to bring along Holland's things, she poked around in the canvas satchel and found two clean cloths for diapers, a change of clothing, and a glass suckling bottle that bore a narrow, metal teat—just the thing to try and coax some breakfast into the baby. After a peek on the sweet, sleeping bundle, Ella used rags to stop up the sink. She filled a pot from the tap and moved it to the stove to heat.

Meal. Bath. Unable to think of anything else that might help, Ella tidied up the living area and tried very hard not to think of Charlie.

Failing at that, she was glad when Holland awoke.

Ella scooped her up. "Good morning!" she gently cooed.

Holland's blue eyes were wide. Mouth pursed tight as if confused by the foreign apartment. She looked around, and Ella felt a pang that the baby was probably wondering where Charlie was.

"He's off to the lions," Ella said cheerily, and about laughed at the rarity of such a comment. "We will have some breakfast and be on our way, too." Gone were any hints of Holland's tears, and Ella held her close as she filled the bottle, tested the temperature on her wrist, then settled in the kitchen chair with her little friend. It took several tries to convince the baby that the drink was worth tasting, but within moments, Holland drank hungrily. Using the edge of Holland's nightgown, Ella dabbed drips of cream from her chin.

"Is that good?"

The baby licked her rosebud lips. When the bottle was empty, Ella broke off pinches of bread which were happily nibbled. After that, Ella moved to the sink, content with the sensation of Holland snug on her hip and the notion that the baby had a full belly. Ella filled the sink from the tap, then warmed it with what she heated on the stove. When the temperature was just right, she rinsed and bathed a very-quiet Holland who was still looking around as if Charlie might appear any moment.

Bent over at the sink's edge, Ella rested her chin on her hands and watched the baby play with wet, soapy toes. Fearing she shouldn't sit too long in the water, Ella lifted her silky, slick form and held her close.

"Oh, you are a delicious little thing," she said, drying her off. Holland kicked her feet happily. "Are you feeling better now? A full tummy and a good night's sleep? Your papa will be so happy to see your face."

From the bag, she pulled a tiny green frock with boat-shaped buttons running up the front. After white stockings, Ella slipped on the girl's leather booties. Next she gathered up a few scattered items, tucked them all into the canvas bag, and draped the strap across her body before carrying Charlie's little one out the door. The walk to the carnival grounds was pleasant while Ella pointed out the sights to her companion. Holland was yet to make a sound. Just those wide, ice-blue eyes, taking the world in. One soft hand clinging to Ella's neck.

At the entrance, Ella stood beneath the great banner announcing the *Graven Brothers Circus* as she pulled out the dime. Recognizing the woman in the booth, Ella searched her mind, trying to remember her name. Lorelai. That was it.

"Good morning, Miss Lorelai."

The woman looked up, took the dime, then glanced from Ella to the baby as recognition dawned in her round face.

"Why if it's not me 'olland. Lookatcha, love. Bright and chipper for yer ol' Aunt Lorelai."

Ella bounced Holland closer to the woman who gave the baby's pudgy hand a squeeze. "I'm bringing her to Charlie."

" 'E'll be up at the Big Top now. Seein' to 'is lions."

"Thank you," Ella said as the force of the line

about pushed her through the entrance. And now. To go find a man who was taking care of lions.

Nothing to worry about.

But as she drew closer, her heart pounded. It was still early enough that the crowd was building and she remembered that the main show didn't start until one. Ella neared the massive tent with its broad red and white stripes and fluttering flags. She looked around, and spotting a man pushing a small hand cart with garbage cans, stepped that way.

"Excuse me, sir, do you work here?"

"Naw, miss. I just do this for fun." When Ella pursed her lips, his mouth quirked, seeming to regret that. "What can I do for you, miss?"

"Charlie Lionheart." She searched for an approach that might keep him out of trouble. "I'm a nurse and was taking care of Holland. Might you be able to tell me how to find him?"

The man doffed his cap and motioned for her to follow. "Right this way."

"Thank you, sir."

He led them around the colossal tent, and after unfastening thick ties, disappeared through a slit. "You'll want to keep to the seats, miss, as he's got the lions out an' he don't allow visitors at this hour," he called back to her. "But seein' as ya got Miss Holland . . ." He flashed silver teeth then slid his hat back on.

Ella ducked inside, taking care with the baby,

and nearly gasped at the sensation of the cool, still air—the musty scent of dirt and animals and distant rain. The Big Top spread wide and round, rows upon rows of vacant benches. She looked toward the grand center, and then she saw him.

A sweeping curve of fencing circled the arena, rising from the dusty earth to the overhead rigging. And in the middle of it, Charlie was surrounded by two . . . no, three, grown lions. Each of the massive beasts walked around the dirt ring—him in their center. Ella gasped.

The man beside her chuckled. "I'll just let ya watch until he's finished."

She barely remembered nodding her thanks as the man departed. Still holding Holland close on her hip, Ella stared. Charlie spoke in low tones to the animals, motioning them one way or another. A second man, dressed in striped pants and a black overcoat, watched on, his arms folded over his barrel chest as he stood just outside of the ornate bars that were as grand as the ring itself. So wide that the cage could surely house a slew of elephants. The man spoke in a gentle baritone—something about the new latch system—and Charlie said he was still trying to figure it out.

With over a dozen rows of wooden benches ahead, Ella started forward.

"No. You . . ." Charlie said to the nearest lion as it stopped and lay down, ". . . are not listening."

Charlie strode over, knelt, then ran his hand up the side of the animal's tan back, patting his muscular shoulder.

Ella's mouth parted.

"You big lazy oaf," he said.

The other man spoke something to Charlie which she couldn't hear.

"They're done for the morning, La'Rue. That's enough practice." Still dressed in the pants and untucked shirt she'd last seen him in, Charlie sat down in the dirt beside the lion. The massive beast rolled over, reclining his head onto Charlie's lap. With fast hands, Charlie scrubbed the animal's thick mane, laughing as another strolled over and nudged him.

Speechless, Ella could only stand there in disbelief and listen to the meaty slap of Charlie's hand on hide as the great cat stretched out beside him, tail lolling back and forth. The third lion ambled over, mouth hinged open in a yawn, flashing brilliant white fangs. He let out a deep, throaty bellow that shot chills up Ella's spine. The creature ran a huge, pink tongue across the top of Charlie's head. Charlie chuckled and ducked away. Still roughing his hands up and down the lion lounging against him only made the animal roll farther over.

Charlie groaned, but spoke good-naturedly. "Move over, Axel."

Ignoring him, the great cat just sighed. The

curved ears that poked out of his mane looked bigger than Ella's hand. Beside them, the other two lions were rolling and pawing. Charlie ran his palms under the lion's face, pulling gently on his enormous jaw, over and over, as if it were no more than a house cat.

The man in the distance said something, and Charlie lifted his face as he searched the stands. Then Charlie looked right at her and Ella froze. Her heartbeat suddenly in her ears, she remembered that she should have gone to his tent. She thought about standing or speaking . . . or at least doing something, but then he spoke.

"It would be gentlemanly of me to stand up, but I'm being crushed."

Ella rose and moved down to the front row where she sat. Tucking Holland snugly in her lap, she peered through the bars that while strong-looking, did little to block Charlie and his animals from view. The lion lifted his angular face and looked at her with pale, golden eyes. He stared fearlessly—boldly—as a king would.

"I wouldn't look too long. Not directly," Charlie said. "Or he's gonna think you want to take something from him."

Ella averted her eyes to the round ears that quirked when the far side of the Big Top rustled in the breeze. The left ear shivered and Charlie rubbed it. Still staring at her, the lion lifted a black-tipped tail in a slow curve before lowering

123

it back to the dust. Then he started to gnaw on the hem of Charlie's shirt and Charlie nudged the lion's massive head away.

She had no words.

"How did you find me?" Charlie asked.

It was an effort to draw sound to her voice. "A bit of help from Lorelai and another man. I'm sorry if I shouldn't have . . ." She fell silent when he shook his head in a manner that wiped away her worries. She glanced to the lions, now so near. "They can't . . . get out, can they?"

"You ask me this *now?*" He squinted at her playfully.

She bit her lip and watched him another few moments. It was then that she noticed an ornate cage wagon parked off to the side. Painted a vibrant yellow and trimmed in gold and blue filigree, the giant wagon stood backed up against the arena bars.

Ella slid her gaze back to Charlie and his great cats. She'd never imagined seeing a lion in her wildest dreams, let alone just feet away. "Is this what they normally do?"

He nodded. "They're done working for now. We've been going over a new routine and they needed some more practice." He looked down to the one who was still lounging on him. "Especially you, Axel."

The lion pawed Charlie's chest, and with a grin, Charlie shoved it off. "So that's what we do. Earlier, we played. They get their energy out. Usually at my expense." He winced when he shifted and she feared his implication. "And now they'll nap, then later on, the show will start and I'll conquer these wild and ferocious beasts with my charms." His eyebrows bobbed. "To the crowd's awe and astonishment. Tell me you're impressed."

She let out a little laugh. "Have you always done this?"

"Long as I can remember."

The lion rolled away from Charlie and stretched before lounging back against his lap. Enormous fanged teeth began to gnaw and tug at the edge of his shirt again, and Charlie pushed the lion's face away. Undeterred, the lion tried once more.

"I never would have known." Ella shook her head in disbelief. "I would have envisioned a trainer with one of those things." She made a whipping motion and Charlie winced.

"Yeah. Those folks are certainly out there. And most just use them for the sound. But . . ." he shook his head. "My father, he had a theory. That there was a better way. No sticks, whips, or barbs of any kind. Instead of making them submit, to treat them in a way that they *want* to listen. That the circus life can be enjoyable for them. Which means—" with a smile in his eyes, he nodded toward the lounging lion—"that this is the most important part of my day. The performance is nothing compared to this. *This* . . ." Charlie ran his hand through the thick mane, scrubbing hard at the dense, amber fur, "shows them that I am one of them. That I have been from the start. And that I'm going to take care of them. They don't have to fear, which makes my job so much easier." His mouth tipped up.

"And you're not afraid to be on the ground like that with them?"

"I try to stay low when they are," Charlie said. "It keeps them from feeling threatened by me. I'm not here to hurt them."

The lion lifted a wide paw and licked the underside a few slow times, his large, pale eyes on Ella again.

"They've learned over the years that I won't leave them. They trust me." Charlie slapped the soft-looking hide of the great, rounded belly with a few friendly pats. "They're like my brothers." With his head, he motioned down to where the lion had wrapped its massive paws around Charlie's leg. "As you can see, they're quite attached."

"Unbelievable," she breathed.

"To them, I'm not their trainer. I don't even think they know that I'm a man sometimes. Oh, and you should see Axel with Holland." Charlie went to stand. "I'll show you."

Ella wrapped her arms around the baby. "Don't you dare."

He chuckled and settled back into the dirt. "Just you wait and see."

"I'd rather not."

He laughed deeper. Startled to alertness, the lion looked up and pressed his huge black nose into the air against Charlie's chest.

"Jealous, my boy?" Charlie buried the side of his head into the wiry mane and stroked a hand up the thick neck.

"Now I know why your hair always looks that way," Ella said.

His brows fell—face serious. "Does it look . . . funny?"

She took in the sight of his ever-wild hair. The way it always stood on end. Untamed. "You didn't know that?" Ella couldn't fight the smile.

He ran a hand forward through the brown locks. "Always?" But as he stood, a sparkle in his eyes told her that he knew as much. "I should get these boys settled before they fall asleep."

Charlie nodded to his partner who whistled toward the back of the tent.

Several workers lumbered in, one calling direction to a massive elephant who wore a thick-strapped harness across both back and chest.

Ella gaped.

Holland flapped her hands.

"She's more in love with the bull man than me," Charlie quipped as he unfastened a trap door in the fencing while the man leading the elephant rounded his charge to a halt in front of the wagon. The solid, dusty feet moved back two steps, and then the man pulled something from his pocket. The tip of a wrinkled, gray trunk dabbed at his palm, and with a flap of giant ears, the elephant ate its reward. Finished, the animal dipped its trunk then lifted it up in a salute. Holland babbled as the bull man reached up to fasten hitch to harness, and it was all Ella could do to hold the squirming baby who was bent on joining them.

"Don't wear yourself out, little one," Charlie cautioned.

Holland cooed and blew bubbles. The elephant trumpeted in return.

After setting a ramp into place, he hefted up a bucket and tossed small chunks of what was surely meat into the wagon. Then he let out a soft whistle and his cats all lifted their heads. "Kristov, up! Axel up!"

In turn, each maned lion lumbered up the ramp, tails swaying lazily behind them. The third vanished into the cage wagon, and it was all Ella could do not to faint when Charlie climbed in as well and shut the door.

"I'll be right back," he called to her.

The lions flopped down in a rustle and immediately set about rubbing faces and licking manes while Charlie dispersed bright straw that one of the circus hands carried to him. The elephant pulled the giant wagon from the arena and out through a slit in the striped tent.

When Holland started to fuss, Ella whispered that Charlie would be back.

And within a few minutes, he was. He strode across the dusty ring, brushing straw from his pants. Grinning at the pair of them, he gripped Holland under her arms and lifted her to his chest.

Charlie kissed a round, pudgy cheek before thanking Ella for the help. "I have to go get ready for the performance now. Would you like to come for the show? I'll save you one of the best seats in the house and even give you your money back if the trainer gets eaten."

A smile bubbled up. "Who could refuse such an offer?"

He wet his lips. "It will be Holland's nap time, and instead of eating at the cookhouse this evening, I thought I'd—well . . . if you'd like . . ." He scratched the back of his head shyly. "Regina said she'd help me make you supper. If you'd like. It wouldn't be much and you could certainly say no, but I sure would like to repay you for last night."

Ella looked up into pale eyes that watched her with hope. "I'd like that. Very much."

When he grinned, a light in his expression took that hope and did something funny to her heart. They walked out into the sunlight where the rich,

129

buttery scent of popcorn was thick in the air. He shoved his fist into his pocket only to pull it right back out which sent several things spilling to the ground. He bumped against her, his arm brushing her skirt, as he quickly knelt and plucked up a scrap of paper and a penny.

"What are you doing?" she asked.

"Honestly? I have no idea." Chuckling, he tossed the scrap in the waste bin. He flipped the penny and caught it before sliding it back out of sight. Then he sobered quickly. "It didn't seem like I was trying to hold your hand, did it?"

Despite herself, she laughed.

Then he halted in his tracks and she heard his quick intake of breath.

Ella stopped too and Charlie glanced at her with a hint of regret. Perhaps wishing she'd kept walking because a wisp of a woman had stopped in front of them with a fiery, potent stare. Her ebony hair was pulled into a severe bun. Wrinkled mouth pursed taut, small eyes snapping as she shifted her glare over to Charlie. With a flick of his wrist, Charlie doffed an imaginary hat.

The woman rolled her eyes. A heavy perfume scent surrounded her and a large man stood a few feet away, meaty hands clasped in front of him.

"I'd like to talk to you." Her voice was thick with a foreign accent.

Charlie made a show of snapping his fingers.

"I'd *love* to." His voice dripped with mock-enthusiasm. "But I have a show."

The woman handed Charlie an envelope. He took and folded it, then tucked the envelope in his shirt pocket. Ella realized the scent wasn't perfume. She remembered it from a patient she'd assisted in the men's ward last fall. It was opium.

"Perhaps you can *make* time. Later. Unless you're simply *too busy*." The slip of a woman glanced at Ella again. Her dark gaze fell on Holland.

Charlie shifted the baby against his waist. The woman's eyes tightened and then she tugged an ornate watch from her bodice. She checked the time, looked sharply at Ella once more, then walked on. Charlie stared straight ahead as she left. Ella glanced back and watched the woman weave through the masses. The large man followed her.

With a tip of his head, Charlie motioned for Ella to walk with him.

"Who was that?" she whispered.

"Just an old friend." He gave her a half smile. She twisted her mouth to the side, and as if knowing she wasn't buying that, he moved closer. Free hand in his pocket, he spoke while looking at the path. "Have you ever worked for someone you really didn't like?"

She felt guilty to confess, but he spoke before she could.

"Kind of like that good doctor of yours."

Ella wrinkled her nose.

"Exactly." He thumbed over his shoulder. "Just like that." He gave her a lopsided grin, but his eyes were shadowed and she sensed it was worse. "And let's just say that now we don't have to worry about you being seen anymore."

TEN

Seated in the front row, Ella gripped the edge of the bench tighter. The air in the vast, striped tent was heavy and thick with the tantalizing aroma of concession treats, the springtime scent of earth, and the rich, humble smells of animals. From the center of the Big Top, the ringmaster announced the first act as cheers and whispers drew to silence. The ring emptied, draining of the clowns and jugglers who had entertained the crowd while seats filled. An overture, Ella realized, because with Charlie's massive cage still assembled front and center, it took no guessing as to what would come first. A thrill pulsed through her.

The Big Top fell hushed as several men dressed in workman's clothing inspected the tall, wire fencing. A herald of the danger to come. Even so, a trio of aerialists dressed in tights, corsets, and little ruffled bloomers slipped through the opening in the cage, jogging into the center of the ring. Their white button-up shoes made nary a sound as brazen whistles shot out. Ella recognized Ruth, the bold redhead from the other day.

Reaching for the three strips of cloth that suddenly unfurled from the overhead rigging, they quick-wrapped their wrists and ankles and climbed in synchronization. With bated breath, Ella watched the women wind the striped fabrics as they rose. Reaching the high rigging, they pulled up the remaining silk, hammocked themselves into sitting positions, then pressed fingers to their painted lips with a collective, playful, "Shhhh . . ." Amusement filtered through the stands.

Finished, the workers slipped out the open gate, leaving the three women to sway overhead like a trio of doves in an ornate cage.

Just then a child in the row behind Ella cried out. "Look, Mama!"

Charlie, dressed in his center ring finery, strode into the arena, as tall and dashing as ever. Face powdered and painted with two jagged teardrops under his eyes, he walked with stoic authority, tall boots forging a fresh trail straight toward his audience. Ella didn't know a single man could hush a packed house with no words, but . . . then there was Charlie Lionheart. The side of her mouth pursed in a smile. Behind him, a dozen more workers bustled in, burdened by three massive crates, which they gently placed inside the fenced area before exiting. The gate creaked closed and a latch was pressed into place. All alone, save the three pretty faces above, Charlie used a brass-topped cane to softly tap each box. Appeared to check that they were locked. Murmurs filtered through the stands.

Anticipation bright in the air, Ella nibbled the end of her thumb.

Charlie rattled one of the locks. Eyed the keyhole. He patted down his coat. One gloved hand slid into his pocket, then the other. A few chuckles spilled around. Ella's smile deepened. Outside of the fencing, Charlie's partner edged closer to the gate and rested a hand on the latch in silent question. Charlie gave a theatrical shrug, and turning away from the audience, strode the way he'd come, through the gate, latching it behind him. Curious murmurs rose.

Then he stopped abruptly and snapped his fingers. Charlie headed toward the seated spectators. He started on the far left of the front row and began a search—poking in the reticules of giggling ladies and even made one man empty his pockets. Chuckles spread and Ella could feel it. The audience . . .

In the palm of his hand.

And here she was sitting among them. Because he'd asked her to. Vulnerability and innocence in his face as they'd stood in the sun. The sheer recollection of it warmed her cheeks. What on earth was she doing? Spending her days at the circus—with a lion tamer. One who was but feet away in his emerald coat, top hat perfectly askew, an amused curve to his mouth. So fetching that she was feeling very nervous as he drew near.

He shuffled his hand along the edges of dress hems that brushed the stands and to a snickering child, lifted his small shoe in search of the key. To Ella's relief, he strode right by. A few steps later, he slammed to a halt. Then turned. And pointed to her. Ella's heart shot up.

Pacing back, he folded his arms and frowned, eyebrow raised. He held out his gloved palm.

When she simply sat there wide eyed, he tapped his foot impatiently.

Baffled, Ella patted her bodice, then peeked under the seat. Arms still folded, Charlie made a show of growing impatient. The crowd laughed. His green eyes twinkled at her. Fearing her face was as pink as it felt, Ella reached into her dress pocket and there it was, the cold press of metal. Recalling the way he'd brushed against her, she pulled the key out and handed it to him. Charlie took it, and grinning, dipped her a bow. Then he straightened and flashed the key high. Laughter turned to applause and Charlie winked at Ella before hurrying back.

He was going to pay for that.

Charlie strode to the nearest crate, unlocked it, then repeated the motion with the other two. Just as he stepped away from the last box, guttural bellows broke the silence. The audience gasped. Charlie slid each lock free with dramatic flair. Hesitated. Then flung down the doors. With easy movements, he climbed onto the center box and walked to the front edge, his polished boots tall and thundering.

Utter astonishment filled the Big Top as the lions ambled out, tails swishing, jaws flexing in yawns. Ignoring the rows upon rows of spectators, the lions pawed at one another. Charlie let them romp for several minutes as *oohs* and *aahs* swelled. He'd told her earlier that each of his cats topped out at over five hundred pounds. Every ounce of that weight and strength was circling in front of him now.

Just then one of the aerialists lowered an ornate banner that read in bold-faced lettering, *Rules of Lion Taming*. A hush fell and Ruth unfurled a second banner—*Starring A Very Naughty Lion Tamer*. The hush bloomed to snickers and Ella smiled as Charlie still appeared oblivious. He gripped the edge of the crate and hopped down into the dirt. A crouch absorbing the shock, he rose slowly.

A little voice spoke from nearby. "Is he gonna get eaten, Papa?"

"I don't . . . think so," came the father's wary response.

The largest of the cats lifted his head and looked at Charlie. What had Charlie called him? Axel.

Another banner inched down. *Rule Number 1: Never Turn Your Back On A Lion.*

With a cheery whistle, Charlie set about easing

crate doors closed. Hinging locks into place, his back to all three lions whose gazes were trained on him. Then they began to follow. Muscles edged their legs, massive paws beating quiet prints into the dusty earth. Murmurs rose as they drew closer, circling Charlie. The thickest one licked his chops. As though just sensing their presence, Charlie stopped his work. The woman beside Ella covered her mouth with her hands.

Still nestled in her knotted silk, Ruth lowered another sign. *Rule Number 2: Always Carry A Big Stick.*

And with his back still to the trio of great cats, Charlie patted his pockets, flexed empty hands . . .

The crowd drew in a collective breath. Standing discreetly beside the gate, his partner smirked. The lions closed around Charlie, and though Ella had seen him with them earlier, the nervous energy penetrated.

Charlie pulled something from a crate—an oversized book by the looks of it. He held it in front of his face and flipped forward a few pages, then turned, book poised, title in grand gold lettering. *Lion Training for Beginners.*

The crowd laughed.

At Charlie's feet, the largest lion lay down and another strode off. Near Charlie, the third lion sank down. Nose still in the book, Charlie sidestepped and sat between them. He lounged against one and propped his boots lazily on the back of the other. Licking the tip of his finger, Charlie turned a page. Snickers tiptoed through the audience. The third lion ambled back, the strap of a canteen in his jaws. Without looking at the animal, Charlie took and uncapped the canteen, then swigged. Still seeming engrossed in his book, he turned another page then looked slowly over at the audience. As if just remembering the hundreds of pairs of eyes on him, he snapped to attention and rose.

He tugged at his coat, chin high, appearing very official and then flipped furiously through a few more pages before tossing the book aside. He scratched his head, then with a raised finger, seemed to have a new idea. He spoke to the lions and motioned them into position. They obeyed, standing in a line of muscle and manes. He gave each of them a gentle touch on the nose and signaled by a dip of his retrieved cane. A low guttural sound rose from the center lion, followed by the others, and within a moment, they roared. A blood-thinning sound. Muzzles scrunched, sharp teeth on display, their stomachs clenched. The rumbling aftermath shattered over the applause and fevered awe that filled the tent.

Ella could only shake her head in disbelief.

Charlie stepped around them, held up his hands to settle them, and they slowly sat back down. Then he raised his cane like the baton of a band leader and seemed about to do something when another banner eased down from above.

Rule Number 3: Watch Out For Aerialists.

Folks snickered.

Grinning, Ella leaned forward and rested her cheeks in her hands.

Just then, one of the dangling women tossed an object down with a thunk. Ella realized it was a leather ball as it rolled and stole the lions' attention. All three of them lunged after it. Seemingly confused, Charlie turned and strode after them. To Ella's astonishment and the crowd's delight, he wrestled the ball free, taking a good knock in the chest by the feistiest lion. Charlie looked unfazed, and by the time he had the great cats arranged in a row again, one of the women slid down her silken cloth and must have dropped something worth nibbling on before climbing back up, because a lion bounded over and gobbled it up.

Charlie's shoulders sank theatrically and he covered his face with his hand. When he had the lions lined up a third time, he raised his cane to direct them when another aerialist dropped a treat. This time two lions bounded away. The quicker one snatched it up which had the other batting at him with a fearsome set of claws. The first lion bared his fangs but backed away.

With feigned dismay, Charlie strode over to the victor, gripped him by his upper and lower jaws, and spread the mouth wide. Gasps shot out at the sight of the huge, hinged jaw, more so when Charlie stuck his face past the open fangs to peer inside. Knowing her eyes were as round as saucers, Ella pressed her hands over her mouth. Charlie pulled back, and facing the stands, held up his hands in question. Countless fingers pointed toward the top of the tent and he lifted his painted face to the ladies for the first time. They giggled and swung. Fists to his waist, he shook his head disapprovingly.

There was something about their actions that felt spur of the moment, but Ella sensed it was all rehearsed. The aerialists twisted and twirled on their silk strips, watching Charlie playfully and laughing aloud now that they were caught. Arms folded over his chest, Charlie watched them back. Heads tilted upward, the lions did too. Axel swiped a huge tongue over his jaws.

A gentleman from a back row hollered out, "Makes ya wonder who wants those little ladies more—the lions or their trainer."

The audience guffawed and even Charlie pointed at the man with a stern yet playful scowl. Folks laughed harder.

Charlie strode to one of the massive crates and bending, gripped the underside and heaved it onto its narrow end with a heavy slam so it stood taller. Awed by his strength, Ella sat motionless as Charlie started to shove another one of the great boxes beside it. Feigning struggle, he whistled and his lions ambled over, each of them placing their heads to the wood and appeared to help. Folks cheered and Charlie grinned. Finished with the stair step effect, he flashed a naughty smirk and motioned Axel, the largest lion, up the boxes.

No longer swinging, the aerialists held palms prayerfully beneath their chins. Each as angelic as could be.

Shaking his head, Charlie motioned Axel up to the next crate. The huge lion bellowed at the women, his tail swishing back and forth. With quick swivels, the aerialists climbed farther out of reach. A loud thrill swept the audience. With a metal stand on his shoulder, Charlie climbed and set the stand for the lion to rise farther. Axel bounded up onto the shiny platform and gave a swipe of his paw. Unable to go any higher, the trio of ladies squealed and a collection of gasps filled the stands. Ella glanced across to where Charlie's partner lingered outside the fencing. Though his stance was easy, he scanned the performance like a hawk, wooden club now in his grip. Ella had to peel her gaze away from what looked like the glinting nose of a pistol at his belt.

She pressed fingertips to her lips, nearly missing the subtle touch Charlie gave the lion between his shoulders. The animal looked over to the crowd and roared. Once . . . and then again, splintering the air. Ruth's painted lips tipped open.

Charlie motioned to one of his lions below. The animal turned, went into his crate, and returned with the stick of a wooden sign quirked crookedly from his jaws that read, *Say Please.*

The audience laughed, and in unison, the three women squealed a *please!* Delight washed through the stands. Ella clapped along with all the rest as Charlie feigned disappointment and signaled Axel back from their hunt. He righted the crates and in the animals went. He clicked locks and the aerialists slid down the silks, landing with perfect precision on the boxes. The crowd cheered and Charlie motioned to the women who did a little bow, then he bowed as the audience stood in thunderous applause. Ella joined them. Charlie flashed her a wink and she gave him a small wave.

With a sweep of his hand, Charlie's partner signaled for the workers running into the ring to retrieve the oversized crates. While the three women tossed one last wave toward the crowd, Charlie disappeared out through the part in the curtain. Turning quickly, the ladies joined him and a new act rushed in.

"Well, that was fun," Ruth snapped. "I just about stepped in elephant—" She pranced over a lounging clown and flung him a glare. "Hey laddie, find somewhere else to sit next time." Her voice fell to a mutter. "Stupid joey."

Someone was in a good mood. Removing his top hat, Charlie trailed her through the press of clowns and acrobats.

Even as he heard the clatter of the fencing being disassembled, he watched the roustabouts tote away the lion crates.

Someone called a greeting to him. "Nice work, Preach!"

Not seeing who it was, Charlie shot a wave in that direction as he headed after his boys. Passing the flyer troupe who stood chalking their hands, Charlie patted one of the young women on the shoulder whose sunny smile always reminded him of Jessamine—Mimi.

He paused to wish her well, a habit he'd taken on since Mimi's death, but Ruth turned and shoved a fingertip into his chest. "*You* are not supposed to improvise."

Rolling their eyes, the other two aerialists steered from the storm.

"Who improvised?" Charlie countered.

"Oh, let's see . . ." Hand propped on the curve of her corseted hip, Ruth all but glared at him. "The wee stunt with the key?"

Charlie grinned—remembering the look on Ella's face. He stepped aside for an acrobat who toted a dozen metal hoops.

Ruth frowned at him. " 'Twas the lass you were with the other day."

Charlie ignored her, but concern slipped into her expression and was warranted, for there was a fine line in the sand and he'd just stepped way over it.

"What are you doing?" Ruth hissed.

Really, he had no idea. "Don't get your ribbons in a twist. If I'm not mistaken, you blew a kiss to a section of soldiers in Detroit last year and missed a very important cue."

"I did not." Though the fire in her eyes said otherwise.

He didn't have time for this.

Pocketing his white gloves, Charlie headed toward the menagerie tent where he helped load the lions into their wagon. Since grown lions only spent about five hours of the day awake, they circled one another, weaving in and out, before flopping down. From nearby, zebras chattered—a hee-hawing laugh sound that Charlie was so used to he barely noticed. One of the giraffes dipped her long neck and sniffed at Charlie's pocket. With nothing to give her, Charlie smoothed a hand along her neck.

Han quirked his head, and remembering how he had favored his left paw near the end of the act, Charlie checked the leathery pad. Finding a burr, he plucked it free. Han licked Charlie's fingers, then his own paw.

The lion licked his hand again, and though the grit of the massive tongue was painful, Charlie held still. The cat's eyes were closed and Charlie watched him without speaking. Sired by his father's own, Han was bred in captivity just like the others. While they had a longer lifespan than those in the wilds of Africa and Asia, Charlie often imagined what it would be like to see his lions walk out across an open plain. Though it wasn't the same, he paid a few laborers to set up the performance arena outdoors as often as he could, which meant a few hours of regular sun for his cats. Circus goers enjoyed seeing them that way and the lions loved it.

Charlie stepped toward Axel who he'd gotten as a cub the year his father had died, and even now could still remember being on the stock car of the southbound train, holding the little bundle of fur that would keep his life afloat when everything else went dark. Something Charlie aimed to return for Axel. Hope. Freedom.

Not just for Axel. For all three of them.

"I promise I'm working on it," Charlie said gently as he ran his thumb under Axel's jaw.

Next he checked water basins, then tuned an ear toward the roar of the crowd, awaiting the familiar sounds that would indicate the matinee's end. The ringmaster, Mr. Graven, would expect him to be at his side for final bows. A hunch told Charlie that it was because the ringmaster was more than pleased that he had extended his contract for another four years. With handsome offers from both Ringling *and* Barnum & Bailey, Charlie certainly had his choice.

When the boom of cannons rocked the air, Charlie adjusted his top hat then slid gloves on, covering the tattoo there.

He strode back to the Big Top to where Mr. Graven stood in the wings. After a friendly pat on Charlie's back, the ringmaster explained that despite having run aground in muddy Roanoke, ticket sales were high and Charlie's act a bright favorite.

Charlie nodded his thanks. Especially since the ringmaster never raised an eyebrow over the fact that Charlie insisted on working with his cats his own way—including a refusal for them to be displayed on the midway between shows. While Charlie didn't care if it posed a problem, his mandate never detracted from the carnival atmosphere; people still flocked to the ticket booth in droves, and Mr. Graven paid him a handsome salary.

"To think that three decades ago we were little more than a dog and pony show," Mr. Graven said with a tug on his red, brass-button coat. No doubt relishing that the troupe's growing caliber had catapulted the Graven Brothers Circus into prominent standing nationwide.

Keeping P.T. Barnum on his toes.

Charlie fell in step with the ringmaster as they strode toward the curtain. The silver-haired man twisted the end of his mustache, speaking of how the show must always go on. "Let's do 'Animals from Around the World.' Keep changing things up for the house."

That one was easy enough. Charlie only had to keep his lions from wanting to eat two bull elephants instead of three aerialists. After Ruth's mood today, he'd take the twelve-thousand-pound bulls any day.

As Charlie stepped through the back corridor of dressing rooms, he spotted the very woman lounging against a side pole. She always waited for him, sometimes more subtly than others. Charlie halted as a roustabout tried to offer Ruth a pile of lacy handkerchiefs and more. She ignored him, so Charlie let the poor fella off the hook by taking the tokens of affection.

The worker grumbled as he adjusted the round of lunge rope crossing his thin chest. "We need to hit the road. Rubes'r gettin' way too friendly." When the hopelessly besotted roustabout peered toward Ruth, Charlie smirked, then leaned in to whisper loudly to the lad, "I wouldn't waste your time with that one; her bite is even worse than her bark."

Ruth stuck her tongue out at him.

A note crinkled on the top of the pile, and

turning it over, Charlie read, *"To the pretty lady with the red hair."* He eyed Ruth.

Adjusting the silky slip of a kimono that draped her shoulders, she snatched it from him, read, then tossed the card in a waste bin. "Manky local."

The final applause erupted. Charlie set the things aside and stepped toward the gap in the striped tent. He tugged at his green velvet coat then smoothed the brim of his glossy hat. "Remind me to never write you a note."

Ruth slipped off her covering, baring cream-colored shoulders above her ivory, bone corset. "Well, if it was from you, I wouldn'a tossed it."

She gave him a little look as Charlie strode into the applause-filled ring, her snapped, "Have fun in *Hicksville,*" trailing him.

ELEVEN

With the sounds of delight still floating along the air, Ella worked her way through the throngs of people back to Charlie's tent. The show danced in her memory, the energy still buzzing around.

After the audience had thinned, Charlie had slipped into the stands toward her, only to be greeted by several young boys, all peppering him with questions. He'd tousled the youngest boy's hair. Kneeling in front of the stair-stepped lads, he passed back easy banter with them even as he slid Ella a winsome glance that was edged in apology. With a smile, she had slipped out quietly to let him finish.

Now clouds dimmed the air and a rising breeze shook the sides of Charlie's tent as she drew near to it. Ella stepped inside to find Regina mixing dough in a bowl and Holland stirring from her nap.

Ella settled down beside the baby's bed, but spoke to Regina. "How did your afternoon go?"

"Very well, *mia cara*."

While she worked on supper, Regina chatted about it in that motherly way of hers. Holland squirmed and seemed uncomfortable, so Ella pulled out a picture book, and with the baby lying on her side, held it in view. Holland touched a picture of a tiger and the girl's nose creased playfully as she stroked the striped sketch. Ella kissed that tiny finger which was so much cooler than it had been the day before.

While the baby was still showing signs of discomfort in her throat, the infection was fading. Ella offered her a sip of water and Regina declared that Holland had eaten a fair bit of porridge that afternoon.

Suddenly the tent flap moved aside and Charlie ducked in. He held out a white rose to Regina. "My dear." Then he slid his hand behind his back and pulled forward a pink one, which he lowered to Ella. "For the lady."

Ella was stunned afresh by his powdered face. The jagged, charcoal teardrops below his eyes that made his charm all the more intriguing.

"Oh." She remembered the way the flowers had fallen into the arena at the show's end. "Might you have a secret admirer?" she teased gently.

With a grin, Charlie pulled forward his other arm revealing a mixed bouquet. Then he tugged a messy array of perfumed calling cards from his breast pocket.

"I have a hunch he's blushing behind all that makeup," Regina said.

Charlie pointed at her. "You be nice."

"*Which* reminds me," Ella said, "I can't believe you did that!"

He feigned shock.

"Sneaking a key into my pocket . . ." She squinted at him as he tossed his coat aside.

"It wasn't that sneaky," he laughed. "I dropped all my stuff *and* bumped into you. I'm usually much smoother with things like that. I think you make me nervous . . ." His eyes sparkled.

More so when her cheeks flushed. To try and cover it, she told him how much she enjoyed the performance.

Grinning, Charlie tugged off his vest. At the washstand, he moved his shaving kit aside then filled the basin. He dabbed oil to his fingers and scrubbed his skin clean. Splashes of soapy water dampened his face and hair. Water dripped onto the shoulders of his shirt as he grabbed the towel.

His face clean, he bent and kissed Holland's head. "And hello, little one." Kneeling beside her bed, he kissed her cheek. "I have a flower for you too, but I'll have to save it." He rose. "I need to go change. Just make yourself at home, Ella." He climbed up the trio of crates and stepped into the wagon, closing the curtains behind him.

A pot of water heated on the stove and Regina brought over the dough she had prepared earlier. She turned it out on the low work surface that was no more than a wide board balanced on two barrels. She patted the dough with a wooden pin and set to work rolling it out. The light in the tent dimmed and Ella peered through the open flap to see the wind softly winding its way through the camp. Clouds pushed across the sky.

Ella brushed at her hands and rose. "May I help you do anything? I could set the table."

Charlie emerged wearing a fresh, dry shirt. He and Regina looked at her in unison.

Oh, yes. There was no table.

"Why don't you just sit and let us do something for you for a change. Remember," he pointed at her, "this is our treat."

He and Regina set to work, and Ella settled on the crates in front of the wagon to watch. Regina rolled and cut rounds of dough and Charlie helped her stuff them with a filling Regina had beaten together. All the while Regina scolded his technique in phrases laced with Italian. The passion in her voice mixed easily with Charlie's chuckles. At the stout woman's direction, he added salt to the boiling water. Too much, it seemed, when the water foamed and Regina swatted his arm with her wooden spoon.

Charlie grinned at Ella as Regina lowered small dumplings into the water. Him standing tall and solid in his crisp shirt, costume pants, and boots, her on a wooden box—they made quite a pair.

"You will like Regina's cooking," Charlie said over his shoulder. "She uses garlic and onions and her peppers."

Regina pointed at him with her spoon. "Don't you start in on my peppers."

Charlie let out a deep laugh that warmed the room. A few raindrops tapped on the canvas overhead. He rinsed his hands, and with the air dimming further, went to light the lantern.

"He is just sore about it because of my peppers and the way he has to load the plants into the wagon every time we move on." Regina motioned toward the ornate green wagon.

"It's quite a task." Charlie moved to a wooden crate that sat on the grassy ground and pulled out a jar of silverware, followed by tin plates.

"It keeps you from becoming a fat old man, my boy." Regina's dark brows danced.

"Regina has a small garden outside. Pots and pots of things." Charlie rose. "She's Italian, and that seems to be the way they do it. A wise old man once said, 'Don't ever befriend an Italian Gypsy or you will be toting around a great many things.'" He ducked when a snip of pepper went sailing past his head. "And watch out for their tempers."

"Were you born in Italy?" Ella asked Regina.

She nodded. "I came here when I was a young woman. My feet were barely on American soil when I married a *carradore*. A wheelwright who was with this troupe of traveling performers. I had traveled so little myself, but felt right at home with the circus. Here I am, thirty years later." She reached up and patted Charlie's forearm. "With this one and his sweet *bambina*."

154

Those threads of joy wound tighter within Ella's chest. "And you are both Gypsy by blood?" She glanced from Regina to Charlie.

"I am not by blood," Regina said. "But in life. Now Charlie here is Roma, and the Romani are—"

"Both clever and good looking," Charlie interjected.

"I was going to say prideful," Regina countered. "But now I see that I didn't need to."

Ella giggled.

Regina peered playfully up at Charlie before shifting her gaze to Ella. "There is much Romani in this company, which is why our banners are so big. And why we linger for three days in each town. They're never in a hurry."

"Vain I will accept, but are you calling me slow?" He spoke down to Regina, but winked briefly in Ella's direction. "You're missing the whole point to what we believe. It's about *l'amore*. A wise old man also said that, 'If you're passionate for something, why rush?' "

The little woman propped a fist on her hip. "Oh, stop making things up. Better yet, tell that to Mr. Graven the next time the Ringling Brothers go flying by on the rails."

He grinned and Ella could see it—this Romani blood in him with his dark brown hair, sun-kissed skin. Vivid green eyes that were like nothing she'd ever seen before. Because of that, she

155

wondered if his parentage wasn't more mixed than he let on.

When the tent fell quiet, Ella peered around the tall, dashing subject to his stout companion. "What you're making smells delicious."

Charlie moved beside Regina and held out a plate. Using a slotted spoon, she drained the dumplings and plopped several onto the plate. From a small pot on the back of the potbelly stove, she drizzled what looked like a cream sauce onto the mounds of glistening dough.

Charlie carried the plate to Ella along with a fork and napkin. Their fingers touched, shooting warmth into her arm. "Thank you," she said.

With a soft expression, Charlie went back to the stove.

"What did you say these were?" Ella asked.

"Ravioli." Regina said the word fondly as she filled another plate.

Ella tucked the steamy, heavenly-smelling dish in her lap and waited as the others got their own meals and settled around—Charlie on the little wooden bed with Holland, Regina on a chair near the stove. With his crates under her, Ella touched her toes together. She picked up her fork and stabbed a ravioli only to see Regina bow her head. Charlie too.

"Our heavenly father," Charlie began.

As quietly as possible, Ella set down the fork.

Holland reached for Charlie's plate and with his

eyes closed, he gently caught her hand in his own. She tried to reach around it and he smiled softly at her antics even as he spoke. "We thank you for this food. And for the hands that have prepared it."

Ella looked over at Regina who, with eyes closed, wore a soft smile.

"And we thank you for Ella, our company. That she's helped make Holland well."

Ella swallowed hard.

"And for taking care of Holland, keeping her in your mighty grasp." Charlie finished with an "amen" and lifted his head.

Mute, Ella nodded, her appetite stilted. When he began to eat, she took a small bite. The dumpling was creamy and rich, and though her stomach suddenly felt unsettled, they *were* good. "These are incredible, Regina."

The woman looked up from her meal. "Thank you, my dear."

Slowly, Ella ate another thinking that she would like to learn how to make them. Realizing she was eating without speaking—and Charlie was watching her with that same look of amusement—she dabbed at her mouth with the napkin.

"My friend has some questions for you," she said.

"From Margaret the Captive? For me?" He cut a corner of cooked dough and offered it to Holland. She plucked the small morsel from his palm then pushed it into her mouth.

"She wants to know if your last name is really Lionheart."

He gave a crooked grin and stabbed a ravioli for himself. "I'll be sure to tell her, the next time I see her."

"Charlie!" Ella said with a laugh.

"Oh . . ." He looked up again. "So this might be for *your* benefit as well?"

Feeling her cheeks warm, Ella held his gaze. "Possibly."

He settled his back against a tent post, and being much too big for Holland's bed, propped his tall boots on a nearby crate. "Yes. My name really is Lionheart."

Ella thought on that, then slowly shook her head. "And you are a lion tamer. What a coincidence."

"It's not a coincidence." He stirred his food around with his fork, eyes down. He looked over at Holland, then back to Ella. "My father joined the circus when he was sixteen."

Ella tried to imagine that.

"As the story goes, he was running away from home. Why . . ." he speared a ravioli, "I don't know. He never spoke of his life before that. I think he didn't see eye to eye with his father. So he joined the circus. And he changed his name."

Lionheart. She almost said it aloud.

"You can be anything you want to be here." He slipped a pinch of glistening dough to Holland

158

who grasped it with pudgy fingers. "If I had a name before Lionheart, I wouldn't know what it was. My parents never told me. So it is the only thing that I have to give Holland." His muted smile was bittersweet, gaze still on Ella. "And whoever else might have need of it."

Her heart hurt a little, struck by the simplicity of that—and the depth.

"He wasn't the first person to change his name around here. Not everyone who joins the circus does it because they want to. Some join it because they have nowhere else to go."

Ella looked at him a long moment. Then remembering her food, made herself take a small bite. Still pondering his answer, she must have thought overlong, for he spoke again.

"Any other questions from your friend? Nurses really are nosy creatures."

If Ella had a pepper in hand she'd have thrown it at him. Instead, she just thought back over Margaret's wonderings. Ella hesitated on Holland's name—something she'd been curious about herself, but after the story he just shared, it didn't feel right probing there. Margaret's other question of how long he had been with the circus was now answered, so Ella searched her mind to see if she had any others.

But she was feeling distracted. Ever since his prayer. "You are a religious man?"

Her inquiry seemed to take him by surprise.

"Would you have preferred me something else?" When he looked back at Ella, there was a seriousness threaded in the glimpse he gave her. "I simply talk to God."

Ella drew in a shuddering breath.

"Because I am not a good man by nature. And I hope to make the years here count for something." He was looking at her with such conviction that she couldn't glance away. "It's something I want to try to be because it's right. And it gives a better life to Holland, and anyone else who has to put up with me."

Ella looked at Regina. The stout woman was watching Charlie with shining eyes.

"I am nothing without God," he said. "And I don't ever want to try to be."

"You see what you started?" Regina said good-naturedly to Ella. "This is why they call him *Preacher*. Just like his father before him."

Preacher.

And his son.

Ella set her plate down with a clatter. No, no, no . . .

She needed to go home now. She stood on shaky legs, gripped the edge of Charlie's wagon to steady herself, then stepped down to the grassy floor. From her side vision, Charlie stood.

"Ella?"

Home. Now.

Alone.

Lanterns bobbed past the tent and in the distance, the peculiar pumping of a slow accordion was drowned out by the clatter of balls and wooden pegs. A crowd of men guffawed and a bell clanged, signaling a prize.

Was she swaying? The room seemed to spin and she reached for something, only to take hold of Charlie's arm when he stepped beside her. His other arm slid around as if to steady her, but Ella startled at the strength she felt there.

Charlie pulled away, his face puzzled and pained. "Ella, are you okay?"

"I need to leave," she whispered.

"If you wish . . ." His voice matched his confused expression. "I'll walk you."

"No!" She moved away from him, memories of old punching her square in the gut. "I'm quite fine all on my own." The room was still spinning, but Ella whispered a distant thank you to Regina. She didn't look at Holland. Didn't want to see her face. Her heart couldn't take it. The only thought she had led her ducking through the tent's opening and into the growing dusk of evening. Wind tugged at her hair, and she'd taken but steps when Charlie called after her. A few more and he was there, gripping her wrist.

Just as the other man had done.

Like the igniting of an electric light, fear bolted through her, hot and sudden. Ella pulled, barely registering his gentle touch until he tightened his hand. She almost screamed.

"Let go of me!" She yanked and hit his chest as hard as she could.

"You're going to fall, Ella." His voice all but pleaded, but he did as she asked.

And she went tumbling into the grass. Ella scrambled to her feet. And ran.

She ran and ran. Her hair whipped into her face, and in the failing light she nearly tripped over stakes and ropes as she hurried through the camp. She heard Charlie behind her, his boots heavy and quick.

And suddenly she was fifteen again and the night was horrible and dark.

A scream rising in her throat, she knew she couldn't outrun him. She whirled, standing low. "Don't touch me." Her chest heaved.

Charlie slowed, his hands held up peaceably. His eyes were wide. Shocked.

He stepped forward and she moved back only to bump against the side of a wagon.

Throat closing off air, she crouched against the wheel, voice small. "Please don't hurt me." Tears stung fiercely.

Pain flooded Charlie's face as he lowered himself so he wasn't much taller than her. "Ella, I would never hurt you." Two more slow steps and he knelt a reach away. He looked about to move closer and she pulled her knees in, trying to become as small as possible against the spoked wheel.

Lowering her face, she pressed palms to her eyes and fought the sting of tears. What was happening?

"Ella, what's wrong?" Charlie's voice was so filled with worry, tears came anyway.

She shook her head and wiped damp palms on her skirt. What was coming over her? She ran a sleeve over her cheek and heaved in a shaky breath. Where was she? She wanted to go home. But this strange place gripped her in both a growing darkness and a rising wind.

"What can I do for you?" he whispered, easing closer. His fingertips grazed the side of her shoe. Ella flinched but forced herself to take deep breaths. She tried to fight off the memory of Charlie's prayer—his declarations about God— but couldn't.

Fear slid cold through her heart. Charlie was nearly twice as big as her. Just as the other man had been. The one who had offered to carry her hymnal as he walked her home from church that night. Then tried to hold her hand. The beginning to an avalanche. A crushing strength that, even after all her fighting, had left her no choice but to try and close her mind. And her heart, and try not to feel or think or . . . or . . . her chest heaving, she couldn't draw air. Terror needled her.

Oh, God. This is what you do to me.

Then a whispered voice broke through. "Are you scared of me, Ella?" Soft. Broken. Charlie pulled his hand away and shifting to a crouch, took a small step back . . . and then another.

Ella peered at him. This was Charlie. She took a breath, her whole body shaking as the fight left as sudden as it had come. Guardian to Holland. Another breath. She tried to conjure the memory of his gentle touch with the baby, tried to absorb the way he was on his knees again—no taller than her.

He was searching her face—no doubt trying to make sense of what was going on. "You want to go home now." He said it as a fact and she nodded. "Okay. We'll get you home." He looked around and tugged at his hair.

A pang of grief struck her.

"Just . . . don't move. Just give me a moment. We'll get you home." He rose and moved back a few more steps. At the nearest wagon, he called out to someone. Light pierced the air as the door opened and a young woman appeared.

And suddenly Ella wasn't fifteen anymore. Because the prayer she had prayed that night— to not be alone—was answered. She looked to Charlie as gratitude and guilt flooded her.

The stranger descended the steps. Her hair cascaded down her back . . . to the ground where it puddled. Her feminine profile peered up at Charlie in clear trust. He spoke to the girl who bound up her hair, tying it securely with a strip of cloth. After nodding to what he was saying, the young woman walked toward her.

A kind face, cool in the first traces of moonlight, drew near. "Hello, Ella. My name is Angelina and I'm going to walk you home."

TWELVE

Charlie watched the way Ella kept swiping that bit of hair from her face only for it to fall back again when she looked over her shoulder at him . . .

Something she'd done more times than he could count.

Angelina explained to her why he was following along. To make sure they both got home safely. Ella nodded. Peeked over her shoulder again, remorse in her eyes.

Hands in his pockets, Charlie walked along, a fair gap between them, his heart in his boots. He tried to recall what he might have done or said to give her fear, but for the life of him, he couldn't think of anything.

Angelina spoke softly, and Charlie could only hear a word here or there in her Russian accent. They walked on until the dim lights of Ella's apartment building reflected through the misty darkness. Slowing her as much as it did him. Halting beneath the three-story brick structure, Charlie gripped the back of his neck and watched Angelina and Ella walk up the stairs.

He leaned against the bricks and tried not to think about how he was going to be late for his night show if he didn't hurry. A glance at his pocket watch said it started in less than ten minutes. He folded his arms over his chest. Unfolded them. Paced.

Counted the seconds for Angelina to return and not really wanting her to appear when what he wanted to do was speak to Ella, he strode up the stairs and into the building. Knowing he had three more flights to go, he took the steps two at a time, making as much noise as a herd of elephants. He rounded the hallway and slowed so as not to frighten her.

"Ella," he panted.

She blinked up at him and her eyes were clearer than before. Gone were the tears. No, they were coming again, but this time he felt her pain, not fear.

"I can't just leave like this," he said.

Angelina walked quietly down the short hallway to the dark window where she peered down.

Having no idea what to say to Ella, Charlie gulped. "I know you don't owe me a thing. Not a thing. You've done so much for Holland and for me. And you have every right to walk away and you don't ever have to see or speak to me again."

She swiped a tear from her cheek.

"But if you would maybe . . ." His nerves getting the best of him, he swallowed hard. For in that moment, he knew. That his life would never be the same. Not since this woman had walked into it. He clenched his fists at his sides, heart pounding. "If you would let me try and make it right, I would . . . I'd thank you."

Another tear, another wipe. Her chin trembled. "Charlie—I—" She blinked up at the ceiling and blew out a breath. "I don't know what to say."

He opened his fists. Closed them. Blast it, he wanted to hold her. But he stood his ground, willing his boots to not move so much as an inch.

Ella pressed the pad of her thumb to her mouth. The mouth that was so small, but full like a doll's. Like it shouldn't be real. But it was real. Everything about her was real and he wished that there was some way . . .

"I'm so sorry for tonight," she whispered. "I owe you an apology. I just don't know what to say."

"Please don't feel the need to apologize. If I've done anything to you—to frighten you—I want to make it right."

She quickly shook her head, more tears coming. "No." It came out shaky. "You haven't done anything. I just . . . I just . . ." She ran her hand up the side of her sleeve and he could see in her face—the way she seemed somehow smaller—how spent she was. "There's an explanation that I owe you."

And here he was out of time. "May I call on you tomorrow?"

Down the hallway, Angelina was still giving them privacy in her sweet way.

He didn't dare look at his pocket watch to see how late he was. "If Margaret won't be home, I could bring Angelina."

The silence stretched on until only his heart was pounding in his ears. Finally, she nodded gently. "All right." She moistened her lips and looked back at him. "And Margaret will be home, but . . ."

He waited, sensing she was about to say more. Some slip of a word that meant she trusted him, but truly, he didn't want to get her alone.

He just wanted her to not be afraid of him.

"I'll come?"

She nodded again. "Please."

"Would the afternoon be okay? About four o'clock."

"Four o'clock."

He spoke the words in a breath of relief. "Thank you, Ella."

Ducked in the wagon, Charlie shuffled through his things looking for his billfold. The horse-drawn caravan creaked as he strode to the other side, still hunting. The billfold was something he rarely used, so he didn't spot it until looking in a box that held clean socks and undershirts. He'd been paid in full that morning, so he slipped the crisp bills into the leather fold and slid it all in his pocket. If this was the last time he was going to see Ella—something he was really trying not to think about—he couldn't bear the thought of not paying her as promised. She'd done so much for him and Holland. So much.

The wagon creaked as he climbed out.

Charlie strode across the circus lot and onto the city street, his sights on the row of buildings that would lead him the few blocks to Ella's. Past shops and then a bank, clatter came from what had to be the iron works. Beyond that, a train whistled a lonely sound. A coal wagon was stuck in the muddy wheel ruts in the road, men working it loose just as he'd been doing the last few days at the fairgrounds.

Across the street, a few people looked his way, gazes lingering. Charlie peered down to make sure he had shed all the pieces of his costume. He'd taken off his velvet coat and vest but kept the white shirt as it was the best he had. And he was certain he'd scrubbed all the paint from his face. Using his thumb, Charlie checked that his shirt was neatly tucked after all his banging about in the wagon.

After a few more steps, he checked his collar for good measure.

He'd been distracted today and didn't trust his judgment just now.

Even during the show it had posed a problem. When he'd forgotten to give the signal during the finale, La'Rue—bless the man—had stepped in and saved it. A mistake Charlie had never made before and one that had him garnering worried looks from more than just Ruth.

All the acts had to keep performing to get by, so he needed to pull himself together one way or another. Thanks to Mr. Graven arranging railway excursion discounts within a forty mile radius to the circus lot, the stands were fuller than ever with new droves of people willing to pay twenty-five cents and upwards for a seat in the matinee.

Because the growing crowds inspired new twists, La'Rue had suggested the stunt they'd been working on. While Charlie feared Axel wasn't ready, the lion had proved him wrong, leaping across a gap in stands two feet farther than what Han and Kristov could reach. Charlie owed the rascal a fat steak. The elephants nailed their own signals and the audience had been on its feet.

A victory, yes. But with every flower or bouquet that the roustabouts picked up, and with every lacy handkerchief, Charlie knew looking up into the stands, hearing the cries and cheers, that it wasn't real. It didn't last. Not the fans, the flowers, and certainly not the smiles from women who were curious about his interludes.

He'd allowed himself to indulge in that one summer. To kiss young ladies in the shade of the Big Top as the sun's heat clouded their thinking that he would be any kind of lasting presence. Them walking away with nothing other than a good story to tell and him standing there empty, wondering if the next conquest might fill the void. He would never remember a name for each girl he'd kissed. Each heart that had momentarily beat against his, so while Axel was but a cub, and with Angelina's help, Charlie had vowed to save any kind of wooing for the woman he meant to marry. It had been a long and lonely few years, but worth it. And now he was thinking of Ella.

She was doing something to him that he'd never experienced before. He couldn't bear the thought of losing her.

But who was he fooling? Who was he to Ella? A Gypsy in a *mud show*.

And that wasn't even the worst of it.

Reaching her apartment, he took his first deep breath of the day. Regina was seeing to Holland's nap, and he couldn't thank the woman enough. His heart beat faster with every step he climbed until he was walking down that hallway again. Charlie cleared his throat, which did nothing for his nerves, and knocked on Ella's door with the back of his hand.

Soft voices filtered through, then it opened.

Margaret peered around the door. "Hello." Such an everyday word, but her eyes took him in as though he were Goliath.

"Is Ella here?"

"Oh, yes, come on in."

She led him to the sofa and he sat, feeling like an oaf on the dainty piece of furniture. With Ella nowhere in sight, he glanced at the closed bedroom door.

Margaret stood there watching him, wringing her hands. Finally she motioned toward the room. "I'll go fetch her."

Charlie nodded. Feeling like his palms were sweating, he ran them along his pants. Margaret vanished and he tried not to count the minutes but was pretty sure that one turned into two then into three before the door opened again.

He glanced up, certain he looked as desperate as he felt.

As Ella stepped out, light from the window hit the white ribbon that held the end of her braid. She gave him a little smile that was so weak he thought he was going to be sick. God help him, he needed the words.

She walked over to a settee and tucked her pale blue skirt beneath her as she sat, eyes on the floor. They were glassy and growing wetter the longer the silence lived on.

Finally, she peered straight at him. "Hello, Charlie."

Words failing, he dipped his head. Remembering his billfold, he thought about tugging it out, but it didn't seem like the right time.

"I'm glad you came."

He stared at the ground and feared what

emotions might live in his face. He needed to say something. *Come on, man.* "About last night . . ."

But she was holding up a hand, silencing him. "Please. Let me explain."

The bedroom door closed and Charlie realized Margaret was giving them privacy.

"I've gone around and around as to whether or not I should tell you this, and once I decided to, I've been searching for the right way, but I fear I don't know what that is."

He straightened slowly.

Eyes closed, she twisted her fingers in her lap so tightly her hands were turning white. "So I'll just say it."

He stared at those hands as she spoke.

"Charlie . . . I had a son." Blue eyes lifted to his, the lashes dark and wet.

He tried to keep his face as stone. Oh, God, please don't let him do the wrong thing. His heart jerking, he slowly nodded. Retraced her words. Tried to get them to make sense. For a hundred different reasons.

"Five years ago."

A slow breath in. A slow breath out.

"That's one of the reasons I'm here. I left home because I couldn't bear the way people treated me. Their whispers. Their looks. Suggesting clear enough what they thought of me." Her voice turned thick. "And I was just too sad."

Her pain lit a flame in his chest. "I'm so

sorry," he said softly, not knowing what else to say. Forming a fist, he ran his thumb over his knuckles, worrying a path he didn't know how to fill with words.

"Charlie?"

He shifted his boots. Stared down at them. She said *had* a son. He wished he knew how to ask in a way that wouldn't hurt her. "Are . . . is he . . . did he not survive?"

Her mouth trembled small around the single word. "No."

Words failing him, Charlie searched her face. His throat was hoarse so he coughed once into his fist. "What—what was his name? Your son." It was all he could think to say, for she'd given life to a child. A person. A soul . . . and he was gone from her.

She looked at him as though no one had ever asked that. "I didn't give him one."

Her regret seemed to fill the room, so Charlie blinked away rising questions.

"Charlie." Ella moistened her lips again and drew in a shaky breath. "I don't know how to say this."

Leaning forward, he rested forearms to knees and clasped his hands. Bowed his head.

Her voice quavered. "Being . . . with a man . . ."

He swallowed hard and after another breath, made himself lift his head.

"It wasn't . . . it wasn't something I wanted

to do." She looked away and that bit of hair fell across the side of her face again. She tugged at a pinch of skirt. Over and over and over . . . "I was forced."

The blood slowed in his veins. He blinked. Tried to breathe.

And failed.

Tears pooled, spilling down her cheeks.

He forced an inhale. His mind and heart racing, he rose, moved to her in a few steps, and knelt. "Ella." Her name bled from him.

She ran a sleeve over her eyes. "I was so ashamed." Her chin trembled harder.

He spoke her name again and it felt so insufficient. In him was a burning, rolling anger toward a man he could kill with his hands this very moment—all beat back by a pain he didn't know existed. Not while looking at her face, those eyes. Heard in her voice. Witnessed the way she'd cowered against the wheel and pleaded for him not to hurt her.

His stomach churned.

"He was a few years older than me and I had trusted him to walk me home one night from a choir practice. We were all to sing for Christmas." Her voice was wooden but soft. "I thought he was a friend and I thought that everything was all right."

The anger rolled again, rising.

"He . . ." Her throat worked and she blinked

back more tears. "What you need to know about last night, Charlie—" She shook her head. "It wasn't because of you. *It wasn't you.*"

He hung his head; his skin on fire when she placed her warm hand to the back of his neck, pulling him closer. He rested his fist on her knee and pressed his forehead there.

"He was the preacher's son," Ella whispered.

Charlie's eyes closed. Fist so tight his palm burned. *Oh, God.* There wasn't a word in the space of his mind to express what he was feeling, for mixed with the desire to tear that man limb from limb was the burning ache to comfort her. Then he felt her shaking and looking up, saw that she had covered her face with her other hand. Sobbing.

He rose to his knees, and when she didn't seem afraid, touched her arm. She bent forward, pressing her face to his shoulder. His hand slid to the back of her hair, holding her. Ella's small frame shook, mouth muffled against his shirt. He held tighter, wishing there was some way he could take the pain and bear it for her.

She sat that way for a long while and he dared not ask what had happened to the man. If somehow justice had been served. It would only be for his own benefit—some way to make his hands stop shaking with the desire of doing it himself.

"You have to know," she tipped her head, "that

177

you are one of the most kind and considerate men I've ever known."

Something snapped in his heart; the fear that he had lost her.

"And I don't know what came over me. I've always kept away from the church since then. I've felt guilty about that, but it's always paralyzed me." She sniffed and fumbled the folds of her skirt for a handkerchief, finding a small square of cloth. "The thought of going into one. Or even being around people who are . . . what you might think of as holy."

A preacher's son. He wanted to cup her face and tell her that there was a world of difference between the light of Christ and the black of which she'd been shown, but this was not the time. Ever the preacher, he curbed his tongue.

Regina's words rushed to his mind. *That's why folk call him Preacher. Just like his father before him.*

The title—the way she saw it—pierced him. "That's why you ran," he whispered.

"I'm so sorry." Regret laced her eyes.

"Please don't be afraid. Please don't leave us . . ." He tried to bite back the last words, but they slipped out. He hoped maybe she would think he was referring to her nursing Holland.

She probably didn't, which was why she was gaping at him. "Leave you? Charlie, *you're* leaving. Any day." Her face flooded with something that had his heart nearly still in his chest.

"I'm sorry. I shouldn't have said that. It's not fair to you—"

"Charlie, do you ever stay in one spot? Do you always move on?"

His mind whirred so he rose slowly and took a step back. Women had asked him that question before. But it had never fallen from the lips of someone he had already begun envisioning a life with.

Charlie grasped for reason. Clawing at it and failing to gather but mere scraps. Those he pieced together and formed into words. "I have to leave with the others. I'm in a contract."

She nodded and her cheeks went rosy. The shift in conversation stumbled him. Why were they talking about this all of a sudden? Clueless as to what to say next, he waited until she rose.

"I'm sorry, I—"

The bedroom door opened and Margaret stepped out. Already dressed in her nurse's uniform, she gave an apologetic smile. She moved to the kitchen area, took up her coat from the chair, and draped it over her arm, clearly leaving.

Which meant he should be the first to go. Charlie looked to Ella. "We *are* leaving in a few days." Never had those words lashed into him before. "And I . . . I know Holland would love to see you again. And I would too." A sting in his left wrist, Charlie rubbed at it.

Ella blinked up at him.

"You're welcome to come by if you'd like. Sometime tomorrow."

Mouth lifting in a soft smile, she nodded. "Thank you."

He needed to leave because suddenly he was thinking about pulling her close again. Right here where he was standing. And that he couldn't do. For a million reasons. All of which pushed him toward the door, the words to his lips, "I'll leave you now." He stepped into the hall and turned just as she pressed her cheek to the jamb. "And oh . . ." Would this sound forward? "Everything's taken care of at the entrance for as long as we're here."

Ella's brows lifted. Would she understand what he was saying? What he meant. That he wanted her with him. For as long as he could.

"So just find Lorelai. It's all squared away for you to come as you please."

Margaret glanced to the clock, then stepped closer toward the door.

"Thank you," Ella said. "I'll come. I promise."

He sealed her face in his mind. Her words.

And later, with the stars out and the night crowd seeking their thrills, the dark didn't feel as black. The torchlight not as sinister.

For as he sat there, bare back against the bars,

failing in giving the crush of onlookers any kind of the show they paid to see, save himself, he simply held onto the sight of Ella's face in his mind. Of Holland's and Mimi's. Thought of all that God had blessed him with.

And he said a prayer for Ella. No, a plea. For her to have the comfort she needed.

Deep beneath that was the sorrow that in a few days, he'd be gone from her. But it was for the best, because sitting this way, bared from the waist up and lit by the light of a dozen flames, he was jarred afresh by how horrifying he would be to her. If she knew . . .

Charlie looked at the crowd with coal-blackened eyes and a pair of ladies shrieked in terrified delight.

Night air crept through a gap in the tent, prickling his skin. The skin that was covered in ink drawings so permanent, so rare and gruesome, people paid good coin to gawk at *The Beast*. Someone poked a bony finger into his waist. Another pried at his forearm for a closer look at the novelty of his flesh. Anger usually consumed him here. Spurring him to fight back. But as clammy hands probed his skin, Charlie simply lowered his head. With his cuffed hands hanging limp at his sides, the sensation of his wrists being chained and bound not beating him tonight, he repeated the hymn in his mind over and over.

Rock of Ages. Cleft for me . . .

These nights of calm—rare as they were—were the nights that kept him sane. Made him realize that although his face was painted, eyes darkened to look as eerie as possible, he would get through this. For just four more months, he could do this.

For Holland—for her freedom—he would pay the debt.

Though his tainted body might be caged, his mind and heart didn't have to be. He had Ella to thank for that tonight. And God.

Closing his eyes, Charlie let the sound of the crowd fade, and for the first time in days and no doubt to Madame Broussard's dismay, he simply sat there. And he sat in peace.

THIRTEEN

With an early evening sun warm on her shoulders, Ella approached the tent. The flap was open and tied back, no doubt inviting in the sweet, spring air.

"Hello," she called out, and clutching a fresh loaf of bread, ducked through. She froze at the sight of Charlie sitting on the edge of his wagon-bed, a needle in the air, thread tethering him to his task.

She smiled and his mouth pursed a bit sheepishly. Regina was near, cutting a length of braid trim. Ella stepped that way first and held out the bread along with a whispered apology.

Regina's small, pudgy hand slid to Ella's back with a little hug. "Thank you, *mia cara*. And you've nothing to feel sorry about."

Charlie was watching Ella and she thought about all that had passed between them yesterday. All she had shared. Spotting Holland asleep on her wooden bed, Ella tucked hands behind her back and stepped toward Charlie. He touched the collar of his shirt, then the buttons at each of his sleeves.

Even sitting he was still higher up on the wagon. She peered at what he was doing and saw Holland's tiny sweater.

"Loose button." He dipped the needle again. "Some nurse popped it loose the other day."

Now it was Ella's turn to smile sheepishly.

He pulled a pocket watch from his vest and glimpsed it before glancing back at Ella.

"Was this a bad time to come?" she asked.

"No." He said it too quick and she feared it might have been. He seemed to regret that as he said, "Holland will be awake soon and you two can visit."

"How was your show?"

The side of his mouth tipped up. "It was good."

When his gaze moved around the tent, she let hers wander again and it was then that she noticed jars of flowers scattered about. "Oh, my."

With fingers that looked practiced, he loosed the needle and slid the flash of silver into a small sewing box that was carved with Regina's name. The hinged box sat beside a basket that held rich-looking fabrics, one cut in the raw shape of another center ring coat and tails. This fabric, a deep burgundy, was finer than any cloth Ella had ever seen.

Using his teeth, he snapped the unused thread then tucked everything away.

"You do that just like my mother," she said.

Smirking, he set Holland's sweater beside him. "Tell me about your family. Where do they live?"

"Um . . . about sixty miles north of here. Just

184

past Clifton Forge." Though maybe he wouldn't know where that was.

"And are you an only child?"

"I have five brothers and sisters."

His eyes shone at that.

"It was a full house and I loved it. I miss them."

"I'm sure they miss you. You came here to be a nurse?"

She leaned her back against the ledge of his wagon. "Someone was always falling down and scraping something or bruising something and they would come to me." She would draw them close, set them on the kitchen table by the sunny window, and tend their hurts. A kiss, a few words of comfort, and they'd be back on their way—out into the mountain air. She told him as much, and he listened as he dragged a basket back to where he was sitting. He set about folding clean diapers and small blankets. Ella helped him.

"So it's just you here. All alone."

She nodded.

"I'm really sorry about your job, Ella. I can't help thinking you'd still be there if it weren't for us."

The light in the tent grew dimmer; the sun surely dipping behind the distant buildings with early evening. "Don't worry." She attempted one of his signature winks. "It was quite thrilling to quit. I've never done anything so irrational."

185

"I'm a bad influence." Then his eyes shot wide. "Oh!" He stomped up the crates, vanished into his wagon, and returned with a billfold. He pulled out several bills and handed them over. "For you. *Thank you.*"

"I don't want it."

He held it closer. "Please. You've done so much. And all those items you brought. More teas . . . the *ice* . . ." He regarded her with clear insistence. "None of it was free."

She tucked her hands in her lap. "Please put your money away."

He seemed displeased and looked about to speak when a little shriek pierced the air. They both looked to Holland's bed. She was sitting upright, blue eyes bright, a smile on her round face. Charlie rose and picked her up. He nuzzled her neck and she dissolved into giggles. Then he plopped the baby in Ella's grasp and she gratefully accepted the squishy, warm bundle.

Regina made tea and Holland was soon crawling into every corner of the tent. Charlie snatched her back each time. Some sort of game. Except for when she crawled too close to the potbelly stove. He plucked her up, scolded gently, and as Holland's chin wobbled, he kissed her forehead and rubbed a hand across her curls. The baby was soon distracted with the bread Ella had brought. The dinner hour flew by as they picnicked on thick, warm slices as well as the hot tea Regina fixed.

The sky was black now, tent sides rustling. A lantern bobbed past the canvas and Charlie was peering out as if his mind had drifted into the dark.

"Charlie." Regina reached up to touch his waist. "It's almost time, my dear."

After a moment, he spoke as if he'd been holding the words on his tongue. "Ella, I have to go soon and do another show." He turned and stepped toward the middle of the tent. "I'm going to be a little while and I don't want you to go home alone in the dark." His eyes seemed troubled. "Would you mind waiting and I can walk you when I'm finished? Or else I could find someone to accompany you. There are some good people here."

So serious was his expression that a reply lodged in her throat. "Of . . . of course. I don't mind waiting. I'd like to—I could go with you. I've been wanting to see this show—"

The jar Regina had been holding thudded to the grassy floor. The stout woman bent for it, scrutiny drifting to Charlie.

He gripped the back of his neck. "Um, this one's not much to see. I, uh . . ." He paced to the far side of the tent and knelt to shuffle through a small crate. His back still to Ella, he turned his head to the side as he spoke. "Why don't you keep company with Holland and I promise that I'll bring you both a surprise." Swiveling on his knee, he looked at her.

"A surprise." Ella said it with marked curiosity, hoping to set him at ease. Something was wrong and she didn't know what it was. "I'll wait here. But is . . . everything all right?"

He nodded gently. "Thank you, Ella."

Rising, he stepped back to his wagon and gathered a pair of brown pants, the tin, and a slip top shirt. One she'd never seen him wear. She couldn't imagine him in anything but his usual garb—snug collar, buttoned sleeves. He set the pile by the tent flap and seemed about to leave, then he returned to where Ella and Holland were sitting. He bent and kissed the baby's hair, lingering, eyes closed.

When he turned, he stunned Ella by running his knuckles down the side of her arm, finishing with a squeeze of her hand. His touch sent a jolt of longing straight through her.

"Thank you for being so good to Holland," he whispered. "And to me." The last words felt added on—as if he didn't want to say them.

As if he was certain he didn't deserve them.

With night crickets chirping all about, Ella's hands moved beside Holland's as they built a little tower of blocks. Ella took care to give it a strong base, thinking it would last longer, and

Holland took care to prove that it was much more fun to knock it down. Over and over. Laughing, Ella stacked the blocks again, and with a squeal of delight, Holland pushed it over. She clapped pudgy, dimpled hands. Her round cheeks worked as she sucked a piece of licorice drop.

After leaving them to their game a little longer, Regina finally scooped Holland up with a sorrowful declaration of bedtime. She set about changing her and Ella rose. The laundry basket was still on the edge of Charlie's wagon, and thinking to help, Ella pulled out one of the last blankets. She glanced around at Charlie's sleeping space. His things were scattered about—in a way that hinted at organization, but there was a calamity there and she knew how he could rush about so.

"Doesn't he ever make his bed?" Ella asked, amused.

Regina's countenance was bright. "He's lazy because of the curtain. And I . . ." she held up her small hands, "do *not* go in there. I fear if I did, I would never come out alive."

At muted footsteps in the grass, Ella turned. The tent flap moved aside and Charlie ducked through. His wet hair suggested a recent wash up, green eyes unlike she'd ever seen. He glanced around—his expression empty, vacant.

Regina moved to his side and traded a dark cloak for a cup of coffee. She patted his arm and gave him a tender smile. It seemed to jar him, because then he was thanking her and taking Holland back. With the baby pressed to his chest, he sat on the rug and leaned against the box bed. Quietly, Ella sat beside him.

"I owe you both a surprise." He cast Ella an apologetic look and she shook her head.

Letting his eyes close, Charlie inhaled slowly. Holland lay against him, still and quiet. Her blonde curls brushed his chin.

"Did you know," he said softly as if they'd been in conversation all night, "that a few years back I almost left the circus?" He propped the coffee cup on his knee.

"Where did you want to go?"

He stared down at the dark brew in his hands. "I wanted to be a farmer."

"A farmer."

He turned the cup to hold the handle and took a sip. "There's something very steady about farming, no?"

She thought on that a moment, wondering if there might be more to the story. "It would be a very different life for you."

"Yes." The muted plodding of a horse and owner moved past the tent, fading into silence. "But I can't keep Holland with me unless she becomes part of the company. Either as a worker of some kind—a costume mistress like Regina— or a performer like the rest of my family was.

190

Otherwise, I would have to find a place to put her and I just don't think I could do that."

"Truly?"

He nodded. "Some of the performers leave their children to be raised by relatives to go to school and have a normal life. Visiting them when they can. The strong man has three sons that live with his wife in Tennessee. He sends them every dollar he makes. It's sad, but it's the way it is. It's the rules—no one can stay unless they serve a purpose. Chances are, Holland will love to perform, but is that the best life for her? The one she'd want? I just don't know."

Ella could nearly feel the burden it placed on him.

"And for the lions. Some of the animals around here will get a long and peaceful retirement, but some won't. In a few years, Axel will begin to show his age and they won't allow him in the spotlight anymore. He'll be replaced by a younger cat and that's the way of it. If I have the power to give him and the others a restful end of their lives, I will." He smiled sadly. "There are very few places that would take a lion in its retirement. There may be a zoo gracious enough, but I'd rather carve out a home where they can live out their days without being on display. Even then, some lions face a much swifter, much more profitable end."

"I'm so sorry."

"It's just the way of it." Fingertips to his forehead, Charlie rubbed them back and forth as if to wipe away memories. "My father had no say in his lions' futures, and because wealthy hunters were willing to pay a few thousand dollars apiece, some became trophies."

Ella fought to contain her shock.

One of Charlie's hands slid slowly up and down Holland's small back. "My father found a way to do something about that and so I've tried to follow in his footsteps. I want my boys to know life in a meadow or a field. The sunshine. Because of that, about a year ago, I bought all three of them outright. Paid their head price."

"What does that mean?"

"It means that they're mine now. And they won't die for a rich man's sport." Eyes down, his expression went thoughtful. "I want them to be fat and happy and old when the good Lord is ready to take them. So I have a bad habit of burning through my bank accounts. And I don't mean too many trips to the haberdasher." He made the motion of putting on an invisible top hat, then smiled gently. "Though that has been a problem in the past."

Ella thought of him that day at Dr. Penske's with mere coins left in his pocket.

"So instead of having the funds to buy a house somewhere, I have a bunch of cats." Though his words were laced with humor, Ella could see—feel, really—that he wouldn't trade that for anything. She was so proud of him for that. When Holland sighed, small shoulders rising and falling, Charlie kissed the top of her tiny head.

"My papa is a farmer," Ella said.

He looked over at her which made sitting beside him suddenly feel very close. "Is he?"

She nodded.

"I would like to meet him one day."

One day. There would be no one day. And as she looked at him, had to remind herself of that.

His expression shifted—holding something back. He gave her a mischievous smile. "So . . . that . . . we could talk about what a troublesome little creature you are."

She elbowed him. But a thrill went through her at the thought of him and her papa sitting. Talking. Charlie not vanishing from her life. "And now. Do you want to be in the circus?"

He looked down at his coffee again. "Sometimes not. Then other times I can't imagine doing anything else." He pulled his knee up and rested his forearm there. His gaze dipped to her mouth then back to her eyes. "No matter what, the lions . . . they need me, you know?"

Yes, she knew that need.

Hand to the rug, she shifted forward. Her fingers brushed his and she slid them away, hoping he might not have noticed.

A peek showed that his eyes were open. Staring. Almost searching for something to say.

"How many more days until you leave?" she asked.

"With the roads still drying and wagon repairs, probably three."

The number did something painful to her heart.

"The hostlers have already left to adjust the next round of billing. What are you doing tomorrow?"

Sometimes he spoke in a way that made her dizzy. She was beginning to wonder if that was on purpose. "I'll probably try to find work again. I haven't had any luck yet and was thinking of going back to the hospital. They may take me as a laundress." If she was fortunate.

His brow dipped.

She felt humbled by the confession, but there it was.

"Tomorrow's Saturday, so I'll have some shows, and then Sunday . . ." He rubbed at the callouses on his palm. "We have church in the morning, here. Would you . . ." He rubbed at his other hand. "Would you like to come?"

She shook her head. "No, thank you."

He sat quiet for a while. "There are some people I would like you to meet. And who I would like to meet you. If you should change your mind, we start about nine. You could sit on the bed with Holland." Forming fists, he set them on his knees. "I understand that you probably don't want to come and that's okay." He looked at her again. "Truly, I understand. I just want you to know that you're welcome."

"I'll think about it." She said it for his benefit. When he flicked a glance to her, he seemed to know as much. "If you have any time tomorrow instead, in the afternoon, I would love to introduce you. You don't have to come or meet them, but just if you're free and would like to."

She nodded thoughtfully, wondering why he would want to introduce her to people who would never see her again. Sitting here—next to him—the notion made her throat tight.

"I hope your job search goes well."

"Thank you," she said in a small voice. "I do too." She smoothed the hem of her dress against her ankle then looked around, realizing that Regina was preparing for bed. "I should get home."

He stood and moved toward the flap. "I'll go fetch Angelina."

"It—it's not necessary. Truly."

"I want to." He said it with such sincerity that she rose slowly, bid goodnight to Regina, and followed Charlie out into the night.

FOURTEEN

Dressed in her white chiffon blouse and a simple taupe skirt, Ella stood in the entrance of the steamy basement. Several laundresses worked with quick, red hands. Fingers clasped together, Ella tried to swallow her nerves as she waited for the head laundress to consult Dr. Penske, for only moments ago, Ella had asked if there might be a position available.

The soaking tub billowed steam as a woman sprinkled in washing soda. Another tub let off the scent of quicklime, and Ella could recount every ratio and usage for the bottles and boxes lining the shelves beside the great wringer. Yet her boots felt like they were standing on thin ice and not the thick, slabbed floor.

More so when the head laundress returned. "I'm sorry, Miss Beckley. We just don't have need of another laundress."

Ella let those words fall into place knowing full well that they were just. She had walked out on the doctor when he'd told her not to. She searched her heart for a dash of regret and finding none, simply nodded. "Yes, ma'am. Thank you."

The basement felt a long distance from the third-floor children's ward, but the memory of all that passed there was suddenly quite fresh.

Letting herself out, she peered up the flight of stairs, remembering how Charlie had nearly crashed into her on that top landing.

Ella headed out and in the direction of her apartment, but an afternoon at home felt more like a weight than a blessing.

There was nothing left to clean in their apartment and no book could distract from the fact that it was time to pen a letter home. Tell her parents that she'd quit her job and ask for the funds to make rent. Or better yet, to simply buy a train ticket back to Clifton Forge, just a few miles from her parents' farm. This city was feeling less and less like home. Worse yet, it was about to lose the very ones she ached to keep.

And she had been alone for so many years. She hadn't realized just how much she missed family, until she saw all that Charlie and Holland and Regina were.

As she walked, Ella weighed her options. She could stick it out, which could prove fruitful. Ask Margaret to cover her for another month while she continued her search. Earlier that morning, Ella had inquired at the newspaper office but lacked the typing skills to be considered. Now she decided to walk a few blocks and see what she could find. One of the photography shops advertised for a clerk. Ella ducked in, but upon speaking with the owner, learned that they were looking for a young lad who could work for a low wage and make quick errands.

It was all she could do to smile and nod before leaving.

She hurried past a saloon, and the other businesses on this street looked just as comforting.

When she veered onto Commerce Street, Ella peered across to where three women were gathered. They looked weary—perhaps having just finished a night shift of some kind. Their dresses were plain and stained. They chattered away to one another before one bid farewell and started down the road. Perhaps heading to Brick Row, two blocks away. It hadn't slipped Ella's mind that such a living may end up as her only option. She couldn't expect Margaret to carry her weight, and while the housing in Brick Row was surely cheap, Ella feared the dangers that part of town held.

Was it a move worth looking into?

She didn't think so. Not when she had a mother and father she missed desperately. Siblings who she ached to see again. Ella swallowed the bitter taste of regret. Loneliness.

Angling towards home, she hurried across the road toward Campbell Street and tried not to think of what it would be like to have a little family of her own. Somewhere in a quaint house far from the bustle of the city. The picture included a man with golden-brown skin and pale green eyes. A sweet-cheeked baby sitting in the center of their bed, a stuffed tiger in her chubby grasp.

Ella slowed to a stop, pressed fingertips to her forehead, and closed her eyes.

"Some lettuce for ya, miss?"

Startling, Ella looked over to realize she'd stopped in front of the grocer's.

"Oh, no, thank you." She had exactly thirteen dollars to her name, so fresh salad was most definitely not on the menu. Ten of those dollars would cover this month's rent and the other three would see her through another few weeks of necessities. Coal, milk, and groceries. And then . . . she had no idea.

She'd tucked a dime in her reticule for a new block of ice, and with the iceman due soon, Ella hurried back to her apartment and settled down on the steps until the wagon came. She paid the man her coin for a small block, and he kindly carried it up to the apartment. When he was gone, she pulled out paper and pen and set about writing that letter. But what to ask for?

Rent money or a train ticket. Either would burden her parents.

Then she remembered Charlie's offer of money. Much more than she'd spent on his behalf, it felt impossible to accept.

Oh, how she hated money! Ella dropped her

head in her hand. After writing half of the letter and abhorring every word, she decided to finish it that evening and traded the pen in her hand for the cool touch of the stair railing as she climbed up to the roof. Perhaps a few minutes in the greenhouse was in order. She plucked the strawberries that were finally ripe, pleased with the red handful that easily filled a handkerchief.

Holland would enjoy such a treat. Charlie, too, and Regina. The notion need only circle her mind once more, and then she was downstairs in her room. Tired of being starched and pressed for job interviews, she dug through Margaret's ribbon box and unearthed a cheery, blush-colored sash. As billowy and soft as a tumble of chokecherry blossoms, Ella tied it about the waist of her skirt and formed a festive bow in back. Her braid was windswept so she tucked a few loose strands into place and bound the end with her favorite ribbon. Then her feet were carrying her across the street and along the three blocks that led to the fairgrounds, strawberries now nestled in a small basket.

She found Lorelai just as Charlie told her to and the plump woman waved Ella on through.

"The lad's paid yer way, love."

"Thank you." A little thrill shot through her at the thought of seeing him. And the way he was waiting for her.

Ella walked across the grounds, taking in

the sights, sounds and sweet, buttery smells all around the striped Big Top and beyond. As the noise and festivities faded away, she passed the red circus wagon, thinking of Angelina and her kindness. A moment later, Ella was being greeted by Regina just outside of Charlie's tent. *"Ciao, mia cara."*

"Hello."

The small woman hung an apron on a clothesline tied between two wagons. The low draped line was already half full. Regina's skirts, damp at the hem, were bustled up around her knees as if she'd been stomping on the laundry in the wash bin. Holland sat in the grass, poking green blades into her mouth, and Ella kept busy keeping them out, which was no trouble once she used the berries as distraction. Red lipped, Holland crawled into Ella's lap and settled there.

Kissing her warm, blonde curls, Ella wished her heart could hold this joy always.

Regina tipped over her wash basin and leaned it against one of the brightly painted wheels of Charlie's wagon. Hands to her stout hips, she tilted her face back and closing her eyes, stood in the sun for several moments. Ella watched the small woman with a full heart. Thankful for all that she did for Charlie and Holland. The goodness that she poured out on a pair of people who needed her so desperately.

Suddenly Charlie barreled around the corner,

tugging off his top hat as he vanished into the tent. He thunked about for a moment, no doubt looking for what he needed to clean the paint from his face. "Little Joe's under the weather. Lost his voice," he called back, seemingly to Regina. "The village needs a talker until Sam finishes his show and can take over. I told them I'd fill in for a few hours, so I've gotta get ready."

Water splashed in the basin. Trickled as he scrubbed.

"You won't have time to rest at all," Regina called. "And you have company."

The water silenced. Charlie stepped back out, running a towel over his hair. He glanced around, eyes settling to where Ella knelt on the grass. "Well, hello."

"I brought strawberries," she blurted.

The side of his mouth curved up. "That's nice."

"She brought them for sharing, Charlie," Regina scolded amiably.

With him standing there, lit by the sun, Ella saw him again as she had in her dream. Her hopes. But just as quick, she made herself circle back to reality. *Oh, Ella. You cannot have this.*

"And now you're leaving." Hands on her stout hips, Regina shook her head.

Smiling, Charlie looked at Ella. "She doesn't like it when I spiel for the village." Clearly in a hurry, he ducked back inside.

Ella picked up the baby and followed him in.

"Because . . ." Regina straightened her skirt as she followed. "He gets no rest."

After smacking a theatrical kiss to Holland's round cheek, Charlie started on the buttons of his vest. "I'll rest tomorrow." He yanked it off and tossed it beside his coat on Regina's partition. "Now . . ." Rubbing his hands, he looked at Ella. "Would you like the grand tour? I know you haven't seen much of this place, and if you want to come with me, I could show you some of the sights." He loosened a portion of the tent canvas tucked under the wagon wheel and from the dark space tugged forward what seemed a rather heavy chest. He shoved it into the center of the make-shift room with a grunt. "So what do you say?"

"Um . . ."

He cast an impish glance at Regina. "Maybe it's not a good idea after all." He squinted at Ella. "I don't even know if you can juggle. Probably can't even sing. Come to think of it, I doubt you could hop on one foot without falling over." He slid a black and white striped garter onto his wrist, then tugged it up his shirtsleeve so that it wrapped his upper arm.

Laughing, Ella shook her head. "What are you talking about?"

"If a talker's gonna have an assistant, they might as well be talented. But maybe you can just enjoy the sights."

She liked that idea. The time spent with him.

His face went serious. "Unless you came here for another reason?"

She had to fight a smile. More so when his eyes filled with mischief. He palmed a trio of small balls and slid them into a canvas sack, followed by a deck of cards and other items.

"What is all that for?" she asked.

"That," he said, moving the sack aside with his boot, "is what I'll be doing."

He picked up a green silk scarf then tossed it aside for a thinner, red one which he tied around his neck, sliding the knot just off to the side. He buttoned up a glossy black waistcoat, then clipped a shining pocket watch to the vest.

Digging around in the chest again, he tossed aside a thick plume of a feather, a bowtie, and last, a curved cane. Finally, he lifted up a small, tattered top hat. He slid it on his head, tilted it to the side . . . down . . . and in that charming way of his, he smiled at her.

Ella stared at him, wishing she could hold back time.

He slid on black fingerless gloves, tucked a coin inside each wrist, then wagged his fingers theatrically as he studied the contents of the chest. "Oh!" He dug around then lifted a small wooden box. He pulled out a cigar, stuck it in the side of his mouth, then gave Ella a playful wink. Rising, he shoved his mess *mostly* inside the chest. "Ready?"

Out of the tent they walked side by side. Charlie tugged at his waistcoat then slipped the cigar into a hidden pocket. As they left the camp of tents and wagons, drawing toward the midway and other public paths, spectators passed to and fro. Children with treats in hand pointed to the many wonders to be seen, and men in bowler hats trailed behind, ladies on their arms. Ella wondered what it might be like to walk in such a way with Charlie. She couldn't help stealing a glance at him only to realize that he was doing the same.

It was a look that stole straight into her, straight to the place in her heart where she knew she should put a stop to what was happening here, whatever this was between them. But for the life of her, she didn't want to. Maybe these days with Charlie were reckless, but how could something reckless make her feel so . . . whole?

Suddenly Charlie stopped.

Ella peered up to see that they were standing in front of a partition made up of banners and great sheets of draping canvas. Colorful posters advertised the different acts to be seen within. She perused them and from the corner of her eye saw Charlie yank one down, crumple it. Pocket it. He slid her a glance that had her wishing it lasted longer for all that lived in his expression.

But then he tapped his cane against the largest poster of all. Not so much a poster, she realized, but a canvas banner that hung from above his head to the ground. Stepping closer, she ran her fingers over the ornately painted words, her heart heavy.

Living Freaks.

He was beside her. "I just need you to know something. I'm going to be saying things that will be very harsh. Maybe not to other people, but to me it feels that way. The acts that I'll be talking about are my friends. They're the very people I want you to meet."

"I see."

"Do you?"

She could see how important this was to him.

"I only do this so that the village gets business and in turn that will take care of them. This is their livelihood. My job right now is to turn as many tips as I can. Maybe even clear the midway. But, please . . . just know that I don't think of the exhibitioners inside this way. I'm just doing a job that has to get done. And it's for them."

She touched his arm, struck by his sensitivity. "I understand."

A burden seemed to lift from his shoulders.

Peering back up to the banner she read, "Village of Oddities. Sideshow Spectacular." She quietly read the rest. *Living Freaks. The Greatest Human Oddities Known to Man.* So this was what Charlie would be announcing to passersby.

"If you feel like wandering around outside of

here," he began, "there are some exotic birds in that marquee over there and just beyond are the elephants. If you don't mind sawdust in your shoes." He pointed to a gray tent nearby. "That's a fun little comedy show which I think starts soon. And that one . . ." He motioned toward a larger brown tent that, by the sound of it, was housing a rowdy crowd. "Please don't go in there." He looked around a moment, looking about to say more. "I need to get started." He gave her a crooked smile then walked to the entrance of the partitioned sideshow.

A large man ambled up and exchanged a few words with him. By the way the man was touching his throat, Ella sensed it was the talker who'd lost his voice. Charlie patted him on the back, and with a nod of thanks, the man stepped to the side. Charlie turned. "Ladies an' gents!" he bellowed.

Ella's jaw fell at the change in his voice.

"Step right up 'ere and see the world famous Village of Oddities. One a the *great-est* shows on earth!" Charlie arced a hand toward the entrance. "Feast your very eyes upon a man with no arms, no legs . . ." He rambled on and a small crowd gathered.

From his pocket he withdrew the deck of cards and she realized he'd slipped his sack aside already. He fanned the cards out to the promenaders standing around. "Could use a bit 'o help. I've lost me queen, an' I'm feelin' lonely without her."

Chuckles shifted through the press of people and several stepped up to draw a card. Finally, a youth waved what must have been a queen overhead. Charlie tousled the lad's hair and gave a grand gesture, admitting him in with no cost. The boy all but ran inside and his parents had to pull out coins to follow.

And to a cluster of giggling young women, Charlie strode over and made a show of pulling a nickel out from behind a redhead's ear. "For you, love." He winked.

The girl blushed and Ella nibbled her bottom lip, knowing just how charming he could be.

He gave the girl her admittance fee and grinned down at her three friends who went over to where they paid their own way. With more giggles, they hurried in to keep up with the one who had just been admitted into the private village. Charlie flashed Ella a mischievous smile as if to say, *that's how it's done.*

Enjoying the sun on her shoulders, Ella walked over to the man she thought was the talker. He stood in the shade and smirked at something Charlie said to the crowd. Ella introduced herself as the nurse who had tended to Holland, then asked how he was feeling. He hoarsely told her of his symptoms, and fearing that it was the same infection, she shared the remedies that worked best. She promised to send over the herbs she had left.

His thanks was quiet, but so filled with gratitude, she only wished she could do more.

Leaving him to save his voice, Ella moseyed around awhile, seeing the colorful birds in their gilt cages and then the elephants just beyond. Not really wanting to watch a comedy show, she circled back to the village where Charlie had a rapt crowd's attention as he called out the mysteries of the human body they could see within.

Ella got in line and followed the people through the entrance. When she got to a panting Charlie, she pressed a coin into his hand and looked up into his handsome face.

He regarded her with open pleasure. "Be on your best behavior, lass," he said loudly.

Ella blushed but gave him a little salute. "Yessir."

Inside the village, she walked through the various tents and looked upon the people displayed, but with each face and *oddity* exhibited, each name, her heart grew sadder. She tried to think as the other spectators might—simply to look upon the strangers for entertainment sake. She wondered if she would have before knowing Charlie. She hoped not. And now, knowing that those on display were his friends, she passed through the village with a heavy heart.

Beautiful voices spilled from a white tent and Ella stepped that way, past the sign with elegant text and a picture of Angelina and her sisters. The three young ladies sang from a decorative stage, their voices stunning and the harmonies holding the audience's rapt attention. The song was slow and melodious, one she'd never heard before. Spotting her, Angelina gave Ella a little smile. Her hair draped her right shoulder, plunging to the floor in glossy waves. As did her sisters'. The viewers watched in hushed rapture, and Ella savored two full songs before slipping back out.

A fire breather sipped from an amber bottle, and she ducked as he moved a torch near his mouth and shot a flame for the spectators watching. Their applause ruptured as Ella hurried along until her feet drew her to a tent she hadn't noticed before. Perhaps because there was no crowd moving in and out. Stepping nearer, Ella saw marks in the dust as if a sign had stood there but moments ago. She peered up to a board dangling from a chain across the entrance of the tent. It declared that the act would begin at six and that an additional fee was required. Some kind of finale?

Like bats from a cave, a pair of kids darted out, under the rope, but not deep enough when they knocked it to the ground. They giggled as they ran off. Ella glanced around and then picked up the end of the rope. She went to fasten it back in place when she noticed how still and quiet the air was inside. The tent completely empty.

She tilted her head, peeking into the dim stillness. Not empty.

There in the center was a wagon, much like Charlie's or Angelina's but instead of wooden walls, it had bars. All around stood torches on stands, unlit but blackened. Carefully lowering the rope back to the earth, Ella took a few small steps into the tent. On the plank floor of the wagon metal chains draped about. She stepped nearer, daring not to touch the bars, only to see that those chains were shackles.

Shackles. A pain struck her heart. Surely they didn't . . .

Surely they didn't put a person in there.

Just beyond the tent, the sisters' singing was soft and sweet. Wanting to be free of this tent, Ella slipped back out. The warm sun greeted her as did the call of birdsong.

"Miss Ella?"

She spun around only to peer up at a man on stilts, a box of bagged popcorn in his hand. He plucked one free and held it down to her. "From Charlie."

"Oh. Thank you."

The man tipped a striped hat and ambled away. Ella pinched a kernel and the buttery goodness melted on her tongue. The breeze stirred her hair as she circled around to the entrance of the sideshow to where Charlie worked. She smiled at the funny accent he was feigning and the tricks he did for the youngsters. The way he drew the ladies in with his charms, the men with his dares. Did the man never run out of stamina?

Ella settled on a bench with her treat. Charlie worked a few more minutes, then another man, dressed much like he was, stepped through the crowd. Perhaps his replacement. They swapped handshakes, then Charlie strode over to her. The sun glistened on his skin as he tugged the garter from his arm. He leaned in to whisper, "I hope I haven't spoiled your dinner." He took a pinch of popcorn.

She squinted up at him. "Which reminds me— you haven't eaten. What would you say to me making you an early supper? And Holland and Regina if they'd like to come along."

He grinned, and with that sparkle in his eye, doffed his top hat, then pressed it to his heart.

FIFTEEN

They returned to his tent to find a note that Regina and the baby were off to the market. To Charlie's relief, Ella settled down in the grass outside the tent while he changed into regular clothes in his wagon. With a few hours of daylight left, they headed toward the circus entrance and passed through.

"I never seem to see any other performers going out this way," Ella said.

"Maybe they just never leave." She didn't look convinced, so Charlie motioned the way they had come. "There are other ways in and out for us."

"But you don't use them?"

"I like to think that I can go this way just like anybody else. It annoys Lorelai to no end. Plus . . ." He looked at Ella after they crossed the street. "It would be prudent if I didn't take you any other way."

She wasn't the first outside woman to come and go from the back lot. He couldn't risk people thinking his pleasure in her company was of a different nature; he meant to protect her with all the dimes this cost him. Folding her hands together, she walked quietly beside him, cute as a button in her blouse and skirt. Bound like a present with that bow cinching her waist.

Much too distracted by the sight of her, Charlie made himself look down at his boots as they walked.

His gray tweed waistcoat suddenly feeling snug, he tugged at it and said a silent thanks to Regina for ironing his good shirt yesterday. Having dressed in a hurry, he slid his thumb along the side of his waistband, checking that the hem was neatly tucked. Ella glanced over just then and tripped a little over a crack in the sidewalk. Charlie tried to hide a smile as he opened the first floor door for her. On the stairs, she mused aloud as to whether or not Margaret would be home.

He sure hoped so. It would make things a lot less complicated.

No answer came when she called out for her friend. "She'll be back soon, I'd imagine."

"Shall I wait?" he asked, hesitating in the hallway.

"No. Come on in."

He did and left the door ajar. Folding his arms, he crossed to the window and peered down at the street. Wagons passed in front of nearby businesses, and in the lot beyond a pair of children tugged a kite from a spindly tree. Charlie wasn't used to being so high up. Or peering out of glass. He tapped it with his finger. "You have a nice view here."

"Thank you. I've always loved it."

At a thunking from beside the stove, he turned to see her lift the lid off the coal bucket.

He stepped closer. "May I?"

"Thank you."

Kneeling, he cleaned out the ashes for her. Then he added kindling and let that burn for a few minutes before sprinkling in a thin layer of coal. By the time flames crackled, Ella opened the small oven door and slipped her hand inside.

"It'll take a bit to heat and then I can put this in." She motioned to some kind of baked dish she was making.

"Can I do anything else?"

"Nope. Just make yourself at home."

Back at the window, he looked out again. He tapped the glass once more, enjoying the feel and sound of it. Wrists sore, he rubbed gently at them, careful to keep his cuffs in place.

Several photos hung along the wall and he studied them. A man and woman, seated in front of a two-story farmhouse, each had a countenance much like Ella's. Her parents perhaps?

The longer Charlie looked, the more he saw the resemblance. She was a perfect mirror of the pair of them. "You look like your folks."

She smiled. Then she asked of his own parents and Charlie told her briefly of his father, Jacobus, a Dutchman, and his mother, Koštana, a Romani flyer. The memories sending a twinge through his chest, Charlie looked back to the photos but could still envision them both. He favored his mother's coloring, her passionate temperament. She was like the wind and had taught him to be the same. But it was his father who had taught him to be steady. To never take a step unless it was carefully thought out. To treat a spirit—be it feline or human—with deep respect.

How he missed the man. Even now the words often spoken between them rushed to Charlie's mind, in particular, the week before his father's death.

"How will you go to a lion?" his father had asked, biting back a cough. They'd stood shoulder to shoulder in an open air pen for what would be their last time together. *"No matter how big. No matter how small."*

"Humbly," Charlie answered, while Axel, just a cub then, dozed in the folds of Mimi's skirt outside the fencing. And Charlie easing his hands along the warm hide of Braam, the nine-year-old lion that had sired all the others.

His father had tipped back an old top hat. *"And you will go to them with strength."*

"With strength." Yes, by the sweat of his brow, his back, he was learning that too.

"And you will go to them when you feel no fear."

No fear. The hardest part when feeling the power of muscle beneath your palms. Looking into the yellow eyes of a maned king. A deep-soul wild that would never change and wasn't meant to.

His father's voice faded away, but the wind of that meadow—of the open plains, his life—clung to memory. Charlie held it all close as he studied the rest of Ella's photos. Took in the faces of her family. The farmhouse—quiet, steady. Unmoving. His eyes traced from that to the papered wall. Still standing there, he slid his hand along the firm surface. He listened but heard not even a breeze. Gave a gentle push but it didn't budge against his hand. He listened again. Silence.

Ella watched him with a curious expression.

Just then Margaret called out and he turned to see her toting a crate of groceries inside. The way the girl was buckling under the weight of it, Charlie hurried to take it from her.

"Thank you." She panted the words even as she gawked at him openly.

He carried the crate to where she asked. Margaret thanked him again, then chatted easily as she set about putting the groceries away. Charlie fell quiet, leaving the conversation to Ella and her roommate as he continued to wander around the small apartment. A wall sconce hung loosely, which would be dangerous when lit, so he asked Ella if she had a screwdriver.

She looked up from where she was setting plates on the table and Margaret offered to fetch the tool. The girl dug in a low cupboard and held one up.

Charlie moved closer. "Do you have a smaller one?"

A bit more digging and she found one.

"Thanks." He walked back to the sconce and loosened the screws to tighten it straighter. He felt Margaret move in beside him.

"Do you always go around fixing people's things?" she asked.

He gave her a smile. "Occasionally."

When he finished, Margaret wiggled the sconce. "Oh, that's much better."

She pointed to the one on the other side of a hanging mirror which was almost as bad. Charlie handed her the screwdriver and told her to give it a shot. Tongue sticking to the side of her cheek, Margaret tightened it.

"See?" he said. "Now you can handle just about anything. And now your apartment might not catch on fire."

She laughed. "You've saved the day."

"Ya flatta me, miss."

Margaret giggled and took the tool. "He's funny," she said to Ella.

"He has an endless array of accents." Ella's smile warmed him through.

Margaret's brows pinched and she looked at Charlie. "Why is that? I can't quite place where you're from."

He settled down on a stool beside Ella. "I'm not from anywhere." Looking back at Ella, he let his gaze filter over her blonde hair that draped against the nape of her neck to her mouth that was suddenly pursed. "That's funny she'd wonder, Ella, because I was pretty sure I'd answered a few questions for someone . . ."

"What questions?" Margaret asked, breaking his stare.

"They must have gotten lost in circulation."

"All right," Ella whispered. "Maybe I was minorly curious, myself."

Realizing he hadn't answered Margaret's direct question, Charlie turned a bit on the stool. "I'm from all over. Most cities you can think of, I've been there. Countless times."

But Margaret didn't seem to hear him as she looked to Ella with a goofy smile. "Hmm. We're going to need another chair. I'll . . . go . . . fetch one from Mrs. Brewer." She stepped toward the door but not before Charlie noticed the googly eyes she gave Ella.

Ella's ears pinked as she focused on the dough in her hands. Charlie coughed into his fist. He sat a few moments, determined not to watch her anymore while she worked.

Finally, Ella's busy little hands stilled. She didn't move and Charlie broke his own promise and skimmed his gaze to her.

"Everything okay?" he asked softly.

Her eyes danced over his. "You're leaving."

So simple a phrase, but with it coming softly from her—with such a pained look in her expression—it had him suddenly trying to remember his own name. He drudged up the only response he could stumble upon. "Yeah, I am. We break everything down tomorrow night."

Though she hadn't finished, she wiped flour from her fingers. "I wish that wasn't so," she whispered.

Charlie had to swallow hard to find his voice. When she simply gripped the edge of her work surface and bowed her head, he moved to stand. "Ella—"

"I have a chair!" Margaret sang from the hallway. Charlie nearly slid off the stool. "And I'm bringing it in!"

He centered himself back on the seat and ran a hand through his hair. Ella plucked up a piece of dough and formed a crooked biscuit. Charlie felt Margaret eyeing them curiously as she nudged her way across the room before plopping the chair in front of the table.

Charlie sat another minute before rising and walking around the apartment again. Margaret started chatting—asking all about the lions, and he answered everything she threw his way from what they ate, to whether or not he gave them baths. That was good because he needed a distraction just now.

Margaret asked where he lived in the winter, and with Ella listening on, he described the troupe's off-season compound in Louisiana. He countered with questions of his own learning that Margaret and Ella had known one another for all of two years and that while Ella had once played the piano, Margaret had as much musical ability as he did.

Suddenly, Ella was calling them to the table. Charlie sat where she directed, and when she dipped her head, she seemed to wonder if they should pray or not. Charlie sat silent. There was no need for her to do something she didn't want to on account of him.

But then she spoke. "Would you bless the meal, Charlie?"

He studied her a moment, those words putting him at a loss for his own. Bowing his head, he spoke a brief blessing then silently thanked the Lord in his heart for her gentle offer. And that God might protect her. Bless her. Aloud, he spoke a soft amen.

Margaret passed him the basket of biscuits. "So Charlie, how long have you been on this good earth?"

He squinted at the brunette. "Are you asking how old I am?"

Margaret glanced to her friend. "Do you know?"

Charlie interjected, "How come I don't get to ask as many questions as you do?"

221

"You can ask anything you want," Margaret said, bobbing her brows.

"How old are *you?*"

"Nineteen," Margaret answered.

Charlie nodded at that, then glanced at Ella, for truly, he'd been wondering.

"You don't know how old I am?" Ella asked.

"Am I supposed to?"

She smirked and he was glad it was light or he would have missed that pretty blush blooming. He wasn't about to tell her that he could find out by checking her teeth. A rather impressive ability when you were seven. He had a hunch this was different.

"I'm twenty," she said.

Twenty. His gaze lingered, which only made the color deepen. Then he thought of her five years prior and that piece of math made him very sad.

"How old are you?" she asked.

Margaret made a show of propping her chin in her palm.

Despite himself, Charlie chuckled. "I have six years on you," he said, discreetly pointing to Margaret. And to Ella, "Five on you."

Ella seemed pleased with that as she scooped casserole onto his plate.

"So Charlie, where to next?" Margaret asked.

"Charlottesville. With our sights on Baltimore. Then up the coast from there as the summer continues." He felt Ella watching him as he spoke.

Margaret folded her arms on the table and leaned forward. "How far do you go?"

"Not sure, but no matter what, we always finish the summer on Coney Island, in New York. Then move south before winter."

Margaret's face brightened. "Coney Island . . . you've really been there?"

He drew in a deep breath and held it before letting it out with, "Bunches of times."

"*Really*. What's it like?"

He poked at his food. "Crowded. Thousands of people come in and out every day. There's a hot air balloon you can ride and a carousel and even a race track. *Lots* of sideshows." They didn't call it Sodom by the Sea for nothing. Many sins known to man just a nickel away. "It's wild and noisy. People looking for fun . . . and thrills and roller coasters. Me, I lost some money last year playing cards with a kid named Houdini. Never play against a magician, even a young one."

Margaret chuckled and Ella looked amused.

"Depending on the season's contract, we're usually there for a two- or three-week run." Maybe it was the Gypsy in him, but he always felt trapped there. He much preferred the open land, wandering from town to town. He wasn't fond of Coney, and feeling like a downer, he searched for a positive. "The sea is nice. I like that part. And also the fireworks."

Ella gave him a sweet smile.

He took another bite of the potato casserole. "This is really good, Ella. Thank you."

"My pleasure. I'm happy to see you eating something."

"You're not hungry, Ella?" Margaret asked.

Charlie looked over to see that she was only pushing food around on her plate. "She ruined her dinner with popcorn," he said. "I told her not to, but she doesn't listen—"

Ella scrunched her nose at him, and when she poked another bite around, he wondered if it might be for a different reason. Good grief, he wanted to talk to her. Even if just to tell her . . .

Her head lifted. "What time do you have to go? For your night show?"

An answer came way too easily. "It's cancelled."

"Cancelled?"

He gave her a half shrug. "It happens from time to time." He didn't say any more and was glad when Margaret cut in.

"Then you must stay," Margaret said, squeezing his arm in a friendly gesture. "I want to hear more about this Houdini."

Damp dish towel draped over his shoulder, Charlie stacked the last plate. They'd left the dishes to sit while they'd talked over glasses of iced, mint tea, and Ella had told a few stories from home. Then, just minutes ago, Margaret had excused herself. Rather on the early side, Charlie thought, but he wasn't about to complain. And he knew he owed her a thanks for it. Having Ella alone, even for just a few minutes, was something he'd been aching for all day. Not wanting to overstay his welcome, he set the towel aside and tried to find the words.

Remembering the jars of herbs she'd set by the door for him to give to Little Joe, he eyed them. "I won't keep you long, but I just want to say thank you for the meal and all that you've done for Holland. It's meant a lot to all of us. I don't know what we would have done without you."

"It was my pleasure."

He could see that she meant it.

"You're welcome to stay a little longer, unless you need to get right home," she added.

Best to step out that door and thank her for a fine evening before this got any messier.

But, fool that he was, he slid his hands in his pockets and shook his head. She seemed to think a moment, glancing first at the bedroom door where Margaret was, then around at the tiny apartment. "Come with me. I'd like to show you something." She plucked her coat from the back of the sofa and glanced back to see that he was following her.

SIXTEEN

She led them down the hall then up a narrow stairwell that closed in tighter the higher they went, then suddenly, Ella was pressing against a door and a gust of night air rushed overhead.

"This is one of my favorite spots," she said.

Charlie followed her as a cool breeze swept over the flat rooftop of the building.

"I come up here sometimes at night. More often lately, I confess." A hint of embarrassment tinted her voice.

Puzzled, he let her lead him to the edge of the roof. She leaned on the wall that met his waist. Then he realized what she had a bird's eye view of. Air lodged in his throat.

She looked over at him. "Have you ever seen that before?"

Charlie swallowed hard. He stared out through the darkness where in the distance lived the glow of the circus. Countless lanterns and torches lit up the place he'd called home since the moment he was born. He drew a slow breath. "Not like this."

"It's beautiful, isn't it?"

He nodded, slowly leaned forward on the wall . . .

And missed his parents.

Missed Mimi.

Ached for Holland even though she was safe with Regina. And he wished with all his might that he wouldn't be leaving Ella. Overwhelmed, he wet his lips, desperate for the right way to say this. Then he remembered what he'd rehearsed. He turned gently to face her. "I spent some time the last couple of days looking at a few maps. I was thinking that maybe when we come back down south in the fall, that we might come fairly close to this area again."

Her eyes widened slightly.

"But they're not going to risk this road again. At least not anytime soon." He moistened his lips once more. "There's something else I realized." Rising nerves crawled across his shoulders. "We're heading to Charlottesville next, like I told you, which means that we'll be going past Clifton Forge by a fairly close distance. About fifteen miles."

"What are you saying?"

"I'm saying that I could take you home. Should you want to go."

Ella glanced around for several seconds.

Were her eyes getting wet?

"You can think about it," he added. "No need to say anything right now. I just wanted you to know the option was there should you want it. I could easily speak to the *powers that be* and hint that you're nursing Little Joe's sore throat so he doesn't get a fever like Holland did. There's a particular sideshow operator who would really like her talker not to lose his voice. Or die. And a nurse around for that would be handy."

Eyes still wide, she simply nodded as if soaking all that in.

"And if that's what you wanted, I would like to do it."

She pressed hands to her cheeks and drew in a heavy breath.

"Will you think on it?"

Ella nodded. And he prayed for God to strengthen him for whatever her answer might be.

They stood silent for several minutes, then she motioned him over to a low block rise in the center of the roof. They settled beside one another. Her coat she laid aside.

Ella was quiet for a long while before speaking. "I haven't been home in almost four years." An ache lived thick in her voice.

So he decided to say this before he changed his mind. "Home to me has always been with my family," he said softly. "Probably because it's the only kind of home I've ever known. My parents passed on and then losing Mimi this last year, home has been with Holland. And with Regina. I wasn't looking for more or asking for more." He looked at her. "And then when I'm with you . . . I have that same feeling. That feeling of home."

The moonlight was soft on her face as she peered up at him. "I don't know what to do with that."

She didn't say anything. Didn't so much as move.

And now his heart was really pounding.

Charlie ran his wrist over his forehead. There was a lot more he needed to say. *A lot more.* But she rose to her knees and sitting back, faced him. Her hand brushed against his. Taking it. Pulling it from his thigh and lifting it. His heart hammered in his chest as Ella held his hand with both of hers, cradling it close. Bowing her head, she kissed his knuckles.

He closed his eyes.

"I don't know how to tell you how thankful I am for you." Another kiss brushed his hand.

Charlie turned his hand, running his thumb over her lips. He wanted to kiss her. Wanted it with everything inside him. But somehow bigger than that was the knowledge that he couldn't just take it from her. Not if it wasn't something she wanted to give. He lowered his arm and looked over at her. Her eyes were wide and searching.

God be his strength, for he was suddenly feeling very weak.

Charlie pressed his palms to the edge of the bricks and cleared his throat. He looked out over the tops of the dark buildings, wishing he wasn't so aware of her sitting beside him. He gripped the ledge tighter, willing his hands to keep from wanting to touch her, hold her. Even brushing that bit of hair away from her face felt wrong.

"Charlie?" she whispered.

"Yeah?"

"Are you all right?"

He nodded but it felt like a lie.

Lightly, she touched the side of his neck so softly that it shouldn't have awoken every bit of his skin, but it did. And then she shifted closer to him, her small hand sliding up to the side of his face, over his ear. He had to remind himself to breathe.

Slowly, she pressed a kiss to his forehead.

Don't move. Don't move. Don't move. It was his cry. Over and over. For he wanted to move and to pull her close . . . draw himself to her. But not wanting to alarm her, he sat there as still as stone, all but his heart which was pounding so loud she had to hear it.

He closed his eyes again and felt Ella's knees bump against the side of his leg which meant she was as close as she could get, her hand still cradling the side of his head. She seemed to be meaning to do something.

Don't. Move.

His chest heaved.

"I want to kiss you, Charlie," Ella whispered. "But I've never . . . I don't know how." Vulnerability softened her voice. Mixed with something very womanly that had him gripping the bricks tighter.

He had to clear his throat again. "Okay." Gosh, that was a stupid answer, but his mind was suddenly feeling very blank right now. And then a surge of grief filled him when he realized what she was saying. She'd never kissed anyone. Or been kissed. Despite all that she'd been through . . .

She had been taken. But never loved.

Something broken grated over his heart and he had to shove away other emotions. The kind that had his hands flex with that fighting desire and he had to silence it, letting her words move through him again. Finally he looked over to realize just how close she was.

"May I?" he asked.

She nodded.

Drawing in a deep breath, he lifted his hand to the side of her face, fingers finding her hair. She felt so small, so fragile. In so many ways she was, but she had a strength.

Made more clear when she dropped her gaze and pulled herself closer to him. Still on her knees at his side. Waiting.

He moistened his lips and adjusted his grip on the side of her face, trying with everything in him to be slow and gentle. He leaned toward her.

Then realized she was trembling.

The ribbon at her waist was smooth beneath

his other hand. But the quake he felt there said that this would be so much harder on her than it would be on him.

"Shall I stop?" he whispered.

A moment's hesitation and she shook her head. "No."

His thumb felt against her lips again and he waited until she seemed calmer. To his surprise, her eyes closed.

He nearly kissed her in that breath, fast and firm and achingly swift, but he had to pull on every ounce of his self-control for his touch to be as feather-light as possible. His father's teaching was the only thing keeping him sane.

You will go to them humbly. Humbly.

You will go to them with strength. Strength.

You will go to them without fear.

No fear.

And then his lips met hers. She was soft and she was silk. His mind and heart whirled with all that she was to him. Like the dripping of wax to an envelope, he felt a press and a pain and a freedom that something had just sealed inside him. He held her that way for only a heartbeat, then pulled away. But she slid her hand behind his neck and tugged him back. Kissing him.

And then his world went white. Everything but her . . . gone.

From head to toe she was perfect and there wasn't a single part of her that was *less than.*

Overwhelming was the desire to tell her that. She was a precious gift to be given. All of her. As was this, a kiss. He knew what value it held for her. And she was giving it to him, of all people.

He told himself not to move. Was utterly still—save his mouth against hers. He didn't want to stop, but he pulled back. Her eyes were still closed, her breathing heavy. The sound of desire or fear, he didn't know.

Finally she looked up at him so beautiful and so pure that he was suddenly very glad he'd pulled away. A little farther would be good. He inched back, hoping she wouldn't notice or take offense. If she only knew . . .

"Ella," he breathed. He wanted to say all that he needed her to know, but it wasn't the time. Made more clear in the way he felt her sorrow tinge the air. A bitter sweetness that he couldn't begin to understand.

And he was glad he'd stayed quiet for then she gripped the collar of his shirt and her face changed. Those very lips trembling. She let out a little sob and with every tenderness he felt for her, he pressed her face to his shoulder, holding her there. He was pretty sure she swiped a tear.

Knowing of nothing else to do, Charlie closed his eyes. Thanked God for her. Held her and prayed. Silently pleaded that she would be safe and healed and whole.

SEVENTEEN

Ella woke before the sun. Restless, she wandered to the kitchen and fetched a drink of water. Knowing her tossing and turning was loud enough to wake Margaret, she settled down on the window seat and peered out. At this hour, the circus grounds were completely dark. Torches, lanterns, and fires having long since been put out. She thought of Charlie asleep and Holland in her small wooden trundle with its carvings and figures that were so like Charlie's wagon, she wondered if the same hand hadn't replicated it. And she wondered if it was his.

She nibbled absently on the end of her finger. The memory of him about did her in and it felt silly to blush in an empty room, but there she was, doing exactly that.

His church would begin in a few hours and unmade was the decision of whether or not she would go. She didn't want to go. Not to church. She didn't want to be a part of it or anywhere near it, but there was something in the way he'd asked. The way he always took such care with her. So gentle. So careful. Something about him was different. Something that had her wondering how . . . and why.

· · ·

An energetic breeze whipped the flags overhead as Ella drew nearer to Charlie's tent. A hush hung over the circus grounds at this hour, on this day. The ticket wagon quiet. Front booths not even open yet. If it weren't for Lorelai, Ella knew she wouldn't have even been admitted. There had been a difference in the streets of Roanoke this morning as people headed to Sunday service. As was she.

Ella pressed a hand to the bodice of her best blouse. She'd pulled her hair back in a low bun—nothing that could be construed with any hint of vanity—and she'd polished her shoes because that's what one did on a Sunday, and she tried to think particularly nice thoughts because that was also something one did before church. At Charlie's tent, she was happy to see the flap open. Someone was singing—rather off key. Peeking in, Ella saw Regina combing Holland's short, damp hair. The singing was a man's voice.

It couldn't be . . . no. It couldn't be Charlie.

But where was he? Ella looked around and the sound was coming from the meadow on the back side of the tent. "Good morning," she said to Regina as she ducked inside.

Surprise registered in Regina's features. "Good morning, *mia cara.* How lovely to see you."

"Thank you." Ella twisted her fingers. "Charlie invited me."

"I'm glad he did."

The breeze rustled the tent, carrying with it Charlie's voice. "My name is *graven* on his hands. My name is written on his *heart*."

"Is that . . . is that him outside?" Ella asked.

"He's loud, no?"

"What is he doing?"

"He's getting ready."

Charlie sang on. Ella pursed her lips and listened. "What is he singing?"

Regina listened a moment. "This one is 'Before the Throne of God.' "

"He's quite animated."

Laughing, Regina tugged the comb through Holland's curls one last time. "Wait until he gets to 'Jesus Paid it All.' That one will be next."

"Does he always do this?"

"Yes. Just like his father before him. Though . . ." Regina's eyes sparkled. "His father managed to sing on key."

Despite herself, Ella smiled. It was rather colorful, his singing. But then she sobered and tried to pay attention to the words—each one marked by his passion. A passion she never knew a man could possess for God or even a song about him.

Perhaps it was her imagination, but his pitch sounded truer.

"One in himself I cannot die. My soul is *purchased by his blood*. My life is hid with Christ on high. With Christ my Savior and my God. With Christ my Savior *and . . . my . . . God!*"

No. It had definitely been her imagination because a dog howled in the distance and from somewhere else a man hollered, "Shut up!"

Regina's shoulders shook in a silent chuckle. "Charlie has conviction, no?"

Ella nodded. More than she'd ever heard anyone sing—or try to sing.

He fell silent and Ella slid to the floor beside Holland's bed. From beneath, she pulled out the baby's basket of toys and began to twirl a little metal top. The brightly-colored top whirred, and rolling onto her tummy, Holland slid off the bed and crouched beside Ella, little ruffled bloomers covering her padded bottom. Those chubby, rolled legs that peeked out from beneath her dress were so tempting that Ella had to tickle them. Holland giggled and squirmed then reached for the top and tried to give it a spin.

Then Ella heard Charlie singing again, softer this time.

"I hear the Savior say . . . thy strength indeed is small. Child of weakness watch and pray. Find in me thine all in all."

The top tumbled and Ella twirled it again, listening.

Holland kicked her feet cheerily.

"Do you like that?" Ella whispered. "Your papa is singing."

Holland patted her hands on those chubby legs, then suddenly Charlie quieted. A moment later he was ducking through the canvas opening, brown hair wild and windblown. When he spotted Ella, astonishment dawned in his face. She straightened her skirt and thought about standing, but with Holland pressed against her side, she stayed put.

"You came." He crouched beside them, forming a crooked triangle on the rug. A gentle smile spread across his face. "I'm glad."

She dipped her head shyly.

Then his jaw fell. "Uh, how long have you been here?"

"For a while." She nibbled her lip to keep it from betraying her.

"You didn't happen to hear that, did you?"

She laughed a little. "You have quite a way with . . . words."

Dropping his head, he tugged at his hair. Then he rose and strode toward his wagon. Looking over his shoulder, he pointed at her. "That was a dirty trick."

Ella held her hands up innocently.

"You could have told me," he muttered to Regina, but the woman only rocked and grinned.

Charlie got to work straightening his bedding. He pushed his black boots off to the side, and after fiddling around with his mess, just closed the curtains altogether. He was nervous.

Was he uneasy about church? Or was it her? Perhaps it was the two combined.

Holland babbled and Ella patted her back. "What was that, my sweet?"

The baby jabbered and patted her hands on her legs again.

"Are you singing like your papa?" Ella asked.

Charlie turned and looked at them.

Dropping her gaze to the rug in front of Holland's bed, Ella retraced her words. Then she looked up at Charlie. "I'm sorry. I meant uncle."

He slowly shook his head and she could see that she had pleased him with *papa*.

Ella held his gaze for several moments. "You are a good one."

The side of his mouth tilted up.

"The benches, Charlie," Regina said.

He snapped to attention. After heading outside, he came back with two small wooden kegs then went out again and returned with a thick board. Charlie did this until two benches were formed. Then he was gone again, longer this time, only to return with Angelina, her two sisters, and a clutch of folded chairs.

Angelina beamed at Ella. "Good morning!" The young woman knelt and greeted Holland too, then introduced her sisters, Danielle and Evangeline. They seemed older than Angelina, by a few years perhaps. All of their dark brown hair was equally as long and thick, except today, they wore it braided and folded in half, bound by thick strips of ribbon. Even doubled back on itself, it fell past their hips. The three of them sat in the chairs Charlie set down.

Remembering his promise that she could sit on Holland's bed, Ella did just that, pulling both baby and basket of toys up beside her. She wanted to slip her feet up, tuck them beneath her skirt, and become as small as possible, but she pressed palms to the mattress and forced herself to stay calm. Charlie was moving about, setting chairs in place, and when he looked at her, he regarded her with clear pleasure. Sending her thoughts back to the night before. So much so that she blushed.

Well, this would never do. *Churchly thoughts, Ella.*

Next, the heavy-set man from the day before lumbered in, so large that he barely fit through the tent opening.

"Ey! Little Joe!" Charlie called from where he was setting his Bible on the crate steps.

Several others had trailed in as well, but Ella couldn't fully see them. Joy stirred in her at the sight of the friendly face. Larger than any person she'd ever seen—she could already tell from their brief encounter that Little Joe's heart matched his size. He spoke a hoarse greeting and today wore a strip of cloth across his chest that went over his shoulders. When he turned, Ella nearly gasped at the sight of a man nestled in a sling against his back. The bald man had no arms, and from the way he was cradled by the fabric . . . no legs either. Suddenly she remembered him from one of the tents she had wandered into the day before. Except now, he appeared much happier.

His sleeves were folded and sewed flat to his sides. A wide smile lit his face. Ella remembered Charlie's words when she'd first met Regina. *Don't stare.* Ella dropped her gaze to the grass at the tent opening then lifted it gently as Little Joe hefted his companion out and set him on a chair. Charlie sat beside them, greeting both men, and was soon laughing about a story the armless man was telling. Charlie slapped him on the back then jumped up from his bench.

"Oh! My manners! Everyone," Charlie arced a hand toward Ella. "This is Ella. She's the nurse who cared for Holland."

The three sisters waved and Angelina's mouth tipped up.

"Nice to meet you, Ella," the man with no arms said.

Ella smiled shyly. "Thank you, and you too."

Charlie stood behind the two men. "Ella, you know Little Joe from the village." Charlie patted him on the back. "And this is Arnold. One of the finest men I know."

Arnold beamed and Charlie gripped the man's shoulder.

The three other people who had come in were

each a little different in shape and size as well. Ella also recognized them from her hour spent exploring the village. Charlie made introductions and Ella greeted them with handshakes when they offered. The final person to greet her was a giant of a man, so tall that he had to bend almost in half to shake her hand in his massive fingers.

Ella couldn't remember his name, but he had kind eyes. He sat on one of the benches—in the back, which seemed to be some kind of a joke as humorous remarks shot his way. A few more people came in, one she recognized as a juggler from the matinee and the other two she hadn't seen before. They greeted one another as old friends and settled into place.

Ella let her gaze scan across the room. At the far side stood Charlie, his expression now wistful as he stared down at his boots, hands in his pockets. A thousand words traced his dipped brow—more lost in thought than she'd ever seen him. Then he looked at her, gave a muted smile, and reached for his Bible before sitting on his crates.

"We left off last week at Matthew chapter eleven." Licking his thumb, he turned the thin pages forward. As if finding the spot, he settled the small book on his thigh and asked if someone would like to pray. Arnold volunteered.

Ella closed her eyes when everyone else did. It was nice, Arnold's prayer. He had no hands to fold and yet his words felt truer and more eloquent than many of the prayers she'd heard over her life.

When he finished, Charlie lifted the book and held it to read. "It says, 'Come unto me, all ye that labour and are heavy laden and I will give you rest.'"

Ella listened carefully.

"'Take my yoke upon you, and learn of me; for I am meek and lowly in heart.'" Charlie tipped his head to the side and seemed to collect his thoughts. With his free hand, he adjusted the collar of his shirt, then reached over and fiddled with a sleeve cuff. His gaze filtered over the room of people—over Ella. "'And ye shall find rest unto your souls.'"

He looked down at the book again, but at the way his eyes were wide and searching, she sensed he wasn't reading the text. But his heart. A heart that she sensed held pain, when his voice grew weak. "'For My yoke is easy . . . and My burden is light.'"

EIGHTEEN

Standing with Angelina and her sisters, Ella laughed as they told her a story of Charlie from several years ago. Something about a cow and a mud puddle. They had nearly reached their climax, voices shrill with excitement, when Charlie stepped into their circle and held out a hand.

"Now that's enough of that, I'll have you know," he blurted.

"We were just getting to the best part!" Danielle said, and though her face was youthful, her voice held a richness that had Ella thinking she was the oldest of the three women.

"The best part of that story is 'The End,'" Charlie interjected.

They laughed and Ella smiled up at him.

"You three are a bad influence on her." He feigned a whisper just for Ella. "Don't believe a word they say about me."

"Oh, I just hope they have more stories," Ella teased.

Angelina's dainty brows danced. "We have quite a collection."

"You know?" Arms wide, Charlie ushered them away from his tent which only released their chorus of feminine giggles. "That's all for today. Bye-bye."

The sisters waved at Ella, then thanked Regina for the cake she'd served after church. They'd sat outside eating the lemony confection while Ella had wandered over to Little Joe to see how he was faring and to feel his forehead for any signs of a fever. She wished she'd had the forethought to bring him some ice as that had comforted Holland so.

Charlie hoisted up a wooden plank that had served as a bench, then carried it out. Returning, he hefted one of the barrels and took it out as well. His steps were a little slower when he came back, expression somber. "Before you go, Ella, I need to speak with you. It's kind of important, so not just now. Once we get the baby settled, would you have some spare time?"

She nodded. His smile was sad, sending a cool sensation into her toes. He hoisted the other barrel, placed the bulk of it to his shoulder, and strode out into the sunshine.

A moment later, he rushed back in. "She's here."

"Who?"

"The Madame."

In a whoosh that took Ella's breath away, he scooped her up and strode over to the wagon. Ignoring the steps, he lifted her onto the mattress. "Stay very quiet. Don't. Make. A sound." He slammed the curtains closed.

Ella crawled to her knees and shoved the hair

away from her face. Peering through a slit in the curtain, she watched Charlie grab up her shawl and stuff it under Holland's mattress. He and Regina exchanged a guarded look.

Uncertain, Ella shifted deeper into Charlie's bed until the hard side of the wagon was against her back. She glanced around the dim space to try and make sense of this. Charlie's abundance of clothes and top hats was scattered about, his essence everywhere. She went to look through the slit of light, but something drew her focus back to the sidewall of the green wagon. Markings. She squinted. Tallies. Dozens . . . no . . .

She touched the scratches in the wood.

. . . hundreds of them.

Ella pulled away just as a woman stepped into the tent.

Charlie stood in the center of the room, arms folded across his chest. The woman looked around, then finally pierced him with a glare. Ella leaned farther back but still saw the slight, pale-faced visitor through the tiny opening. Her black hair was piled up into a fashionable bun. Ella recognized her from the other day before the show. The thin woman took her time surveying Charlie's tent.

"Traveling alone, I see," Charlie said.

"You would like to think so."

Ella couldn't place the woman's foreign accent as she spoke to someone just outside. A large man pulled a chair in front of the tent opening. As if to keep guard. His arms were like tree trunks and he sat with a creak, the wood sounding about to snap.

Still in the center of the tent, Charlie gave his female guest a dark little smile. "It really is a shame when they don't come house trained."

Ignoring him, the woman moved along one side of the tent. She lifted a cloth, glimpsing underneath. She turned a jar of flowers, slowly . . .

"I'll thank you not to touch my things," Charlie said. "But say, as fun as this is—"

"I've come for my explanation. I was missing an act last night. He just . . ." a bony hand fanned in front of his face, "didn't appear."

Ella put fingertips to her mouth and closed her eyes. *Oh, Charlie.* He'd stayed with her.

"Would you like to tell me why that is?"

"I got hung up." Charlie snapped his fingers. "Promise not to let it happen again."

"Who is she?"

"I don't know what you're talking about." Charlie moved out of view again and Ella tried not to even think about shifting. "Coffee?" he asked. "It's nearly fresh."

"Oh, shut up." The stranger's dark eyes lingered momentarily on the wagon before skimming elsewhere. "I've already seen you with her so you can just stop your game." She stepped closer and Ella's heart shot into her throat. "It would seem we have a problem on our hands. If I'm not mistaken, we had a little understanding."

"I'm rather aware of that understanding, and if it helps you sleep at night, that lady is just a nurse. For Holland. Who was very sick and is better now, thanks for asking."

The woman cast a dismissive glance to where the baby was playing on her trundle bed. "Hmm." She moved as if to pick her up.

But then Charlie was there, a look so fierce, Ella's skin prickled. The side of his large hand was pressed to the woman's knobby one as they stared at one another.

"I'm not going to take her," she said condescendingly. "Probably couldn't even keep her fed, the fat little thing."

Charlie didn't so much as move.

The woman rolled her eyes. "You are so theatrical."

"You can get out of my tent now."

"And you can remember to honor your contracts." Her expression tightened. "Or I might forget to honor mine." She strode toward the slit of light, glancing dismissively at Holland. "Then where would we be?" With silent steps, she left.

Rising slowly, the giant of a man followed her.

Charlie stood in the entryway a long while. Ella's heart pounded, and with her legs aching, she finally allowed a small shift. Charlie strode back to the wagon and opened the curtain on one side. The brightness hurt her eyes and she blinked against it.

Standing there squarely, he searched her face.

"What was that?" Ella breathed.

He reached to help her down, but she stopped him. Not help. Answers.

"She works here and her name is Madame Broussard." He reached for her again. "Please?"

Ella shook her head.

Charlie rested his elbow on the side of the wagon and leaned forward. His fingers slid into his hair. "Ella."

Pulse rising up her throat, she braved the words, "You said before that you work *for* her."

He nodded.

She remembered how hard he had labored to draw a crowd. "That's what she was doing then, the other day. Paying you."

Then he was leaning toward her, face down, eyes closed. "Can you give me a moment?" He took a few slow breaths and she could see he was trying to find the words. "Please."

Still on his mattress, Ella inched forward, drawing closer.

"She wasn't paying me," he finally said. "That wasn't money. It was a list of instructions."

"I don't understand."

"I'm just going to say this," he whispered. After casting a glance over his shoulder at Regina, he turned to Ella. "Do you remember . . . do you remember that I told you that Mimi died which is why I now have Holland?"

Ella nodded quickly, feeling a sliver of fear at how distant his eyes were.

"She—Mimi—died when the baby was five weeks old."

"Yes."

His eyes implored hers. "But I didn't get her from my sister. I got her from the woman who was here. She acquired the baby from Mimi's husband in a business deal. They have a contract stating that Holland is hers."

"What?"

He tipped his chin up and looked at Ella—grief so heavy in his face that her blood went cold. "It's a story that I can tell you. But it's complicated, and right now, there's something I need you to know."

But Ella couldn't think clearly. The chills pierced her heart. "Holland . . . belongs to her?"

He shook his head. "Not anymore." He peered up at her with anguish. So much so that she thought she was going to be sick. "I do."

NINETEEN

Her face went cold. "You what?"

Charlie swallowed hard. As if unable to bear her shock, he lowered his head in his hands and stared at the ground.

Regina rocked in her little chair and stilled when Holland crawled over to be scooped up. Hefting the child into her arms, Regina rose and told Charlie she would give them a few minutes. She ambled out.

Ella climbed down so she could turn and face him.

His sorrow was palpable as the tent fell silent. The cool breeze that slipped in the only thing that moved until Ella touched his arm. "Charlie?"

When he finally looked at her, his lashes were wet. Her blood thinned. Stomach lurching, she tried to speak.

As though summoning his courage, his throat worked. "There's something I need to tell you. I didn't do it sooner because there didn't seem a point. But now there is."

Tipping his chin up, he loosened the button of his sleeve cuff. Something he had never done before. Not even when he washed. With barely a sound, his mouth moved—words Ella didn't catch. One of his songs? One of his prayers?

What was happening?

He appeared to fight a battle with his fingers a moment, then slowly rolled the cuff back. Once . . . and then again. His golden-brown wrist was darkened by markings—everywhere. The same type as the script on his hand. Splashes of black that stained every inch of his skin.

Ella's knees nearly buckled.

He rolled the sleeve up to his elbow, showing that his forearm was covered entirely in gruesome ink drawings. Tattoos, he'd called them. How far did they go? She opened her mouth but nothing came out. He didn't look at her as he loosened the button of the other sleeve. Peeling back the fabric. Showing her his other arm was as horribly marked as the first.

Her eyes grazed over the twisting, coiling shapes engraved on his skin. Her stomach rolling, the words were thick on her tongue. "Are there more?"

He nodded. His hand lifted to the button at his collar, and then he dropped it. He lifted it again, then lowered it, blowing out a breath. Sweat glistened on his brow.

Heart hammering, Ella took a step closer and then another. She studied the width of his white collar that was always buttoned so high and tight. Why had she thought so little of it before? She'd simply assumed him very modest. Then her hands were moving there. Her shaking hands. Gently he stopped her. His eyes on her were broken as he tipped his chin up again and loosened the top button. Her head went woozy and he moved to the one below. Freeing it.

Then he dropped his hands at his sides. Before she could change her mind, she peeled his shirt away from his collarbone only to see more markings. Tears blurred the sight as he loosened another button, then one more. She pressed shaking fingers where the two sides of his shirt met against his chest, and carefully, she brushed the fabric aside. *Oh, God.* She traced her eyes where the pictures continued down his abdomen, thick and solid, to the waist of his pants. Ella stepped back, nearly stumbling.

"Ella." His voice was bleak.

The room spun.

She needed to sit down. Needed to wake up from this dream. It couldn't be real. Not Charlie. He hadn't done this to himself. "You gave yourself to that woman," she breathed.

"Yes."

"Like this?"

"It was the lesser of two evils." His voice was terribly dark.

Her mouth worked to speak, but nothing came out. Tears stinging her eyes, Ella motioned toward him. "And Holland?" she whispered.

"Is mine now."

She nodded furiously. "That's . . . that's good.

That's so good." Her chest heaved for air as Holland's safety whirred in her mind alongside the darkness he was baring.

"I've startled you." The words slipped out broken.

"No. No." Ella willed herself to reassure him. But air wasn't coming. Or maybe it was coming too fast. The whole world blurred.

"Ella, a deep breath." Charlie's voice was distant.

His hand gripped her arm. Was she falling?

She was a nurse, training should have her stronger than this. Despairing at what he had done to himself, at the misery Holland had been facing down, her mind swung to the science of it. "It's permanent. Forever?"

"It's indelible."

"Done with a needle."

"An electric one."

"Are you in pain?"

". . . not anymore."

Relief spread through her, but he stepped forward, closing the gap between them. His hand slid to the side of her neck, fingers into her hair. "Ella, you're not my nurse."

"No." Tears welled. At his touch, his body, his reality—she didn't know. Surely it was all of it, and what *was* clear was that he'd deceived her.

I'd like to—I could go with you. I've yet to see this show and I've been wanting . . .

This one's not much to see.

Peering up at him now was like being under water. She could see the surface—see the sun— but it was all out of reach and her lungs were on fire. Steadying herself, she backed away and quickly gathered up her things as he watched on. Ella hurried out, uncertain as to what it was she was truly running from, but with his footsteps behind her, feared she was about to find out.

Charlie grabbed her arm, slowing her. He didn't want to hurt her, but there was no way he was going to let her go. Not in this moment. She stumbled to a stop and turned to face him, but still gripping her arm, he led her away from the tents and wagons, to the outskirts of the lot. He said nothing and was glad that she was silent as he walked her out and away from people. The hilly meadows swallowed them up and still he led her on until she could scream at him and no one would hear it.

"What are you doing?" She panted the words calmly, but her eyes were doe-wide.

"If you will just listen, I will tell you. And stop *running away*." Pacing a moment, he quickly finished buttoning his shirt, then turned to her so fast, she stumbled back. "This is why I don't tell people. This is why I don't make friends with people like you."

"People like me?"

"Yes. People like *you* who think that this . . ." He motioned to his chest. "Who . . ." He couldn't say it. Couldn't name how she had to see him for her expression declared that he was right. A part of his heart snapped. He knew that he was revolting. Gentlemen in bowler hats shouted it at him every night while women in high-collared gowns squirmed in his presence. He didn't need Ella to writhe as well.

Making a fist, he pounded it against his forehead, one too many times it seemed when she looked about to run again. Best to just say it. "When Holland became Madame Broussard's ward, I had to get her back." He let that breathe again, hoping it would be enough for Ella to stop looking at him like that.

"What would this woman want with her?"

Of anyone, Ella would know this world wasn't always a good place. "A little girl is very valuable to a woman like the Madame. She could have sold her . . . or made her a part of her show one day." Or a million other things he still had nightmares about. "Madame has unconventional ways of making her money." He could see Ella's wheels spinning. Trying to piece it together. "And when she stated a price, I had nothing else to give."

Wind whipped a strand of Ella's hair across her face and she pushed it back. "I don't understand that."

Of course she didn't. Because the crowds' beloved lion tamer was splashed across half the banners in this place. Making him the highest paid performer here.

Charlie closed his eyes and forced himself to speak calmly. "I went to Madame Broussard and told her I would do anything to have Holland. She considered that and stated her price." An insurmountable sum that he could never hope to obtain, not after he'd purchased the lions. Something the Madame knew as well. He told Ella as much. Except he left out the messy bits—what Olaf was capable of with those fists of his. A strength Charlie had tried to take down, leaving them both black and blue—and inspiring Madame to tuck Holland away in the city they'd been in with one of her cohorts. "I asked what it would take to find her. And this . . ." he touched the shirt over his chest, "is that price."

"Forever? This contract—"

"No, not forever. Holland's first year." Just enough for the Madame to see him broken.

He was less than four months away. The wretched woman wanted him to continue and would give him a bulk of the profits, but he wanted no more of this nightmare.

"Only it's longer," she whispered.

Right. Because he could never wash himself clean. He peered down at her. "Ella, please." It came out a plea, and when she simply stared back

257

. . . and stepped away . . . everything crumbled within him. "Do you want me to explain this further or do you want to go home?" He didn't mean that to be harsh, but God help him, he was losing his mind with her looking at him like that.

He knew this day would come.

He knew it.

And he'd tried to never let himself get close to someone. He'd learned how to keep to himself. Had taken great pains with it. He'd learned to become a shadow. Even when he'd laid Holland down on that hospital bed and this nurse had helped them. Showed him kindness—more than he'd ever received from an outsider. He'd tried to keep his distance.

Standing here now, he let his eyes rove her face, fearing it would be the last. Because Ella was looking at him just like that—like he was the shadow he had learned to be. Like he wasn't real. Not a person.

Finally she spoke. "I'll go alone. I don't want you to have to walk me."

Sure she didn't. Which meant he needed to ask . . . "And when we leave this place? Will you be coming?"

That doctor had thrown him out of his hospital.

Surely Ella could throw him out of her life just as quickly.

It was fair. He was an aberration.

Her study of him was teary, gaze falling to

his chest then the span of his shoulders. Charlie reached up and touched the collar of his shirt to make sure it was secure. The irony.

"I *will* be coming." Her voice was small.

The words nearly had him taking a step forward. Made it a battle to stand his ground. "Truly?" Aching to touch her, he kept his hands at his sides. No sense in reading any hope into that. What was he to her? What was he beyond the empty, glassy look in her eyes, her pained expression, and the tremble of her mouth?

He was nothing really. Had the posters to prove it.

She nodded, a tear slipping to her cheek. Swiping it away, she shifted as if to go. "I will see you later." But she didn't look at him as she spoke, and he knew that he had lost her.

Whatever had grown between them over the last days—severed.

A thousand questions shadowed her profile as she turned away. Each one would be answered if she'd but give him the time. But they didn't have much time. He didn't want to let her go, but knew it best. He'd just piled more at her feet than she'd ever bargained for. He didn't want to think of what it would feel like to be in her shoes. Watching her walk away across the field, he couldn't even imagine what she saw in him now.

The sheer notion had him walking back to camp, sights on the red vardo.

Seeing the three sisters outside getting their fire ready for the evening, he walked past them and to the side of their wagon. He hated mirrors. Had not a one, save the tiny looking glass. Not since the bargain with Madame. On the rare occasion he needed to check his appearance, he always came here and they always welcomed him. The mirror hung on the outside wall and he unlatched the wooden doors that protected it. Charlie took a deep breath as he shoved the red shutters aside and found himself staring at his reflection.

Angelina moved nearer. He glanced at her a moment then started on the top button of his shirt. He worked his way down, sliding out of the white cotton and bundling it in his hands. He couldn't look up into the mirror. Angelina said not a word. She'd seen him this way before, many times. As had Evangeline and Danielle who watched on. Their expressions quiet. Eyes sad.

Charlie forced himself to meet his gaze in the glass. Took in the dark drawings that he rarely looked at this way. From the waist of his pants and up, they covered him, spreading across his chest and the curves of his shoulders, folding down over his back. Ornate and intricate and each one carefully chosen. The only pure skin showing was that of his face and neck, his hands. Well, one of them. He reached up with that hand and touched the Dutch windmill over his heart. And thought of the very girl.

"Would you do it again, Charlie?" Angelina circled around him and settled down on the wagon step.

Charlie looked back to the mirror. Hating what he saw. But yes. For Holland. For Mimi. "I would."

Eyes wet, Angelina gave him a smile that hinted at hope. "Then God will make a way for you."

TWENTY

Ella couldn't remember when she'd started running, but by the time she reached her apartment, her chest ached for air. She hurried up, not stopping until she had climbed the stairs that led to the rooftop and was pushing back out into the late afternoon sun.

Bending, she drew in a deep gulp of air. Straightened. Held it.

Charlie Lionheart. She squeezed her eyes closed and pressed her hands there for good measure. Ella exhaled. And saw his face. Wind struck her—yanking at her hair.

What was her life before Charlie?

It was quiet. Simple. So safe it was empty. She'd taken care to make it that way. There was a routine and a plan. Everything always fell in order day in and day out. She had a job. A paycheck. But her heart—

Slowly, Ella sank to the brick rise behind her. How long she sat, she didn't know, but just as she finished recalling Charlie's story, the door creaked open.

"What are you doing?"

Ella turned.

Margaret walked toward her. Bundled in her robe, she'd had yet to dress for the night shift. "I saw you coming up the street and then you were storming past the apartment. What's wrong? Is it the end of the world and I just don't know it?" Margaret reached up and fingered a rag in her hair, tugged it free, and a curl sprang forth. She pulled another rag loose. "Well, there's someone here to see you. It's a girl." Margaret lowered her voice to barely a whisper. "With *very* long hair."

Ella angled toward the doorway just as Angelina appeared. The young woman clasped her hands in front of her. As if sensing something amiss, Margaret headed off but not before flashing a worried look. Ella tried to smile but knew it had to appear as forced as it felt.

Angelina crossed to the brick rise, tucked her fashionable, floral dress beneath her, and settled down on the ledge. She sat quiet for several moments before speaking. "Since you came to us, I've put myself in your shoes. Wondering what you would think and feel if you were to know." Angelina smoothed the lap of her dress, playing with a stubborn crease. "I said nothing because I knew Charlie wanted to do it himself." She tipped her head to the side. "I think we both understand him enough to know that he would have wanted to be the one to tell you."

Ella nodded.

Angelina's expression was soft. "Though he has been to many places, there have been no others that he's had to tell."

No others.

"I confess . . ." Angelina twisted her mouth to the side. "I confess I was surprised when I saw that he had brought you home to care for Holland. He has never allowed a woman into his life. Not even his tent, as perhaps you have learned. A very guarded man, Charlie. For as—energetic as he is—he *has* led a quiet life." Angelina's dark brown eyes blinked back a wet sheen. "He cares for you in a way unlike I have ever seen. You have been the only one . . ."

Ella's heart shattered even as joy attempted to string the pieces back together. She touched her forehead, spent and aching. The breeze stirred about them as Angelina's face turned toward the horizon. Not knowing what else to say, Ella let a question bubble out of her. "Have you never thought of Charlie as anything more than a friend?"

Angelina's cheeks appled. "He is a *handsome* one." Her expression turned a touch sly. "And quite charming, even, I think, when he doesn't mean to be. In truth, I have more love for him than is good for me." She let those words air a moment as she tipped her chin toward the sky. "But I have a husband."

"You do?"

The girl's face went wistful and Ella could see a new light there. "We all do. My sisters and I left Russia a few weeks after my wedding. For

264

our people, it is common to marry as soon as a husband is chosen. I was still a child, as was he, so we had never even kissed."

Ella was pretty sure she was gaping. She forced a swallow.

Angelina patted her hand knowingly and smiled. "Though he and his brothers woke to find us gone, they have since written us many letters. And we write back. So many over the years." Her expression turned playful. "You could say that all of my sisters . . . we now have sweethearts."

Could that mean love? "Will you one day be together?"

"Soon. They are coming to America to join us." Color tinted Angelina's cheeks in the way of a young bride.

"My sisters and I have learned that we were matched with good men. We always pray that they are safe and well. Though . . . if it weren't for our vows, Charlie would have had his hands full with the three of us." Angelina's face, while jovial, held a wistfulness. "So we have all learned to love him as a brother. And we've all prayed that God would bring him a good woman." A clear joy shone in her eyes. "Truly, we are glad that He has brought Charlie you."

Ella dipped her head. The sheer thought of that made her ache for him all over again, but her mind kept circling back to the grievous sight of his skin and all that he had hidden from her.

"Charlie told me yesterday that you were considering coming with us. That we might be taking you home." Angelina's brows furrowed tenderly. "Is that still true?"

"I—I believe so." Ella twisted her fingers together. "But it's all so much."

Angelina reached over and squeezed her hand. "But remember. It is not a marriage proposal from Charlie. It's simply a few days to take you home."

Angelina stood and walked over to the railing. "It's an interesting thought to imagine," she glanced toward the circus, "that tomorrow, standing here in this very spot, that will all be gone." The wind lifted, barely moving her bound hair. "I only ever think of where we are going, not what we are leaving behind." She gave Ella a sad smile. "For it is rare for us to have something to leave behind."

Ella stared out to where the tops of the circus tents glowed beneath the late sun, flags fluttering in the spring breeze. And thought of Charlie. The memories pierced her. Beginning with the moment he first slammed into her life—Holland safe in his arms. All the days Ella had spent beside him. But . . . "Those markings. What he's done."

Angelina nodded gently. "It is a severe thing that he has done. His life, it will never be the same."

Ella had seen in Charlie's broken eyes how true that was. All for those he loved.

Angelina walked back and sat. Taking Ella's hand in both of hers, she gave a loving squeeze. "It is hard, no? When a part of a person is spoiled. Especially that which cannot be reclaimed." Angelina's glittering gaze held a sweet sadness as she slipped a bit of Ella's hair behind her ear. "Perhaps it is best, truly, to discard that person entirely. For what do they have left of worth?" Her expression was both humble and pained as she placed each word with care.

Forcing Ella's chin to tremble. She tried to fight it, but the sting came. "How do you know this?"

"I know nothing of you," Angelina squeezed Ella's hand again and peered at her, "but what I saw in your eyes that night by the wheel."

Ella blinked quickly.

Regret and pain slammed her chest in a hot gush. Bowing her head, she didn't speak for several minutes and Angelina was simply still beside her. A comforting presence. The edge of Ella's sleeve was damp by the time she knew what she needed to do. She needed to pack her belongings and brave what newness tomorrow might hold.

Finally, Angelina made to stand. "I should go before I'm noticed missing."

Ella lifted her head slowly.

"You may know that the road is passable again.

So tomorrow is the closing day of the circus. Having stayed longer than usual, we've settled in more than we tend to, so there's more to do. We'll begin breaking down this mess we've made of your town. The next day, we'll leave at first light. My sisters and I are joyed to have you coming with us."

Swallowing a swell in her throat, Ella stood to give Angelina a hug, squeezing the young woman tight, wishing that their paths might not separate. She said as much, and when Ella pulled back, Angelina's eyes were sad. Gone was the confidence, the mature light. She seemed on the verge of tears now. And so very young.

"Do you remember that night? The night you ran away from him? Yet he came with us to make sure you were safe?"

How could she forget? Cold, Ella wrapped her arms around herself.

"Charlie's contracts are very binding. If you turn from him now . . ." Angelina touched fingertips to her own heart. "You will be going where he cannot follow."

TWENTY-ONE

Margaret squeezed her so tight, Ella squeaked.

"You must write and tell me *everything!*" Margaret squealed.

"Are you sure that Abigail is going to board with you?"

"Will you stop worrying about me?" Ella crammed two books into her carpet bag. "This is crazy. Margaret, please talk me out of it."

"Are you kidding? You must go. Because if you don't . . ." Margaret fastened the ties of her nursing apron. "I will." Finished, she smoothed the pleats of the gray dress, reminding Ella of all that had changed. "I mean it. If that man looked at me the way he looks at you, you better believe that my bags would already be packed. I'm already horridly jealous. Don't make me hate you by letting him get away."

Smiling, Ella stepped in to help with Margaret's back buttons. "I'll do my best."

The girl spoke over her shoulder. "I can't believe I have to go and when I get home you're going to be gone."

Ella slipped the last button into place, and Margaret turned and hugged her.

"Thank you for everything," Ella whispered.

They exchanged a few final words then with three kisses to Ella's cheeks, Margaret hurried out, waving and swiping tears all the way.

Alone, Ella turned back to her carpetbag. The circus was leaving at first light, but Angelina had invited her to come tonight to settle in. Glad for that chance, Ella crammed in her second pair of shoes, followed by stockings and undergarments. Next went in her box of herbs and medicines where it would ride safely. By sheer will and strength, she rolled up two skirts, squashing them in before adding a trio of blouses and buttoning the bag snug.

Carpetbag in hand, Ella lugged it down the steps of the building—her sights set on the circus grounds. A stirring of excitement shot through her when she drew near enough to see the lowering flags. The thrill was mightily tempered by a heavy dose of nerves. But she lugged her bag down Campbell Street, through the carnival lot, and into the camp where tents and wagons were moving and changing.

Coiled ropes lay wound about, and the clatter of stakes being piled rang out from several directions. Amidst the chaos, she spotted Angelina coming toward her.

Someone moved in the distance. Charlie.

His untucked shirt was bright and white under the afternoon sun as he walked along the outside

270

of his tent, carrying a washtub. Bound snug to his back in the sling was Holland.

Ella glanced back to see Angelina waving her over to the red wagon. After joining her, Angelina spoke. "Is that all you have?"

Ella peered down to the carpetbag in hand. "I need to go back to fetch just a few more things." She followed Angelina up the four little steps into the wagon and was suddenly swept into a world of cupboards, fringe, and light.

"Oh, my." The rounded ceiling was papered in a soft floral print and the walls, built of narrow boards, painted cream. At the very back was a raised bed where tiny curtains pulled back to show a stack of quilts and brightly-colored blankets. Below the bed nestled four quaint cupboards where copper pots and pans winked at her.

The wagon creaked gently when Danielle joined them.

Ella stepped down the narrow carpet runner that was underfoot. "What do you call these wagons?"

"It's a caravan . . . or a vardo. Not *quite* as big as your apartment."

"It's *lovely*." Ella touched a wooden counter built into one side wall and beside that a white iron washstand. Opposite stretched a narrow bed, petite table, and two spindly chairs. Hatboxes of every shape and size filled nooks and crannies, and little drapes shuttered things from view. Square glass windows let in light. Hinged and opened out, they invited in the spring breeze.

"I never knew these could be like this." Ella looked up to where glass was laid in the ceiling, letting in even more light.

From behind her, Danielle spoke. "Ah, you have seen only Charlie's, no?" Her Russian accent was thicker than Angelina's.

Ella nodded, thinking of his oversized mattress spread on the floor, pillows and blankets scattered about. His tallies scratched into the wall.

Danielle's pretty mouth twisted up, dark eyes sparkling. "Charlie's is a storage wagon." She made a motion with her hands to indicate the way the broad side folded down. "Though he fills it with much clutter."

The sisters knew him well.

"He says it is because he does not fit on a bed this size." Angelina winked playfully. "But I doubt that is really the reason."

Ella sensed that Charlie didn't have a wagon like this because of propriety. This was an intimate space indeed, and he honored Regina by setting up the tent and tucking himself away. A feat that caused him much work each time he moved on.

She followed the sisters back out into the sunshine only to stop short in the middle of the steps at the sight of Charlie standing there, breeze tousling his shirt. Ella made her way down the last two steps and felt his gaze on her as she circled past him. Charlie looked to Angelina. "Evangeline said you needed me."

Angelina mentioned concern with the glass in the roof.

"Is it loose?" he asked.

"It seems to be."

Focus on the grass at Ella's feet, he unknotted the sling across his chest and eased a sleeping Holland to his front. He handed the baby to Angelina. Freed of the sling, he gripped a carving on the side of the red wagon and swung himself up to a ledge. Ella couldn't see what he was climbing, but he was suddenly on the roof, boots taking him down the wooden center to the raised section that was filled with small panes of glass.

He crouched and felt the narrow hut with his fingers. "Yeah," he finally said. "The leak's coming in here." He rattled off several tools and Angelina lifted a side hatch.

Nearly lying on his stomach, Charlie reached down and took the small tools she held up. Angelina stepped back and shaded her eyes from the early evening sun, and with the baby still on the girl's hip, Ella squeezed Holland's bare, pudgy foot.

A smile bloomed in the little girl's eyes. Charlie worked for a few minutes without speaking.

Seemingly finished, he tossed the tools into

the grass and climbed back down. "It'll hold for now," he said, tucking the tools away. "I'll need to get some tar and we can seal it up better at the next town. And one of the gutters is loose. I'll fix that too."

Angelina thanked him and he took Holland from her. He didn't so much as look at Ella as he turned and left. Ella drew in a deep sigh. She was going home. And now, she would not be left wondering what might have been, but when she looked back to Charlie's camp only to see him using his forearm to shape a coil of rope—and watching her darkly—she sensed she already had the answer.

Now with an empty crate before her, Ella slipped in her brush and comb. Next went in books, a nursing encyclopedia, and some bedding which mounded over the top, so she pulled the books out and used them to weigh the quilts and sheets down.

Then that was everything. Her world in a crate and a carpetbag and she was beginning to feel like a Gypsy. She almost laughed at the idiocy of this. It would certainly be a story to tell her grandchildren.

So as she toted her crate for her final trip to the circus, she prattled off a list of practical reasons for doing this.

Reason number one—she hadn't the money to

274

get home. There wasn't a train ticket in the world that could be hers without writing home and burdening her family.

Reason number two—she was freeing Margaret to have a roommate who could actually pay her share of the rent. This reason was selfless indeed.

Reason number three . . .

Well, he was tall and charming and he deserved for her to fix what she'd broken. But before she could imagine what that might look like, her attention was stolen by reason number four. Because reason number four was pudgy and sweet and crawling away from Charlie's tent this very moment. Setting down her crate, Ella hurried over.

TWENTY-TWO

"And where do you think you're going, young lady?" Ella scooped the blonde bundle up. "Are you moving on without your papa?"

Holland squirmed and fussed, so Ella set her in the grass and knelt beside the girl who clearly wanted to crawl around. Ella watched her for several moments, then suddenly Charlie barreled out of the tent. He shot his gaze around, spotting them.

He exhaled, chest rising and falling rapidly. Kneeling beside Holland, he ran a palm down his face. "I couldn't find you," he whispered to the baby.

Holland bounced pudgy fists on her knees, not a care in the world.

Charlie's shoulders sank in a heavy sigh and then he looked at Ella. "I was loading a trunk into the wagon, turned around, and she was gone." His fear was palpable.

Hoping to comfort, Ella said, "Little ones have a way of doing that."

"I'm not used to this crawling business yet." He kissed the top of Holland's tiny ear, then in a motion so brief she nearly missed it, the back of his hand touched Ella's. "Thank you for watching her."

"Of course."

He pulled Holland onto his lap.

"Where is Regina?" she asked.

"Getting water."

"I can keep an eye on the baby for a while. I'm not all that helpful to Angelina, I don't think. Unless you count knocking over a tower of boxes." Oh the sight of all those ribbons and petticoats tumbling everywhere. "And I almost broke a window when I tripped over the floor rug a bit ago."

A smile lifted his mouth, but he seemed to try and fight it. Pale green eyes took her in. "I'm a little more worried about you than the window."

She looked down as a jumble of yearnings shot through her. Laced with the memory of his ink-stained body was that of his kiss . . . his kindness. And the two were not cooperating in her heart. So she simply said, "Please. I'd like to help."

He plucked a blade of grass. Tore it in two. That wall returning. "Thanks." He rose and brushed at his pants. "I shouldn't be much longer because I need to get ready to go soon."

His last show in this town. Not so much a show, she realized, but an exhibition.

She rose with Holland and he ran his hand over the baby's feather-soft curls before stepping away. A wide-open meadow beckoning, Ella meandered around, rocking the baby.

Regina returned with a bucket of water and a

277

cheery greeting. The stout woman bustled in and out, folding things and shaking things, and even asked Ella if she would like to walk over with them for supper. Ella politely declined, which would have been easier if Charlie hadn't walked by at that moment, watching their exchange.

Evening swept in slow and cool. Two early stars glinted in the dimming sky. Ella turned, swaying Holland farther out into the meadow where other wagons were being filled. She rocked Holland there. Gently sang all the songs she could think of.

By the time the horizon had dimmed and the air was fragrant with the scent of supper cooking, a chilly breeze pushed her back to Charlie's tent. He was loading a thick coil of rope into the wagon, so Ella changed Holland into a nightgown, and with a kiss on her creamy shoulder, buttoned it up snug. She tucked the baby into her low bed and Holland gripped the threadbare stuffed tiger before rolling onto her side. With a sigh, she peered back up.

"I'm not going anywhere, little one. Go to sleep."

The tent flap moved aside and Charlie appeared, a sunset pink behind him. He seemed tired as he stepped to the washstand and wet his hair. Droplets struck his shirt. He took the makeup tin from its low shelf and hefted a crate over by Regina's chair. The small woman ambled in, and soon the pair was settled in their spot. Charlie straddled his crate and Regina lifted the tin onto her lap.

Words tumbled into silence as Regina handed Charlie a can of pomade. He ran some through his hair, but instead of slicking it back as he did for the matinee, he tousled it then wiped his hands clean on a towel.

"More," Regina mumbled. "Madame Broussard will not be pleased with that."

"I do not care what she is pleased with."

"You will *take heed* to care." She tapped the small can. *"More."*

Charlie glanced at Ella and she realized she shouldn't be here. She made to stand, but Holland whimpered. When Charlie gave a reluctant nod, Ella knelt again.

He dipped pomade then mussed his hair more. From the larger tin, Regina pulled a pencil, charcoal, and small brushes. Ella didn't dare speak as she watched their silent exchange. A rhythm built on trust between two people whose lives had wound together since Charlie's birth. And here she was watching—an outsider.

Charlie closed his eyes. Scooting to the edge of her chair, Regina smeared soft pencil beneath his lower lids, and using her finger, smoothed it about to create shadows. She did the same to his top lids, then followed this with strokes from the charcoal, darkening the flesh dramatically and smudging it down the tops of his cheeks. Blacking every bit of skin there. Making him look haunted. Sinister.

Finally, Charlie's eyes opened. And found hers.

Ella checked her breathing. Made sure her face held no hint of what passed through her. Sorrow . . . and to much dismay . . . fear. Her chest rose and fell with it.

Candlelight flickered off him as he rose and she had to remind herself that it was still Charlie. The one she had laughed with, whose singing had filled the morning air.

His eyes were on her as he slid into a dark cloak. The pale green of them, all that she recognized, and even that vanished into shadow when he pulled the hood forward. His voice was low for Regina. Ella couldn't hear what was said, so fiercely blood pounded in her ears. Then with a sweep of the tent flap he was gone.

Holland stirred gently, well asleep, and unsettled, Ella reached out and smoothed a blonde coil of hair away from the baby's ear. Using the towel Charlie had wiped his hands on, Regina cleaned her fingers.

"I don't understand," Ella whispered.

Regina's rag stilled as Ella rose to her knees, then stood.

The woman looked up sadly. "He would not want you there."

Nodding, Ella thought on Regina's words as

she bid farewell and walked to where the sisters were eating supper. And she thought on Regina's words as she ate and later helped carry dishes to the back of the cook tent. Then as the sisters set about brushing and braiding their hair for bed, Angelina laughing to Ella about how it would take the better part of an hour, Ella thought on it one last time. She exchanged a few quiet words with Angelina, and with a squeeze of Ella's hand, Angelina told her that perhaps a little walk was in order, then whispered to bring a nickel.

Ella thanked her.

She headed to the sideshow by memory, for what lingered of the circus was much different at night. Unsavory characters were everywhere and she was not by Charlie's side this time. Aloneness crushed in. More so now that she knew where he was.

Ella kept her head down as she walked, then hesitated just beneath one of the torches that flanked the entrance to the village.

"You seem like a lady lookin' for a bit of a thrill."

At the strange voice, Ella glanced over to the man guarding the entrance.

Sitting lazily on a stool, he leaned against the partition behind him, grungy boots up on the booth. A bowler hat sat low on his head and his cheeks were eerily rouged. Mustache oiled and curled into twists. "The *blowoff*'s already started, but there's still time to catch it." He replaced the cap on a metal flask.

"The what?"

With a finger, he tipped his hat back then eyed her from head to toe. "The blowoff. The finale. No children allowed." Using a brass-topped cane, he tapped the bottom of a poster that listed all the sideshow acts Ella had seen earlier beneath a heading *Sideshow Spectacular*. Ella stepped closer, glimpsed words that hinted at Arnold and Angelina, then farther down where she read of conjoined twins and the tall man. The last act was surrounded by a moon and painted stars, hinting at its time. Written in bold font where the man's cane had rested was—*The Beast.* Charlie.

Ella skimmed over the brief description, barely grasping hold of how it depicted him as a wild man. Tattooed and savage, assuring the audience they were safe even as it beckoned them to one last show at the cost of another five cents. She swallowed hard, her heart aching for Charlie.

As if taking silence as hesitation, the man spoke. "Aw, don't be scared, Miss Do-Good. Show's gone tomorrow and we ain't comin' back. And don't worry, ladies like you are always throwin' a stink over the great injustice of it all." He lowered his voice, brow dipped indignantly. "They let him out of the cage afterwards." He flashed a brash wink. "So watch yourself."

Sick on Charlie's behalf, Ella paid and stepped across the small courtyard to the tent in the distance. From somewhere else, a harmonica filled the night air. Part of her hoped that Charlie was finished because the hour was late indeed, but by the press of people in the tent, that hope died. The sound of music was trampled down by the chatter within. Ella stepped up to the tent and was met with the backs of several men. She went to move around them, straining on her toes to try and find Charlie. Her hands brushed tweed and wool as she pushed her way through.

"Excuse me." She inched past, their gazes like oil on her skin as she did.

One of them suggested something that had her moving away quicker. In the distance, she heard the rattle of chains. Smelled the stench of cigars. Beside her, a pair of young ladies clutched one another and giggled.

Another man tipped a flask. "Show us your face, Beast! Or haven't you got one?"

"Don't rile him up," someone called.

"Hey, that's what we paid to see," the man replied.

The crowd laughed.

Swallowing a sour taste, Ella wanted to scream as she fought toward the front. Shout for them to move out of her way. She wanted Charlie. Was desperate to see him. To know that he was all right. That he wasn't hurt.

For she'd been in this tent before and knew what it held.

She squeezed forward several more steps, then looking up, slammed to a halt against the wagon. Knelt in the center was the one man she ached to see. Bound by chains and bars.

Air failing her, Ella stepped forward. His head was down . . . defeated. Above his brown pants, he was bare. Shockingly so. The planes of his body—strong and lean and imposing—on display. Piercing her, pulling her forward. Making her want to call his name. To shove the people from the tent. Did they not know? Not care?

That this was Charlie. Holland's papa. Her *papa*.

The tattoos drew comments from the crowd. Ridicule and sneers, even questions. Charlie sat silent. Showed no reaction and she was certain he'd grown good at ignoring it. Or perhaps only good at pretending. He shifted and a chain rattled with muted thuds.

Then she saw his bound wrists. Recalled the way they always bothered him.

Heart bending on itself, Ella touched the bars.

Charlie's eyes—blackened with the smudges—appeared almost hollow as he lifted his head and looked out over the throng of people as if seeing something worth holding onto. Torchlight flickered on his painted face. His lips continued to move. Perhaps praying. Maybe a hymn.

"He's mad," someone muttered.

As Charlie knelt on the wagon floor, chains dragged across the wood planks and he clasped his hands in front of him. Tears stung her eyes.

She thought of his smile. His laugh. The sound of his singing on a cool spring day. Holland in his arms—her little cheek pressed to that strong chest. The girl's place of safety and rest and assurance that yes, there was a person in this world who would stand up and fight for her. And Ella had known the feeling herself when she was with him.

The distance killing her, Ella slipped her hand through the bars. His ornate forearm rested just there. Gently, she touched him, fearing too late that he might startle. Charlie snapped his arm away, rose, and moved to the other side of the narrow plank floor in a clang of chains.

"You've scared him," the man beside her said, brows furrowed in disappointment. "Hey, Beasty. Come here." The man reached through and snapped his fingers. When that got no reaction, he pulled at the nub of his smoldering cigar and flicked it at Charlie. It hit him, and then the boards, smoking against the wood of the wagon. "Fetch, boy. Or do you have a litter of beasties to do that for you?"

With a growl, Charlie turned and kicked the bars so hard, the whole wagon shook. Ella covered her mouth. The man barely had time to yank his hand back before Charlie kicked again. Metal groaned and the people reveled. In a flash, Charlie was on his knees. He gripped the man by the collar and yanked his face against the bars.

Charlie drew himself nearer, voice chillingly low. "You have *no* idea."

When he loosened his hold, the man stumbled back. Charlie dipped his head. His lashes blinked over and over and he spoke softly to himself, finishing with a sideways glance right to where Ella stood. Recognition dawned in his charcoaled eyes. Shoulders rising and falling, he sank lower on his knees. Ella almost reached for him. So sinister were the smudges of his skin, so dark the face she knew and loved, that her mouth went dry. In what bespoke countless words, he slowly turned his head to the side. She gripped the bars and dared not whisper his name for he was silent himself.

Staring at her, his eyes grew wet. The crowd was growing hushed.

Then he jerked his head toward the exit. He wanted her to leave. She could feel it. See it in the way his brows dug together, pleading. The murmurs rising again, several hands reached through to touch him, but the fight was gone as he simply looked down at her. She'd baited him; no longer did he push the hands away. He didn't so much as move.

Stomach rolling, she backed away—for no

other reason than to free him. As if to mark the late hour, a man with keys at his belt extinguished the first of many torches. Feeling the poke and jab of the remaining crowd, Ella took several more steps. Charlie's stare followed as she backed toward the exit.

Turning, she hurried into the night and slipped from the village.

Had there ever been a night this black? Sinking onto a bench, she looked around at the eerie, thinning crowd and thought of home. Of meadows, creeks, and the cool damp woods. She ached for it, hating this moment. Because it was Charlie's reality every night. Ella watched it all pass by. The dark shapes and shadows of townsfolk ebbing and flowing as the sideshow slowly drained of patrons. She didn't know how long she sat there, but the place was near to empty, most of the tents folded down when she rose, chilled through.

Arms folded tight, she hurried toward Charlie's camp, toward the glow of campfires. Suddenly a shadowed figure caught up to her and a hand cupped her elbow. Ella yelped.

"You had no right to do that." Tall and looming, Charlie pulled her forward.

Even as she swallowed her heart, Ella's feet skittered to keep up. "What *was* that?"

"That was none of your business."

He led her to the red wagon. Brought her all

the way to the bottom of the steps, then let go. Turning, he strode toward his own.

She ran after him and walked backwards to face him. He steered around her.

She followed. "They chained you."

"The people need a good show."

"Isn't there some kind of regulation against this?"

"Welcome to the sideshow." He let out a single, dark laugh. "Do you really think that there is a regulation against a man with no arms and no legs on display for people to pay to see? So they can laugh at him?"

Words failed her.

"I'm a grown man, Ella. I make my own decisions." He stopped so quick, she tripped over a tent stake, catching herself on a rope.

"The lesser of two evils." She fought the urge to rub her ankle.

He looked at her. Hard.

So he thought she'd forgotten about that?

"What do you want from me?" he asked.

"I want to understand."

"For what? Your own benefit? Or is there some reason why my business is your business. Because the way I understood it . . ." His voice fell too soft to wake others. "Why did you come there?"

"I needed to know."

"Know what?"

"Who you are."

"You know who I am." He stepped into the light of his tent opening and then ducked inside, letting the tent close.

She hesitated only the briefest of moments before following him in.

TWENTY-THREE

Ella blinked into the soft light of a lantern that burned low as if waiting for him. The space was hemmed in silence, Regina asleep behind her partition. Holland bundled on her bed. Charlie reached up and pulled back the hood of his cloak, keeping his face toward the ground. Ella searched his profile. "A few days ago I thought I did," she whispered.

He winced, and when he glanced around, the light illuminated Regina's handiwork with coal-black coloring. Ella checked her fear. It was just Charlie. She tried not to think of how he'd startled the crowd. Startled her. How fearsome he had been. *It was just a show,* she reminded herself, and tried not to think of how the muscles of his chest and arms had coiled tight with his grip through the bars. How he towered over her now.

Ella gulped. A man not of hatred, she reminded herself. But of brokenness.

Overwhelmed, she dropped her gaze, peering down to his hands, his wrists instead. "You're hurt."

"I'm fine." After tossing the cloak aside, he sank onto a crate.

"May I look at them?"

"I assure you, *I'm fine*—"

His voice clipped to an end when she knelt and traced her fingertip past his raw skin where the iron cuff had worn. "This needs salve. I have some. Please, let me." When he said nothing, she slipped away, crossed to where the red wagon sat, and quietly knocked.

Angelina opened the door. "You don't have to knock, silly goose." She motioned her in only to reveal that Danielle was brushing the end of Evangeline's hair.

"Oh, goodness," Ella breathed.

"It is long, no?"

Evangeline's hair puddled to the floor and into the aisle of the wagon.

"And a bit crowded, I'm sorry. Why don't we sit out by the fire?"

Ella motioned back the way she came. "I need to fetch something for Charlie, but then I'll be back." She pointed to the box just behind Angelina.

"Oh, yes." Angelina pulled it down and handed it to her. "We have to do this every night and morning. I fear you may regret coming with us." Smiling, Angelina held the door open and Ella promised she wouldn't be long.

The case clutched tight, Ella walked back. Charlie sat in the same spot, looking too tired to move. So as not to wake the others, she circled him and his crate and sank back to her knees. The case she nestled in her lap. It clicked open and she hunted for the tin of salve.

"How much longer?" she asked. "For you. With all of this?"

"About four more months."

"Would they . . ." She reached for his hand and he let her take it. "Would they have done this to Holland?"

"Blast it, Ella," he muttered.

So she stayed silent.

He sighed, and after rubbing the side of his face against his shoulder, spoke low. How he wasn't sure of what would have been done to Holland. But that he was certain it would have been worse. "Madame makes her money by exploiting people in cities all over the country."

Ella watched his face, uncertain of what he meant.

"Whether it's the burlesque dancers or the tall man, they're here by choice, and they make much of their profits. But Holland would have been different."

Closing her eyes only amplified the despair in his voice. Ella glanced to the baby curled up, asleep in her bed.

"The moment Madame could have begun making money on that little girl, she would have." As if not wanting to talk about it, he moved to the washstand, wet a rag, and returned.

Gently, Ella took it from him. His shoulders sank.

"Sit, please." She pulled over Regina's low chair for herself. When he didn't move, she touched his sleeve. "Will you let me look at your wrists?"

He rolled back the cuffs. Loosening the top of his collar, he spoke as if to converse with the grass at their feet. "Does this make you uncomfortable?"

"No." The wrong answer because he freed two more buttons and pulled the shirt overhead and off.

He tossed it aside, and whatever he had wanted to prove worked; suddenly her heart was in her throat. He watched her for several heartbeats. Whatever this test was, she clearly failed because his gaze raked from her to the crooked stove pipe rising up and out.

He motioned with his hand between them. "You were only Holland's nurse. And I thank you for what you did. But we both know there's nothing more to it than that."

Yet she could see that though the lie came easily, it wasn't true for him.

And for her?

She searched his face, looked past his blackened eyes, and saw the man who had been taking her heart in what she could only name as love.

Then her eyes grazed his body. Grief laced

293

through her again—at all he'd given up. Marred with needle and ink. But the grief ran deeper, sharper.

Burning right through her walls that she had so carefully built around her heart.

Because she knew what it meant to be damaged. Not only in one foul moment with pain and horror so fierce, she could vomit all over again, but daily, yearly. Bit by bit, dying, not healing. And here he was, scarred beyond repair, and no amount of his faith would make it go away.

He was marked. As was she. Which had her wanting to ask him to put his shirt back on. The desire strong, she voiced it. Slowly he rose, picked it up, and loosened the rest of the buttons. He slid the shirt on and fastened it up, stopping only after he'd rolled the cuffs back.

When he sat, she eased his hand to her lap and dabbed the cloth on his wrist. Next, the melting of salve to his skin. Before she could finish, he turned his hand long enough to squeeze hers. To hold it.

"I'm sorry about last night," he whispered. "I shouldn't have kissed you like that. Not without telling you first."

Was it only last night that they'd sat on the roof? Her giving him the only thing she had left to give a man? She swallowed the burn of tears, consumed with her love for him and the way it mixed with the heaviness of loss. Of shock and broken hopes. Of his body and all that he'd done to it. The crushing heat and the crowd's ridicule. All for a little girl who she knew he would die for.

When the silence stretched on, he leaned forward. "It's still me," he whispered.

She looked at him, and blackened eyes implored for words she couldn't speak.

His head bowed between them. "Please see me."

Her hand moved, reaching for his hair. Some piece of him that might make sense. She felt the oiled ends, felt the grit of the carnival grounds.

As if knowing as much, he said, "I should go. I need to take a bath. I can walk you on my way to the creek."

"That is where you go, then. It's so cold . . ."

"I bathe there because I never know when *you're* going to show up." He motioned to her, silently proving his point. "And it helps me calm down."

Ella glanced to the baby when he did.

"I'm sorry that I almost kicked you. I didn't know—"

She shook her head.

"I really am sorry. And the others . . . Ella, I'm not angry at them." He tipped his head to the side, light dancing along the line of his jaw. "Well, not entirely. I just—sometimes I panic knowing I can't get out. Or if they throw things at me. I wish I could tell you that I'm always on my best behavior, but . . ." Head lowered, he shook it.

Her heart was in a hundred pieces. "You have to do this every night."

"Only during the carnival."

"Why do they chain you?"

Charlie let out a slow sigh. "A question for another night, Ella." He slowly shook his head and she could see that he was utterly spent.

Remembering the rag, Ella lifted it slowly toward his face. A question.

In answer, he closed his eyes.

Breath bated, she gently wiped at the ebony smudge that darkened one eye. She folded the rag over on itself, wiping the rest somewhat clean before moving to the other. The charcoal had smeared, she could only guess from sweat, since it had dried in rivulets down his temple. She slid the rag there, wiping the darkness away some.

For an unnamed reason, she ran her fingers over his forehead, down the side of his face, to his neck. His throat worked and he moistened his lips.

"There you are," she whispered, letting her hand still where the last smudges had smeared. The place where his reality began and no amount of wiping would make it go away.

No doubt feeling it, his eyes opened. "I want you to know that you don't have to come with us. I won't hold you to anything. You're not trapped."

"I don't want to stay here." Not if that life meant that he wouldn't be in it. Ella didn't know how to make sense of that.

They sat in silence for several moments. Wind rustled the sides of the tent, and the snapping of a nearby flag echoed back.

His hand slid forward on his knee—hesitating. Then the words *Carpe Diem* caught the lantern light as he tucked a strand of hair behind her ear. "You're *so* beautiful." His voice held such ache and longing that she rose before it could melt the defenses she was already thrashing against.

At the washstand, she took her time rinsing the rag. She returned and settled back on Regina's chair then pulled his other hand into her lap. Dabbing at the raw skin with the cloth showed that the flesh hadn't torn. At least not tonight, as it *was* scarred. With careful fingers, she smeared salve into his skin. Ella lifted a quick glance. "Does that hurt?"

He shook his head, uncertainty heavy in his eyes.

This man deserved such gratitude, and while he had it in Regina, Holland's bright smile—even others, Ella longed for some way to acknowledge what he'd done. He'd displayed such honesty, such strength about them it practically hung in the air, tinging it with truth—vulnerability.

Though small, so insignificant to what he deserved, Ella pressed the side of her face to the back of his hand. Coming tears tightened her throat. His skin was so warm, so right against hers.

His breath hitched to silence and he slowly pulled away. "You should go." He looked more taken aback than his words allowed.

Nodding, she shifted to a stand when he did.

Without speaking, he led her from the tent the short distance to Angelina's wagon. The air nipped at her arms and she ached for a bed. He moved a little closer and the chill lessened.

"Sleep good, Ella." He stopped and let her walk the last few feet alone to the red wagon. Sensing that he was already gone, she had to force herself not to look back as she slipped inside.

TWENTY-FOUR

Ella woke to the gentle sounds of Danielle and Evangeline moving about in the small space, brushing their floor-length hair. Evangeline spoke softly, her voice holding a hint of shyness even with her sisters, and she was perhaps only a few years older than Angelina. Evangeline's face was tilted toward the window, and with each sister arranged so, Ella decided that Angelina was the most darling, the most sunny of spirit. Evangeline, so like a fawn, was as lovely as she was gentle, and Danielle, with her dark hair and exotic eyes, ever so elegant. Surely Charlie noticed all of this as well. She wondered if their marriage vows had ever been difficult on his own heart.

Still in a chemise and corset, Angelina sat at the table, sipping from a dainty teacup. Her locks had been unbraided from a night's sleep and now lay to the floor in glossy waves.

Danielle gripped the bottom of her own hair and ran a brush through the ends. Her countenance was cheery as she looked to Ella. "Did you sleep well?"

"Very well, thank you."

"Don't feel the need to get up just yet." Though she was the oldest, Danielle didn't seem but twenty or so, and her scrunched nose was full of spunk. "As you can see, there is nowhere to walk." Her hair covered the floor around her feet when she released her grip on it to brush higher up.

Ella folded her legs in and bundled her blanket snugly around her waist. She was thankful for the narrow bed and generous hearts. Danielle had given up her space, joining her sisters on the large back bed which, although wide, had to be crowded with three. Their smiles hinted that they didn't mind at all.

Ella watched Danielle run the brush down her hair in long strokes. Her own felt utterly disheveled. "Do you do this every morning?" Ella asked.

Evangeline nodded. "We must. Oh, you should see how grumpy Angelina gets if hers snarls. Helping her is not a task anyone would envy on those mornings." Evangeline winked and Angelina chuckled.

"How I envy you," Evangeline said to Ella.

"*You* envy *me?*"

"To have such short hair. So easy."

Ella felt her own braid that went down to her lower back. She'd never thought of her hair as short, but now, after seeing all the sisters went through to maintain their length, she could see why it was such a novelty. The three of them tucked and bound their hair in tidy folds that was truly a feat in itself. Ella changed out of her nightgown and was thankful for the helpful hands on the buttons of her dress, returning the favor for Danielle.

Ella thought of what Angelina had said the night before. Of how these young women with the dark, sparkling eyes and almond-hued skin were fond of Charlie, yet bound by vows made as girls. When Danielle peered at Ella, her expression was kind. Caring. Clear was the heart of a young woman who had been learning to be like a sister to a man who had touched her heart so. Ella was humbled by the graciousness extended to her by these young women who had walked beside him for so many years.

Outside, they shared a humble meal of bread and cheese since the cookhouse was nearly packed away.

Bread in hand, Evangeline strode off across the meadow. She returned but a few minutes later, leading a massive black and white horse on a line. With fur draping over his hooves, the horse's feet looked like white bells. Tall and thick and patched with opposing color, he was a creature unlike any Ella had seen.

"He's beautiful," she said as Evangeline drew near.

Evangeline stroked the horse's white mane. "Thank you. We keep him stabled with the other Vanners and ring stock." She pressed the side of her head to the horse's neck lovingly, and after a few more strokes, led him to the front of the wagon where she tethered him, allowing plenty of room for a morning graze.

Danielle bent and freed a piece of wood chalking one of the wagon wheels. "As you can see, Evangeline has a heart for horses. I see to the business side of things. Finances." She moved to the next wheel. "And Angelina keeps everything clean and organized because she is not very good at sums. Or horses."

Angelina's giggle carried through the open wagon window.

Smiling, Ella turned to see if anything else needed to be gathered up when she spotted a green wagon moving past.

Charlie walked steadily across the meadow. With Holland snug in the sling against his back, he led a horse that looked just like the sisters'. His wagon followed slow and creaking like a great ship on a grassy sea. Ella must have watched him overlong when Danielle stepped beside her.

"He's not leaving." The young woman smiled.

Ella felt her cheeks pink, for she'd been wondering the very thing.

"He's one of the lead wagons, with the lions. So he has to get in line earliest. We're nearer to the end of the caravan, so we still have a few minutes." Danielle gave her a sly wink. "Well,

Ella. It looks like you've run away and joined the circus."

Ella glanced the way she'd come. To the rise of buildings that led back toward her apartment, and already she felt a sting of tears at missing Margaret and everything that had been home. But Ella looked back toward Charlie, more than thankful that she was not standing on top of her apartment building watching that very wagon disappear out of sight.

Never had the spring sun felt so warm. The road beneath his feet so right. Charlie gripped Siebel's line and knew it had something to do with a particular woman. The black and white Vanner following steadily along and with Holland still asleep at his back, he kept an eye out for his spot in the caravan, just behind his lions.

He neared Ruth's wagon that she shared with the two other aerialists. She stuffed something in a carpetbag, her white ruffled skirt a sharp contrast to the dark little moccasins she wore. Seeing him she straightened and propped a hand on her hip. "Me mare's a bit sluggish today. Has been the last month or so. 'Tis growing steadily worse."

"Don't buy such a lazy horse next time." Charlie led his own onward, but felt Ruth glaring at him.

"They continue to pen that louse of an animal

with my mare." She flung her hand toward Siebel.

"And?" But by the look she flashed him, Charlie already knew. He slowed, fighting a smile.

Her fist returned to her hip. "If my horse foals, t'will be that horse's fault. *Again!*"

Charlie held up his hands. "I assure you it's not. The first time, maybe. But . . ." He shook his head gravely and felt a mite sorry for poor Siebel.

"Ne'er do well," Ruth muttered and adjusted a latch on the side of her wagon. "If she foals, I'll be selling it and you willn'a see a single dime from me."

He grinned and motioned toward Siebel. "This is the face of a saint." A very gelded saint.

She gave him a squinty look.

As he walked on, Charlie rubbed the scruff of Siebel's neck. "Don't worry. I'll make sure your name gets cleared." The horse let out a snort and flicked his tail.

Charlie led them onward until he spotted the caged wagons that held his lions. Thanks to La'Rue marking his spot, there was a gap in the caravan awaiting him. A bit too small, so Charlie led Siebel in at an odd angle. "Whoa." He pressed against the horse's neck and the Vanner stopped. Hands in his pockets, Charlie strode up the line to see how his boys were doing.

Kristov lay with his back pressed against the

bars, golden mane sticking through the slats. Han was asleep as well, but Axel looked up. The lion rose lazily and moved to where Charlie stood and leaned against the slats. Charlie scratched his thick fur.

"Hey, boy. I'll have you out of there soon, all right?" He hated to see the lions caged. It was his least favorite part of this job. How he wished he could just romp with them in the meadow.

"Soon," he said, scrubbing harder at Axel's hide.

Charlie moved his hand back a few bars and gave the lion's hindquarters a firm pat, then poked around in their food stores and slipped the boy a piece of meat. He didn't know how many lion tamers there were in this country but knew that every one of them would tell him to never feed an adult lion with his bare hand. He also wasn't supposed to sit down with them and he was quite certain wrestling was frowned upon. It wasn't that Charlie ignored the rules—he just preferred to trust his instincts. One of the most valuable lessons his father had taught him when working with these cats. And if they were his friends, he treated them as such.

If one of his boys had wanted to eat him— they'd have done it long ago.

When Axel lowered his head to the gap between two bars, Charlie touched his own to Axel's, honored each time the five-hundred-and-thirty-pound cat greeted him so intimately. He had always known Axel to be the alpha of the three males. But Charlie sensed that Axel saw him as the alpha—a position of honor that Charlie treated with great care.

He braced himself as Axel lifted his white jaw and ran his tongue up the side of Charlie's head. Children often asked him what a lion's tongue felt like. He always explained that it was rough like a housecat's but ten times worse because a grown lion's tongue was designed to pull the flesh right off an animal's bones. Feeling like he'd just been attacked by sandpaper, Charlie groaned good-naturedly and ducked away.

A few more pats and a "love you too," he stepped back. With Axel still watching curiously, Charlie slid Holland forward to his chest. She was awake now, and upon seeing the great lion, stuck out her hand which Axel sniffed. Charlie let her babble and Axel talked back—a *wuh-ooow* that had Holland beaming. All the lions saw her as Charlie's cub, and he always took care to let them see her close to him. And to let her interact in safe ways. If he was a part of their pride, then Holland was too. Though the only lion he ever allowed her this close to was Axel. For when it came to the five-year-old male, Axel was an old soul.

Each of his boys had a different personality and Charlie knew them as well as any family. Axel had a sensitivity and protectiveness that made

Charlie trust Holland in his presence. The animal was patient, not flighty in the way Kristov was or as rambunctious as Han. Charlie played the most with those two and loved them for it. But Axel was his other half; if Axel were a man, he would have been Charlie's brother.

And Han and Kristov? Well, they were two partners in crime, but he knew their soft spots—Han's literally being just under the shoulder, and Kristov was putty in his hand when Charlie rubbed his belly or napped in the sun with him. Kristov was his favorite to wrestle with and Han had eyes so vivid that Charlie could sit and watch him for hours.

He gave Axel another firm pat as the great cat lay down. Holland had been slung at Charlie's back around the eldest male since Mimi's death. Though Charlie doubted his sister's maternal instincts would have had her approving, it was Mimi herself who had sat as a mere tot with their father and the very lion that had sired Charlie's own. Perhaps not the best way for him and his sister to have been raised and perhaps not the best way for him to parent Holland, but it was the only way he knew.

Enjoying the stretch of legs, Charlie walked farther up the line, past the wagon that held the striped Big Top that was covered with canvas and tightly bound. In front of that, the king pole ran up the center of its massive wagon—all sixty feet of the pole being led by an eight-horse hitch. Charlie greeted the canvasman, and then seeing the front of the caravan begin to move, walked back to his wagon.

From somewhere behind, a woman was singing a Psalm. Several others joined in. Charlie took up Siebel's lead rope, and with Regina settled on the back stoop of the wagon, clicked his tongue and the horse walked on. Charlie listened, sparing the world his voice. Holland was round and soft against his back. A small bundle of warmth that seeped all the way to his heart. Reaching back, he gave the mounded sling a gentle pat and tried to make sense of how one person could love another more with each passing day. That was surely what was happening to him. He wished Mimi were here to hold her. To know this feeling.

The day passed smoothly, and by the time the sound of song was but a memory, energetic children now tired and lounging on vardo porches—watching where they'd been as opposed to where they were going—the sun hung low in the sky. Charlie saw the wagons up ahead begin to circle. Around them spread a broad grassy knoll, and in the distance, a glittering, snaking strip of silver meant a river wasn't far off.

Charlie waited until they were parked, then paid a bored-looking roustabout a nickel to tend to Siebel. Holland and Regina were contentedly eating slices of pickles in the tall meadow grass, and as much as he wanted to go and check on Ella, he turned all his attention to the big cats, and more particularly, the cleaning of their cage. A job he wouldn't mind leaving to a laborer, but it was always hard recruiting men to climb inside a cage with fifteen-hundred pounds of lion. Which meant he had the privilege of shoveling manure every single day.

Charlie grabbed what he'd need, and with a roustabout on hand, freed the lock to the massive, barred wagon. His boys were asleep, so Charlie pushed aside the metal clasp and eased the door open just enough to climb inside. He closed the door carefully behind him, then reached through the bars for the shovel.

Three maned heads lifted and they blinked sleepily as he moved about, shoveling out old straw. Energized by his presence, Axel rose to watch more closely while Kristov—the pest—made it his obsession to jump on Charlie's back with his front paws. Charlie kept pushing him off only to have the beast do it again. He gave Kristov the strongest shove he could manage. So hard it might have appeared rough to an outsider, but it was scarcely a nudge to a giant like Kristov, and if Charlie didn't treat them with ferocity now and again, they'd stop thinking of him as a lion. A sucker for roughhousing, Kristov nudged Charlie's side with his broad head and Charlie indulged the cat in another playful shove.

After fetching fresh straw, the tall, spindly laborer handed it to Charlie. By the time it was spread about, the animals were back in their napping positions, Han gnawing on the end of a rope, Kristov gnawing on the center of a bone.

Crouching, Charlie gave the rope a playful tug. Paws to the rope, Han smashed the tattered fibers to the floorboards and flicked his long tail, letting out a low guttural sound. With a grin, Charlie tugged a few quick times. Han let out a snort and Charlie gave a firm yank, pulling it free. "Ha!"

But his victory lasted less than a second because the whole wagon shook when Han pounced on the end. It was enough to make Charlie fall, and with massive jaws, Han ripped the rope free, flopped back down, and set to gnawing again. This time while lying on Charlie's leg. Charlie chuckled as he sat up. With firm hands, he scrubbed Han up and down his mane. A few seconds of that and the cat closed his golden eyes, lazily lifted his jaw, and the rope was momentarily forgotten.

Charlie kissed the side of his muzzle then struggled to a stand.

"Are they crowded with the three of them in one cage?"

He looked down to see Ella standing there—at such a safe distance that he smiled. "Um . . . sometimes they ride separately. But lions like to lay on one another, so they get cranky if I don't keep them together."

A silk scarf bound her hair back and it caught the soft breeze blowing over the meadow grasses. She watched quietly as he set about filling up their water bowl to the brim.

"Would you like to come closer?" he asked.

Quickly she shook her head. "Will . . . will they eat now?"

"No. Tomorrow."

"What will you feed them?"

"Well, they'll start with a salad and then a chilled soup . . ."

Ella smiled.

Charlie winked. He'd made it a habit of making light of their diet to passersby. He'd only been joking to those children about zebra meat. The menagerie was well cared for, so unless an animal somehow died healthy, they took no part in his lions' supper. Venison or goat were the favored meats, but they ate what was fitting in different towns and cities, and the circus kept grazing stock for that very purpose. He explained all that to her as tactfully as possible.

"In Louisiana, the farmers bring me any livestock that's died of natural causes. We try to only take from what's already been lost—but I also have to be selective. If we have to take an animal's life for these lions I make sure that I'm the one to do it." When she remained quiet, he gripped a hand around one of the bars. "Does that make you unhappy with me?"

"No. I suppose . . . I suppose they'd have to eat in the wild."

"Yes." And what most people didn't realize was that his maned brothers were designed to be less quick with their prey than he was.

"Have you ever thought of freeing them?" she asked.

"Are you writing an article for the newspaper or something?"

She smirked. "I just want to understand."

He looked at her—more grateful for that than he could say. So much so, that he climbed down and locked the door before striding over to her. "I think of it every day of my life."

Ella peered up at him.

"But they were born in captivity, not taken. I dream of them in the wild, but even if I could get them to a land where they could roam freely, they'd have a high chance of death because they'd each need to fight other males for lionesses. Maybe even each other."

Ella glanced from the lions then back to his face.

"They also wouldn't know to avoid humans, which would not end well for the cats."

Sorrow filled her eyes.

He didn't mean to concern her but rarely had the opportunity to speak freely. Speak truth into what people understood so little about. "So I do my best for them and make sure they get lots of sun and air and places to roam. *And* that they get to spend some time with lionesses a few times a year." Her jaw fell a little, so Charlie added, "They're very affectionate. Lions."

"Is that so?"

"Yes." He wasn't about to go into detail so instead explained the courtship. The way the leader of a pride pressed the front of his head to a lioness's. To tell her that he saw only her. With Ella standing so near, Charlie touched his forehead down to hers and she smiled up at him. Which was gracious considering that he probably smelled like manure. He took a step back. "So . . . have you come to talk about these fellas, or did you really come to tell me how bad your feet hurt?"

Ella circled around him, avoiding the cage that was still yards away. "I promise to keep all aches and pains to myself."

"Then you're half Gypsy already." Unsheathing his knife, he brushed his thumb against the blade several times to check the sharpness. At the supply box on the back of the menagerie wagon, Charlie pulled out a length of rope and cut a fresh piece which he tossed in to Han. "Don't worry. The soreness is something you get used to."

She fingered something in her palm, nodding slowly.

Charlie realized his blunder. No, she wouldn't be getting used to this type of travel. Why had he said that? Tomorrow would be her last day with the caravan. He cleared his throat, but Ella spoke before he could.

"Danielle mentioned that there would be dancing tonight. I don't know how you all manage it."

He closed the supply box. "You don't feel like dancing?" Charlie reached over and gave a gentle tug on the scarf that bound her hair. "Maybe you're only a quarter Gypsy, then."

Ella laughed and backed away a step. As if just remembering the scarf herself, she unknotted it. "I'm terrible at it so will just sit and watch."

"Terrible? Then you'll have to learn a thing or two."

Smiling, she tugged at the slip of silk and her blonde hair tumbled free. "Does that mean your dancing is better than your singing?"

He looked at her, pretty sure he failed to hide his smile—and his heart. "You'll just have to wait and find out."

TWENTY-FIVE

With two blankets in hand, Ella walked beside Evangeline who was still straightening the scarf on her tresses.

Each of the sisters had braided and bound up their locks in thick buns at the napes of their necks. Wrapped secure with colorful scarves, the silky fabrics draped their backs. They'd combed and measured their hair but an hour ago—a feat within itself that Ella helped with. Shortly after, she'd gone off in hopes that Little Joe could spare a few moments for a quick checkup. He'd happily settled on the axle of his wagon while she examined his throat and encouraged continued use of the teas and tinctures. Most of all, rest whenever possible. Passing by, Madame Broussard had eyed them skeptically.

Now night was settling. A few steps ahead, Charlie carried Holland on his shoulders. He wore a clean shirt and dark suspenders. Hair damp, his worn top hat sat at an odd angle thanks to the baby's pudgy hands. He swayed as he walked, drawing giggles from the little girl.

Beside him, Regina ambled along with a basket on her hip. Circled around were dozens of blankets, and within that, set out of the way, two pianos flanked one another.

"Oh my!" Ella slowed.

Charlie turned.

"There are pianos . . . in the meadow."

He walked backwards. "The circus is very good at moving things."

In the distance, countless instruments tuned—fiddles, banjos, and what sounded like an accordion. Two young women ran past, tiny trinkets jingling from their ankles, and a trio of children somersaulted down the shallow slope.

"You do this often?" she asked.

"Life is short, no?" He seemed amused by her awe. "And we try and be on our best behavior when we're in town so we take advantage of a full moon now and again when we're on the road."

He plucked Holland from his shoulders and Ella gladly accepted the wiggly bundle. She caught the scent of soap on Charlie's skin before he stepped away. When Ella pressed a kiss to Holland's creamy neck, Charlie smiled down at them.

The smells of supper pulled them forward, and though Ella was hungry, she felt guilty at the notion. Supper was communal, and she assumed that whoever operated the circus provided the meal. Since she wasn't a performer or earning her keep in any way, taking a plate felt wrong so she kept to the blanket she spread out and watched Holland do her darndest to chew on her toes.

Standing above them, Charlie spoke. "I can take her back if you'd like."

"I'll be hard pressed to let her go."

He winked and strode off.

By the time the last hints of daylight had been snuffed out, Angelina and Danielle were settled beside her, plates and forks in hand. Danielle gave Ella a meal, insisting that there was plenty to be had. Evangeline and Regina joined them, and by the time Ella was partially finished with her supper, she looked around wondering where Charlie had gone off to.

Clusters of people lounged about on a patchwork of blankets and Ella finally spotted him across the way with the man she recognized as his partner and fellow lion tamer. Charlie sat with his knee pulled up, eating and laughing with the folks surrounding them. Keeping some distance. For her sake or his?

Holland pulled at the bread in Ella's hand, so Ella pinched off another bite for her.

Minutes later, with Angelina and the baby immersed in a game of peek-a-boo, Ella rose to stretch her legs, her sights on the pianos nearby. She touched the polished wood of the nearest instrument, which sat at a complimentary angle to the other. Her fingers ever so tempted by the sight of the keys, she smoothed her skirt and sat on the wooden bench.

Her heart did a little leap and she ran her

fingers across the cool ivories, not so much as pressing a one. Then she moved her hands into position and pushed softly. Perfectly tuned, the instrument sounded heavenly. She played only a C. One simple chord, but she eased it into an A minor. The sweet sound lifted her lips and her foot found the pedal, only daring to steal a few bars since the piano wasn't hers. With the tune still vibrating, she pulled her hands into her lap.

"That's *very* nice."

Ella looked up to see Charlie stepping closer.

"Thank you." She pressed a single key. "I haven't had a piano for years." She swiveled to face him. "Just touching these keys makes me feel home again."

He settled beside her and pressed one and then another, making a funny sound. "And soon you will be."

She clasped her hands between her knees. "Very soon."

"And I've kept you alive this long. I'm feeling quite proud of myself." She could tell his humor was covering something deeper, but before she could make sense of the look he gave her, Charlie rose and motioned for another man to take his seat. With gartered arms and a bowler hat topping his red shock of hair, surely one of the pianists.

"Are you going to come dance with me?" Charlie asked her.

He said it so easily, her smile bloomed. "I assure you I'm quite terrible." She turned to face him fully. He stepped away, giving her a sly look of distrust, then paused. "Say. Do me a favor, then?" A harmonica began in the distance and he adjusted his top hat. "Keep an eye on this for me. Just so no one steals it." A mischievous sparkle lived in his eyes.

Baffled, Ella watched him go.

Wanting to give the pianist his space, she went to stand, but the man patted the seat. "Please," he said. "And I heard your fine playing so my feelings'll be hurt if you don't help me out." His wink was friendly.

Settling back onto the bench, Ella watched the thickening crowd of circus folk as they filled the meadow. Laughter and cheers rang out. Several ladies ambled into the middle of the grassy area garnering more than a few whistles. They playfully called for someone, and one of the women waved her arm to draw that person forward.

"Come on!" the woman hollered. "We wanna dance!"

A fiddler appeared, playing a cheery lick, and others vacated the blankets for the field. Lanterns bobbed as people brought them along, lighting the space—helping the moon.

And then everything went silent, save a harmonica that blew long and low. Ella craned her neck to see a man in a gray top hat bent over, both hands clutching the little instrument in front of his mouth. An eagle feather split the band of his hat and his red waistcoat glistened.

Women walked into the circle, skirts swaying, some barefooted. The tune picked up, an energetic rendition of *Auld Lang Syne*. A guitar joined in, picking a sweet, sweet sound that had the women swaying and turning.

A banjo twanged into the song, speeding up the pace until shrill whistles pierced around. Then Ella spotted Charlie. He was just on the outskirts, arms folded, laughing with a cluster of men. A woman bounded past them, fringed hem swaying over her bare feet, and with a flick of her hand, she reached up high and knocked Charlie's hat free, caught it, then put it on herself.

Charlie hollered after her, but the shout melted to a grin. Ella wondered again what he'd said about keeping an eye on it. The woman's tapping feet carried her away as fast as the banjo and she seemed rather pleased with her conquest as she clutched up her skirts and spun.

Charlie's eyes found Ella's through the crowd and she laughed.

As if that had been his cue, Charlie moved toward the dancers that were now a colorful blur of feet and skirts, all golden in the glow of the lanterns. Countless voices, including the man beside her, sang so loudly, Ella understood why they waited until they were in the middle of nowhere.

We two have run about the slopes,
and picked the daisies fine;
But we've wandered many a weary foot,
since auld lang syne.

Every pair of hands clapped to the quick rhythm, and suddenly everyone called out, "We'll take a cup o' kindness yet for auld lang syne!"

Then the banjo raced back in and the dancing started—even more vibrant than before. Charlie strode slowly through the crowd, as if looking for the right partner.

The woman with his hat pranced past and another woman came along and plucked it away and put it on herself. She shook a tambourine against her hip as she jigged toward the center of the gathering. The hat didn't stay long as another feminine hand stole it. Except this victor had her sights on a finer prize when she danced up to Charlie. He took her outstretched hand, twirling her in front of him. The woman's bright skirts spun and he let her go just as all the instruments went soft.

Then the great gathering parted and a man stepped into the center, holding his hands up for all to quiet. An instrument was slung at his back. The music faded, changing to a different key and a slightly quicker tempo.

The new song but a whisper.

After sliding a mandolin forward, the man teased a strum. Somewhere in the distance a cowbell clanged. The musician crouched low, stomping one foot. He played faster and the song raced into the night air—countless instruments joining in with a burst that Ella felt right through her. The noise flooded the meadow.

If ever joy had a sound, she'd think this was it.

A tambourine rattled high in the air, followed by another, and beside Ella, the pianist pounded away at the keys so loud and fast that her jaw fell.

Suddenly everyone sang out in a great shout— words she couldn't understand. Ella swung her foot to the music. Everyone, including Charlie, sang out again, and Ella listened closely. It was another language. They kept singing as though they'd learned this song from the cradle.

"What are they saying?" she hollered to the piano player.

"It's French! Cajun." His hands pounded away on the keys. "Ever been to New Orleans?"

Ella shook her head with a laugh. "No!"

The man smirked. "You stick with us and we'll change that!"

Ruth swaggered past Charlie, and to Ella's surprise, she wore his hat. With a wink and a brazen roll of her shoulder, she climbed atop the far piano with as much ease as she climbed her silks. Two men as stout as Regina clambered up behind her as if they did this kind of thing every day. They tapped their feet in a funny dance. Wagging a finger in the air, Ruth clutched up a bit of her dress and turned in a cheeky circle before someone hollered out and Ruth took the hat and flung it toward them.

Charlie reached for it but missed.

Ella clapped along to the music as everyone sang out in French again. Two men with black skin waved trumpets side to side, playing with all their might. And somewhere beneath the night sky a cowbell clanged and the mandolin raced along fast and sassy.

Singing along, Angelina swayed past. She winked over at Ella before taking up Charlie's hat from the latest keeper, and with exaggerated flair, nearly set it on her own head. Then Evangeline took it and did the same, followed by Danielle. Charlie made a show of covering his heart with his hand and acted about to faint dead away.

Ella glanced over to where Holland was asleep in Regina's lap. The sight was obscured by twirling couples. Fringed skirts and dusty pants. A carefreeness that had Ella's foot bouncing. Suddenly Lorelai bobbed past and Danielle set the hat on the large woman's head. Nearby folk whooped and hollered, and Lorelai grinned from ear to ear as she shuffled by Charlie who was rather busy dancing a jig with a trio of little girls who'd taken him by the hands. He bellowed a laugh when he spotted Lorelai, and Ella had a hunch by his sheepish grin that he was blushing.

To Ella's surprise, he staggered over to where she sat on the bench, his mouth near her ear, panting over the hammering pianos. "Last time I give you a job to do!" Grinning, he jogged back to the dancers where he pulled Lorelai close in a flamboyant jig, his hand to her plump back.

Beside Ella the piano player sang as loud as he could. His hands slammed the keys in a blur. Beneath her, the piano bench trembled from the sheer noise of it.

"I thought this was a duet!" he hollered, eyes bright with challenge.

Feeling the ragtime all the way down to her toes, Ella turned on the bench and wiggled her fingers over the keys, trying to catch the notes and tempo. Then she tapped the ivories, taking a moment to catch up—and gasped at how quickly she had to move her hands. She played along as the man raced around with so much flair, her mouth fell.

His gartered arm pressed against hers in a friendly manner, then he slid her a grin and bobbed his head to the music as if to keep time with her. Happiness tugged her cheeks. Then to her shock, the man rose and slid his feet back up on the seat, crouching. Laughing, it was all Ella could do to keep her fingers moving.

Suddenly there was a hand on her own and it

was Charlie, pulling her to her feet. He swept her up in a dance, close and fast and strong. His hat was back on his head and he hollered over the noise. "You were supposed to watch it for me!" He was breathless and his shirt stuck to his skin.

"I tried!" she hollered back.

The sweet night air clung to him and his eyes sparkled. Holding the small of her back firm with one hand, he reached up, slid off the top hat, and set it on her head.

Around them, cheers and whistles shot out, followed by a few theatrical complaints from several women. Ella looked around and her cheeks went to roasting. Charlie was looking down at her as if she'd just given him the moon. The music softened, Charlie slowed them, and to her surprise, pressed a kiss to her cheek, sending a heat that made her knees weak. More cheers spread, and fearing she'd never recover, Ella plopped his hat back on his head.

"Is there some secret to this thing that I should know about?"

"Maybe."

"But you're not going to tell me, are you?"

"Nope." When the music drew soft and sweet, he slowed them. Dipping his head beside her own.

Ella looked from the hollow of his throat to just below where his shirt wasn't fastened as high and tight as it had always been. That's when she realized why. Because there were no rubes around. Just her.

Tipping his head slightly, he looked at her. Gave a gentle smile, his face so very near, the shadow of his hat shading them both from the moon. The music seemed to hush. Or perhaps it was her imagination. Perhaps it was only in her mind that all she could hear was the sound of her heart . . . could only feel the way it was reaching for him.

TWENTY-SIX

The day passed in a blur. In the morning, Charlie visited with the lions, ducking inside their cage, and while Axel gnawed on the sleeve of his shirt, Charlie made sure the new roustabout understood how things operated with the big cats. The ashen-faced lad nodded and Charlie made a mental note to check back in the afternoon to make sure he was still alive.

Back at his wagon he saw that Holland was awake. Regina was feeling poorly so Charlie dressed the baby and slid her in the sling, which not only kept his hands free but helped conceal the fact that he hadn't combed her hair.

A fact that Danielle noticed anyway. And remedied.

He was grateful when the young woman offered to keep Holland for the morning, freeing him to turn his attentions to Siebel. The Vanner acted uncomfortable, pulling the wagon with a slight limp, and Charlie checked his hooves to find that he'd thrown a shoe. At the noon break, he led the horse over to the farrier and had the shoe replaced. By the time they were on the road again, Regina was feeling better. Which was a relief because Charlie knew that the moment they made camp, he would need to wash laundry and soak diapers, which meant that later on when he laid down, it would be a miracle to get back on his feet.

Even as the first stars appeared, Charlie drug his bedroll out of the wagon. More than a bedroll, really, for it was his mattress and half a dozen blankets, all sloppily tied together with a rope. He lugged the massive bundle over to a gnarled oak tree, near enough to his menagerie wagon to keep an eye on the lions. They were dozing now, but in the late hours of the night, they'd begin to roar. It was mostly a gentle bellow, one that he and the rest of the company were used to, but this close, it would be loud enough that he'd sleep with a couple of pillows over his head.

He set his mattress down, spread the bedding somewhat straight, and went back to lug over one of his crates. With a low, crooked branch holding the lantern and the line of sheets he'd washed drying in the night air, it almost felt private.

At the sound of the bell, Charlie grabbed a bar of soap and slung his towel over his shoulder, eager to be free of trail dust. They always tried to camp near water, so be it a creek or spring, it made the rest a lot more pleasant, and as was their tradition come nightfall, the women bathed first. It wasn't until a cowbell clanged—signifying that the women were finished and dressed—that the men would draw themselves down. Maybe they were just Gypsies, but they took pride in being clean.

The men sounded like clumsy oxen in their heavy boots as they worked their way down the shallow hill; the women lithe and gentle with bare feet. Wanting very much to spot Ella, he forced himself to keep his focus on the grass as he walked. It really wouldn't do him much good seeing her in the moonlight. Charlie tried to ignore the flirty banter that passed back and forth, particularly of that between husbands and wives, as the two groups passed on the grassy slope.

Tired, he undressed in the dark and waded into the cold water. He wanted to complain but fought the urge. If several dozen women could brave this water, by golly, he would too. And now he wished he hadn't thought of that. Or of Ella. Charlie ducked down and let the water close over his head. Freezing, he straightened and swiped his hands through his hair. He soaped and rinsed quickly, then climbed back up the bank, not really wanting to linger or hear the crude jokes that always happened to spring up from these grassy banks like reeds. He toweled and dressed, then started back. With one hand he gripped his boots and with the other, ran the towel over his hair while he walked.

His shirt hung unbuttoned. Maybe it was lazy, but he spent so much of his days with it so snugly done that now and again he just wanted to feel free.

In the near dark, he set boots and towel aside, then knelt on his pallet bed and reached into his crate for the box of matches, lighting the lantern. Last, he found the map and after setting it aside, reached into the crate for his Bible. Charlie propped his pillow up against the tree, settled against it, and pulled up a knee to do some reading. Cocooned from the breeze by the wagon and the drying laundry, he settled deeper into his bed and rested an arm behind his head.

From all along the river's edge, the twitter and chirps of exotic birds kept an easy, familiar rhythm with the yips and squawks of monkeys. If those animals quieted, he'd hear the throaty mewl of a giraffe here and there. The breathy pants of the tiger's chuff. Accustomed to the menagerie's orchestra—the very breath of distant jungles, and dry plains—Charlie felt it lull him toward slumber.

He read for a few minutes then sat up. Maybe a shift in position would keep him awake.

"Charlie?"

He looked up to see Ella standing a few feet away. Her braid draped her shoulder, dampening that bit of blouse. She held a sweater in her hand and slid it on. Suddenly forgetting how to speak, he simply watched her step nearer.

"Are you all right?" she asked.

He took a moment to rub his palms over his eyes. "Um, yeah. What are you doing here?"

"I was wondering if we could talk."

"Uh . . ." He glanced around a moment. Thinking. Stalling. Deciding. Then he pulled the last of the items out of the crate, turning it over. He set it down for her just in front of the hanging sheets. He motioned to the makeshift seat. Which was stupid. Because he really should just ask her to leave. At least tonight. They could talk in the morning. Over breakfast.

For he was tired. Had let his heart grow raw tonight.

And she was so pretty.

Lantern light was only making her more so. Driving deeper the pain that she was leaving him tomorrow. Charlie ran his hands through his hair, at a loss for words. Because the temptation to fall to his knees and tell her that he loved her and to ask her to stay with him . . . was burning too brightly. Too strong.

Forming a fist, he pounded it gently against his forehead.

"I'll leave." Plucking up the hem of her dress, she turned to go.

"Will you just give a man a second to think, Ella?"

She halted and he took another breath before motioning toward the crate again. Folding her hands, she sat and her gaze filtered over his space, then back to him. She seemed to be searching for something to say. "What are you reading?" she asked gently.

"Psalms."

"Oh."

"It's a book in the Bible."

She tucked her thumbs inside the sleeves of her sweater, and folding her arms, leaned forward. Her expression was kind. "I do know that, Charlie."

Right. Of course. He set the book aside and said a heap of a prayer that he could do this without losing his mind. "I was looking at the map this afternoon." Kneeling forward on the bed, he dragged it across the blankets and sat with his legs folded in. "And it looks like . . ." He ran his pinkie down their route. "It looks like tomorrow, sometime late morning, I'll take you off this way." He drew his finger up into the mountains there. "Home."

She nodded mutely, but he sensed a thousand words in that head of hers.

"It will probably take most of the day, but we should get there by dark. I'm hoping."

"Thank you, Charlie."

Somewhere in the distance, children laughed. A mother quietly shushed them.

"It's my pleasure." He said it without emotion, for truly he meant it, but grief at the impending loss of her was dragging him under.

Suddenly, she was tipping her head to the side, studying him. Remembering that his shirt was unbuttoned, he went to fasten the collar but she motioned for him to stop. When she moved off her crate and knelt beside him and his mattress, Charlie's heart pounded. She sat there, studying his skin so intensely, he wished he could read her mind. Or that she might speak. Say what it was she was thinking.

Then she gently reached up and touched her fingertips to his heart. Staring at the dirt, he swallowed hard.

She whispered his name, and when he looked at her, saw wonder there. Her finger slid along his skin, making it feel alive. Charlie looked down only to see that she was tracing the outline of the Dutch windmill there with its broad blades and sturdy base.

"Holland," she whispered.

He struggled to find his voice. "If something was going to go there, I wanted to make it count."

Then her hand slid to his shoulder, inching his shirt back. In his mind, he knew what she was touching. First the whale . . . and then the three kings—wise men—and the Christmas star. Others . . .

"Are they stories?" she asked.

"A few. Some I chose and some I didn't."

She slid her hand gently down his arm, pulling the shirt free even more. About to lose his mind

333

with her doing that, he slid out of the shirt and set it aside. She knelt closer, studying him.

Her blue eyes took in the black ravens winging below his collarbones and across his chest to ships on a stormy sea. A sea serpent wrapped its scaly tail around one of the vessels, dragging it under. He held an inhale as she reached up and touched the lighthouse on his other shoulder, tracing fingertips down the path of a curving chain to where mermaids swam around an anchor . . . down his bicep, to the hollow of his elbow. He let out a quiet breath. Tucking her hands in her lap, she silently studied the tattoos on his abdomen with only her eyes, and he was glad for he would have had to stop her. Her lips were pursed and he tried to read her expression.

He touched the waist of his pants and then his thigh. "There are no more." There hadn't been time. She didn't ask, but he just needed her to know.

She nodded thoughtfully.

Gently, she pressed on his shoulder, hinting that he turn. He angled away so that his back caught the lantern light. She felt along his shoulders and he knew all of what she touched. Egyptian dunes, fishermen's nets, David's stone and sling. More of the stories. Her touch trailed down his spine. Down the leafless tree with its winding, twisting branches, where the snake coiled and roots stretched out to his waist. Her fingers slid to the lion's face that covered his lower back where she lingered ever so slightly. Chills covered his skin, and as if feeling it, she pulled away. He reached for his shirt.

"They'll fade some with time," he said needing to break the silence. "It's been less than a year, so they're still quite dark." He hoped that might comfort her.

But why it mattered, he really didn't know.

Ella was looking down at his chest where the windmill covered his heart. An exact copy of the landscape from one of the postcards Mimi had kept in her satchel. One of the few things they had of their father's previous life. The place his sister had always dreamed of seeing.

"Is Holland her given name?" Ella asked.

He only ever wanted to be honest with her, so he tipped his head. "Not entirely. But it would depend on who you asked."

Ella's eyes skimmed across the windmill again.

"And really, none of us use our birth names with rubes. Most of us have a spare."

She looked at him, her thoughts nearly tangible. Which meant she heard what he was saying. Remembering the day they met. Her with that hospital ledger.

"Your name, sir?"

"Charlie. Lionheart."

He spoke quietly. "Aren't you going to ask why that is?"

She shook her head and a soft smile made him love her all the more for it.

Slowly he leaned nearer, his head beside hers. "And my name really is Charlie," he whispered. "I gave it to you that day because—I don't know. Maybe it was how you were treating Holland. And me."

He heard her mouth part in a smile. Stealing a little glance proved it.

"Well . . ." His voice was still soft. "Actually, it's Richard, but let's just stick with Charlie, all right?"

She pursed her lips sweetly, and much too tempted by the sight, he leaned back. Then heard Axel roll over with a throaty sigh . . . and a snort.

Ella looked past Charlie and her eyes shot wide. "Oh, my goodness! There's a lion." She rose and stumbled as she backed away.

At the shock on her face, Charlie laughed which only brought another sleepy snort from the beast behind him.

"Why didn't you tell me there was a lion there!" she cried.

"There's actually three. You didn't see them?" He beckoned her back, but she shook her head and he looked over his shoulder to see Axel laying the closest, mane poking through the bars, with a goofy, oversized housecat-sleeping smile. "There is no way on God's green earth that he is going to hurt you."

But with the look she threw him, he pushed himself to a stand. Still chuckling, he finished with his buttons then slid into his boots, ignoring both laces and buckles as he plucked up the lantern.

"Come on. Let's go where you won't get eaten." Besides, he had something to tell her and this space felt too intimate because the words he needed to speak were more so.

TWENTY-SEVEN

The night didn't feel dark. Not with the moonlight overhead and countless fireflies blinking above the tall grass, dipping and rising in the inky air. Ella was quiet as they walked, seeming to take in the sight of the glittering green bugs that lit up across the high meadow. As they walked, Charlie ran his hand up the side of his sleeve, remembering her touch. The markings. Each one being pricked into his skin.

Rushing his mind back to New York last year.

Mimi was gone from this earth. Holland but weeks old. His brawl with Olaf still fresh on mind and body when he'd agreed to take Holland's place and Madame had sent him to New York to arrange the deal.

By fine carriage, she'd taken him to a building that might have held all the airs of a prestigious hotel if it weren't for the ladies who had ushered them in. Dressed in bright silks and satins, cheeks unnaturally pink, eyes tired . . . then curious. An establishment that offered services aplenty, quiet at that noon hour.

Charlie had halted in the entryway. *"I don't know what you think you're doing—"*

Madame Broussard had held up a hand. From her leather satchel she pulled a pristine sheet of paper and offered it over. He read the contract, his stomach churning at the sight of what he was going to sign. The one that would make him a part of her show. So why had she brought him here?

"It would be rather cold of me to not offer this . . ." She handed over a different contract. *"An alternative, and I must say, a rather attractive one."* She tapped his shirt against his chest with her closed fan. *"But you'll need to take that off. Don't be prudish or I'll lose my patience and it's already thin."*

He would never forget the wretched sensation of standing there in the great parlor. The air ripe with perfume. Lavish furniture dripping with finery. Even the women leaning over the balcony were done up in pearls and ribbons. Powder and lace covering not nearly enough. Charlie feeling no different with his shirt aside as the two madames had studied him, conversing quietly behind their fans. Calculating.

Madame Broussard had never looked so pleased.

They'd stated sums. Figures. Then names— prospective clients. *Lady Olivier in New Hampshire. Mistress Chastain's oldest daughters in Boston.* The list went on. Women in every city they would visit that following season.

And as the procuresses pondered, more women had melted out of every nook of the upper floors.

Some lounging in rapt silence. Others whispering on the stairs. He'd tried to avert his eyes, but everywhere he looked, white-hot light spilled from the glass dome in the ceiling glittering on corsets . . . ruffles . . . lace. Women leaned forward on railings while others drew so near he was certain they could hear his pulse. He turned his focus to the marble beneath his boots.

Rock of Ages cleft for me.

Bind my wandering heart to thee.

He'd thought the words over and over—the tangle of hymns a prayer, a plea.

"But he is virtuous," Madame Broussard was softly saying.

Then the other Madame, her accent thick. *"So you have brought him here to see which of my beauties will change his mind."*

He'd blinked at the floor. The door. Then up into eyes of every color scattered around. Of all the moments of his life, save losing Mimi and Holland, that had been the bleakest.

"And his past?" the woman asked.

"A poor man's son," Madame Broussard said, then more softly, *"and he has a little girl."*

But not soft enough when more heads turned.

"You said he is vir—"

"The child is his sister's. He is . . . how do you say it? Her guardian."

Never had he felt so many eyes on him. The procuresses had stood there studying him. And all around, fans fluttering, little whispers. Some he wished he had never heard.

"Getting from one place to another is no trouble—he is with the circus," Madame said. *"The man who tames the lions."*

Murmurs hushed into silence as every eye in the room stared at him.

All save the beat, beat . . . beat of his failing heart.

"His name?" someone asked, and then a young woman in an ivory gown was moving closer.

Hands at his sides, Charlie had fisted them, praying the Madame wouldn't . . .

"A Mr.—" Madame Broussard tapped her cigarette over a glass dish, *"Lionheart."*

The word whispered around the room. An echo. His soul on its knees. The young woman sat on a settee and glanced up at him. Leaning forward onto the curved arm, her gloved fingers brushed beneath her chin, eyes fixated—pretty face so pale, it made his heart hurt. She studied him for a long moment and the room was quiet.

What did she see?

Was the story that bled into his heart making its way to his brow? The one his father told him as a boy. Of Christ's temptation in the wilderness.

Was this his wilderness? His soul for bread?

The words blew in on the breeze from the overhead windows, floating down to him on traces of perfume.

The devil taketh him up into an exceeding high mountain, and sheweth him all the kingdoms of the world, and the glory of them; And saith unto him, All these things will I give thee, if thou wilt fall down and worship me.

He looked to Madame—to the two different contracts in her grasp. Would she stop before his knees hit stone?

He knew the answer to that, which was why he glanced back to the courtesan. The young woman continued to take him in. Searching. Probing. Her eyes on his skin were filled with sorrow as if she knew what the Madame had planned.

And so like a lifeline, she rose and turned ever so slowly in a circle for him. Her saddened glance to his face nearly pleaded with him to choose her. A kindness. A mercy. He let his gaze linger from the folds of her silk gown to the tumble of red hair spilling against her neck. The madames' whispered murmurs sounded more pleased the longer he looked. Their dark heads tipped together as they stood beneath a mounted tapestry declaring *Carpe Noctem*.

Seize the night.

And him not knowing that for his defiance, those curling, coiling letters would be the very first tattooed to his skin.

But all he could think of in that moment was the little girl—just weeks old—with no mother to hold her. No father to protect her. All she had in the world was him, a man who knew nothing about raising a child, but he was certain it would begin by walking out those doors.

"He . . ." The young woman's gaze danced over him. *"He wants to leave."* Her voice, grieved, was laced with something more. Wonder.

Charlie looked at her. An unfathomable story in the courtesan's eyes, he knew she had been a girl like Holland once.

Unbunching his shirt from his palms, he had slid it on. Taking the pen Madame held, Charlie dipped ink and signed the bottom contract. Olaf was still at the doors as he walked toward them, but the large guard didn't stop him and Charlie wondered what kind of signal the Madame had given.

As Charlie had walked back to his hotel, he'd fought the burn in his throat over what he had just done, of what was to come; a burden that he and he alone would bear. And the next day, Madame Broussard had brought him to the artist. The one known for both skill and innovation with his invention of the electric tattoo needle.

It was the first time in Charlie's life he'd ever been alone. Each night in that tiny hotel room, Madame and her massive guard across the hall. She certain he wouldn't run since the very thing he needed most was a little girl hidden away, awaiting him.

The needle to his skin for hours every day,

the pain had been so great he couldn't lie down. Couldn't sleep. Spent hours sitting on the floor in the middle of the room, a fever slicking sweat to his skin as his body fought to reject the ink. Just under three weeks the tattoos had taken. And on the final night, he lay awake, facing the wall. Stared down an emptiness he hadn't known was possible. A hatred for Lucca so strong, he ached to sate it.

Stared at the black words of *Carpe Noctem* etched onto his forearm.

Then to the vow he'd countered hers with.

He looked at Ella now. Searched her face, praying to have the words. For though he'd never wanted to tell a creature of those days— and he knew this wasn't the time—he wondered if perhaps he could find the way for her to know that there was no place God could not go. No chasm too deep where He couldn't reach down . . .

Charlie wanted to take her hand so badly, he had to cram his own in his pocket, then realized that if he didn't pay attention to what he was doing and stop walking, he'd lead them to the next state. He stopped abruptly, trying to get his bearings.

"Why don't you sit down," he said.

Ella sank in the grass and smoothed her dress around her knees.

Charlie knelt across from her, sitting back on

his boots. "So now I know why people are always reaching out to touch me."

Her expression changed. "Oh, Charlie, I'm sorry. I didn't even think of that."

He shook his head to void her apology. He had no words to describe how different her touch was, and it was just as well, because he *really* needed to not think about it right now. He coughed into his hand, to clear his throat and head. When that failed, he chuckled and looked at her. "You are a very distracting woman."

"*I'm* distracting?" A smile tinged her voice. "And what would you be? There was a lion two feet from you and I didn't even notice."

He grinned. "You noticed eventually."

"Eventually."

Charlie tugged on his hair, then circled his mind back to what he wanted to say to her. "Ella. There are two parts to me right now. If I'm to be honest, what I'd like to do is spend what little time I have left convincing you of how much I want to be with you and that I think you should really think about wanting to be with me." Despite everything. And oh, he was rambling.

She watched his face closely.

"But there's another part of me that has to stop that thought and to simply tell you something I need you to know."

"All right."

Still knelt, he inched closer so that their knees

nearly touched. From the camp, Axel let out a low, long bellow, followed by Kristov.

Charlie took her hands in his. "Ella . . . there is a God who loves you."

She went to pull away, but he gripped the slightest bit firmer. "Please, just let me say this and then you can walk away forever if you want to." But he could see in her eyes that she didn't. God help him, he needed to find the words. "When you told me that day in your apartment, of what happened, I can't even express to you my sorrow. For your sake." He held out his hands. "I could commit violence, Ella." He'd thought of it a hundred times if not more. "I'm angered by it. So angered."

She slipped her fingers free of his and he could see that he was losing her. That she was about to run. If not in body, then in spirit. He tried to not feel fear over that.

"But then I try to think through your mind and your heart and . . ." He reached out to grip the back of her head. "I need you to know what an incredible person you are. And also, that as a woman, you're perfect."

Her bottom lip trembled.

"Do you understand what I'm saying?"

She nodded gently.

"You are so precious to me," he whispered as a tear slid down her cheek.

"But there is a part of you that isn't whole."

When she blinked quickly, he reached out and nearly pressed his fingertips to where her heart lived. "It grieves me to think of why that is and I can't go another minute without telling you that there is a God. And he loves you so much. He *aches* for you. He can be a jealous God, and at times even angry. I believe . . ." with his whole heart . . . "that He is both of those on your behalf."

She peered up to his face.

"I don't know why this happened, and I confess that I sometimes wonder about God's ways. What He allows to happen. But, Ella," he lowered his head to peer up at her, "do you think that you are a different person now than you were then?"

She nodded and he hoped she didn't think he meant in body, so he said as much. She nodded again.

"When I am gone from you I will be praying for you. And that prayer," he said taking her hand, "will be for you to be whole again. Right here." He touched his chest. "For you to have peace." He gripped her hands in one of his and held them tight. "That man stole something he had no right to take from you."

She turned her face to her shoulder.

"And he has the power to take more from you, if you let him." He slid his arm around her, his hand to her back where her heart beat against it.

347

His voice was suddenly very small. "Please don't let him take more."

She tilted her face down, her braid brushing his arm.

"The Bible speaks of both God's wrath and His mercy, and He will fight this battle for you. Do you think you could trust in that?"

She pursed her lips and he could see the indecision on her face.

"That God is not against you, Ella." Charlie smoothed her hair away from her face. "He is *for* you."

Gently she nodded and he knew she needed time to ponder that. Perhaps quite a lot. So soft, so melancholy, the lions' roars rose one over the other. Claiming their territory. Calling for him to come back.

"My Bible. Do you think I could give it to you? For you to keep?"

She seemed to think on that a minute. Finally, she spoke. "You keep it. Truly." She twisted her fingers together, eyes down. "Because you can do so much good with it. You help people. And I'm just one person."

Her words pulled at his heart, but if he were to be honest with himself, he expected her to say something like that. He grappled for some way to encourage her. But then she was speaking.

"But do you think you might write that part down for me? That you read on Sunday. The one about being weary?" She tucked her hands in her lap. "I'd like to read it again."

His throat was so tight, the answer would scarcely come out. "I'd be happy to." There seemed no more space for words, so he simply pulled her close and she leaned into him, the side of her face to his shoulder, him holding the back of her head.

Charlie closed his eyes, knowing he needed to say one more thing. A first for him, and it would be nothing but the truth. "I love you, Ella," he whispered.

With her hip in the grass beside his, she curled against his chest, suddenly seeming very small. He sensed he had overwhelmed her, so he just held her, not even caring for an answer. He really didn't want one, for it would make what he had to do tomorrow all that much harder.

He would take her home. And he would leave her there.

TWENTY-EIGHT

Standing in the red wagon, Ella looked over to see that Angelina was as downcast as she. The morning had flown by, it seemed, and now with the dinner hour almost over and Charlie's maps declaring that it was time for the pair of them to turn northeast, it was time to say goodbye.

"You will be in our prayers." Angelina's eyes were wet.

Ella nodded fiercely. "Thank you." She swiped at her own cheeks. "I wish I could write you. This place Charlie mentioned where you stay in the winter?"

"I will give you the address." Angelina took a scrap of paper and jotted it down. "If you tell me where I can send *you* letters, I'll do that too. It would be a joy. Perhaps I can send you a photo of my husband and I one day."

The thought was so bittersweet that another tear slid down Ella's cheek. Combined with the joy of knowing Angelina would one day have her sweetheart, was that of Charlie. And what the time ahead might hold for him.

She hugged Danielle and then Evangeline, unable to believe that she was truly leaving. But she'd known this day would come. It was time to go home. It was time. She'd told herself that over and over last night while the sound of exotic animals flooded the night air. The knowledge that Charlie was but steps away.

And that he loved her.

Feeling more tears coming, Ella wiped at her eyes and glanced around the cozy wagon once more. Took in the lace, the fringe, and the faces of the three sisters she'd come to care for. So very much. Knowing she had another goodbye to say, Ella sucked in a deep breath and forced herself down the wagon steps.

Earlier, she'd bid farewell to Little Joe and the other people she had come to know. Now, she looked across the way to see Charlie loading another saddlebag onto his black and white horse. He'd borrowed another horse to pull his wagon, and while he hadn't told her as much, she sensed he'd paid one of the laborers to see Holland and Regina and his wagon safely along in his absence. Charlie was to be gone only two days. She'd heard that soon, the caravan would pull into Charlottesville and the matinee would need its showman.

She drew closer as he slid a pistol into one of the saddlebags, followed by a box of bullets. Inside he'd already placed her things, including the hair wrap Angelina had given her as a gift. One Ella would treasure always.

Charlie finished strapping another blanket

in place when Regina called him over to the wagon. He spoke with the small woman, then carried over a crate which seemed to hold food. With practiced movements, he tucked a few jars and little bundles into the saddlebags, followed by a knotted sack. Sensing Charlie was close to finished, Ella went to stand by Regina. She reached down and took the woman's warm hands.

"Thank you for everything," Ella whispered.

Regina waited for Ella to bend down then touched the side of Ella's face. "A joy to know you, *mia cara*. A *joy*." Her thumb slid back and forth with motherly affection.

Ella soaked in the sight of her face, knowing how she would miss this spunky woman. Charlie asked for the matches and as Regina stepped away, a different voice had Ella turning.

"Knock, knock." Madame Broussard came toward them, her black hair pulled back tight, a cameo at the throat of her dark green blouse. She looked at Ella so coolly that Ella felt it wise to step away.

"So the time has come," the woman said.

Charlie yanked a strap tight and tucked the loose end in. "What do you want?"

"A warm welcome for starts." With a flick of her wrist, the Madame lifted up a scrap of paper, silencing him. To Ella it was so small pinched between two fingers, but at the way Charlie suddenly went mute, a shiver of fear slipped through her.

"This is the best yet."

Ignoring her, he moved around to the other side of the horse. The Madame followed him and spoke in quiet tones. Charlie shook his head, his voice low and controlled, but Ella heard anger there.

The woman said something sharp and glared at Ella. Charlie's gaze lifted as well—for the briefest of seconds—before answering the Madame. Now he was really angry.

He walked around the horse and she followed, still speaking. Finally his hands stilled in their work. Charlie rested them on the saddle. The woman watched him several moments, then she slipped the paper in his shirt pocket and strode away. Charlie didn't move. Head bowed, he stared at the ground.

Ella came to his side. His eyes were closed. As if sensing she was there, he looked over at her. "We need to be going. You should say goodbye to Holland."

Ella knelt beside the carved bed and looked down at the girl that had been swept into her arms one snowy day. Lying on her side, hands clutching a worn blanket, Holland was asleep. Pink lips puckered. Black lashes fanning her pale skin. Ella brushed her mouth against the silky, round cheek and whispered a prayer for her.

Then another for the man who was more papa than her father had ever been.

At the side of the wooden bed was a basket, and Ella pulled out Holland's blue knit cap, turning it in her hands. Charlie stood quiet in the doorway as Ella felt the wool then reached for the tiny sweater, cradling both to her chest—remembering. She looked down at Holland and slid her hand along her warm back. "I love you," Ella whispered.

Tears blurred Ella's vision, and blinking them back, she let her finger trace the carvings in the side of the petite bed. Moons and stars and little doves. Her thumb grazed over the hand-hewn letters of *Holland Lionheart*.

Leaning forward, Ella pressed her lips to those golden curls—feeling the warmth of the baby's skin. Hearing her gentle exhales. The lump in her throat was nearly more than she could bear. "You take care of your papa, all right?"

From her side vision, she saw Charlie run a hand down his face. He stepped from the wagon and crossed away, both hands in his hair.

Ella pressed a kiss to Holland's silken neck and slammed her eyes closed. Her arms trembled as she gently held the baby close for one more heartbeat.

Then she rose.

Let Charlie help her down from the wagon.

And barely remembered him leading her toward the horse.

"I'd like to walk," Ella said. "Which way?"

Charlie pointed northwest, and using her palms to wipe her eyes, Ella started in that direction. She couldn't stop to think. Couldn't do anything but walk because she had to. And to stop and think too hard about it, would change her mind.

So she walked . . . and walked . . . and suddenly Charlie was beside her, leading the horse.

He didn't speak and she was glad. It was all she could do to keep breathing. The meadow rose, and above loomed hills and trees which grew darker as the land neared the sky. Ella swiped her sleeve over her eyes. She told herself to keep walking, lasting but a few minutes, until she was sinking to the ground.

Charlie knelt beside her, his hand warm and strong to the side of her head, pulling her to his chest.

"I don't know how to do this," she whispered.

She shouldn't have spoken the words, not with the position she was putting him in. It felt so selfish. He was taking time to bring her home—all which that entailed—and here she was, on the ground.

His hand slid to her shoulder and squeezed it. "Let's get you on the horse," he said softly.

She knew he needed to hurry, so she let him help her up. "I'm so sorry."

"Don't be sorry."

When she placed her shoe in the stirrup, he gripped her waist and lifted her toward the pommel. Ella pulled herself into the saddle and sat, arranging her skirts as best she could. Her gaze fell to Charlie as he moved around to the other side of the horse, took up the reins, and silently led them on.

TWENTY-NINE

The land slowly mounting, Charlie led Siebel across another knoll, so thick and lush he'd have thought it had swallowed them up if it weren't for the trees in the distance telling him they would soon climb higher. Ella rode a ways, silent and sniffing, that sleeve of hers continually dabbing at her eyes. This was killing him. He slowed the horse, dug around in his pack, and handed her a handkerchief.

After the horse bobbed along a few more steps, she recovered some and asked him to let her down. Charlie gripped her waist and lowered her. She walked at his side, not so near that he might think her his, but near enough . . .

"That should be the road," he said as the land rose into the looming mountains. It didn't really look like more than a rabbit trail, but this had to be the spot. Ella walked on ahead and crouched in front of a small, crooked sign. Weatherworn and time beaten, she ran her fingers over the name of the pass that Charlie couldn't read until he drew closer.

"This is the one," she said.

They walked on, the trail firm and grassy as if few had passed on it since the last snow. The air was warm, heavy. Spring flowers budded on both sides of the trail with nary a stone underfoot. Charlie sensed that as they climbed, that would change, but for now the horse had an easy way of it. Though Siebel's shoe was repaired, that lingering limp made each *clomp-clomp-clomp* slower than usual. Proved more so as the day wore on.

The trail continued to narrow. Saplings grew tall on each side, nudging him and Ella together, and Charlie minded not one bit. The breeze whistled through leafless branches, rattled budding blossoms.

Over his life, he'd grown adept at gauging miles. An awareness for time and distance; it was nothing but miles that had always separated them from one town to the other. Each traveled on foot. As a boy, he knew how far to run, how heavy he needed to pant, before he'd reach another mile marker on certain roads. He knew now that he and Ella had gone about four on the steepening path. Confirmed further by the way everything was changing. Dark green shrubs draped along both sides of the road, and some kind of mist was settling around them, cooling his skin, coiling the ends of Ella's hair.

"What is this place?" he asked.

"Just a hollow." She held out a hand, letting the mist weave through her fingers.

"But this is a cloud," he said matter of factly.

A little light in her eye made him think she was trying to replace tears with smiles. "It happens sometimes as you rise."

"Oh. I don't often go into the mountains much." Really not ever, but he felt like an idiot to confess that.

She turned back around. A leaf in her fingertips, she twirled it one way, then the other before dropping it. "There's a name for that."

He waited until he caught up with her and searched for his cheeriest voice. "Is it better than rube?"

She smiled gently and told him that it was 'flatlander.'

When her shoulder brushed his, her hand feeling too right beside his, he stepped away, reaching for Siebel's line instead. "Yeah." He examined the area. "I suppose I am."

They crossed into a high meadow, the grass spring green and soft underfoot. A homestead loomed in the distance, the garden dark and plowed, seeds no doubt waiting just underground. Siebel was slowing, so Charlie mentioned stopping for a rest. They walked on a while and then Ella motioned toward a pocket of an oak grove where a fallen log would make an easy perch. Following her, Charlie led the horse to where he could roam, then poked around in the saddlebags for something to eat.

Along with two red apples, he brought over

peanuts in a striped paper bag that actually coaxed a small laugh out of Ella.

"Circus food," she said, a play of brightness in her cheeks as she took the crinkling bag. "In the woods."

Charlie cracked a peanut and tossed the shells at his feet. "Another first. I should have brought some lemonade too."

Her faint smile warmed him.

Nearby, Siebel munched acorns, which was all right, but Charlie knew they would need to be moving on before he ate too many. He gave Ella and the horse a few more minutes of rest then brushed bits of peanut shells from his pants and stood. "We better be going or Siebel's gonna give himself a stomachache."

Ella swiped her hands together and tucked the peanuts into the saddlebag. He assumed she was content walking, and it was just as well for he liked having her near. As the trail climbed into their next mile, the soil darkened. Trees became more and more spindly, stretching skyward in thick groves, all reaching for the sun. Moss grew on the shaded sides of rocks. Squirrels scampered loudly along branches. The path here was rutted with gnarled roots weaving this way and that, so their steps were slow as Charlie led Siebel up the winding trail. The horse kept favoring that front leg. A fact which had Charlie wary.

Afternoon was passing and the first nip of

coolness tinged the air. Then the quiet was interrupted by footsteps and voices. Charlie listened a moment as they walked, wondering if Ella did too. Seconds later, she lifted her head in that direction and Charlie spotted two men striding toward them. With guns slung over their shoulders and a pair of pheasants in a meaty grip, their business was clear.

"Do you know those people?" Charlie asked, more for curiosity's sake. He didn't know how it worked for country folk.

"Possibly."

The distance closed between them and he could sense Ella scrutinizing the strangers. It was just as well since they were doing the same. Having drawn nearer, the hunters slowed. Charlie pressed a hand to Siebel's side, bringing him to a stop.

"Good afternoon," Charlie said when Ella was silent.

"Evenin'."

The man had a point, but Charlie had been trying to ignore that fact.

One of the men looked from him then to Ella where he lingered. His gaze skimmed her blonde hair, her face. He doffed his floppy hat. "Might you be one of the Beckley girls?"

"Yes, sir," she said.

His air was friendly. "Ya look just like your mama."

Her surprised catch of breath held a pocketful of meanings.

The man looked from Ella's bare ring finger to Charlie. Not really wanting to explain the tale, Charlie reached out a hand. "Charlie Lionheart." They shook and the man seemed to size him up. "Pleasure to meet you."

With a dip of his head, the man spoke. "Headin' home, Miss Beckley?"

"Yes, sir. How many miles would you say it is from here?"

The man scratched his balding pate and glanced back. " 'Bout seven."

Not good. Charlie did a few calculations as the pair made small talk about the area, the people. Suddenly feeling fidgety, Charlie was glad when the men bid their farewells.

"You rubes are strange creatures," he finally said. "I thought those men were gonna stay and talk forever."

"We are not strange. They were just being friendly." She gave him a small nudge with her elbow. "And it's not very nice to call people *rubes*."

The side of his mouth lifting, he paused. Then he scratched the back of his head and wondered if she was waiting for a response. Unable to walk away from the challenge, he thought a moment, then spoke in Ciazarn. Knowing she wouldn't understand, he asked her if she knew how beautiful she was in that yellow dress of hers. Her eyebrows tugged together in clear confusion and he laughed.

"If you had a drop of circus blood in you, you'd have known what I just said. So that would make you a *rube*." He paced closer, cupping her face in his hands. "But, my dear," he said softly, soaking in the sight of her stunned face for he was taking himself by surprise as well. He whispered as quiet as he could, "You called me a flatlander, so you started it."

He felt her smile form beneath his hands, saw it, bright like the sun. Mercy, he wanted to kiss her, so he pulled away and clicked his tongue, nudging Siebel onward.

They passed several more farms and outcroppings as the sun drooped below the tree line. Here and there a dogwood was giving up its blooms. Charlie asked about her family and she told him of her parents, Milly and Holden. And while they stopped by a creek to water the horse once more, she described brothers and sisters.

Charlie leaned against a tall, spindly tree, and as Ella rinsed her hands in the gurgling water, she explained that she was the eldest, and then there was Elizabeth and James, the twins, two years younger than her, who had both married and had homes of their own. Next was Connor, who was fifteen. Danny was coming up on ten, and young Beth would soon be eight.

Having learned long ago how to sort strangers, he paired the names and numbers together, then filed them away in the back of his mind. He moved to the creek's edge and filled a water skin, fastened it to the saddle, then took up the horse's reins and motioned for them to walk on.

"Are you doing okay?" he asked.

She gave what seemed like a forced smile. "It's good to be going home."

"I'd imagine so."

"But I will miss you." Her blue eyes followed his movements as he walked.

He wanted to tell her that he missed her too. Already. More than she could possibly know, but he held his tongue, because God help him he was trying to retain some shred of sanity. But he didn't want her words to hang there, so he bent toward her and pressed a kiss to her warm hair, cupping the back of her head ever so gently. He hoped that said what he couldn't.

Perhaps he ought not to have done that. Perhaps it would have been better to harden his heart and let her think him indifferent. But he didn't want any regrets in this life and that would have been one of them.

"Where will you go from here?" she asked.

"After Charlottesville, toward the coast and then north toward Baltimore. Then up, maybe as far as Massachusetts before we come back down to New York where we'll land at Coney." He spared her a glance. "Why? Are you thinking of running away and joining the circus for good?"

She blinked at him.

"Because if you are, I know some folks who would take you."

She nodded, then pressed a hand over her mouth.

Oh, he shouldn't have said that. "Please don't start crying again." But her chin just trembled, so Charlie dug around in the saddlebag and handed her the handkerchief again. "You should ride now."

"Please, I'd rather walk."

"You're slowing down and we still have some ground to cover." He wasn't quite ready to tell her that they weren't going to make it tonight. He was still trying to come to grips with it himself. The fact that—without a shadow of a doubt—the two of them would be passing the night in these woods.

"When do you have to be back?" she asked as shadows stretched long.

"Saturday. I absolutely must be there for the matinee." Two and a half days.

"Will you make it in time?"

"Yeah." He had to. He glanced around. Time to say it. "Look, Ella. It's going to be dark in half an hour. How far do you think we are from your home?"

She surveyed the land around them as if hunting

for familiarity. "I'm not sure. I didn't come this way ever. It was always Papa's doing. How many miles do you think we've gone since we spoke to those men?"

"Three." He'd been gauging them. It was more like two, but he didn't want to discourage her. And now he was feeling like a liar, so he confessed the truth.

"You could ride this horse, too," she said.

"I'll walk, thanks."

"We'd get there faster."

Something he had no desire to do, for even now, he knew that when they came upon her father's house, his heart would be the worse for it. And riding the horse—he couldn't quite handle the thought of her putting her arms around him, or his around her. No. He'd walk. "The horse is tired and he won't be able to handle anything other than you."

She looked regretful for having made the suggestion.

"Look, Ella, I want you to decide. I can get up on Siebel with you and we can ride for a while, but he truly is tired. His hoof is bothering him and this is a different terrain than he's used to which isn't helping. So I don't know how far that'd get us. Or, we can just press on like this. Possibly be there late tonight around midnight or later." He shifted his head at a pesky gnat. "*Or,* we can stop and get settled while we can still see.

We've been following a creek for a while now and just passed an old camp. It's as good a spot as any. Then we would get to your parents' in the morning. It's up to you."

She didn't say as much when she'd spoken of what had been done to her, but by what she shared—walking home from church that night— he sensed it would have been along a wooded path. Perhaps like this. The thought of her being afraid of him churned his stomach and he had to let her know there were other options.

She reached out and patted Siebel's neck. A pink sunset burned over her shoulders. "We can stop. It would be a good idea to rest the horse." Her eyes didn't quite meet his. "And then get an early start tomorrow. I haven't seen my folks in so long, and they're not expecting me, so I don't want to startle them in the middle of the night. It would be best to stop."

He took a moment to let her words sink in. Finally he nodded. "Then we'll stop."

THIRTY

Ella blinked into the growing dark as she followed Charlie and his horse to the clearing he'd circled them back to. The rooted and rutted path mellowed into a small grassy pasture. Charlie dropped the lead rope and stepped to the creek which wound and gurgled beneath thick trees.

Returning, he loosened the buckle of the saddle. "How can I help?" Ella asked.

Charlie glanced around and mentioned something about a fire. "You could gather up some kindling. Pile it right here." He pointed to a ring of stones that looked like it had been used for that purpose many times. "I'll get it going and there'll be some light."

Saddle hefted aside, he clicked his tongue and called the horse to the creek where the animal drank deeply. Charlie gathered up larger scraps of wood and added it to Ella's pile of sticks. She brushed the grit from her hands and dress front as he knelt in front of the stones.

He arranged the smallest scraps together, and using the matches from his saddlebag, had it lit. On his knees, he lowered his face and blew gently on the flames, coaxing them brighter and stronger. Ella turned to keep busy. She focused on the necessities. Food. Something to sleep on.

Probably best not to go poking around in his stores, so she worked his odd knot that held her own gunnysack to the saddle.

He moved to her side. It took but a moment then he had it free. She set the sack aside and tugged out her blankets. The air was fully black now. Fire crackling a halo in the center of the clearing.

Ella looked around. Where to put herself?

As if sensing her uncertainty, Charlie motioned toward the fire. "That's gonna be your best bet."

Clutching up her sack, Ella carried everything nearer to the flames. She set her blankets down, and not wanting to go about making a bed just now—or think of what that entailed—she sat on the pile like a little seat and, feeling the dark all around, watched the flames grow. Charlie carried over a bundled sack and set it near.

"Supper." Next he brought over a bedroll, insisting she take it as he set it beside her. Ella slowly glanced at it.

"It won't bite, Ella."

An easy silence settled as Charlie tethered the horse to a low branch. He spoke soft and low, coaxing the horse's leg from the ground to examine that hoof.

Charlie lowered the animal's leg again and stroked his side. Then he glanced around and said, "I'm going to go fetch some water." With deft hands, he rummaged about in his things and took up the canteen before heading off.

He was gone a lot longer than it would take to fill the jug and he returned with wet hair. His shirt was dry but clung to his skin as if the latter were still damp.

Ella pulled her knees in and gripped her ankles, staring at the fire. A heavy longing for Holland made cracks in any rest the quiet might have offered. Thoughts of home were the thread stitching all things back together. But the thread didn't feel strong enough.

Charlie leaned toward her and freed the jar of dried apples from the sack. He popped the lid, let her take a handful, then took some for himself. She broke a piece of dark bread and gave him the larger portion. He sat opposite her, and with their simple supper formalized, she nibbled on a piece of sweet apple.

"You look just like the Princess and the Pea sitting there on that perch of yours," he said.

With a soft chuckle, Ella shifted on the mound of bedding. "I'm not terribly used to sleeping outside." Feeling more a field mouse than a princess, she unraveled her braid only to work fingers through it and bind it back up with pins from her sack. A swipe at her forehead caught traces of grit there.

It would be nice to see her folks tomorrow somewhat clean. She mulled on the idea a few more minutes. "I'd like to wash up myself."

He looked at her as if surprised she'd be so brave. "Um." He peered off to where the creek was. "I promise I'll sit right here and won't move."

Of that she was surprisingly certain. Ella rose and shuffled through her things for soap and rag, as well as the cotton hair wrap Angelina had given her, which could serve as a towel. She strode off, and with the night enveloping all around, glanced back at Charlie.

"Would you like me to walk you?" he called.

"No, it's fine." But she looked into the blackness that shrouded the creek. Just to follow the sound of the water perhaps . . .

She took a few steps, but then Charlie was striding toward her and on ahead. Ella's eyes adjusted to the pale moonlight until she could see her feet. Then Charlie's hand was on hers.

"There's an embankment here," he said. "Watch your step."

She did, but nearly stumbled on a root.

"This here," he said when they reached the bottom, "is a little pool. It's not real deep but it's freezing. So don't drown, because I do *not* want to have to come and save you."

Ella smiled. "I promise not to drown."

He turned and pointed the way they'd come. "You can see the fire? That's where I'll be."

"Thank you."

He strode back up the bank into the clearing where he settled beside dancing flames.

Now. How to do this? With the darkness and *not-quite* aloneness, she was inspired to stay in corset and petticoat and sponge bathe along the edge.

But mercy that water stung.

She scrubbed vigorously at her arms, savoring the feel of being clean. Hair already pinned up, she ran the cloth over her neck and shoulders, trying not to dampen the lacy straps of her chemise. Water trickled as she washed her face. A chill taking over, she snatched up the scarf and ran it over her skin. She glanced toward the fire where Charlie sat, arms still on his knees. He broke a small stick in two and looked about to throw a piece into the flames when his face turned her way. Shrouded in darkness, Ella didn't flinch.

Perhaps he'd heard her grow quiet.

"I'm not drowning," she called out.

His chuckle was soft.

Sliding back into her dress brought the regret at having not fetched a clean skirt and blouse. But with sleeping on the ground, perhaps it was best to leave that for the morning. A few buttons later, she heard a slow, thrashing sound. Something heavy ambling on the opposite side of the creek. She snatched up her boots with stockings still tucked inside and strode up the bank. The circle of the fire pulled her nearer to him and she sat so close that her hip brushed his.

"It's probably just someone's pig," he said calmly. His gaze flicked to the darkness where she'd been, then back to her, lingering.

It took a few minutes to thaw and then she plucked a stocking free of her boot, and turning sideways, poked her bare foot out from beneath her hem, slipping the soft cotton over her toes and past her heel. Charlie inched away some, giving her space. Hands safely hidden beneath her skirt, she tugged the stocking up her calf, sliding it snug above her knee.

His eyes followed the movement.

Her fingers grazed the little garter clips at her thigh, but she wasn't about to even *attempt* those with him watching. Fighting a blush, Ella pulled the other stocking free. Her eyes lifted back to Charlie. Oh, why hadn't she done this out of sight? She couldn't very well hobble into the dark with one stocking on. As if realizing her struggle, Charlie glanced away. Ella slipped her toes into the other stocking and tugged it up that bare calf. Finished, she straightened skirts and forced herself to tuck her hands in her lap.

Charlie glanced back to her, his eyes taking her in for such a long quiet moment, her heart began to pound. Then he blinked quickly, picked up his bread and tore a piece.

She made sure her skirts were righted.

"Don't worry, Ella," he said quietly as he stood. "You're modest."

He moved to the opposite side of the fire and sat, not looking at her.

Minutes passed in silence. Every so often, he circled a hand around his wrists. A habit, she'd once thought, but now she knew why.

Every muscle hurt as she rose. Ella rummaged around in her box of medicines and pulled out the salve. Knowing it wisest, she removed the lid and simply handed it to him.

"Charlie. Why do they do this to you?" She settled opposite him again. "Why the bars, those chains?"

It wasn't until he'd rubbed the ointment into his skin and placed the lid back on the tin that she realized he wasn't going to answer that. Water gurgled in the creek, and around that, the gentle sound of Siebel tugging up grass kept an easy, chomping rhythm. Wind rustled along the treetops, all the sounds ebbing and flowing together until his gentle voice rose over it all.

"My sister was a flyer. A trapeze artist."

Ella lifted her head.

"So was Lucca, her husband. But he was an addict. Liquor, opium—whatever he could get." Charlie tugged a suspender from one shoulder, then the other, letting them hang loose. "He pushed her too hard, too soon. Some say her death was an accident, but I say it was something that could have been prevented."

Ella thought back to the show under the Big Top. The way the flyers flipped from one swinging bar to another—a woman trusting a man to catch her. The clap of hand to wrist. Flesh to flesh. The poof of powder and the cheer of the audience. A feat of strength and perfection that was the careful precision the circus balanced on. She recalled a net below, but grief coiled to think of it failing Holland's mother. Of everything failing her.

"When Mimi fell, she was gone instantly, they say. Someone came and found me and it's all a blur. We realized that Lucca was gone. Everyone searched, but . . . nothing. I thought he'd taken the baby with him, but then rumor spread that she was with the Madame."

"And her father—?"

"Walked away a rich man. I assume he fled the country, though I don't know. Holland was already gone—hidden away. And I'd been baited by Madame and her cohort."

"Baited?"

"I'm not certain but Holland may have just been a means to an end for her. Which was why I didn't ask anyone to help me. They would have fought for her, but it would have cost them their livelihoods and Madame would have just searched for another way."

"What do you mean?"

"I, uh . . . it's—" He ran a hand down his

lightly-bristled jaw a few times. "It's hard to explain delicately."

When she assured him she didn't mind, he blew out a slow breath and studied her a few quiet moments, eyes unflinching as if weighing a heavy decision. Then he spoke. Told her the story. Of wealthy women who didn't shy away from scandal and how he'd stepped into the middle of it all. He told her of a brothel and then weeks spent in a hotel room. Hours upon hours with the needle because he'd refused to give himself any other way. She was nearly speechless when he finished.

"The Madame protects her assets," he continued. "Whether it's keeping scissors out of Angelina's reach or making sure that Arnold always gets brought to his stand on time, she's very protective of what she can make a profit on. And because the nature of my contract is much different than theirs, I knew the Madame would have been unhappy to find you in my tent. With me."

Her jaw fell a little.

"I hope that doesn't make you uncomfortable."

"Would she have thought—?"

"She would have thought what she wanted because to her nothing should be given. Not if it could have a fee. And I think she's been waiting for me to defy her on that." His brow unfurrowed, glance tentative. She was surely staring at him because his mouth quirked up the tiniest bit. "I've shocked you."

Ella fought to keep her expression as quiet as possible. "No. I appreciate your honesty. Please don't be afraid," she said, meaning it.

With slow fingers, he peeled at the bark of a stick, flicking the bits into the fire, then finally the stick itself. The coals popped and he wiped hands to pants. "What I hate is that the women there were surely there for many reasons. I had opportunity at my fingertips to choose another way, but . . . may I ask you something?"

She nodded.

"Would you be able to envision another way for yourself? If you were desperate?"

Ella searched his eyes. What did she see there? A pained and unbridled empathy. "I—I don't know. I've never thought of it before."

"If you thought of it now."

Surely the answer lived in her soul, but even that felt like a well that went far, far, far down within her. Even the longest stretch of rope felt as if it would come up dry. "I don't know, Charlie. Why do you ask?"

Reaching over, he pulled a blanket nearer and unfolded it. It wasn't until he'd settled onto the dark wool that he spoke. "Because I can still see their faces."

His hand brushed against the cuff of his sleeve, agitating the skin as if it itched.

"You have compassion," she said softly.

But he looked at her as if all he had was sorrow. "The only one I could make a difference for was Holland." He rubbed his hand across the cuff of his sleeve again, pushing it up his forearm.

"Surely you made more of a difference than you realize."

He shook his head, looking doubtful. But she saw such strength in the man before her and water gurgled into that deep, deep well. Wetting the rope—breathing a whisper of an answer to her soul.

Brow turning pensive, he lowered his sleeve, but the images—the drawings—still flooded her mind.

To take such a burden upon himself. She hadn't even known such a choice was possible prior to a few days ago. Not to this extent. Until working for Dr. Penske, she'd never heard of a tattoo, let alone seen a man who was covered with them. Her attention was lost in it all until Charlie reached over and brushed a bit of hair away from her neck.

His touch having shot an electric current through her, Ella struggled to speak, but the truth rallied. "I am proud of you." She thought of all the names the crowd called him. Declarations that he was less-than.

She'd had such words thrown her way. Disgraceful. Unworthy. Ruined.

"Ella, I spend some time in very aristocratic circles. And those people would be mortified to discover who sat at their dinner table with his smart tie and his top hat. I know that Mr. Graven will do anything to keep my secret for that very reason, and I know that a father would surely never give me permission to marry his daughter. I know all of these things. But I'm going to hope anyway." Charlie moistened his lips. "Maybe I don't look like I should, but I'd like to think that this . . ." he pressed a hand to his shirt where it covered his abdomen, "isn't too much for God."

She circled his words, slowly. As if from a distance. But they struck harder than she liked because of the truth there. She thought of the tender way he'd spoken about her heart and the way she'd locked God out of it. His plea still surrounded her.

Please don't let him take more. Ella shifted, peering up at the sky.

"Which makes me thankful every single day that He'll have me." His grief was tangible.

Tears stinging her eyes, she blinked them away. "You're worth having, Charlie."

She peered back down just as the words visibly jarred him. He leaned forward, stoking up the fire, and it wasn't until he'd sat back down that he spoke. "You should go to sleep. We've got some ground to cover still tomorrow."

When she slipped between her blankets, he laid

down, still a few feet away. Settling on his back, he clasped his hands behind his head.

Turning toward the sky, Ella stared back up at the glittering, black spans between the treetops that hemmed the clearing. She closed her eyes, feeling the heat of the fire, the softness of this bed, and the sounds of the woods that had once filled her with fear. All of that was swathed in the comforting peace that goodness *could* win. It wasn't until she was starting to drift that she heard Charlie's gentle voice.

"Good night, Ella."

THIRTY-ONE

Morning came with birdsong. Blinking awake, Charlie looked over to the fire, the cold coals. He'd meant to tend the flames through the night, but exhausted, had slept too deeply. Somehow in the night he and Ella had come together like magnets, so he pressed his hand to the ground and pushed himself away. In the gray light of dawn, she lay in her bundle of blankets, hair wild in the dew and calling his fingers. Her brow furrowed as if she was dreaming. He wanted to smooth his thumb there . . . some way to ease her.

Charlie rubbed the heel of his hand over his eyes and forehead.

Last night he'd lain awake, just listening. When the forest quieted, he'd been awake for a different reason. It was his father who'd taught him to cling to hymns in times of doubt or fear. Charlie had been waiting twenty-five years for God to bring him to his bride, and last night— laying so close to the very woman he prayed it would be—he'd had to think on the words to many a hymn indeed. Somewhere between "Be Thou My Vision" and "Fairest Lord Jesus" he'd finally drifted off.

He woke with the words still in his head.

Now he rose and headed down to the creek. He

drank deeply, then stood and watched fish gather in the shallow pool.

From a tree behind him, a pinecone clattered to the ground. Charlie turned and walked back just as blue eyes blinked open. Ella spotted him and slowly sat up.

"Did you sleep all right?" he asked, not sure how to greet a woman waking up on his bedroll.

"I did." Clearly chilled, she pulled her knees in. "And you?"

"Well, thank you. Are you hungry?" At his saddlebag, he pulled out one of the little savory turnovers Regina had baked. He held it out to Ella and her eyes widened in surprise.

"Regina made them," he said. "She saw what kinds of things I was going to feed you and took pity."

She smiled up at him. "I'll have to thank her."

Dropping his focus to his own turnover, he nodded soberly. "I'll be sure to tell her for you." He rose and started putting things away while he ate. Then while Ella rolled up her bedding, he saddled Siebel. The black and white gelding seemed rested and Charlie patted his thick neck. He thought of the lions, feeling a void in his routine without them. He'd probably pay the consequences when he got back. The cats had a rambunctious way of letting him know when they'd been missing him.

Charlie turned to see Ella beside the fire,

tugging the pins from her hair. Several strokes with a bristle brush and she piled it low and secure. Rising, she gave him a shy look. "I'd like to change my clothes."

Rubbing his hand over his mouth, he glanced around. "There's some shrubs there."

She gathered up her things and he turned his back. He finished saddling the Vanner and secured the saddlebags again. He'd add Ella's things next, but he wasn't about to turn around to find out if she was done. A few minutes later, footsteps announced her return.

She wore a dark skirt, an airy white blouse, and a sash, reminding him of the night he'd kissed her.

A glance down also reminded him that he was just a Gypsy.

One who was standing there in his untucked, wrinkled shirt and boots with more buckles than boots ought to have.

He wanted to tell her she looked nice, but didn't know if she would smile or get shy—or Lord help him—start crying again, so he just secured the last of her things in place.

Starting off, they walked side by side, and he couldn't even bring himself to make small talk. The silence was right in its own way. He was thankful to simply be with her. By the time the sun had crested the tops of the trees, he asked her if she wanted to ride.

"No, thank you. I'd rather walk with you."

She had a sweet way of being honest, so he knew she meant it. Which had him reaching down, brushing his hand against hers, taking it gently in his own. She didn't pull away, and to his surprise, she slid her fingers between his as if to hold on. They walked on a long while. Whether one mile or two, he didn't know so distracted he'd become, but the road was smooth and steady, giving them no need to pull away. The sun rose higher, filling the air with warmth as morning turned into noon. Hours passed much too quickly, and as Siebel grew steadily slower, he knew it was time to rest that hoof.

But then Ella whispered, "We're almost there."

He had no response to that, so simply held her hand in his as they walked down past a bramble of berry bushes that were taller than his head.

Suddenly Ella drew in a quick breath. There in the distance he saw a house.

She turned toward him, eyes glassy. "Charlie."

He released her hand and looked to the house, a pain rising so fiercely, he couldn't remember how to speak. So this was it. He swallowed hard, knowing he couldn't very well just stand here. A goodbye. He needed to form a goodbye. "I'll leave you here," he finally said.

She shook her head, chin trembling. Unable to

bear the sight, he went about loosening her things from the saddle, but his fingers were trembling so bad that the knots wouldn't be coaxed loose.

"Not like this. Please," she said.

"It's for the best, Ella." What did she want? Him to walk her to the door? Introduce himself to her family? He untied a knot.

She shook her head no again. "Please."

Patience failing, he asked, "What do you want me to do?" This was killing him, and the sooner he turned around and left the better.

"Do you think you might stay for supper?"

He spoke before he changed his mind. "Do you think you might marry me?"

Her lips parted.

If not, there was really no point in her inviting him for supper.

He couldn't bear kindness. Not when he ached for more of her. Her wide eyes searched his face so intently that in two steps he was before her, hands to the sides of the face he loved.

Lowering his head, Charlie pressed his mouth to hers. Not calm and patient as he had the night on the roof. But urgent. Hungry. Her hand gripped the front of his shirt, the other pulling at his waist. She kissed him fervently, but even then her shock was tangible with eyes wide and hands trembling more than she probably realized. From somewhere, a door opened and closed and it was just as well because he'd told himself he wouldn't kiss her until she was safely home. And here they stood, a few brief seconds not nearly enough. Though he knew he shouldn't—plain sight or not—he eased three kisses down the side of her neck. The pulse of her throat pounded against his thumb and Ella dipped her face as if overwhelmed.

"I didn't say that to startle you," he whispered. "I'm genuinely asking you." Charlie forced his feet back, releasing her. She stumbled but he cupped her elbow.

Her shock was tangible, chest rising and falling.

Heart pounding in his ears, he rubbed at the back of his neck. There was probably a much better way to propose, but they were short on time.

And he had to know.

She was simply watching him, tears forming in her eyes. His stomach churned as moments passed. Why was she crying? Girls usually said *yes* if they wanted to.

Didn't they?

He'd tried to convince himself that maybe he didn't repulse her, but his defenses crumbled. What was he thinking?

He was in a freak show in the circus, for Pete's sake.

Standing here, seeing her grief, he knew he'd only been deceiving himself. Had been for months now. Trying to still think of himself as no different than any other man. Worthy of a bride. And like an idiot, he'd just asked a woman to marry him. And not just any woman. Ella. His Ella. To bind her heart and flesh to him. His chest rose and fell with the weight of it, heart thrashing against his ribs. "You've only known me for a week, and I know it's a lot for me to assume that it would be enough."

Her eyes were wet and shining—regret clear. He was going to be sick. She stepped closer. "Charlie . . ." her voice quavered. "I . . . I . . . this is so fast."

"Ella, is that you?"

The strange voice jolted Charlie. Ella turned just as a man was walking toward them. Hair misted gray and pulled back with a cord, his face was slightly weathered but he was by no means an old man.

It had to be her father. Charlie adjusted his grip on Siebel's lead rope.

"Papa?" Ella stepped forward then quickened into a run, belting into his embrace so quick, the tenderness struck Charlie square in the soul.

"Ella." The man ran his hand down the back of her hair, and lifting her off the ground, turned in a slow circle. The man's shoulders shook as he buried his face against her neck. "You've come home." His arms seemed to tighten. Then her father lifted his head and looked at Charlie . . . and lowered Ella back down.

She brushed a bit of hair from her face and turned back to Charlie as if just remembering he was standing there.

Really, the earth could swallow him whole now and he'd be happy.

"Papa, this is Charlie. Charlie Lionheart."

Expression wary, the man stepped forward and extended a meaty hand. Charlie wiped his own on the side of his pants and shook the firm grip.

"Charlie, this is my father."

"Pleasure to meet you, Mr. Beckley."

"Likewise." The man said it kindly then looked to Ella as if seeking answers.

"Oh. I've been in Roanoke, as you know . . ." She seemed to choose her words with care, and for the life of him, Charlie was glad she didn't look his way. "I knew it was time to come home and Charlie here is with the circus—"

"The circus?"

Ella nodded and Charlie could sense her nerves. "He's a lion tamer."

Those silver eyebrows shot skyward. So that's where she got it from. Mr. Beckley glanced over at him.

"Yes, sir," Charlie said. "Our troupe was in Roanoke and my niece was ill. Ella tended to her, and thinking I might . . . thinking I might be of service in getting her home to you, I came along to see her here safely."

Ella's father studied her a moment. "You traveled with the circus?"

She nodded sheepishly.

He gave a laugh. "You've got some explaining to do, daughter." When she blushed, he added, "And a few stories to tell, I'd imagine."

Her eyes lifted to Charlie's face and everything in him hurt.

"A few stories," she said, her voice holding all the bitter sweetness that he himself felt.

"Any one in particular I might need to be knowing about just now?" Mr. Beckley glanced between the two of them.

Ella gave a little shake of her head. Her gaze flicked to Charlie then back to her father. "We're not . . . we're not married," she said.

Her father looked his way and Charlie wondered how clear the view was from that front window.

"No, sir," Charlie added.

The man rubbed the side of his jaw. "Hmm."

Probably really clear. Charlie adjusted his grip on Siebel's reins again.

"That horse looks tired," Mr. Beckley said.

Charlie shifted his feet at once regretting this moment and relieved for the distraction from all Ella didn't say. His question—if she might have him—still hanging between them. "He's accustomed to it."

"Why don't you rest him a spell. You'll join us

for supper?" Her father's face was stern. "I'd like to meet the man who brought my daughter home all the way from Roanoke."

Hearing a challenge there, Charlie swallowed hard. "Yes, sir."

Charlie watched as Mr. Beckley held the front door open for Ella, and never had he heard a room in such a tizzy. Charlie hesitated, but the man motioned him forward, those eyes on him at once welcoming and searching. Inside the house, a woman was hugging Ella. Holding tighter than he'd ever seen someone be held. Charlie stepped back, nearly bumping up against a window. The woman and Ella exchanged words and tears and even laughter. It had to be her mother.

Charlie had never felt so tall and awkward. He'd always been good with crowds. But not this kind. Aside from the occasional business dinner or Ella's apartment, he'd never been inside someone's home before. He'd certainly never met a woman's family.

Ella turned to him. "Mama, this is Charlie Lionheart."

The woman looked his way and her husband added, "He's with the circus."

From the hallway, a young man emerged. "The circus!"

A little girl was close on the lad's heels, followed by another boy. Ella gave them all

390

hugs and the girl clung to her as she introduced them to Charlie. He tried to hang onto the names afresh, but his pulse was racing in his ears . . .

"You're from the circus?" the older boy repeated.

Words just wouldn't come, so Charlie nodded. He touched his collar to make sure it was securely buttoned. Then his cuffs. Ella watched him sadly and Charlie swallowed hard. He'd never been this nervous before. Made worse by the way Ella's father was studying his hand. It took all of Charlie's resistance to keep from cramming it in his pocket. He finally met the man's quizzical gaze. It was a leveled look that made the room close in. Charlie took a step back, nearly knocking a vase off the windowsill.

Ella's mother gave Charlie a kind smile. "Won't you sit down, Mr. Lionheart?"

He wanted to decline, but then she was pulling out a chair and offering him a cup of coffee. Swallowing his heart, he slowly sat. Ella's eyes were wide and wondering as she slid him little glances. But when her mother unleashed a bundle of curiosities, Ella responded in turn. Ella's brothers and sister were watching him and Charlie realized he hadn't answered that question.

"I *am* from the circus," he said gently to the young man.

"We've never seen a circus before."

Charlie smiled. The conversation easing him, he figured he'd do just that until he could leave. "Well, that explains a few things about your sister, then."

The boy laughed. "What do you do there?"

"I work with lions. Raising and training them."

"Lions!"

Charlie nodded.

The young man's mouth hung open a few moments. "You. Have. A lion."

"Three of them."

Arms still about one another, Mrs. Beckley finished saying something to Ella, then turned back to Charlie. "And what of your family, Mr. Lionheart?"

He looked at the woman and noted how much she resembled her oldest daughter. "I have a little girl," he said. "She's my sister's . . . who passed away last year."

"Oh, I'm so sorry."

Charlie nodded his thanks.

"It's just you and her then?"

"Yes, ma'am. And my godmother who lives with us. She helps take care of Holland as she's just a baby." Charlie turned the coffee cup in unsteady hands. "And me as I'm not very tidy."

Mrs. Beckley chuckled and Ella's eyes were wet and shining. "Holland is the baby's name," she said softly to her mother.

"And how did you come to know our Ella?" the woman asked after a moment.

He'd been waiting for that question. The very subject moved to the table and sat across from him, her sister leaning lovingly against her.

The sight shooting a pain through him, Charlie turned his attention to Mrs. Beckley. "I met Ella about a week or so ago." Just saying that out loud made him realize why she was prudent in hesitating. Charlie swallowed a lump in his throat. "Holland was real sick. We came to Roanoke, slowed down by weather, and so I brought her to the doctor's." He looked over at Ella, thinking of how he'd almost crashed into the nosiest nurse he'd ever met. His heart hurt at the memory. Throbbed really. But people were watching him and waiting, so he spoke. "And Ella took care of her."

"She's the most delicious doll you've ever seen, Mama," Ella added.

Mrs. Beckley laughed. "You say it as if you could eat her with a spoon."

Charlie smiled, missing her even more.

Mrs. Beckley's face turned thoughtful. "And she's not here?"

"No, ma'am. She's back with the circus. They're about a day ahead of me. I'll be catching up with them in Charlottesville."

"A day and a half, I'd say," Mr. Beckley cut in.

Which meant he needed to be going. Charlie's

heart suddenly thundering, he fought the urge to run his hand through his hair. He didn't look at Ella as he spoke. "Might I . . ." He looked at her father who'd grown quiet. "Might I speak with you a moment, sir?"

The room went quiet as the man exchanged a glance with his wife, then with Ella.

Swallowing his nerves, Charlie rose and straightened to his full height. He felt everyone in the room looking at him. Losing the battle, suddenly all he saw was Ella. He sealed her face in his mind, holding it there. Praying it would last. This little nurse. The one who'd taken him and Holland when no one else would. And her . . . so strong yet so filled with hurting it broke his heart. He wanted—with everything inside him— to be able to hold her heart and fight the sorrows for her. To bear them for her. But he couldn't, and if he tried, he would only be adding another.

It was time.

Mr. Beckley was stepping out into the yard and Charlie forced his face to keep from revealing all that rolled inside him. Soaking in the sight of Ella one last time, he stepped away and followed her father out into the sunshine.

THIRTY-TWO

Ella stood at the window and watched the closed barn door. Charlie and her papa had disappeared there over half an hour ago. What were they talking about? She touched the glass, hating the distance, knowing it would grow if she didn't hurry up and answer him. And oh, how she longed to answer him. She hated the look on his face that her silence and surprise had borne.

"I do believe my daughter is in love," her mother said.

Ella didn't even know where to begin, so full was her heart with thoughts of Charlie and the time they'd shared. All laced with sorrow at the rush of this. The decision. What he'd asked and what she needed him to know. Never had she felt so small and so on the verge of change.

The children inquired about her time with the circus as if four years in Roanoke were much less fascinating than the last week and a half. Delighted by their endearing ways, she answered them, soaking in the sight of their faces—all that she'd missed.

Yet she couldn't be in two places at once.

Her heart torn in so many ways, Ella was grasping at it, trying to put it back together in the only way that felt right. And that was with

Charlie. She glanced out the window again to the closed barn door. It had almost been an hour now.

Knowing she should do something to pass the wait until his return, Ella helped her mother wash dishes and put them away. Some things had been moved to new places which was making being useful a bit of a challenge. Especially with her thoughts circling around the men in the barn and how she was going to explain all this to her parents in a way that made sense.

There was a clatter and a crash, and Ella turned to see that Beth had dropped a jar of beans. They splattered every which way. Ella knelt beside her sister and together they scooped them up. Her mother handed down a bowl and Ella filled it to rinse the beans. Seeing several under the table, she crawled over and plucked them up, lowering the handful into the bowl with a clang. She found a few more under one of the chairs and pointed to where Beth could fetch the ones that had rolled to the foot of the stairs.

Ella went to straighten and hit her head on the table. The door opened. She rubbed at the spot and sat back, eager for Charlie.

In the doorway stood her father. He stepped in . . .

Closing the door behind him.

Ella tried to stand but her legs didn't move. "Papa?" When he looked down on her, she gripped the table's edge and pulled to a stand.

The room felt as though it tipped. "Where is Charlie?"

Her father seemed to decide how to answer that. He held out an envelope and Ella didn't move. She glanced to the window then back. He held the envelope out farther. She took it as she rushed to the door, her head light.

"He's gone, Ella. He left a few minutes ago."

No. She tugged open the door and hurried onto the porch, scanning the yard for some sign of him. Since they'd gone to the barn, she ran that way, crammed the envelope in her skirt pocket, and shoved open the massive door. Empty. Empty. Empty. Each stall.

This place.

Empty.

"Charlie," she breathed the word broken on a sob.

She ran back out and turned in a circle. She started down the road. Running. Running as fast as she could. *Please, God, let him be on foot.* But there were no boot prints. Only that of a horse. Perhaps a galloping one. Her heart pounded and her head, so, so light, spun. Still running, she called his name again. And then again.

Grief pooling in her chest, she couldn't breathe.

For the trail sighed empty. A great vast hush of it. Slowing hope to a halt and sinking her knees to the rutted path where fierce hoof prints spoke just what her father had. He's gone.

The land around her blurred and she saw nothing but his face. The whipping of flags rushed her mind. A sound that didn't live here, save her heart. Ella bent lower, face twisting, and she remembered the coolness of an open field. His hand on hers. Those pale green eyes smiling. Fireflies and his whispered *I love you.*

Charlie. She called his name. Tasting it. Needing him.

His words from the trail rushed her. *Do you think you might marry me?* A question spoken so abruptly, she'd barely grasped it. But as each word tumbled into place, realization dawning—what he was proposing, *giving her*—she'd sought the answer. Though fast-blooming were the buds of these days and their time together, the root of him ran deep. One she could never pull free. He had to know.

That yes. She would.

A piece of her ripped away. A heaviness pulled her closer to the ground and she sobbed against her wrist. The air grew cooler then warmer as light danced, the breeze playing in the clouds . . . pushing all things on.

Suddenly remembering the envelope, Ella sat up. She wiped her eyes with a sleeve then tugged it from her pocket and tore inside.

She slipped out the single sheet of paper, hand shaking so badly that she couldn't read it.

Vision blurring, she had to wipe at her eyes

again. More so at the sight of his tidy, masculine script at the top half of the page.

Come unto me all ye that labour and are heavy laden.

And I will give you rest.

Ella heaved out a sob.

Take My yoke upon you and learn from Me, for I am meek and lowly in heart, and you will find rest for your souls. For My yoke is easy and My burden is light.

The paper trembled as she ran her finger over his words.

Matthew 11:28-30

She realized something was tucked behind the paper. She slid it aside. A postcard. The sketch of a Dutch landscape. Tears pooled and she squinted, forcing them to fall as she turned the postcard over.

You are loved and you'll not be forgotten.

- Charlie

THIRTY-THREE

Late summer, 1890

Charlie felt the sun warm on his face. Warm and hot and perfect. With his eyes closed, he could feel the wind ripple across him, wave the dried grasses. Laying there, Axel's great side beneath his head, the lion's stomach rose and fell in a quiet sigh and Charlie with it. In the crook of Charlie's arm, snug against his bare chest, Holland slept peacefully.

He was so content he could fall asleep himself, but he dared not, so he forced his eyes open and had to blink against the white light of noon, a glorious blue sky. He should be finishing packing. He had so much to load. But this moment was too precious. Until he got to Coney Island, Philadelphia was one of the few cities where the lions would be able to securely stretch and sun, even feel the grass against their fur. So he was going to delay as long as he could. Charlie closed his eyes again. His sigh matched Axel's.

Holland shifted. Her curls brushing his cheek.

A man's gravelly voice broke the quiet. "Crew wants to break this down, so I've been ordered to load 'im."

Charlie squinted one eye open and looked over

to see a roustabout just outside the enclosure. Careful not to disturb beast or baby, he hefted Holland to the center of his chest, pressed his hand against her back, and sat up. Her eyes didn't so much as open when he rose to his feet. She'd grown over the last three and a half months but was still nothing to heft. She'd yet to take a step on her own, and with her first birthday just two weeks away, he knew that time wasn't far off.

He carried Holland out, and still holding her flush to his skin, thumbed a corner of his dangling shirt snugger into his waistband. He ought to put it on, but Holland was so comfortable, he ignored it. If the Madame saw him, she'd pitch a fit—for according to her, no one gets a free show. But there were no rubes around, so he simply went over the routine with the roustabout and made sure the man knew how Axel was to be loaded.

"I'll come back to check in once I get hitched up and the baby settled." Charlie walked through the bare carnival grounds. Troupers milled about, getting ready to leave, no one giving him a second glance. People knew who he was here. He was one of many—all strange in their own way—and it was a rare thing indeed that he could be outdoors without his collar snug no matter the time of year. So he savored the late August breeze on his shoulders and Holland's sleepy breathing as he walked to where he'd left his wagon.

Tethered to the side of the green caravan,

Siebel was nibbling grass, and Charlie grinned when he passed by Ruth whose mare looked a little rounder in the belly. He lifted a hand in greeting and Ruth scowled in that playful way of hers. They'd been pestering one another since they were kids. He supposed some things never changed.

He knew she wasn't all that mad—not that she had a right to be—since once they set out on the road, she would most likely offer to carry Holland a while. He always let her but had a feeling her intentions were more wifely than motherly, which made him a bit uncomfortable. Usually, he sought out Angelina or her sisters when he needed an extra set of hands. And when it came to Holland learning the feminine arts, he'd certainly be as choosey.

As he walked on, Charlie blinked against the noon glow and thought of Ella. The way she used to hold Holland and walk beside him. He thought of what she might be doing. What she was thinking. If she was missing him.

For he was surely missing her.

The caravan had two full days of travel ahead. Two road-weary days and it would be that much closer to Holland's birthday. Which meant it would happen while they were at Coney since they'd be there into September. And then the contract would be fulfilled. A light pooled in his chest, so bright that he nearly laughed with the feel of it. He was almost done. Almost free.

The circus would soon turn south again, and as he'd told Ella, they would begin their descent for the winter. A few entertainers would head to east coast boardwalks, and while Charlie had done that himself in years past, he now spent his winters at the circus compound in Louisiana. Since Holland had come along, he was trying to learn how to settle down some.

Last winter, while others in the circus lounged or peddled or even told fortunes, he'd spent three months breaking up scrap metal in a yard near New Orleans for fifty cents a day. Swinging a sledge hammer didn't pay much, but it kept him strong and gave Holland a few quiet months away from the midway.

It also meant he'd still be a pauper come spring, just as he'd been when he charged into that hospital in May. He smiled at the memory of Ella's shocked face—she'd had a bundle in her hands. Busy little bee. He sobered at the memory of having but coins to pay. Then her kindness. Her goodness. The way she'd followed him that snowy day and showed them compassion. How she let him sleep on her floor—truly sleep—for the first night in days.

He needed to stop this. His chest was con-stricting something awful.

Charlie focused instead on hitching up the wagon. Regina settled on the back porch of the caravan with Holland. The woman's black and white hair was pinned up in a high bun. Dark eyes bright and snappy. The pair of them prettier than any of the ornate carvings and trimmings.

Charlie slid into his shirt then led both horse and wagon to his spot in line. A quick check on the lions, then he went back just as the caravan was setting off. The noise and busyness of Philadelphia behind them, he breathed a sigh of relief. He didn't much like this place. It only reminded him of losing Mimi.

The day before, he'd visited her grave. Had let Holland crawl around awhile in the grass there. Her gripping the little stone to pull herself up to a stand. Charlie had sat near and ran his hands over the letters of *Jessamine*. Remembering how shattered he'd been. How he'd hated Lucca with every fiber of his being. First for the loss of Mimi, then for what he had done to his daughter.

And as Charlie had sat there, Holland plucking up blades of grass, him turning a dandelion between his fingers, he'd prayed for God to take away his hatred of that man. That he could be free of the disdain that had him once lusting for revenge. Now with Holland in his arms and him determined to keep his sister's memory alive, Charlie had simply asked Holland if she knew how beautiful her mother was. The baby had babbled at him, poking a finger in the grooves of Mimi's name.

Holland didn't remember; she never could. So Charlie told her. And he would always tell her.

He turned the memories over in his mind. Those of Mimi. Those of Ella. And he knew the two would have been friends. Mimi would have welcomed Ella like a sister, for that's the way she was with everyone. And Ella . . . why, she'd have asked a million questions and Mimi would have answered every one as Mimi dearly loved to talk.

A sting in his eyes, Charlie chuckled to himself.

When Holland grew too fidgety for Regina, Charlie took her. The caravan rattled on. Pots and pans and baying animals. Children's laughter. Birdsong and the breeze whistling through the spokes of the wheels. An elephant trumpeted.

Charlie let out a contented sigh. One that became many as the miles wore on. He felt Holland in her sling. Wide awake, she was tugging at his shirt to be freed, so he swayed a bit as he walked, hoping to keep her content a while longer. Amazed once again at the notion of her walking beside him one day soon. Her small hand in his.

The thought made his heart soar and ache at the same time.

My, how she was growing. With her birthday near, Charlie had drafted up a contract. Not so much a contract, he supposed, but a statement of faith for the Madame to sign. He'd spent ten dollars for a solicitor to make sure it was binding.

After poring over it, the solicitor had looked at him over thick spectacles and said it would be another ten because of the illegality of it. The latter sickened him, made him dislike the man quite significantly, and having no choice, Charlie had dug the money out of his pocket.

Unable to stomach the man thinking ill of him or Holland's fate, Charlie explained the story and the solicitor had appeared genuinely intrigued. So much so that next, he waved the extra rate.

Charlie liked him a little more then. He'd walked from the office with a grin, a document he could rest in, and rather glad he had the knack for weaving a whale of a tale—even a true one.

He hadn't known how to legally adopt a child, and even then, was pretty sure he lacked what was required. He didn't have a birth certificate and would bet anything that his last name wasn't legal, either. Charlie had also asked the solicitor what he could do about that. A few more forms and fees and Charlie had been on his way to changing that.

He was no one to anyone in this country, nor was Holland. The very reason Lucca had gotten away with the selling of her in the first place—a baby born in a tent last summer. Her first cries lifting the ears of tigers. She might have been a field mouse for all society knew of her.

And Charlie didn't wholly trust the Madame, so it was all he could come up with for some kind of assurance of peace. That and a hearty dose of prayer.

Those prayers carried him the rest of the day, through the circling of the caravan. As the first stars appeared in the night sky, he pulled Ella into those prayers. Covering her and Holland in the only way he knew how.

Charlie carried Holland to the cook tent, filled a plate heaping with stew, and walked back to their camp where he settled the baby in his lap on the back porch of the wagon. He stabbed at the smaller bits, feeding her first before polishing off the rest himself. Regina was off visiting, and already he could hear the tuning of instruments. There would be music and dancing within the hour. Not in a dancing mood, he tucked Holland into her bed that he always loaded within easy reach. By the time she'd drifted off, Regina had returned.

"Would you mind watching her?" Charlie asked, running a hand into his hair to try and set it to rights. "I won't be gone long."

"Certainly." Regina eyed him curiously.

This was something he'd been waiting a long time for. He ducked into the wagon, careful to take light steps. He pulled on his waistcoat then ran pomade and a comb through his hair before looking for his papers, finding them just where he knew they'd be. With the documents folded in hand, he headed back out.

Standing beside the wagon, Charlie felt Regina watching him as he buttoned up the waistcoat. He ran a bit of pomade into his hair and combed it off to the side. With no mirror he turned toward Regina. "This all right?"

"*Molto bello.*"

The night was warm, but he suddenly felt chilled. He slid his free hand into his pocket as he walked, then pulled it back out. Fingers running together, he tried to calm his nerves.

In the distance, a guitar plucked along slow and sweet. Throwing romance into the air that still held the warmth of the sun. A song for the Gypsies. Vagabonds who had come from ancient India, Greece, Russia, and so many other places. Along with the guitar, a woman sang soft and low. Charlie didn't catch all she said—but he recognized the *Romany* language, for his childhood memories were fragrant with those words and his mother's pretty mouth. Her ebony hair and golden bangles.

Missing his mother, Charlie lowered his head.

The bohemian song was lilting as another woman joined in harmony. And he knew a love song when he heard one. Charlie looked in that direction as he passed. Firelight flickered off their tanned faces, little dark-haired children playing around. Just as he and Mimi had once done.

Looking on, he spotted his destination. The

vardo in the distance was ornate—a rich burgundy with gold paintings and scrollwork that even in the moonlight was prominent. The Dutch door stood closed despite the warm night, but light glinted through the two narrow windows. The steps were slung up for the night as if to say, *you are not welcome.*

Reaching it, he pulled down the little ladder and slid it into place, because this was a meeting he would have.

Thirty-Four

He knocked. Soundly.

Heard a shuffle, and then the top of the Dutch door parted and he moved lower two steps so it could open wide. Frowning, Madame Broussard looked down.

"I'd like a word with you, if you please," Charlie said.

Her wrinkles deepened when she pursed her mouth, then he heard a click of the door lock. She walked away without opening it. Rubbing his fingers over the documents, Charlie blew an exhale before letting himself in. Inside, he was hit with the stench of opium—a sweet, tar-like smell that churned his stomach. He glanced around for Olaf and guessed by the snoring mound on the bed that the man had already had his share. From the narrow fireplace mantle over the inset stove, Madame pulled something from a glass dish and popped it into her mouth. She held the dish out to Charlie and he shook his head. Likely nothing more than some kind of sweet, but he wasn't about to take a thing from her.

Her eyebrows inched upward as if waiting for him to state his request.

Charlie opened the paper in front of him. "This is for you to sign."

"Sign."

He nodded, determined not to lose his nerve. "To make sure that you are a woman of your word. Which of course you are."

"A contract."

He shook his head. "An agreement." He wanted no more of contracts and this woman.

Madame studied him from head to toe, and Charlie was more than a bit glad that Olaf was gone for it. She narrowed her eyes as if sensing as much. Did she not know the man and his habits were as easy to read as a clock? This would be Olaf's worst night of all. Away from the fairgrounds with little responsibility, he was always a goner by sunset.

"It's a statement of faith," Charlie began, "that states she is legally mine." He was using the term *legally* a mite loosely, but she knew that as well as he did since this whole situation had grown under that light.

"Why would I sign such a thing?"

"To confirm that our contract is fulfilled on Holland's first birthday."

"Antonia," she countered. "And that would be Bassi and not Lionheart."

He made no response to that.

She spoke on as if expecting as much. "That contract is sufficient."

Not for him. "I'd like my own copy. In my own terms." Something that she couldn't tear up or

411

burn. He handed it out to her. "You're welcome to read it."

From the mantle she pulled down a pair of spectacles and Charlie took a step closer to the door, desperate for a breath of fresh air. Already his head was starting to hurt. Studying the paper, she took several minutes to read it.

Finally she spoke flatly. "I do not know that I want to sign this."

"Then I don't know that I want to perform on Coney."

Her gaze flicked back to him. Coney Island was one of their greatest profits out of the year. Money was ripe for the taking. A city laced with sin that never slept. Where people craved their entertainment—many a diverse form of it.

"You can't tell me that and you know it." She folded the paper closed.

Forcing his expression to remain calm, Charlie kept his breathing steady. "You'll sign that document. And I'll be on my way. And then I'll give them their show and you'll get your profits."

She studied him with a gleam in her eye—calculating.

"Nothing less. Nothing more," he added.

Her eyes tightened.

He motioned toward the declaration in her hand, thinking also to the contract she'd drawn up with Lucca when the man had wanted to flee. Charlie had watched it be torn up with his own eyes, but he didn't trust that the Madame hadn't another copy of Lucca's arrangement hidden somewhere. Charlie had no way of knowing.

So he'd taken care. "This little girl . . . Antonia Bassi . . . who's even going to believe that's her real name? I can't think of anyone around here who knows such a child."

Madame looked down at his document where the words *Holland Lionheart* were written clear as day right beside his own name. "Do you really think your tricks are going to get her anywhere?"

"It's not a trick." He smiled.

"Your sister was a fool. More so with that silly nickname—"

"Which has been submitted to the state of Louisiana, along with her papers that are being processed." Birth certificate, everything. When he got back this winter, he would need to pay the registrar a visit, but for now, the wheels were in motion. The solicitor had told him that formalizing adoptive kinship in a court was rare, but Charlie would do that too if necessary. He said as much.

Madame's eyes narrowed, and she glanced around her vardo from Olaf to the mess on the sofa, the mantle, then back to Charlie who she took in again so thoroughly, he had to force himself not to shift his feet.

Always the Madame.

She pulled off her spectacles. "You think you

are so different . . ." She waved around her dwelling. "But one day you are going to rot away an old man."

He made no response.

Her hand, still aloft, was shaking. Face more placid than he'd ever seen. For the first time in his life . . . the first time since this nightmare began . . . he pitied her.

"I'll ask you to sign that now." Using his thumb, he tucked at his shirt against his hip. "And just so you know, I had no way of paying her hospital bill in Roanoke."

Her mouth twitched.

"So really, I'm doing you a favor. They were quite displeased. The whole place in a tizzy, actually. So should you pass through there again, say hello to the doctor for me."

Madame rolled her eyes and yanked the agreement from his hand. "I'll be glad to be done with that fat little thing."

Charlie grinned which seemed to only annoy her further.

Her slender hands groped along the mantle as if searching for a pen. She found it, and seeing the inkwell, Charlie handed it over. From the bed, Olaf let out a snore and Charlie felt a warmth in his chest that this was almost finished. Pen dipped and then she scratched the tip across the line. Charlie slipped the top paper free to reveal that there was a duplicate. Those small eyes of hers shot toward the ornate ceiling then back at him with a leveled look.

"Almost done," he said gently.

She scribbled her name across the second line and he took that copy as well. He examined her signature then looked at the woman. She stared back. Small and empty.

"I won't take up any more of your time," he said.

He held the papers with care in one hand, then tugged at his waistcoat with the other. He opened the door and went down the steps. In the grass, he turned slightly to see her standing in the doorway. He breathed in the clear air, then tipped the papers in her direction. A thank you.

The night carried him home, music high on the hillside where lanterns burned brightly. There were no words for the joy in his chest, but when he reached his camp, he climbed inside the wagon and ducked low over Holland's bed. Kneeling there, he pressed a kiss to her little bared neck. The skin soft and warm and milky. Then her plump cheek, her ear.

She sighed in her sleep.

"I guess you're stuck with me, Miss Holland," he whispered, and leaning forward, kissed her tiny nose. "But that's okay because I kind of like being stuck with you."

THIRTY-FIVE

Holding the jar in front of her, Ella ladled thick, hot jam into the clean glass. She scooped and spooned until the jar was nearly full, then reaching for another, did the same. At her side, her mother wiped the glass mouths and laid the canning lids in place before carrying them over to the pot of boiling water.

Mama sang as she worked.

Ella listened, hoping it would settle her nerves. Her fingers sticky, she wiped them on a damp rag. Early morning sun spilled through the front windows.

"You don't have to do this," her mother said softly.

Ella nodded. "I know. I want to."

Mama's striped skirt swayed as she turned back to the boiling pot.

Truly, she wanted to.

All she had left of Charlie lived in a small envelope. Something she pulled out and read almost every day. Some way to know that he had been real, him and Holland . . . and everyone. And whenever she did, Ella read the words again. Over and over. Letting them sink into her heart—the truth of them.

Come to me.

And I will give you rest.

She knew it was God speaking. But she hadn't thought of God that way in a long time. A *long* time. And now it gave her hope. It gave her comfort. Even amidst the unknowns that wet her pillow more times than she liked to count. As much as she missed Charlie, as much as it tore her up inside, there was hope. There had to be. Those very words promised as much.

Holding all that hope to herself felt selfish. Today had been a long time coming, and perhaps like Charlie . . . she was nearly free.

She clung to that as she ladled jam into another jar and wiped it clean. Mama set the sealed jars on a folded towel to cool. When they had finished, Ella set about cleaning up the mess. Her father came in from the barn, hung up his hat, and took the cup of steaming tea Ella fixed him. Joy shining in his eyes, he sat at the piano, lifted the heavy lid, and coaxed out a song. His favorite way to pass a restful hour. Especially on a Sunday.

Ella had asked if they could stay behind from church today as there was something she dearly needed to do.

Mama set about making biscuits and Ella stepped toward the piano. She leaned against the side of the dark wood, savoring the melodic sound of his gentle playing. "You've been working hard this week," she said.

He peered up at her. He was a quiet one, her papa.

"And where are the boys?" she asked.

He smiled. "Swimming." Then he looked over at his wife. "Make a few of those biscuits to go?"

Mama said she would. With a question ever in heart, Ella voiced it.

Papa lifted a look that was equal parts guarded and amused. He always did that whenever she spoke of Charlie. And she always asked what they had talked about that day.

Each time, he differed to other avenues. Something about a promise made, a promise kept.

He played softly on the keys. The song slow and soulful.

"What promise did you make to Charlie, Papa?"

He smiled, his thick fingers making a C major before easing into a C sharp.

"You're still not going to tell me what it is," she whispered.

His steady hand slid up the keys, tempo even and sure. A hint of spark in his eyes, he shook his head. "Why don't you play a duet with your father." He patted the bench beside him. "We don't know how many more of these we'll have." His eyes found hers—whole and searching. And she wondered what he was telling her.

Feeling every bitter sweetness of things both

lost and gained, Ella kissed the top of his head and lingered. "Will you save me that spot this afternoon? There's somewhere I need to be."

"I sure will."

She could see how happy it made him. Lost were their duets for so many years. But now . . . she'd begun to play with him again. The hymns he had always loved. She knew how much it meant to him and it meant the same to her.

Thinking back to what the morning still held, Ella took a deep breath, whispered a prayer for strength, then kissed her father's head again.

Within the hour, she found herself walking the path with her mother. Ella had worn her best dress and fixed her hair as nice as she could— pinning that stubborn bit out of the way. The part that always fell across her eyes. What did she need to hide for?

She was done with hiding. And running.

Even so, her hand, looped through her mother's elbow, was shaking. As if sensing as much, Mama reached over and squeezed it gently.

Just like in the kitchen, her mother sang as they walked.

Ella let the words soothe her. Thankful for this woman who she had spent years missing. All while thinking some distance would help her heal. Good and well, and while she would never trade those years in Roanoke, she had a feeling that a little more healing was meant to be had.

With the basket on her arm, she set sights on the trail as they slowly climbed.

Ella's heart quickened, perhaps from the rise in the path, but she knew it had more to do with the cabin nearing in the distance. Set away from others, it was high. Remote.

Lonely.

This hadn't always been his home. Of that she was certain. The reverend had had a fine house near the church. This, set back amidst the pines, was a shack. Ella glanced around, her heart suddenly in her throat.

She realized she was trembling again because Mama gripped tighter. For months—no, years—Ella hadn't been able to shake the dark memories of that wretched night. The way the preacher's son had kept chatting with her at choir practice, then later, calling her *awful pretty* as they had walked the night path. Had kept touching her wrist and her lower back as he strode beside her. The sickening feeling in her gut of being so very alone. Of having no one around to help her.

Ella drew in a quivering breath. She didn't want that feeling anymore. That sinking burden that she was all alone. She knew she would carry the scars always, and never would she forget the little boy who she'd clung to the two hours of his life, but she sought hope that with each step taken, the burden would grow lighter.

For My yoke is easy . . .

It had never felt that way. Not for the last five years. Not with the God she'd pushed away. She now knew what Charlie had meant. *Don't let him take more.*

The reverend's son had stolen enough already, and she'd been letting the rest of her heart die away piece by piece. She'd always thought she had nothing left to give. But now she knew that she'd chosen to see herself that way.

As long as her heart was beating she had something to give.

Ella stepped farther into the clearing and stopped. She looked around at the humble dwelling, then the door opened and a gray-haired man appeared. Her heart twisted at the sight of him. The reverend had always been a good man. She could recall a time that she had truly liked him. He'd been one of the things she'd enjoyed about church. His jovial ways. Jolly smile.

And now he was in a shack high up in the hills. All alone . . . on a Sunday morning. Nary a friend in sight.

For all that his son had done.

Ella felt unsteady as she studied the reverend. The man looked back at her. His son had vanished without being seen again. The congregation had denounced the reverend and she'd been happy about it. As had her family. He was banned from the church and in some ways, so much more. Perhaps it was the right thing for people to do, but she really didn't know.

About a year later, he'd written her a letter, but Ella had tossed it into the fire without so much as opening it. She'd left for Roanoke soon after, needing to be free of this place. *Thinking* she would be free of this place. But the hurts only followed because they didn't live in these hills or this mountain. They'd lived within her. No matter where she went. They bound her the longer she let them.

She looked into the reverend's face now. No longer a reverend to this town, but she didn't know how else to think of him. She scarcely recognized the man at the pulpit from her memories. Gone was his dark coat. In its stead was a flannel shirt, worn and wrinkled. A tattered floppy hat. A lock of silver hair across his brow, a Bible in hand, and a question in those wide eyes.

Turning the jar, Ella barely heard her mother gently say that she would wait there just as they'd planned. Ella told herself to step closer. Just another step. And then another. She repeated that until she was at the foot of his porch, and suddenly her stomach was complaining. Her hands wobbled against the lid of the jar. Ella swallowed hard and realized she was staring down at his boots now. Worn and dusty. She took a little breath, then gently lifted up the jar. Knowing that was no way to give a gift, she forced herself to look to his face.

She'd told herself that perhaps he wouldn't recognize her. That perhaps it would make this easier. But then she saw that his chin—speckled in silver bristle—was trembling.

He looked to the wrapped jar, then to her face. He blinked quickly and tucked the Bible under his arm.

"For you," she said softly, moving up one step just long enough for him to reach down.

The jar, still warm, passed hands.

His eyes turned wet and his mouth worked. Lips pursing over and over as if needing time to draw words from the bottom of a well. "Thank you, miss."

She gave him what felt like a weak smile. "It's blackberry." Her voice sounded so small. "We just made it." A silly thing to say, but all she had.

He turned the jar in his hand. Ran his thumb over the brown paper she'd wrapped it in.

She gave him another little smile and hoped it was better than the last.

That's all she had to do. All she told herself she would do. The only reason why she'd braved this moment. But with him looking at her so—like he was seeing the first sunrise after a storm—she couldn't turn away. She wanted to say something more, but words ran into hiding.

"I . . ." The paper crinkled under his fingers as he turned the gift. "I'm real sorry." His chin was trembling again. "For your hurts." His gray eyes searched the ground at her feet then slid up to her face. "The wrongs."

Her own tears welling, Ella could only nod.

He looked past her and must have spotted her mother when his head dipped in a quiet greeting. Ella took a small step back. Overwhelmed, she turned to leave.

"If you've ever a need of anything . . ."

She paused and timidly glanced back.

"I'd be at your service." He pulled his hat off, silver hair standing on end, and pressed his hat to his heart. "Always. No matter how great."

The back of her throat burned and she barely whispered out a thank you.

He moved down a step, and then another. His gait uneven as if he'd earned a limp over the years. "An' I'm . . . I'm so sorry." He moistened his lips, eyes glassy. "I'm so sorry about the boy."

Ella nodded fiercely, blinking back tears. "He was a sweet one." And he'd been hers for two whole hours. Bundled against her snug and careful. His tiny hand in hers—little chest heaving for air that wouldn't come no matter how hard she prayed.

The reverend's furrowed brow held conviction. "He took after his mama."

She pressed her lips together and could only tip her head in thanks as nary a word would slip past her throat.

She gave him a gentle wave, then turned and walked for what felt like forever to her mother. But never had her steps felt more free. Realizing she was trembling, Ella slipped her arm through her mother's. Mama reached over and squeezed Ella, kissed her cheek, and they walked on.

Letting out a deep sigh, Ella leaned into the strength beside her and closed her eyes. She felt utterly spent. But in its wake was rushing forward a joy she didn't know could live inside her. It hit her chest so fiercely her skin tingled.

Ella felt a smile surface. And now? She didn't know.

But she thought of a sunny meadow. And lions. Wondering if the man with a heart for them would be singing just now this Sunday morning. The thought of it about did her in. A warmth that went down to her heart and pulled at it, making it hurt. Wanting to hear that sound again . . . *just once more* . . . she clung tighter to her mother's arm.

Holland was going to be one tomorrow. Ella wondered if there would be music or dancing. Perhaps even a cake. She smiled at all the mischievous things Charlie would be up to. More than anything, she wished to be there. To hold Holland again. See how she had grown. To see Charlie's face—the joy that would live there that very day. For his little girl was safe . . . and he would be free.

Thirty-Six

"The cake?" Charlie asked, shoving a stack of dirty dishes off to the side of the tent.

"It's there."

"And everyone?"

Regina's dark eyes twinkled. "They're all coming."

"All right, I'll bring her along."

Regina patted his arm and told him she would see him shortly. They were all to meet at the picnic area Charlie had reserved that dawn, far from Coney Island's bathing pavilions and the bustling Iron Pier. Earlier, he'd *rather officially* marked off a tree-shaded section of grass— near to the beach, but far from the hordes of vacationers who dotted the sand like seagulls.

When Regina was gone, Charlie searched for the beaded necklace Evangeline had made Holland for the occasion. But for the life of him, didn't remember where he'd stashed it. He shuffled through a crate of Holland's belongings, tugging out socks and dresses and little ruffly things that the sisters always sewed for her and he was yet to know what to do with.

He plucked out the necklace and set it aside, then his hands stilled at the bottom of the crate. He lifted out her yellow sweater. It was too small now, so there was no reason to keep it, but his fingers grazed his uneven stitches on the middle button and he recalled how it had dangled loose after that nurse had nearly torn it clean off in her haste. That nervous little nurse who kept giving him odd glances and acting like such a know-it-all. Charlie smiled to himself, the melancholy overwhelming.

Holland babbled at him and he snapped to attention.

The baby was on the floor where he'd left her, but she'd crawled over to a tin of cookies and now sat with it in front of her, a half-eaten cookie in each hand.

"What are you doing, my dear!" Charlie knelt, tucked the treats away, and slid them on the shelf.

Holland started to cry, a garbled sound with cookies already in her mouth.

"Hey." He pointed a finger at her sternly.

She stopped, but her bottom lip quivered.

"I said no."

Crumbs were all over her birthday dress as she hung her head. Her new white stockings poked out from beneath the blue checked fabric and jolly red hem. Two front pockets that had been cut and sewn like tulips. Regina's handiwork.

Chuckling, Charlie scooped her up and did a little dance, turning them in a gentle circle. Her hand came around and gripped his shoulder, her other at his neck as she held on. She chewed her mouthful of cookie and he kissed her sticky, plump cheek.

"Happy birthday, Little Miss." He plopped her in the center of his bed then climbed inside. "Now, if you'll just wait a second while I change, we can be off." He doffed his good top hat and yanked off his velvet coat, leaving the costume shirt. Back down the crates he searched for her shoes, then it took him a few moments to fasten them up the side. The buttons were so small and his fingers so big, it was really unfair. Holland giggled as she watched. In jest Charlie asked her where he'd put the button hook but she just pointed to the tin of cookies and said, *"peaz?"*

He grinned as he slid her onto his arm. "How about we go celebrate." He grabbed his father's tattered top hat from the trunk and put it on as he walked out.

Outside the tent, the early September sun was hot, but the whoosh of a distant roller coaster jangled along the seaside breeze. He lowered Holland into the new little wagon, painted a deep plum purple—her birthday present. He'd padded the wagon with a blanket, worried she might fall over, and when he pulled it into motion, she did just that, tipping back into the soft bedding. Charlie grinned, and with wide, uncertain eyes, Holland sat back up.

"Thatta girl."

He pulled the wagon across the noisy midway

where here and there workers and performers waved out to them. A few *happy birthdays* in Holland's honor. Across the paved pathways and away from the bustle of the promenade and sideshows, he led them, the sound of laughter and shouts fading into the crash and swell of the ocean. The air grew cooler and a seagull dipped and swooped overhead. Still walking, Charlie pulled Holland and her wagon to a shallow grassy knoll that overlooked the water, far away from the noise and bustle. He could see Angelina and her sisters, all the others. Evangeline wore a bright beaded necklace that matched Holland's and Danielle waved cheerily.

Blankets lay scattered all around and he creaked the wagon to a standstill where he lifted Holland out and plopped her in the center of it all. She spotted the cake and crawled toward it. Falling to his knees, Charlie lunged and caught her by her little shoe with a laugh. Evangeline came along and swept the cake up, moving it out of reach. He pulled Holland back across the blanket and the girl giggled.

She giggled more as Charlie helped her open gifts. All kinds of girlish things that delighted Holland and the sisters alike. Then there was a tin whistle from Arnold and a wooden box for keepsakes that Little Joe had tied with a bow. Charlie heartily thanked everyone. Regina passed out plates of cake and Angelina poured glasses of frosty lemonade. Charlie had never seen such a feast. Never seen such a pretty little girl as the one smooshing frosting between her fingers and a bit in his hair whenever he got too close. He kissed Holland's hand and made a growling sound as he nibbled at the sweetness. She laughed a deep belly laugh that shot down to his toes.

Then suddenly, the salty wind lifted his hat, tossing it over him and into the dry grass where it tumbled toward the shore. Charlie jumped up and ran, laughing at the sudden burst of cheers and whistles behind him. Which made him glance back to see Evangeline and Danielle sprinting after him—ruffled skirts free around their bare feet. He knew they only followed in jest, but it had him running faster all the same. Down the hill the hat tumbled, farther and farther. Their strides were no match for his, and he got there first, plucked the hat up out of the sand, and with a shake, set it back on his head. Breathless, the two sisters made a show of snapping their fingers in disappointment. Reaching them, Charlie draped an arm around each of their shoulders as they walked back to the grass and blankets.

"You two can be very troublesome when you want to be," he panted. "What would your husbands say?"

They each smiled up at him, their faces shining.

From his spot in the shade, Arnold said, "I think I need to get me one of those hats."

Everyone laughed.

"One day," Angelina said from where she sat on the patched quilt, "you are going to lose that hat for good."

"And then where would we be?" Charlie sank down on the other side of Holland, the shade cooling him from the sprint.

Angelina gave him a knowing smile.

"What exactly is the hoopla with this hat?" Little Joe asked.

Angelina looked at him slyly, beginning the words to the tale that Charlie had heard told all his life. "Some say it is luck. Others . . . magic."

Charlie held up a finger. "But I say it is . . ."

"Love," Regina finished, for they all believed the same.

Beside her sister, Evangeline pulled Holland into her lap. "Tell us the story again."

Holland rubbed her face against Evangeline's pink dress and sighed. Charlie could tell the baby was getting tired, sitting there in the warm, speckled sunlight, eyelids heavy. No doubt she would be asleep soon. Which reminded him that he had somewhere to be with evening not long off. One last show. The thought filled him with both melancholy and joy, binding his chest tight.

"I'm not really much of a storyteller—" Charlie had to duck when crumbs of cake flew his way. "All right, all right. That wasn't true."

"*I* will tell the story." Regina held up a stout

hand. "Because *I* was there." She pressed a finger to her lips, making a show of thinking.

Charlie watched her, secretly hungry for the memories.

"He was standing beside the Big Top, your father." Her dark, sparkling eyes found Charlie. "He'd just finished cleaning up after the matinee. It was a cold day and I was walking with your mother. She was new to the circus. Her first week. A Romani beauty, she was." Regina's face went wistful and Charlie squinted down, overwhelmed by the image of her in his mind.

"We were talking about something—that I can't remember," Regina continued. "One of the shows. I'd been working the dressing room, and of course she was a performer. One of the flyers. She was so talented at what she did and so beautiful. And kind. I remember she was wiping rosin from her fingers . . ." Regina made a gliding motion with her small hand. "But then the wind came. Just snatched that hat right off that man's head." Her hand floated across the air, growing lower. "Until it fell." She looked from Holland to Charlie. "Right at your mother's feet."

"And they say . . ." Charlie arched an eyebrow, missing the two of them so bad it hurt.

"That they were married at the very next town."

The ache grew deeper as he remembered the life his parents had shared with him and Mimi. It had been beautiful and he was blessed to have been part of it. He looked down at Holland who sighed in her sleep.

"So be it luck . . . or magic . . ." Regina continued.

"Or love." Charlie rose and took Holland. "That's 'the end.'" His throat smarted so he swallowed against it. Because he could still remember Ella's wide eyes as he'd taken the hat from his head and set it on hers. Lantern light golden on her hair. Her small hand so perfect inside his. Perhaps she didn't find the hat herself. Perhaps the wind didn't blow it to her feet. But it was hers all the same.

Thirty-Seven

Crickets chirped—a sweet fast sound in the night air.

Sitting beside her sister on the porch swing, Ella's bare feet barely grazed the porch as the wind kept the swing creaking. Little Beth was asleep. A bowl of beans rested on Ella's lap and she trimmed them as Beth slouched against her. Ella kept her fingers moving, savoring the quiet, simple work of evening. Thankful for her family and all that God had given her. Missing Charlie. Missing Holland.

Missing her little one.

As the air cooled, so slowed the sound of the crickets. Papa stood out near the windmill, watching the sunset. Mama had taken the boys in to wash up for bed, and while Ella had thought about following them in, she couldn't resist setting the beans aside and easing Beth down to the striped cushion. Rising, Ella left the porch and headed toward her father.

She stood beside him for several moments, perhaps too quiet when he cleared his throat.

"Where is my girl who is so full of questions?"

Ella smiled. She'd made herself keep constant wonderings to herself this week. "I think about him all the time."

"Do you now?" Amusement lifted his voice. "I dare say, we've all taken notice. It's a special man indeed to do that to my daughter." He winked but there was a depth to his words, his expression, that made Ella know just what he meant.

Across the sunset, a hawk dipped then rose. The windmill clattered a breeze, the iron groaning as it turned west. The air warm and dry. Her father was watching her with a curious light in his eyes.

"Did you know who Charlie was?" she asked. "And I don't mean about the lions." A question she'd never posed before.

Arms folded over his chest, he thought on that, then dipped a nod. "I knew who he was."

"You did?" Ella studied his profile. "He told you?"

After a few more spins of the windmill, he nodded again.

Moistening her lips, Ella looked off at the sunset—the mountains an indigo silhouette against a pink and gray sky. She tried to picture the pair of them talking that day in the barn—all Charlie might have shared.

Her father shifted worn boots. "He was quite a character." It didn't come out as an insult.

"Yes, he was."

"He had a lot to say that day. A fair bit to show me."

Had he truly been so bold? "What did you think of that?" Ella whispered.

Her papa ran a weathered hand over his mouth. "It was quite shocking . . . but . . ." He dipped his head. "It was honest." He glanced sideways at Ella. "There's something to be said for honesty. Especially when a man doesn't have to be."

Ella squeezed his hand. They stood without speaking as she pondered that. "Did he ask you anything?"

"He asked me a great many things." Her father ran thick fingers over her own. "He asked me to take good care of you." A sad smile. "And of course I promised that I would."

Though he had already told her that, she held that thought close. Missing Charlie terribly.

"He asked me what I knew about farming," Papa said.

"Really? You didn't tell me that."

His smile turned to a grin. "It would seem that boy doesn't know a plow from a bag of seed."

Ella laughed—everything she loved about Charlie flooding her chest. "I don't know what to do, Papa. I want so desperately to go and find him."

He looped her arm through his own, patting her sleeve. "That's a big change. Have you talked to the Lord about it?"

"I don't know what to say. What if God says no?"

He chuckled. "I doubt that. He'd have a good time following you there. The creator of the earth is rather adventurous."

Ella smiled. Her father tugged on one pant leg and then the other, then he sank down to the earth. She followed. A calloused hand took her own and he held tight.

"Can . . . can we also pray that he's all right?" She knew where they kept him tonight. His body, his heart. "That he's not afraid. Not in pain."

Papa nodded. And with his strong hand over hers, showed her how to say hello to the good Lord. First a greeting, then a heart of gratitude. Then they sat quiet as the windmill rattled overhead. Papa squeezed her fingers and Ella said what she needed to say. Her voice was awful small so surely Papa couldn't hear, but he held tight, steady beside her all the same.

Torchlight glowed, and though the canvas tent rustled, nary a breeze came in to sweep comfort against this misery.

Charlie knelt on the stiff wagon boards, giving the crowd the display it paid for, and tried to rally his strength. This night need not be hard. It was his last of all. He should feel joy. Nothing but release. So why was he doubled forward, nearly trembling? Perhaps it was the air hovering stagnant over a crowd much more dense than ever. This city of sin that never slept? He was feeling the very heartbeat of it now as their voices ebbed and flowed about him, a few drunken slurs rising over everything else. Even breathing was hard in the hot stench of sweat and revelry. Something warm and wet hit his chest and he didn't even want to think about what it was.

Charlie laced his fingers tight and peered out over the masses.

Rock of Ages . . .

Movement caught his eye. Strange, since the whole tent seemed to jostle and swell. But this flash of color was different. A woman edged nearer, neither in amusement nor fear, but in serene silence. Her face was pale. Stunning. And he knew her the moment he saw her. The courtesan who had turned for him that day under the dome of light. Here on Coney, they were but a short train ride from that very establishment.

Her lashes were white blonde, full lips stained crimson, clear purpose in her eyes. A green satin gown cinched up her bodice. Few courtesans were adorned so finely and he knew he'd been offered the best. Her windswept curls were a flame of red. Skin nearly translucent. She tugged off a black traveling glove so it was with the softest, palest fingers that she reached through the bars, touching him.

"We heard what had been done to you." Her eyes brimmed with tears as if she'd been holding them back ever since. One fell and she swiped it away. "I saw the posters. The circus advertising such a man. And I hoped it would be you."

She'd hoped for . . . *him?* As a man and not a monster?

A faint smattering of freckles touched her cheeks in a wisp of girlishness. A guess would put her at eighteen. Perhaps seventeen. Slowly, she drew closer to the wagon until her face was just inches from his bowed one. Her perfume lifted as the most fragrant oil—freeing him for the briefest of moments from the stench of cheap cigars and stale liquor. Then her whispered voice. "Thank you." Chains rustled as she pulled his fingers nearer to her mouth. Gently, she kissed his hands, one and then the other. Wet eyes peered up at him. "For being the man who walked away."

Lowering his head, Charlie slammed his own eyes closed. Both of her hands were around one of his now. Holding so tight he could feel her pulse. His eyes stinging, he peered at her through blurred vision. The front of her gown pressed against a spoked wheel where it was surely being soiled by grit and grease. Beads of moisture trickled down his spine in the late summer heat. His chest was slick with it. That same humidity coiled the ends of her hair. "May I stay here beside you?" she whispered. "Until you are freed to go home?"

His throat was nearly too dry for words. "They won't allow it." Just him, alone.

Looking grieved, she lifted his palm and pressed it to her cheek which was so silken, so clean, he was suddenly aware of the way the sweat mixed with dust on his skin. How filthy, how stained he was.

The crowd balanced on a stunned hush. Perhaps transfixed by her loveliness. Perhaps astonished at the way she clung to him.

"Don't go back there," he said softly, breaking the rules again by speaking. Their exchange had surely been noticed by now.

From her reticule, she pulled a tiny glass vial and slowly unscrewed the lid. She glanced to a torchbearer who drew near and told her to move away. The young woman ignored the command even as two men stepped forward, surely her guards, because they hemmed her in safety. "There is only one thing I am skilled at, good sir." She blinked up at him.

"And there's only one thing that *I'm* skilled at," Charlie countered. Throat aching for water, he had to whisper the rest. "Yet one day I'm going to try my hand at pushing a plow."

She smiled, beamed really. "And have you a lady to walk beside you, Mr. Lionheart?"

"I do," he said, his throat still hoarse with thirst. Meaning it with his whole heart, he rallied his voice. "I'll go next to find her." The moment he was freed from this place.

The young courtesan's head bowed and to his

surprise, she tipped the vial against her fingers and touched oil to his wrists, sliding the tender concoction beneath the manacles, soothing. She peered up at him and her face held new life. New life that told him, no, she wasn't going to return to that place. "Then I'll pray Godspeed. For both of you."

Hands still tight in her lap, Ella's doubts faded away. She might not have been a practiced petitioner, but it only took one thing to talk to God. Simply the words lifting from her heart. That Charlie was safe on this darkest of nights. That he wasn't alone. Wasn't afraid.

She thought of the crowd that was surely surrounding him now. Prayed that the ridicule and the jeers would be far from him this night.

Would they ever know? The man walked with lions. A fierce legion that would step forward if he but commanded them.

The wind tugged at her hair, stirring the sleeves of her blouse. It was a warm, dry wind, making her think of the end of summer. Of the man she loved coming south again. Closing her eyes tighter, Ella prayed he would find his way back to her and if that wasn't possible, that she would find her way to him.

If it meant boarding a train and traveling to his compound, she would. Perhaps the circus needed another costume mistress. She'd even learn how to juggle or do a somersault if necessary. The sheer thought of it had her laughing aloud, startling a pair of crows. And Papa. His head lifted ever so slightly and he winked.

Surely a strange amen, a laugh, but perhaps her newfound joy was amen all the same.

Afresh in mind was Charlie's teasing about being able to hop on one foot without falling over. Her heart filled with the memory of that day— his funny accent and deck of cards. A million costume pieces bursting out of that trunk. The way he'd drawn in the patrons with his riddles and wit. Made sure Ella had her concession treat. How she hadn't realized it that day, but just like with his boys, he'd taken the time to play with her. Gave her a reason to laugh again. To feel the bars stretching far and away, the world boundless.

If she could just be there once more, she would. If she could just slip her dime into his gloved hand, she would. Not to see any kind of brokenness. But to be a part of the uniqueness and life that no mold could contain.

And there? There she would make sure that he knew just how much she loved him.

Charlie strode into his tent just as fireworks popped. Canvas walls tinted pink and then blue. Accustomed to it, Holland slept as if it were a lullaby. Clad in a nightgown, Regina came around her partition. Without a second thought, Charlie picked her up—something he never did because she hated it. He smacked a kiss to each of her cheeks and Regina tried to kick him, but her foot only tangled in his cloak. Even then he knew she didn't mean it because she was beaming.

The music playing along the night air was a clatter of brass and trumpets and Charlie turned her in a funny dance. After dipping her, he put her back on the ground.

Hands to hips, she peered up with every shred of spunk she had. "Now what?"

"Now?" He climbed onto his bed and took up the thin blade he used to make tallies. His hand shook as he pressed it to the green wood of the wagon. Finally, he touched down and scratched a short line. The final mark. He leaned back on his heels and looked at the mass of cuts. Nearly a year of his life. He glanced around the wagon, the tent . . . to Regina and Holland. And thought on those who weren't there.

"And now?" Regina asked again.

"At the moment." After climbing down, Charlie bent, and taking her small hand, pressed it to his forehead. "I feel like I'm coming down with something. A cough. Maybe a cold. At the very least a fever. Or do you think it's a broken arm? Either way, I've already got the days off to recover."

There was a sparkle in Regina's eyes. "Sounds

like you need a doctor." At the washstand, she wet a rag and motioned for him to sit.

"I was thinking maybe a nurse." Charlie pulled forward a crate and settled onto it.

With slow, steady movements, Regina wiped the blackness from his face for the final time.

"Come with me?" he whispered. After Regina made a few more swipes with her rag, he opened his eyes to see her smiling face.

"I wouldn't miss it for the world."

Thirty-Eight

Morning came and with it the dew. The kiss of early autumn all around, a few leaves slipped along the air as Ella helped her mother with the laundry. Steam rose from the great iron kettle in the yard, and using the wooden paddle, Ella dunked sheets and pillowcases below the sudsy surface. Papa walked across the yard, gun slung over his shoulder. He threw them a wave and vanished over the low hill.

Dip and stir and rinse. The motions filled her morning as Ella filled the line. Her mother cranked the hand wringer, squeezing water out of a petticoat and Ella hung it up. They stopped only to warm beans and bread and then Papa was coming back over the hill, a pair of rabbits in hand. Leaving her mother to plan supper, Ella went back out to finish the laundry.

She stood in bare feet and stretched up to drape an apron to dry, securing it with a wooden pin.

Her eyes lifted over the line, taking in the noon horizon and its emptiness. Ella sank back down and plucked up a pin from the basket. She secured the last pieces of laundry, then slid the basket aside. Wiping her hands dry on her apron, she drew in a slow, deep breath, then lifted her lashes. Took in the empty horizon once again. The one that was empty every day. Every hour.

And then she froze.

Seeing him.

A man . . . walking across the field. Handsome as could be, wearing a gray waistcoat. Brown hair slicked to the side.

Ella didn't move. Her arms froze at her sides and she didn't realize she'd forgotten to breathe until she gasped.

Charlie.

Her chest rose and fell quicker . . . and quicker . . .

She stared at him, the cool press of a sheet against her hand as she peered around it. Pushed past it, feet suddenly moving, carrying her over the dry grass, closer. He seemed to spot her. She knew it in the way he slowed. Stared. Hands fisting at his sides.

She'd always known him to be tall and strong, but standing there in her papa's field, the sun bright about him and the truth pressing against her heart—that he had come back to her—she'd never seen such a perfect, more beautiful sight. And suddenly she was running.

You are loved. And you'll not be forgotten.

She didn't know how long it took to reach him, but then she was colliding into his chest and he hoisted her inches off the ground. He turned in a slow, slow circle before lowering her gently back down. He smelled of summer and all that she loved, eyes so vulnerable it made her ache all over. She touched his jaw, silken and smooth. Let her hand slide up the side of his head, into his hair.

She breathed his name.

He laughed hers loud and deep as if having waited to speak it a long time.

"You came back."

He let out a slow sigh, his eyes soaking in her face. "Well. I'd asked this girl I know a question and she never gave me an answer." He kissed her forehead and lingered.

Ella closed her eyes.

"I don't mind trying again," he whispered. He moved as if to lower himself down.

She gripped his vest in her hands. "Yes."

He stilled.

"Yes . . . please."

He laughed. " 'Yes please' you want me to give it another shot or 'yes please' you want me to marry you?"

"Yes please, I want you to marry me."

He sobered. All his humor vanished and in its place was a man looking down on her, his eyes suddenly glossy as if he hadn't anticipated that truly being her answer. She slid her thumb along the inside of his collar.

He closed his eyes. "You're sure?" he whispered, and she heard how the words broke.

She nodded, vision blurring. Overwhelmed by the thought of having him—him being hers, for all of their days—her shoulders shook. He pulled her close.

"You left me." She nearly said that she wished he hadn't, but knew now that he had been wise. Wise in walking away and forcing her to dig deep and understand what it was in this life that she truly wanted. How he'd given her the time to begin to heal.

"I'm so sorry," he whispered. "Trust me when I say that I didn't want to." He gently pushed her back to peer down. "It's just . . . there were so many things to figure out. It was all so fast for you." He smoothed a strand of hair away from her face. "I see that now. I don't have a house, Ella." Regret lived in his expression when he pulled farther away. "I don't even know how I'm going to buy one for a while yet. And worse yet, I'm still in a contract with the lions for three more seasons with the circus. Years. I could break it, but . . ."

She quickly shook her head. "I don't want you to break it."

He looked at her hard.

"I want you to just take me with you."

"Are you sure?" His brow shadowed in uncertainty.

She nodded fiercely.

"It's just me," he said. "And Holland and a wagon, and really, Regina."

"I love all those people." She swiped at her eyes. "Lots and lots. And I like wagons. If you're in it . . . I like it."

Suddenly he was blushing, perhaps at the notion of her in his wagon.

"Oh, I've missed you." He ran his hand back across her ear. "But that's what I'm worried about." He moistened his lips and cupped the sides of her face. "I want to love you and I want to make you my wife. To be the husband that you need. And I don't want to hurt you or cause you grief." He paused as if needing those words to sink in for her. "I promise, Ella . . . I promise you that I would be so patient—"

"I named him," she blurted, needing him to know how desperately she trusted him.

His brow folded deeper. "What?"

"I named him."

"Who?"

Ella moistened her lips and touched first her stomach and then her heart. "I named him Charlie."

A muscle in his jaw flexed.

"Is that all right?" She stepped closer. "Do you think . . . do you think there could be two Charlie Lionhearts?"

Suddenly his chin was trembling. His eyes grew wet as he pulled them away from hers and sank down to his knees. Ella followed him. He bowed his head and covered his face with a hand. His shoulders shook. The sight of him blurred, for her own tears came.

"I didn't want it to be anything else," she whispered. "I like to think that he would have turned out like you."

Fist to his forehead, Charlie looked at her, his eyes so wet he had to pause to run his face against his shoulder. "Ella." Slowly, he shook his head.

"Will you have me, Charlie?" She slid her hand inside his, twining fingers through ones she had thought about every single day. "I don't want to be without you. Please take me with you."

With his face holding every bittersweet joy she felt herself, he pulled her close. Held her.

Ella sniffed. "I'll talk to my parents. They'll understand—"

"I already did," he whispered.

"You what?"

"I did. I spoke to your father."

"Is that what you were talking about?"

He gave her a coy smile and swiped at his eyes again. "Among other things." He sobered gently. "I asked him a lot of questions and he asked me a few of his own, and the only request he made is that I give you some time."

Overwhelmed, she could barely form the words. "That's why you left."

451

He set his mouth and looked to be trying to collect himself still. "It was one of the reasons. It was for the best. But . . ." He moistened his lips. "I told him I would be back, and last night I got to ask him again."

"You were here last night?"

He nodded. "Just for a little while."

"How did I not know about this?"

"I dunno. You were doing something in the kitchen." He smiled and she knew he'd taken care not to be spotted.

She almost hit him. As if sensing as much, Charlie chuckled.

Ella savored the sight. "And what did you say?"

"Ella." He took her hands in his, kissed each one. "Do you think you could survive without asking a question? For just *two minutes* . . . and let me get this out."

She laughed and sniffed then nodded.

"And now would you be so good as to stand back up so I can do this properly."

She shook her head, wrapped her arms around his neck, and scooted closer.

Laughing, he put his arms around her anyway. He rubbed his face against her shoulder, once and then again. Finally when he spoke, his voice was soft. "Holland. Sometimes she looks around the tent and I think she's looking for you."

Ella pressed her forehead to his temple.

"I think this goes without saying, but you'd be getting a little girl too."

Ella's lip quivered. "I'll take her." With her whole heart.

"I thought you'd say that. And Regina . . ."

"Regina too."

Straightening, he smiled at her enthusiasm. "Regina wants to go home to her daughter in Florida. She's been waiting to for some time now. If it's any comfort, she wouldn't be leaving because of you. She would have left the company sooner but stayed for me and Holland. And now . . ." He shook his head. "She knows that time would be over for her. To everything a season." He gave such a sad smile that Ella's chin trembled. He nodded as if his thoughts mirrored hers. "She's a good woman."

Ever so gently, Ella kissed his forehead.

"So with all that. If you'll have me . . ."

"With all my heart." She kissed his warm skin again. Holding tight, Ella looked over to see her parents standing on the porch and a happy sob slipped out. Ella covered her mouth with her hand. Slowly, timidly, her parents came over. Her mother hugged her. Papa shook Charlie's hand. And Ella saw Charlie looking at her as if he never wanted to look away.

The next day, Charlie bathed in the river and hoped he looked presentable in his best shirt

453

and dark boots. He combed his hair until it was tamed, then, with butterflies in his stomach, hitched up his wagon and returned to Ella's farm, Regina and Holland sitting, the pair of them, on the back porch of the caravan looking like sunflowers with their happy faces.

Never had he been so nervous as he was leading the horse into Ella's yard. Before the gold-painted wheels even slowed to a halt, her father came out and then the children. Last of all Ella's mother. The woman's eyes were already glistening. All of them were dressed up like they were going to church. Charlie handed Ella's father an envelope with a spare document inside. One that bore Holland's name and so much more.

The man vowed to keep it safe.

Charlie glanced around as they greeted him, but everything faded away when Ella stepped from the cabin. Standing there . . . prettiest thing he ever saw in a pale blue dress, her hair softly braided. And he wished his father and his mother could have met her.

For they would have surely understood why his knees suddenly felt weak and why he knew the days of his life would not be empty.

A preacher came then. A plain one—but with a smile that reached his eyes. He seemed to know Ella as a friend. The man stood them together right there in her parents' yard, under the shade of an oak, Holland babbling away in Regina's arms.

The preacher spoke some and Ella nodded. Took Lionheart as her own and with her eyes on Charlie, said that she would have him. Always. And Charlie said the same—his heart near to bursting. The preacher, misty eyed, said that she was his wife and he was her husband. Charlie ached to tell his father that he was happier than any man had a right to be.

Later that evening, surrounded by a quiet meadow, with Regina and Holland settled off a ways in the tent, Charlie lifted Ella into his wagon. He was about to climb in as well, but with her knelt just there at the edge of the mattress, her head was level with his own. So he cupped it in his hands, and closing his eyes, pressed his forehead to hers. Her breath that brushed warm against his face caught briefly when he held them still and steady for a stretch of heartbeats.

Surely a strange way for a man to greet his wife as crickets hailed in their wedding night, but it was the most honest *I love you* that he knew.

Her eyes were bright and wondering when he pulled away, that bundle of blankets still in her grasp. He laughed for no other reason than to settle his nerves. He sensed her own were the same when she blushed.

"You look just like the Princess and the Pea," he whispered, hoping to ease her as the sun sank.

Praying she'd have no fear and vowing to never give her reason to.

She said that was just fine as long as he was her prince. And then the dark had never felt so light, for she was in it, changing him. As he was changing her.

EPILOGUE

Holland Lionheart
Virginia, 1904

There's something perfect about Papa in the lantern light. As if his face was always meant to be seen this way. Sitting here now, looking at him, with Mama and my sisters all around, I think I could likely stay right here forever.

"Tell us the stories, Papa," Priscilla asks. She's a young little thing and cute as can be.

"Stories?" His voice is soft and rumbling. "I don't know that I recall any stories."

"About the circus! The lions!"

"Lions? Ella, do you remember any lions?"

"None that I can recall." Mama purses her lips since she is not a very good liar, you see.

"You're both such a tease!" Priscilla cries out.

She is a chatty one, Priscilla, and she remembers as well as I do the way Axel used to wander into the cabin and startle Mama to bits. Papa would always hear her cry out. He'd run in from the fields, scoop Mama up, and pretend to rescue her while Axel pounced after her apron strings.

Papa's eyes shine. "Do you remember any lions, Holland?" He looks at me, his expression puzzled. Papa is very good at theatrics.

I think a moment, letting the room breathe with expectancy because I am too. "There *were* lions," I whisper.

My sisters squeal and I feel Papa's belly laugh rising up in the way he looks at them all.

"What were they like? Tell us again," little Sonja asks from her quiet place by the fire.

I study each of the younger ones a moment, wishing they could have been with us and the lions. "They were soft." Oh, they were soft. "And warm. I remember always falling asleep against them. The way they would lay there still, almost holding me . . . so safe and so strong, and I remember that nothing could harm me. Not ever. I remember the way they breathed. Their gentle sounds, almost like a lullaby."

Papa's face changes. As if he is remembering too. As if I have given him a gift that only I can give. And it is hard to imagine that there was once a time that it was just he and I. I am only fifteen, but it seems like a lifetime ago, that place. *That* is the place . . . he once told my sisters . . . where he got the markings. Whenever one of them asks him about the drawings that won't ever wash away, he shows her, he answers her. He doesn't hide. Not from my sisters. And I've often wondered if the tattoos had something to do with me, for sometimes when he speaks of them, his eyes find mine. But I don't know.

"The lions!" Priscilla squeals.

I realize then that my sisters are watching me expectantly. But I'm suddenly not in a mood for talking; my throat is tight and it's hard to swallow. Axel is gone now. So is Han and Kristov. Papa buried them old and happy beneath the chokecherry tree. The littlest ones don't remember them, but I miss each of my uncles almost as much as Papa does. "They had very heavy—and *very naughty*—paws."

Papa laughs; he knows it to be true.

"What else do you remember, Holland? Tells us again of the circus," one of my sisters asks.

I smile at the memories, then cough to chase away the ache. I tell them of the sun on the grass and of the wind—ever-blowing flags of colors brighter than you could ever imagine. The sound of baying animals and of distant laughter. The strange accents from every corner of the country. The boom of the cannons and the feel of feathers and sequins beneath my cheek. I look at Nancy. She was there too, but she never remembers.

We left the year after she was born. Mama brought her into this world in a tent on the plains somewhere between Kentucky and Missouri. Papa told me that Mama was brave. He brought her back to her mountains, and with grandpa's help, built this cabin for her not long after, giving her four walls. Roots, he called them. But none of us ever felt fully rooted. Not Papa and Mama and I.

"What else do you remember? Tell us, Papa, how you met Mama," Sonja asks, and I realize that her lisp has faded. I look at my sisters, and even though our blood is not the same, each of them is precious to me.

"I'm afraid," Papa says with a shake of his head, "that I cannot remember. It was so long ago, you see."

"No!" comes a collective cry.

Priscilla jumps up, runs to the chest beneath the window, and searches inside. She scurries back to him, a top hat in her hand.

"What is this?" he asks, feigning curiosity. He turns over the tattered hat that will always be as much a part of him as the lines around his eyes.

"This," Priscilla says with a laugh in her voice, "is so you remember!"

"Oh! Is that what this is?" His brows tug in that way of his. "And what do I do with it, lass?"

"You put it on!"

"Like this?" He sets the hat far back on his head.

Priscilla is laughing so hard, she barely bubbles out a "No!"

"Perhaps like this . . ." He turns it sideways and leans forward on his elbow, flashing a playful scowl.

"No!" my sisters squeal.

"Oh!"

And he gives me a look that has my heart dancing, for I know what is to come next.

He leans forward, sweeps his gaze across the room, and a hush falls over my sisters. From her corner, Mama rocks and smiles. Her eyes are shining.

"Like this." With a slow hand, he pulls the worn hat slightly to the side and down so it shades his eyes in mystery.

He is a handsome man, my papa. The most handsome man I've ever known. I wonder if he knows it too because whenever he wears his hat this way, he winks at Mama like they have a secret. Sometimes he teases her that it is why there are six of us, and then he muses that maybe there will be a number seven. She always blushes at that.

And then my sisters groan and giggle and Papa laughs the laugh of kings.

Mama tells him to behave himself or we're going to need a bigger house.

She is not really my mother, this I know. But I call her such because she has made me hers and I love her for it. Papa tells me of Mimi and who she was, and though I don't know her, I dream of her. I should tell you now that there was a boy, too. Our brother. He was born before I was. Papa calls him his Little Prince. He says that, I think, when he wants Mama to press her face into his shoulder as that is just what she does. And he holds her.

"Oh, now I remember." Papa sighs and his eyes turn wet like two river stones. "I do remember how I met 'very plain and very boring Ella.'"

The whole room seems to dance with giggles. Mama's cheeks are rosy because Papa is looking at her as if he never wants to look away. But he does, pulling us all in with a gentle beckon of his hand. The words written there catch the light. In a whisper of skirts and button-up shoes, we move closer.

"There is a place. Where two worlds collide. Listen." He leans forward in his chair, a hand to the side of his ear. "Do you hear it?"

My sisters all lean in, breath bated, eyes wide and curious.

"I think so," Priscilla whispers.

Papa winks at her. "That, Priscilla, is the sound of a thousand faces and a thousand lands and a thousand stories that will never be told. Where color and wonder give birth to the greatest show on earth. That, my girls . . ."

I smile, for I feel a piece of my heart awaken.

"Is the *Circus*."

Beside me, Sonja sighs. She knows.

That next, Papa will lean forward, tilt his hat a tiny bit lower . . . and he will tell the stories.

AUTHOR'S NOTE

Every story is born in a different way. This one arrived in my life one Sunday morning while in church. I sat there, wrestling over something with the Lord, an angst churning within my head and heart. One that, no matter how much I wished, would not go away. The Lord's answer came through, and within moments, not only did I feel called to write through the anxieties that had been crushing in, but that calling came in the form of a story idea that I had to jot down. Right there on a receipt snatched from my purse.

The tattooed man in the circus.

The rest is history.

At first, the story began as a reflection on *Beauty and the Beast*, and while those threads are still a special part of this tale, something even mightier was at hand as words tumbled onto the page. Something more than I ever anticipated.

The story of a man who, through pain, bore darkness so that others could have life.

A fictional resonance of a very true account: the Gospel. Has there ever been a greater love story than that one?

So the two themes entwined together, becoming *The Lady and the Lionheart*. A book that allowed me as a writer to step out and feel the sun reflecting off the sides of tents. Hear the timbre of workers' voices as they steady wagons. Smell the scents of animals from every corner of the world and watch the lines of town folk form along the midway. It allowed me to experience a world that, in the shade of the Big Top, could be heaven on earth . . . or at times, much, much darker. When it came to the *good versus evil* in this story, the circus seemed an appropriate location for such a battle to wage.

But in life, just like within these pages, the darkest night is not the end. The battle has been won. Light has risen. A new day dawns. And though the act is complete—and the scars are forever there on He who gave His life—we, like Holland, are given hope. We, like a small pride of lions, have had the price paid for our freedom. And we, like Ella, have the honor of being invited as the bride of Christ. What a gift we have been offered. If this book could play a small role in pointing toward that gift—given by a man who did not have to walk the hard,

hard road for us, but who chose to anyway—my greatest hope for this story will be fulfilled. That these pages would point to the One who is the most lionhearted of them all.

With love,

Joanne

ACKNOWLEDGEMENTS

There are so many people to thank for this book, and it's with great joy that I get to sit and think of each of you in turn and how you've touched my life through this process.

To my agent, Sandra Bishop, thank you for rallying around this story in its infancy, and for believing in Charlie and Ella so deeply. To my precious mom who looked at me like I was crazy when I confessed to writing a historical romance about the tattooed man in the circus. It makes it all the more special that you quickly became Charlie's number one fan.

A huge thanks goes to my critique partners, Amanda Dykes and Jocelyn Green, and my editorial team, Denise Harmer and Kara Swanson, for making this story its absolute best. Thanks also go to the early readers for this book: Jaime Wright, Kerry Johnson, Ashley Ludwig, Brittany McEuen, Tricia Mathis, and Joy Harrison. I rejoice when I see each of your fingerprints on the pages of this book. Thank you for helping to make it shine. And to dear Kezia Manchester, thanks for being a most wonderful assistant and delightful helper along the way!

To the amazing team of endorsers—some mentioned above—may I add friends Rel Mollet, Kristy Cambron, Laura Frantz, Sigmund Brouwer, Rachel McMillian, and Lori Benton to the list of awesomeness. Each of you and your words are a gift to me! So much gratitude to Mindy Sato for your friendship that is as beautiful as your calligraphy—thank you for the gift of Charlie's *Carpe Diem* on the paperback cover and so much more.

Out there are several distinguished editors who thought enough of this book to take it to their publishing houses in hopes that it would be chosen. Though the outcome didn't work out as we had all aimed for, your faith and belief in this story was a bigger blessing than you'll ever know.

Somewhere around day one, I asked a friend to talk me out of writing this idea because I worried it wasn't fitting for the CBA. One more thanks to Amanda Dykes for sitting with a gentle ear and a heart of wisdom, then telling me to *please* write this tale because you wanted to read it. Thank you for always being the brave when I run out of brave. I couldn't imagine dedicating *Lionheart* to anyone but you.

And to the God who made mountains. Who made clouds and forests and sunlight and the eagles of the air. To the God who made every image that is forever etched upon my husband's skin. Thank you for restoring my joy when I felt so very joyless about the marks that won't ever wash away. Thank you for sitting me down that Sunday morning and prompting me to deal with my desire to change that which couldn't be changed. For prompting me to pull that old receipt out of my purse and scribble those six words that began everything—all starting with a journey on pen and paper that changed this girl's heart.

SELECTED BIBLIOGRAPHY

Dale, Bruce and McDowell, Bart. *Gypsies: Wanderers of the World*. Washington D.C.: National Geographic Society.

Davis, Janet M. *The Circus Age: Culture and Society Under the American Big Top*. The University of North Carolina Press, 2002.

Dotson, Rand. *Roanoke, Virginia, 1882-1912: Magic City of the New South*. Knoxville: The University of Tennessee Press.

Garbutt, Bernard. *Up Goes the Big Top*. California: Golden Gate Junior Books, 1966.

Harris, Nelson. *Images of America: Downtown Roanoke*. Arcadia Publishing, 2004.

Immerso, Michael. *Coney Island: The People's Playground*. New Brunswick: Rutgers University Press, 2002.

Kasson, John F. *Amusing the Million: Coney Island at the Turn of the Century*. New York: Hill and Wang, 2011.

Maxwell, Anna Caroline and Pope, Amy Elizabeth. *Practical Nursing: A Text-Book for Nursing.* G.P. Putnam's Sons, 1907.

Osterud, Amelia Klem. *The Tattooed Lady: A History.* Colorado: Speck Press, 2009.

Park, Tony and Richardson, Kevin. *Part of the Pride: My Life Among the Big Cats of Africa.* New York: St. Martin's Press, 2009.

Tarcher, Jeremy P. *American Sideshow: An Encyclopedia of History's Most Wondrous and Curiously Strange Performers.* New York: Penguin, 2006.

READER'S GUIDE

1. If you were a part of the circus during the Victorian era, what might your role have been? If you could be a spectator at The Graven Brothers Circus, what, or who, would you most like to see?

2. Ella recalls Dr. Penske's warning that men with tattoos were considered felons since such markings were often obtained in jail in the Victorian era. In 1890, what do you think this type of taboo means for Charlie's life? What kind of risks might a young woman like Ella face as she befriends him? Would you have done anything differently?

3. When the baby's name is changed from Antonia to Holland, what did you sense were Charlie's reasons for this? Isaiah 43:1 states, "Do not fear for I have redeemed you; I have summoned you by name; you are mine." In what ways was this verse paralleled in the story?

4. Each of Charlie's tattoos was carefully chosen—some by him and some by Madame Broussard. With chapter twenty-six being

473

the first time they're described, what did you think about the choice and locations of the images on his skin? What do they say about him? What do they say about Madame Broussard?

5. With a broad cast of secondary characters—both human and beast—did any stand out as your favorites? What was it about their character that drew your heart to them?

6. Though he was but the son of a poor man, Charlie was named after a king. The theme of royalty was continued throughout his story in subtlc ways. Can you recall any instances where this was noticeable? What does the connection of royalty symbolize to you for Charlie's life?

7. In the New York brothel, Charlie recalled the words, "Rock of Ages, cleft for me. Bind my wandering heart to thee," mixing together one line from "Rock of Ages" and one from "Come Thou Fount." What does this say about his state of mind in this scene? What was he holding on to?

8. At the end of chapter 19, Angelina tries to encourage Charlie by saying, "God will make a way for you." Is there a time in your

own life that you had to do a very difficult thing in hopes of honoring the Lord and might have clung to words such as those?

9. When Ella faces her greatest fear by bringing the small offering to the reverend's doorstep, what do you believe that moment meant to her? To the reverend? At the end of the novel, do you think this was the same reverend who performed the wedding ceremony? If so, what did that symbolize to you?

10. The scene of Mr. Beckley and Charlie speaking in the barn is alluded to, but not described. If you could write that scene, how do you think it would play out?

11. Between the final chapter and the epilogue fourteen years pass. How do you imagine that passing of time for the Lionhearts? What might life have looked like for them? Do you foresee anything ahead?

LET'S CONNECT!

www.joannebischof.com
Facebook — Author, Joanne Bischof
Instagram — @joannebischof
Twitter & Pinterest

Or subscribe to Joanne's e-newsletter,
The Heartfelt Post

ABOUT THE AUTHOR

A Carol Award and three-time Christy Award finalist, Joanne Bischof writes deeply layered fiction that tugs at the reader's heartstrings. She was honored to receive the SDCWG Novel of the Year Award in 2014 and in 2015 was named Author of the Year by the Mount Hermon Writer's conference. That same year, her historical novella, *This Quiet Sky*, broke precedent as the first self-released title to final for the Christy Awards. *To Get to You*, her 2015 release, was the second. Joanne's 2016 novel, *The Lady and the Lionheart*, received an extraordinary 5 Star TOP PICK! from Romantic Times Book Reviews and she's pretty sure it's Charlie's fault. Joanne is represented by Sandra Bishop of Transatlantic Literary Agency.

Books are
produced in the
United States
using U.S.-based
materials

Books are printed
using a revolutionary
new process called
THINKtech™ that
lowers energy usage
by 70% and increases
overall quality

Books are
durable and
flexible
because of
smythe-sewing

Paper is
sourced using
environmentally
responsible
foresting methods
and the
paper is acid-free

Center Point Large Print
600 Brooks Road / PO Box 1
Thorndike, ME 04986-0001 USA

(207) 568-3717

US & Canada:
1 800 929-9108
www.centerpointlargeprint.com